Praise for *Code Zero*

'[Exposes] the dark underbelly of social media giants' societal control via the manipulation of data. Elsberg is nothing if not prescient; this is all pre-Cambridge Analytica.' BARRY FORSHAW, *Guardian*

'This may be fiction but it is unnervingly realistic.' *Choice* magazine

'*Code Zero* is a tense tech thriller that reads worryingly real.' *Sunday Sport*

'Marc Elsberg has a sixth sense for burning issues. So sinister and realistic, it will make you download encryption software immediately after reading.' *Glamour*

'A captivating read and a very well-researched techno-thriller.' *Shots* magazine

'This is *the* go-to thriller that ignites topical debate around Google and the right to personal privacy. A nightmare that as Elsberg sees it has long become a reality.' *FOCUS*

'A topical thriller set in the world of online activists pitted against corrupt IT companies who collect and analyse personal data.' *Der Spiegel*

'As with *Blackout*, Elsberg combines a realistic near-future scenar... ...thriller that confro...

CODE ZERO

MARC ELSBERG

Translated from the German by Simon Pare

BLACK SWAN

TRANSWORLD PUBLISHERS
61–63 Uxbridge Road, London W5 5SA
www.penguin.co.uk

Transworld is part of the Penguin Random House group of companies
whose addresses can be found at global.penguinrandomhouse.com

Penguin
Random House
UK

First published as *Zero* in Great Britain in 2018 by Doubleday
an imprint of Transworld Publishers
Black Swan edition published as *Code Zero* in 2019

A CIP catalogue record for this book
is available from the British Library.

ISBN
9781784163488

Typeset in 11/14 pt Sabon LT Std
by Integra Software Services Pvt. Ltd, Pondicherry
Printed and bound in Great Britain by Clays Ltd, Elcograf S.p.A.

Penguin Random House is committed to a sustainable
future for our business, our readers and our planet. This book
is made from Forest Stewardship Council® certified paper.

MIX
Paper from
responsible sources
FSC® C018179

1 3 5 7 9 10 8 6 4 2

For Ursula
For my parents

Know thyself.
Ancient Greek saying

We shape our tools, and thereafter our tools shape us.
Father John Culkin, based on Marshall McLuhan's ideas

We want Google to be the third half of your brain.
Sergey Brin at an event on 8 September 2010

The best way to predict the future is to create it.
Unknown

Author's Note

Code Zero may at times read like a utopian vision, but all the technologies described here are already in use, and the police facilities mentioned in London (Lambeth) and New York (RTCC) do actually exist.

Companies have been using data collection and sophisticated computer programs for many years to predict our future behaviour in many areas, and they can do so with ever-increasing accuracy. This allows them to offer us relevant services – or not. At virtually the same time as *Code Zero* was published in Germany in 2014, scientists admitted to having manipulated the emotions of some 800,000 Facebook users in a secret experiment. More and more applications are popping up for individual use. Growing numbers of people trust in satellite navigation systems ('Take this road to avoid traffic jams!'), fitness apps ('Your recommended distance for the coming week is . . .'), virtual coaches ('Imagine yourself in the following situation . . .') and life management tools ('Alexa, . . .') to make their lives more comfortable, healthier, safer and better. Only the development of lifestyle apps lags a little behind what is described here.

China is introducing a 'social credit system', and police forces are conducting trials with smart glasses for facial recognition and other purposes. Back in 2014, many people dismissed concerns that new technologies might be used to manipulate elections as fanciful. The recent revelations regarding Cambridge Analytica have made this scenario terrifyingly topical. As a result of this (and of the EU's General Data Protection regulation, which came into force in May 2018), companies are now actively discussing business models that allow users to sell their own data – the same kind of models whose implications make *Code Zero* so chilling.

And yet this book is a novel. The characters are fictional, and any resemblance to actual persons living or dead is unintentional or coincidental.

You will find a glossary of selected terms and a list of the main characters at the end of the book.

Marc Elsberg, May 2018

Peekaboo777: Everybody ready? There won't be a safe place in the world for any of us after this.

Teldif: Ready.

xxhb67: Ready.

ArchieT: Ready.

Snowman: Ready.

Submarine: Ready.

Nightowl: Ready.

Peekaboo777: OK. Here we go!

Monday

'What have you got in here – rocks?' groans Cynthia Bonsant as she heaves a packing box on to her new neighbour's desk, almost dislocating her shoulder in the process.

'No end of cool gadgets,' boasts Jeff. 'Product samples for the technology department to test.' He takes a Weeble with blinking eyes from a cardboard box crammed with bits of technical gear and cables.

Technology department! Cynthia runs her fingers tetchily through her short hair, sending finger-long strands splaying in all directions. She pats them back into place as her eyes wander over the new open-plan office where the *Daily*'s print and online journalists are being herded together like cattle. Old and new colleagues are busily unpacking their belongings on to six long rows of desks, piling and arranging their things like workers on the assembly line at an office equipment mail-order company. The monitors are virtually touching; between them, the IT team are connecting the last cables, which spill like intestines from the electronic devices. More and more colleagues enter the room, carrying boxes pressed to their stomachs and elbowing their way through the crowd in search of their desks. A flurry of pictures from international news channels, websites and social media flickers down at them from the

2

gigantic wall of monitors at one end of the office. A ticker message for newcomers runs along the bottom: 'Welcome to the *Daily* newsfloor!'

'Newsfloor,' mutters Cyn. 'Engine room, more like.'

She studies her own packing box. No cool gadgets in there. She plonks the battered tin for her pens down firmly in front of the new screen and lines up her notepad alongside it.

When she next looks up, Jeff's stopped tidying things away and is staring trance-like at his monitor. Other colleagues have also broken off their work on the assembly line and are clustering around the screens in whispering groups.

'This is crazy,' whispers Jeff, scratching his patchy beard. 'Look!'

At precisely that moment, the editor-in-chief, Anthony Heast, rushes out of his office. 'Put it up on the video wall!'

All the monitors have been showing the same footage for some time already: wobbly aerial views of a golf course, scattered roofs in the woods beyond, with the Stars and Stripes fluttering over one of them.

'A drone . . . a drone's attacking him . . .' stammers Jeff.

Cyn recognizes the President of the United States now too. He's positioning a golf ball to tee off. Next to him is his wife, and their two children are unenthusiastically thrashing away at balls on two adjacent tees. A few yards from the First Family, five members of the President's security detail wear bored looks behind their dark glasses.

'These pictures of the President's holiday home have been streaming live on the internet for the past few seconds,' blathers an excited TV presenter from the video wall. 'Shortly beforehand, an organization called "Zero" took to social media to inform the public and the media of the

3

operation. We don't yet know how the drone got through the security system, let alone what Zero plans to do!'

Cyn's heart starts racing as the airborne camera speeds towards the US President. *Hasn't anyone there noticed?* Several colleagues cry out in terror. Even the removal men have now interrupted their work and are gawping at the screens.

The President pulls back his club, swings through the ball and watches its trajectory. He rams the head of the driver into the grass and shouts something after the ball. Not a compliment, Cyn reckons, given the face he's pulling. Suddenly his expression twists, he stretches out his arm and points straight at the camera. He spins towards the bodyguards, then runs over to his wife and children, who are rooted to the spot in terror. Several secret agents rush after him. Two black SUVs come shooting out of the woods. Their tyres plough up the fairway, as the security personnel fling themselves on top of the President and his family to protect them.

A squad of men appear from the trees behind the covered driving range. A few of them hurry over to the First Family while others scan the area nervously or peer through binoculars, tap frenziedly on their smartphones and tablets, or yell into their headsets.

The bunch of agents bundle the First Family into the front car. Divots of soil and grass spray out from under its wheels as the car speeds off into the woods. It's only when Cyn exhales that she realizes she's been holding her breath with all the suspense.

Her pulse starts to accelerate again when the flying camera tracks the vehicle through the gaps in the tree canopy. The second car soon catches up with the first. Men with machine guns lean out of the windows, scouring the sky, until the SUV reaches a compound and disappears into a garage.

'OK,' the TV commentator announces breathlessly when the door shuts behind them, 'the President and his family seem to be safe for now.'

'Is our live ticker ready to go?' calls Anthony, loosening his tie. 'Can we embed the stream on our home page? Headline: US President under attack . . .'

His voice trails off as agitated cries ring out in the engine room. Cyn can now make out the two SUVs on shaky footage showing the inside of a brightly lit garage. The President, his family and their defenders look tense as they clamber out of the cars. They don't notice the intruding drone until a child screams. Everyone starts running again. *As if they've been cornered by a swarm of hornets*, Cyn thinks with a shudder.

Shielded by their guards, the President's family reach the exit, while two watchmen remain behind, helplessly waving their guns around. A fist-sized shadow buzzes around the room behind them.

'Fuck! How did they get inside?' one of them yells as he levels his gun barrel at the camera. The images on the video wall dissolve into a blur of walls, vehicles and people, accompanied by the sound of deafening gunfire. Then the screens go black, leaving several TV presenters talking over one another.

A collective sigh runs through the engine room, and Cyn wonders if it expresses relief or disappointment.

'Shit!' cries Jeff when the pictures return. 'They've got another camera in there!'

A worm's-eye view of a flurry of legs. This hidden camera's lurking somewhere like a beast ready to pounce on a hunter. Cyn realizes she instinctively sides with the little animal. Even though it might be about to murder the President of the USA.

'There are some left, Chuck!' Chief of Staff Erben Pennicott roars into the phone. His free hand clenches tensely. On the computer and TV screens in his study, Erben sees the First Family and their security men reach the exit from the next room. Only two pairs of sturdy black shoes now remain in shot, but suddenly the camera scurries past them and after the President. Gunshots. Screams. For what seems like an eternity, the camera fixes the fear-filled eyes of the world's most powerful man and the dark hole of his screaming mouth.

Goddammit! Goddam and shit! Erben thinks with a grimace. *The whole world's watching these pictures, and they don't show the President in a good light. No authority whatsoever – none at all!*

There's another burst of gunfire and the screens go dark. Erben stares at the screens, still clutching the receiver to his ear. He has no idea who fired those shots. Their own people or the drones? The TV commentators' voices resume their excited chatter. What if the President or one of his family has been hit? Erben runs out of the room.

He sprints effortlessly through the hallways and rooms of the rambling compound. More shots ring out. Another room that could easily accommodate ten people. The double doors on the other side of the room are open. The President's children, flanked by three hefty minders, rush towards him like panic-stricken dwarves, followed by the First Lady, the President and several secret agents. Out of the corner of his eye Erben sees a shadow scampering along between their feet. The group races past him, and the guys with the guns fire randomly at the floor.

'What the hell are you doing?' he yells at the men. 'Where is the fucking thing?' he shouts, his eyes darting back and forth between the live video on his smartphone and various spots around the room.

'There it is!' cries a bodyguard next to him, aiming his gun under a sofa.

Erben forces the man's arm upwards, and a volley of gunfire crashes into the ceiling, bringing a shower of plaster dust raining down on them.

'Quit shooting the place up!' he shouts. He's spotted the little legged robot. Quickly he wriggles out of his jacket and dashes towards the metal spider. He flings his jacket over the device like a dogcatcher's net, and hurls himself on top of it.

'Oh!' gasp several people on the newsfloor disappointedly as the pictures vanish from the monitors. Howls greet the switch to a worm's-eye view from yet another camera. It shows Erben Pennicott reaching under his crumpled jacket with one hand and triumphantly pulling out his fist. A few metal legs squirm between his powerful fingers and after tearing them out with a few swift movements, his hands expertly explore the mouse-sized remains.

'What is it?' asks Cyn. 'What's he doing?'

'What do you mean?' answers Jeff. 'That's a mini legged robot fitted with a camera. Pennicott had his own internet start-up back when he was still a student. He sold it for hundreds of millions of dollars. He knows all about this kind of device.'

Seconds later, the chief of staff holds up something Cyn doesn't recognize between two fingers.

'A wireless card!' Pennicott's deep voice intones from the screens as the security detail frantically search for further cameras. Then he shouts, 'OK, make sure every regional mobile network is shut down right away!'

A dark shadow covers the remaining camera, and the voices are suddenly muffled. Someone's just tossed a jacket over the second legged robot.

'Who or what is Zero?' Anthony roars across the newsfloor. 'Terrorists? You got anything for me, Charly?'

'Internet activists,' says Charly, scratching the back of his head. He's a *Daily* dinosaur; Cyn knows him from the print edition. She'd bet any money that every morning he ticks off the days until his retirement on a calendar and has been for a while now. 'A bit like Anonymous, but much less known. They've posted a few videos online, along with a guide to protecting yourself from surveillance. *The Citizen's Guerrilla Guide to the Surveillance Society*.'

'Well, they're not unknown any more. How daring can you get! I wouldn't like to be in their shoes when the FBI catches up with them . . .'

Cyn listens to her colleagues chatter excitedly for a few minutes until it dawns on them that the fun and games are over. No more broadcasts of unauthorized footage from the President's holiday residence. The removal guys crawl back under the desks to connect the cables and tighten the last few screws.

'What now?' asks Jeff.

'Now turn all that into a story for me!' says Anthony. He's a smart bloke about Cyn's age – a manager and accountant who'd love to be doing something more creative, as his clothes and hairstyle attest. The owners appointed him to this job to 'lead our media group into the future', which of course means online. 'Jeff, Charly, you research Zero. Dig up anything you can find! Cyn will cover the investigation.'

'The internet isn't my field,' she reminds him as he rummages around in a packing case.

Without looking up, he replies, 'The internet is everyone's field.'

'No corpses, no injuries,' Charly says half-heartedly. 'If that's it, then the story'll be dead by the day after tomorrow.'

'But until then we're going to milk it for all it's worth,' says Anthony with fervour, still up to his elbows in the box. 'Where have they got to?' he mutters. 'Ah, there they are!'

Proudly he holds up three small cardboard boxes and hurries over to Cyn, Charly and Jeff with them. 'To help you give the story a modern twist,' he explains.

'Oh, awesome – the latest glasses!' Jeff cries, his fingers already tearing at the packaging. He pulls out a pair of glasses and promptly puts them on. Next, his hand reaches for the smartphone on his desk.

'What are they?' Cyn asks Charly.

'Smart glasses, augmented reality glasses – or whatever else you'd like to call them,' he grunts. 'You can screen things you'd usually only see on your smartphone on your glasses.'

'How long have these things existed?'

'Oh, come off it, Cyn,' says Jeff with some amusement. 'You must have heard of them! Google and others brought out the first models back in 2012.'

'A new manufacturer has lent us a few to test,' Anthony explains excitedly. 'Ideal for the present circumstances.'

'What am I supposed to do with them?' she enquires. 'I'm a newspaper editor. I write.'

'Live research. Reports. These glasses mean you can always keep an eye on your surroundings *and* obtain all the information you need directly before your eyes. These things are the future!'

9

Cyn twiddles the frame in her fingers. 'I'm not a TV reporter.'

'Everyone's every kind of reporter nowadays,' Anthony lectures her. 'And you better get used to that quick, or soon we won't be needing you.'

'If everyone's already a reporter,' she gripes, 'then I'm already not needed.'

'I heard that,' says Anthony. 'Watch out, Cynthia, or I'll take you at your word. Some computer programs can already write articles on their own that are indistinguishable from ones written by humans,' he adds with a laugh, passing so close to her that only she hears him when he hisses, 'You're on my list as it is.'

Annoyed, she turns away from him. Beside her, Jeff is waggling his head back and forth. 'Wow! Wicked . . .'

She studies the frames in her hand. 'Look just like any other pair of glasses.'

'That's deliberate,' says Charly. 'Most people don't like you walking around them with smart glasses on. They're scared of being watched and filmed.'

'And rightly so,' Jeff says with a chuckle.

'They probably record everything they see and hear,' Cyn guesses. 'And then save it somewhere or other.'

'Correct,' says Jeff, giggling. 'Cyn mutates into a four-eyes for a company bent on spying into every hidden corner of her life.'

'You really make it sound tempting! At the moment I'm happy if I can make my mobile work.'

It's true that there's an old-fashioned receiver fitted to the smartphone on her desk, a light-hearted present from her daughter two years ago.

'Come on. I'll set the glasses up for you quickly,' Jeff offers.

She gives Jeff free rein, as this would definitely take her hours, whereas he's able to establish the wireless connection between her smartphone and her smart glasses in a matter of seconds.

'Put them on,' Jeff directs her. 'Sound's transmitted directly to the bone behind your ear by vibrations in the frame of the specs.'

'You're having me on now.'

'Nope. It's a proven technique they've been using in hearing aids for decades.'

'Get moving, ladies and gentlemen!' Anthony claps his hands. 'Off you go!'

Cyn rolls her eyes. 'So who is this Zero?'

'I've got him on screen,' says Charly and manoeuvres his chair ponderously to one side to make room for her and Jeff.

A familiar-looking male face stares out at Cyn from the sinister black-and-white screen. Melancholy yet piercing eyes, a full head of hair painstakingly combed back, a thin moustache on his top lip like a third eyebrow.

'But that's George Orwell!' she exclaims.

'I have a complaint to make today,' the English author explains. 'In 1948 George Orwell wrote a book. He called it 1984.' As Orwell speaks, his face morphs, as though made of rubber, into a pasty-looking bald man wearing black glasses and a grim expression. The timbre of his voice changes too, becoming deeper. 'In it, a totalitarian dictatorship practises comprehensive surveillance over its citizens and tells them how they must live their lives.'

The book was required reading at Cyn's school. That was back in 1989 when not a single surveillance state was in power, and in fact Communism and its informer apparatus were collapsing.

'Ooh, how scary to imagine – a nightmare vision! By the way, the book's slogan was "Big Brother is watching you." Now *Big Brother*'s a TV programme.'

This Zero loves mutating. As one face morphs into the next, Cyn recognizes first the US President, followed by the British Prime Minister, the German Chancellor and other heads of government. It reminds her of a Michael Jackson video from her childhood, but that was far more static. The voice keeps changing too: sometimes it sounds like that of a woman, then a man, and yet Cyn finds the sound pleasant rather than alienating. Its peculiar lilting quality has something of a hypnotic effect on her.

'Now imagine your government for a second. It only wants the best for its citizens. It develops amazing systems to protect every individual: PRISM, XKEYSCORE, TEMPORA, INDECT and Lord knows what else. These wonderful systems collect and analyse all the data they can get their hands on in order to identify in advance any possible threat to their citizens.'

Cyn catches herself grinning. Whatever else, Zero does at least have a sense of humour.

'And how are those governments rewarded? They're derided as Big Brother! So why is the National Security Agency monitoring worldwide phone and internet communications?' The picture changes. Zero is standing in an Underground station in a dark suit and shades. All around him, people are babbling into their mobiles. 'You really think it's fun being buried every day under a gigantic heap of small talk, bragging and other nonsense? You only do this if you really, really want to do the best for people – because you hope that somewhere in that heap you're going to find a terrorist! So, feeling safer now? I hope so! No? Griping, are you? Still calling the state Big Brother, like in *1984*?'

The images keep switching, and Cyn has to concentrate hard. Zero is now a young blonde woman in red shorts and a white top. She runs past rows of numb, grey, ordinary people staring at a grave-faced presenter on a giant screen, swinging a giant hammer over her head as she goes.

'Over thirty years ago, a computer manufacturer launched an ad campaign for its latest model featuring the slogan "On January 24th Apple will introduce Macintosh. And you'll see why 1984 won't be like *1984*." That's the same computer manufacturer whose iPhones and iPads now log where we're standing or walking at every instant. Whose apps search and pass on our address lists. Which bans apps from its App Store when they show, say or do something that Uncle Sam doesn't like. A bare nipple? Heaven forfend! But let's be fair: Google and all the others apparently undertake precisely the same kind of surveillance with their services, mobiles, glasses and sensors.'

Cyn can't help nodding along to this. This is exactly why she's so sceptical about recent technological innovations.

Zero morphs into a police officer and continues: 'Imagine if your government or the police demanded you carry a little box around with you at all times that constantly signals where you are and what you're doing. You'd give them the finger! Yet you're paying the world's data oligarchs to spy on you. That, right there, is consummate surveillance. Please let me give you money so you can locate me and use my data! They could sure teach international spy agencies a thing or two . . .' Zero lowers his voice, his tone more biting. 'Here they come with their Trojan horses, offering you search results, friends, maps, love, success, fitness tips, discounts on your shopping and who knows what else – but all the while, armed warriors sit lurking in their bellies, waiting for an opportunity to pounce! Their arrows strike you

13

right in the heart and the head. They know more about you than any intelligence service. They know you better than you know yourself! But the old question remains: who's monitoring the monitors? And who's monitoring their monitors? But perhaps we already know the answer: everyone monitors everyone else,' Zero chants almost cheerily, wagging his index finger at the camera. 'Little Brother, I'm watching you.' He suddenly turns serious again. 'But not us! Another thing: I believe we must destroy the data krakens.'

'Nice tricks,' Cyn says appreciatively.

'No sweat with modern animation software,' Jeff retorts.

'Zero's published over forty of these videos in the past few years,' says Charly.

'I'll watch them all overnight,' answers Jeff.

'OK. And I'll see what I can find out about the investigations,' says Cyn, packing her handbag. It's past seven.

'Wait!' says Jeff when he realizes she's leaving. 'You haven't heard the best thing about those glasses yet. Facial recognition.'

'What?'

'Facebook and photo software have used it for quite a while. Developers have been holding back with live versions, but for a few months there've been updated versions that let you identify just about any face online. In real time! I'll show you.'

He puts the glasses on, stares straight at her and holds up his smartphone, which shows a picture of her. Beside it she reads:

Bonsant, Cynthia
DOB: 27.07.1972

Height: 1.65 m
Address: 11 Pensworth Street, London NW6
Mobile: +44 7526 976901
Tel: ex-directory (more >)
Email: cynbon@dodnet.com
Profession: Journalist
Status: Divorced, from Cordan, Gary (more >)
Children: Bonsant, Viola (more >), > Freemee profile
Mother: Bonsant, Candice † (more >)
Father: Bonsant, Emery † (more >)
Images: . . .
More Freemee info:
Professional from £0.02 (> purchase)
Analysis from £0.02 (> purchase)

'Everything anyone needs to know,' Jeff explains. 'So who's this young lady?'

'My daughter,' Cyn reluctantly admits. Young people's careless way with the internet gives her the creeps, and she's not at all impressed with her own daughter's online behaviour.

'She's a goth?' Jeff wants to know.

'That particular phase is behind her, fortunately.'

A more recent photo shows Viola with short fair hair. She's turned eighteen and inherited Cyn's slender figure and her father's blond curls. She's worn her mop like a tomboy ever since she let the black of her goth phase grow out and had it all chopped off.

'Wow, she's unrecognizable!' says Jeff.

At least two dozen other pictures show Cyn at different times in her life, including one from her university days. It comes from a platform old school friends can use to get back in touch.

She furrows her brow. 'What do "professional" and "analysis" mean?'

'Information. Analysis. Who you vote for, the kind of products you buy, where you're going on holiday and so forth.'

'How do they know all those things?'

'They have no trouble figuring it out from everything they know about you, me and billions of other people.'

'You must be joking!'

'Most companies do it nowadays,' Jeff explains patiently. 'And have done for a long time. You've got a mobile phone, loyalty cards for supermarkets, petrol stations and hotels, your credit card and all kinds of other stuff. You've been leaving a vast data trail for years. How do you think insurance companies, banks and credit agencies calculate their risks? A credit card company knows with ninety-five per cent certainty which of their clients will get divorced in the next five years.'

'They could have given *me* a heads-up,' Cyn observes drily.

Jeff's mouth twists into a wry smile. 'There are some good sides to it, though. Google can follow the development of flu epidemics or even make live predictions based on searches by people who've contracted the illness, and software like this has also made weather forecasting far more accurate, to give just two examples.'

'People will still moan about the weathermen,' mutters Charly.

Jeff carries on unperturbed. 'You heard about the famous case of Target pregnancies?'

'So famous I missed it,' sighs Cyn. She's longing to go home – it's been a long day – but Jeff's in his element now.

'Years back, the discount retailer Target worked out from data recorded via a huge number of loyalty cards that all their pregnant customers bought specific products at different stages of their pregnancy. Fragrance-free soap, unbleached cotton wool pads and so on. By implication, Target also knows, of course, that if a woman buys this or other product, she's in a particular month of pregnancy. So Target is able to predict the child's date of birth almost to the day.'

'You're pulling my leg.'

'Nope,' Jeff insists. 'It's all about identifying patterns of behaviour. It's called predictive analytics. Nowadays we all think we're individualists, whereas in fact we behave in relatively standard ways – which can be anticipated. It's how the police hunt serial criminals, because arsonists and rapists often repeat patterns of behaviour. Using predictive policing and pre-crime software, they can identify particular streets in particular cities where crimes like drug dealing and burglary are most likely to occur. They can then turn up to prevent them. More and more cities employ such software.'

'Sounds like *Minority Report*,' says Charly. 'Not a bad film, by the way.'

'Preliminary versions are already in use,' Jeff replies. 'In some US states, judges refuse certain prison inmates parole because someone's developed algorithms that have calculated that their particular group is highly likely to reoffend within three years.'

'What if you're one of those who wouldn't reoffend?!' Cyn protests.

'Tough luck,' Jeff says with a shrug.

'They don't get a chance to show they won't reoffend?' Cyn asks in bewilderment.

'Well ... In this brave new world of ours, possibilities and chances are sacrificed to probability. Your future

17

depends more than ever on your past – because your future is assessed on the basis of your past.'

'And they're always assuring us that they're only collecting anonymized data.'

'It was proved years ago that you can identify individuals from anonymized data,' Jeff explains. 'Especially if you combine various different datasets. Our online history, mobile data, and travel and purchasing behaviour produce a unique profile.'

'So they're just lying when they claim that the data is anonymous. And most of us fall for it.'

'Yes and no. They gather the data in an anonymous fashion, but then someone in the data analysis chain plays around with it. They trace it back to you, and then they can figure out your habits and make predictions.'

'So they can look into my future and know what I want?'

'Not a hundred per cent, but often with a high degree of probability. They also know how easy or hard it is to influence you on certain subjects.'

Cyn purses her lips. 'It doesn't work very well, though. I keep receiving online adverts for things that don't interest me in the slightest.' She thinks of all the sponsored links for all sorts of diets that have recently kept popping up on the sites she visits. And she really has no need for them either.

'You receive them *because* it works so well,' Jeff contradicts her. 'If advertisers keep offering you the right things, it starts to seem spooky and you feel as if you're being watched and someone's worked you out. It's known as the "creepiness factor" in the profession. To avoid it, they scatter a few irrelevant offers into the mix from time to time. And then you believe what you just said: that they haven't figured you out – and so you fall into their trap all the more easily.'

Cyn shudders. 'Now *that*'s creepy!'

Jeff rolls his eyes. 'What do you mean? I'd honestly rather they left all the unnecessary crap out of it. It saves a lot of time if they offer you what you want straight away.'

Jeff's generation simply have a different approach to all these forms of media. Just like her daughter. Or doesn't Cyn herself pay enough attention to it? Why does she object so much to the technological innovations of recent years? Her mind goes back to what Zero said. How did he put it? 'Here they come with their Trojan horses, offering you search results, friends . . . love, success . . .'

She turns to leave, but Jeff's effusions are unstoppable. 'Wait, I'll set up facial recognition for you.' Before Cyn can stop him, he's fiddling around with her smartphone. 'There you go! Try the glasses out on the Tube on your way home. The video tutorial explains everything.'

'I don't really want to know.' She drops the glasses into her handbag and says goodbye to Jeff and Charly, her head spinning from all the new information.

Cyn loves playing guessing games about people she doesn't know. Sitting in the bus or on the Underground, she speculates about their jobs, their past, their desires and their family life. Of course she never knows if she's right or not, but she trusts her intuition. So the glasses in her bag are obviously a huge temptation. How good is she at guessing actually?

She sticks her hand into her bag, feels the glasses and hesitates, then takes them out and toys with them. Puts them on. No one pays her any attention.

Within a few minutes, Cyn has worked out how to use the things. She can enter a question by voice, by blinking, by moving her head or touching one of the arms. She can view all the information directly on the lenses instead of on the touchscreen. It floats there in space before her eyes, semi-transparent, like ghosts, and what's more her hands are free, which is practical.

She studies the man opposite and activates the facial recognition software. After a few seconds, several lines of text and symbols appear beside the man's head. Name, age, address. She glances around her and swears under her breath. The internet knows every single person on this bus! *I* know every single person on this bus . . .

She fixes her gaze on one face in the crowd – the device's automatic eye tracking identifies the person she means – and whispers, 'Glasses, identify.'

Within seconds she knows all about Paula Ferguson, a housewife and mother of three who lives in Tottenham and is thirty-five years old. She could find out more, but to do that she'd have to set up an account with a vendor and pay. She switches to a young man with dreadlocks and a wire dangling from his ears. In the blink of an eye she discovers that the twenty-three-year-old Dane is studying at the London School of Economics and listening to Wagner. She admits she'd never have guessed *that*.

Despite some lingering reluctance and a tinge of shame, she's beginning to share Jeff's enthusiasm, fascination replacing her sense of guilt. By the time she changes on to the Tube, she's unmasked over a dozen people. She realizes that her fantasies are often wide of the mark. Yet the reality – or what her glasses pass off as reality – is often no less surprising.

She continues her observations as she makes her way through the Underground station. A woman of similar age comes walking towards her. The glasses display the usual information and pictures. And more: newspaper reports from fifteen years ago show the woman was hospitalized following a serious attack. '. . . A brutal assault . . .' Cyn picks up from an old headline, '. . . lost a foot . . . early retirement . . .' The woman does indeed have a slight limp, she notices, before turning away in shock. Spontaneously she turns the question around. How many pairs of glasses on the faces coming towards her might be like hers? Which of them are currently doing to her what she's been doing on the bus and while changing on to the Underground? Who might potentially be streaming live pictures of her on the internet? She suddenly has a weird sense that thousands of eyes are boring into her.

Cyn sneaks a quick sideways glance at the glass covering a billboard to check out her appearance and study her behaviour. She looks up and suddenly realizes where she is: on a London Underground platform at rush hour. Hundreds of people can see her here, even without such glasses. So can Transport for London's ubiquitous CCTV cameras, of course. *Welcome to paranoia*, she thinks.

Her train rattles into the station. Shoved into the carriage by the press of workers heading home, she heads for an empty seat. The glasses tell her how long it'll take to the station where she needs to get off.

During the journey, Cyn uses the glasses to surf the internet. The US administration hasn't yet published its official response to Zero's Presidents' Day action. Cyn presumes that the mood in certain offices in Washington must be a bit like when a fox has ransacked the henhouse. The media's already cooking up the most ridiculous conspiracy theories featuring the usual suspects plus a few new ones.

Cyn has to stop by the supermarket to pick up a few bits and bobs. She's just reaching for a pack of tomatoes in the vegetable section when the glasses warn her about pesticides.

She leaves the tomatoes where they are and heads for the biscuit aisle. The glasses advise her to buy these biscuits in a different supermarket just around the corner where they're thirty pence cheaper, so she puts the trolley back and heads for the rival shop.

The biscuits there are indeed at a lower price, and the tomatoes are pesticide-free, juicy and organic. She realizes that her prejudices about the glasses are gradually fading, and notes how easy and fun they are to use. She makes her way along the aisles and examines various special offers. The glasses give her some useful recipe suggestions. When she opts for egg sandwiches, the glasses ask her which of the ingredients she has at home and remind her to buy the missing ones.

Standing at the till soon afterwards, she begins to have second thoughts. What's she doing? She only set out to buy tomatoes and biscuits, although she could certainly use all the items in her shopping trolley.

A queue has formed behind her. Lost in thought, she places her items on the conveyor belt and takes her purse from her handbag. The glasses recommend that she get the supermarket's loyalty card, showing how much it would save her on this first purchase.

Another card? Cyn wonders with a glance at her wallet, and instinctively decides against it. She pays with cash. *So much for see-through customers!* she thinks.

'The President is still mad,' rages Erben. Gathered before him are the heads of the US security agencies. They're all used to long meetings, but Erben's gaze encounters only weary faces.

'These jokers have made a worldwide laughing stock of us! And it might have been a whole lot worse ... You all realize, of course, that those drones could have been carrying more than cameras.' His tone is sharp as he continues. 'The President wants to know why we didn't anticipate this attack. He wants to know who these people are. He's insistent that we hunt them down as fast as possible! Orville?' he says, brusquely addressing the head of the FBI. He's struggling to control his fury at these activists. They seem to see themselves as some kind of Monkey Wrench Gang!

'Transmission started at 10.13 Eastern Time,' Orville reports.

The mere thought of this guy's stiff soldier's face makes Erben angry. The operation may have one good outcome at least: changes in personnel, all the way to the top.

Orville plays the footage of the driving range on the large screen on the wall.

'The President's security detail was notified at 10.16 . . .'

The President and his wife duck, their hands over their ears.

'Three minutes!' cries Erben. 'If that thing had been armed, we wouldn't have a president now.'

'It would've had to have been a lot bigger for that, and then it wouldn't have slipped through our security net,' Orville answers. He starts the film again.

'Within another three minutes the bodyguards had the President in the garage. Unfortunately, in all the hullabaloo, a few tiny companions followed them inside.' He pauses the film and points to five shadows swooping down from the treetops behind the car. 'These five drones flew into the garage in the slipstream behind the car.'

'Undetected,' groans Erben, glaring at Orville.

'It all happened very fast,' the FBI director says in his defence. 'Two of the drones were doing more than filming. Five legged robots with cameras were carried piggyback on them, and immediately set loose in the garage. Those things were the size of tarantulas and darned speedy.'

'What if one of them had been loaded with a chemical weapon and sprayed it?' roars Erben. He isn't sure what enrages him more, these activists or Orville. 'We can't rule it out. The President and his family murdered! Images of an ugly fight to the death beamed live around the world! This shit is worse than 9/11 . . . it proves that even the best-protected man in the world isn't safe! Those jerks pierced the very heart of our great nation. They've sown poisonous doubt and undermined trust in all the security measures we've put in place in recent years. No one in this country is safe – that's the message they've sent! Who was steering those damn things, and how?'

'Jon?' the director of the FBI calls to one of the assistant directors, adding by way of explanation, 'Jon's leading the investigation.'

It's an obvious ploy. Orville is hoping to placate Erben with this detail of personnel.

Erben and Jonathan Stem have been friends since college. Everyone in Washington knows this. At thirty-seven, Jon's young for his job. A highly decorated former Navy Seal, wounded several times, with a law degree, he and Erben have made it to the top by displaying the same ruthless self-discipline, if not the same smart appearance.

'We presume it was Zero,' Jon says in his slightly shrill voice, 'via the internet. They channelled the mobile signals through anonymizing networks. Zero was able to pilot those things using a smartphone and the internet anywhere in the world. That's the bad news—'

'But . . .' Erben interrupts him irritably. The President can't afford to lose face like this. If the President's image is damaged, his leading advisers will feel the burn too. Meaning him. 'We're eavesdropping on the whole world and we don't get so much as a sniff of the planning or of the operation itself? What the hell's the point of shovelling billions of dollars up the asses of our intelligence services and their contractors every year?!'

'We're pursuing three main lines of inquiry,' says Jon, trying to bring the conversation back to a rational level. 'First, the drones. We're investigating the origin and path of every tiny part and testing them for classic traces such as DNA, fingerprints, etc. Beyond that, we're of course finding out where the wireless cards came from and who bought them.

'Second, the video stream. It was broadcast live from a YouTube account and also on a dedicated website called zerospresidentsday.com. Probably as a backup, just in case YouTube closed the broadcast down. YouTube channels and websites have to be registered by someone. The associated email addresses, IP addresses and other digital trails were obscured or else are pseudonyms and disposable addresses, but we're already screening them.

'Third, Zero has published a lot of videos in recent years as well as an online privacy handbook called *The Citizen's Guerrilla Guide to the Surveillance Society*. We're naturally examining them all for potential clues.'

'OK,' says Erben. He can hardly ask for more at this stage. Things are kicking off in the Middle East, China is simmering dangerously, the Russians are baring their teeth again and the Europeans are trying to break their shackles of debt. He really does have a lot else on his plate. 'Keep me posted, Jon,' he says in a deliberate affront to the established directors around the table. Without so much as a glance, he turns to go.

The tiny hallway of their flat is dark, with only a narrow strip of light shining from beneath Viola's door.

'Hi, I'm home!' Cyn calls out. She puts the shopping on the table in the kitchen, which is scarcely any bigger than the hall, and lays the glasses down beside the bags.

Only now does she notice how worn out she is from the constant stream of data. She feels a mixture of relief and loss, as though she were painfully but happily kicking off a pair of smart new shoes.

'When did you start wearing glasses?' Vi asks behind her.

Cyn spins round. Her daughter is now half a head taller than her.

'Smart glasses – awesome!' Vi cries euphorically before she's even picked up the device.

How does she know what they are? She and Jeff would get on like a house on fire, thinks Cyn.

'Who gave you them?'

'The editor.'

'The *Daily*'s that tech-savvy? Well I never. Can I try them on?'

'Dinner first.'

Without so much as a grumble, Vi prepares some sandwiches while Cyn goes to the bathroom to freshen up. Over dinner, Cyn asks her daughter how her day at school went, but Vi's only interested in the glasses. Cyn tells her how she got them.

'Oh yeah, the Presidents' Day operation,' says Vi. 'Sick. If they catch those dudes, they're dead meat.'

'Have you heard of Zero?'

'Nah. Not before today anyway. Can I have the glasses now?'

Cyn lets her take them to her room, then settles down with her laptop on the sofa, which takes up virtually the whole living room – and not because of the size of the sofa. She doesn't mind the slightly cramped space. Moving into this flat shortly after Vi's birth had marked a new start. The rent's very low because she's lived here for so long. She couldn't afford to live in London otherwise.

She checks the newswires. There's a terse press release from the White House: the President and his family are fine. No weapons were involved in the attack. The FBI and Homeland Security have started investigations to track down the terrorists.

Terrorists? Cyn wonders. *Of course. Anything remotely resembling an invasion on American soil is immediately branded terrorism. But what's really going on behind the scenes?*

Every single headline mentions the operation, even though no one was killed or injured. Wherever she looks, the media are talking about nothing else. Reactions range from *Schadenfreude* to wild speculation and outrage. The reports are dominated by one photo: the President's panic-twisted features, his eyes wide with fear and his mouth open in a scream.

If Zero's aim was to turn supposedly the world's most powerful man into a miserable little heap in the eyes of the public, then the operation was a success. *He'll never forgive them*, thinks Cyn, and she feels a spark of concern in the pit of her stomach. A hysterical *and* insulted superpower is not to be trifled with.

Cyn has put the kettle on and is enjoying a couple of minutes of peace and quiet while the water comes to the boil for her tea. There's no sound from Vi's bedroom. That would have worried her even a year ago, but over the past few months, Vi has metamorphosed from Lily Munster into Goldilocks. Not so long ago, as an excuse to check on her daughter, she'd have knocked on her door to ask if she wanted tea.

Every now and then, she was gripped by the fear that Vi might slide into a quagmire of depression and drugs.

She no longer feels the need to control her daughter. After years of endless and ugly arguments they're on the same wavelength again, as Vi would say. *She seems to have picked herself up*, Cyn thinks. It's a shame she'll probably be moving out soon when she finishes school. Vi plans to start a law degree in September.

With a quiet sigh, she carries her steaming cup back into the living room.

One good thing to come of the *Daily*'s modernization efforts is the new digital archive containing every published article, which Cyn can now access from home. She searches for recent reports on surveillance, privacy and investigations by the US authorities. There's no lack of material about Wikileaks; Bradley – now Chelsea – Manning, the American soldier who uncovered US Army crimes in Iraq; and of course Edward Snowden's revelations about the National Security Agency's worldwide surveillance regime. Cyn followed the articles for a while back in the summer of 2013, but as usual, at some point she'd had to turn her attention to other, faster-moving stories such as revolutions, civil wars, floods, earthquakes, terror attacks and the financial crisis.

Also, she's a Londoner: she's used to being watched. What can she do about it? Ultimately she consoles herself with the thought that surveillance also brings a degree of safety.

She shakes off a vague sense of unease and focuses on her work. She finds an online report about how US investigators hunted down Anonymous members and a group called LulzSec. Go on the internet without the necessary precautions, she learns, and they'll nab you. Doesn't look good for

Zero, it occurs to her – they'll get them too. In the next article about the film-maker Laura Poitras, to whom Edward Snowden spilled his secrets, she discovers that the two of them were actually able to communicate undetected. Most of the measures they put in place sound technical and complicated, and others are the stuff of spy thrillers, for example, details of how they hid their phone batteries in the fridge. She takes a few notes and drafts a very rough article using keywords.

Only just turned 40, I feel as if I've woken up in a sci-fi story from my childhood . . . Privacy is dead . . . Is privacy dead? . . . Privacy has only existed as a legal concept for about 100 years . . . Is it outdated? Or isn't it being defended robustly enough? Is Zero's kind of resistance to surveillance a last twitch of the corpse or rebellion resuscitated? -> Examples of other activities and activists . . . Fear of terrorism real reason for surveillance or just excuse for control and/or profiteering?

Slowly the article begins to take shape in her mind. She'll write it up in the morning.

Next, she logs in to her account with a dating agency she throws money at every month with no real results to show for it. Her photo is almost up-to-date and she hasn't edited it out of all recognition. The slight auburn tinge to her brunette hair looks good. She shaved a few years off her age to make sure there was a three on the front.

There are five messages in her inbox. She deletes three because of the subject line and one due to its brevity. The last one doesn't sound too bad, even if he's not really her type. She might write back. But probably not.

Shortly before eleven, she starts to flag. She goes into the bathroom, which is so small she can hardly turn around between the shower and the washbasin. She sheds her clothes and, as every morning and evening, her eyes avoid her reflection in the mirror, only to wander over the pattern of taut, twisted swirls of red skin on parts of her left breast and ribs and on the inside of her left upper arm.

She feels a momentary surge of panic that online there might be a photo of the fire seventeen years ago, like the ones she saw today of the woman who lost her foot after being attacked two years later.

She takes a long shower before carefully drying herself and gently rubbing some ointment into the scar tissue. Then she puts on a T-shirt and a pair of pyjama shorts with her comfortable old dressing gown over the top.

She knocks on Vi's door.

'They're so cool!' her daughter cries after opening the door. 'Can I borrow the glasses tomorrow? I'll give you them back in the evening. Please! Pretty please?'

'Well, I'm supposed to use them for work,' replies Cyn, quickly adding, 'although I'm not quite sure what for. I probably don't need them tomorrow anyway, so take them if you like. Don't lose them, though.'

Snowman: Did you see the President's face?

Peekaboo777: Only how he lost it.^

Tuesday

'We want Google to be the third half of your brain,' Zero recites, his face having taken on the features of Sergey Brin, one of the founders of Google.

'Did Brin really say that?' says Cyn. She wheels her chair between Charly's and Jeff's to get a better view of the video.

'A few years ago,' says Jeff, 'when he was presenting Google Instant or something.'

Zero's features melt into a mixture of Sergey Brin and Larry Page's faces. His skull starts to swell, inflating like a balloon.

'It would actually be pretty amazing to have one and a half brains, don't you think?' Zero blathers on. 'Well, apart from headaches, maybe. And Google's vision gives me a headache the size of ten heads. Billions of heads, actually! Your heads . . . What do they say? Don't rack other people's brains.'

The outsized head shatters into smithereens. Another head immediately sprouts from the empty collar and just keeps jabbering away. 'I know lots of people who already use their smartphone as their external brain. Whenever they don't know something, tappity-tap, look it up on Google. Or Wikipedia. Or something else.' His tone turns sarcastic. 'Ever wonder what your brain's for? That's right:

for thinking! Go on, give it a go. Let's have a little think about what Google is. Preferably using the third half of our brain.'

Zero taps something into a smartphone.

'What. Is. Google. Wow! Over two million search results? Ouch! That's too many answers to one question for me. Let's try a different approach. What does Google itself say? "Google's mission is to organize the world's information and make it universally accessible and useful."' His face twists with rage as he continues: 'Oh, for God's sake! How much useful information even is there? Ninety per cent of the information I receive each day, no matter who sends it, is crap! Messages from Facebook or WhatsApp, celebrity news, reality shows, adverts, spam, instructions from my boss . . . The only way you can "organize" that much information is to put it in the trash – but no! Google apparently wants to turn that crap into my brain! Dear Google, I think I'm better off with the two half-brains I've got.' He pauses for a moment and leans forward. 'You can keep your third one. Organize it however you like, shunt shit back and forth, but not into my brain! It's got enough to do as it is, without any of your crap. What do you want with my brain anyway? If you do wheedle your way inside, how do I know you're going to behave yourself? *How* exactly do you organize "the world's information"? By *what criteria* do you make it accessible? *Who* defines them? Who makes the rules? Who writes the algorithms? One of your programmers? In *my* brain? Oh right, of course I'm not allowed to see them. Your computations. In my brain. Trade secrets, naturally. Big Brother's a total amateur in comparison!' Zero cackles. 'And anyway, Google isn't just the third half of my brain, but of my neighbour's too – and boy, is he an idiot! And I'm meant to share the third half of my brain with him like a Siamese twin? And with billions of other morons around the world? Siamese billionlets?' He raises his hand to his brow. 'I think I'm getting another headache. Another thing: I believe we must destroy the data krakens.'

'So let's sum up everything we know about Zero,' says Cyn, leaning back in her chair. 'Charly?'

'Here's the list of the thirty-eight videos he's posted since 2010.'

She skim-reads the titles – *Little Big Brother*, *The Great Reappraisal*, *The Human Rating Agency* – as Charly continues. 'Short, moody sermons about privacy, the extent of surveillance and other threats posed by the digital age and connectedness. Documents about a few small guerrilla operations too. For instance, they decorated CCTV cameras in various cities with gift-wrap bows or masks representing the respective head of state. Until yesterday only a few thousand people had watched these videos. Since the Presidents' Day operation they've received millions of hits.'

'There's been a lot more interest in *The Citizen's Guerrilla Guide to the Surveillance Society* since yesterday too,' adds Jeff.

'That contains tips about how to encrypt data and resist surveillance, right?' Anthony interjects. As always, whenever he's actually in the editorial office instead of sucking up to the owners or the board, he stands around whipping up his editors like an incompetent sheepdog in the middle of a flock of sheep. He continues before Cyn or one of the others can even answer. 'Do we know anything more about this gang? Who's behind it? Where their headquarters are? How many of them there are?'

'No idea,' says Charly. 'They've kept a low profile so far.'

'Secrets – perfect!' cries Anthony, clapping his hands together. 'Secrets breed stories! How much traffic are our reports getting?'

'Cyn's article has the highest number of hits for today's online edition,' says Jeff. 'The topic's hot.'

'Then let's go all out with it,' says Anthony, as Cyn studies the list of videos. She doesn't have a clue about this stuff, but that's Jeff's job.

'Maybe we could turn it into a series of articles,' she suggests. 'Every day we present one of the videos and publish an accompanying article providing more in-depth analysis.'

'That's exactly what I meant,' says Anthony, adjusting his glasses. Cyn wonders when those NHS frames are finally going to go out of fashion – Anthony looks ridiculous in them. 'But don't overdo the text,' he says, shooting Cyn a look of admonishment. 'I want to see cool graphics – animated would be best. And you should incorporate some videos of your own. We'll start with the video you just watched about Google. It's a good introduction to the subject. I want something up by this afternoon, and think of a sexy trailer to go with it.' After these words, he hurries away.

Cyn and Jeff exchange glances.

'Sexy,' she scoffs with a shrug.

'Well, at least he makes his mind up fast.'

'This is the forensics lab,' Marten Carson explains. There are signs of tiredness in his grey eyes. This latest case has kept him busy through the night.

Jonathan Stem walks over to one of the tables, where the components of a drone are laid out as neatly as the salvaged wreckage of a crashed aeroplane in a reconstruction hangar. Altogether there are eight tables in the room, and several men and women in white coats are hard at work examining the parts.

'So far it would seem that Zero's people have proceeded with great caution,' says Marten. 'We haven't been able to secure any DNA, fingerprints or any other human traces from these.'

'They knew what they were doing,' Jon remarks.

Marten picks up one particularly small component with tweezers and shows it to Jon. 'We've made a bit more progress with the wireless cards. We've been able to trace them via the serial numbers. They were bought five and six months ago respectively in Lynchburg and Richmond, both in Virginia. We've already identified the stores. According to our preliminary information, however, they were bought using pre-paid cards, which you can purchase anonymously. Both stores have surveillance cameras, and the staff are looking up the receipts for us. Two of our teams are heading down there.'

Marten leads Jon into the next room where four men are sitting in front of several monitors each. At Jon's command Marten established the central investigation office here overnight. Assistant Director Jon Stem has set no restrictions on the hunt for the authors of the embarrassing Presidents' Day operation. Marten is sure that Jon must have backing from the top, presumably from even higher up than the FBI Director. That's fine by him: all too often in his twenty-seven-year FBI career he's had to work with one hand tied behind his back.

'These are our digital detectives. They're supported by our colleagues at the NSA. Luís,' he calls to one of them, a sturdy man in his mid-thirties. 'What are you working on right now?'

'Three things,' Luís explains, rubbing his hand over his stubble. 'First, we're looking into Zero's YouTube account and the website where he streamed yesterday's videos. The YouTube account was registered with the email address zero@taddaree.com. It's a disposable address, but we're trying to trace it anyway. What's interesting, though, is that Zero uses the same name for his email address. The guys from the NSA are running their programs to check where this or similar addresses have appeared online in the past. They're doing the same with panopticon@fffffff.com, a second disposable address the website was registered to.'

'They're also looking for names and addresses on the same theme such as jeremybentham, bentham, et cetera,' Marten adds, 'for serial variants like panopticon1, 2, 3 . . ., for anagrams and backward versions.'

'How long's this going to take?' Jon wants to know.

'Our programs are pretty quick at things like this,' says Luís. 'If they find something – and they will find something – we'll have the first results in the next few hours.'

'That was still "first", right?' asks Jon.

'Yes,' Luís says. 'We're also examining all Zero's past videos. There are thirty-eight of them in total. We're checking them for the uploader's IP addresses, metadata, the software used, telltale visuals, film snippets, the types of faces and voices used, the power-line hum and so on.'

'The power-line hum?' Jon enquires.

'Recording devices are fractionally influenced by tiny frequency variations in the public power grid. That influence is detectable. So if you know the frequency variations of the grid at a particular point in time, you also know when a recording was made and sometimes even where.'

'And we know the frequency variations?'

'We've built up a database for recent years. Other countries began to do the same after the British proved a murder case that way.'

Jon vaguely recalls the case. 'Have the videos already turned up some results?'

'Not so far. We also have first to modify or write the search programs for several of those tasks. The public has helped us with others.'

'What do you mean?'

'Zero weren't particularly well known before yesterday, but they did have a small online fan club. Some of those fans had already run all the faces and masks Zero metamorphoses into in his videos through image search engines and facial recognition software. About twenty per cent of the faces and almost one hundred per cent of the masks have been identified. It looks as though Zero left only celebrities identifiable. The other faces were either completely artificial, too distorted or composed of several people, whose fragments were very hard to assign to anyone in particular. Good work. In the meantime, those checks have been verified and confirmed by several hundred volunteers.' Luís laughs.

'Do we know what software they use for the animations?'

'3DWhizz,' says Marten. 'We've already asked for every user's registration details, but there are millions of them if we include the taster and free slimmed-down versions.'

'We could certainly reduce that by combining the data with email addresses and other data points.'

'For sure!' says Luís.

'And third?' Jon wants to know.

'Third, there's the *Guerrilla Guide*. It was first published online years ago and has been continually updated. Basic stuff. But there too, we're looking for email and IP addresses and the like.'

Jon gives a quick nod and pats Luís on the shoulder, adding, 'Keep it up!'

Back in Marten's glass cube of an office, from where he can keep an eye on his whole team, Jon glances at his watch. It's an expensive model from a Swiss luxury brand, a gift from his wife to celebrate his most recent promotion.

'When will the teams get to the wireless card stores?'

'In about an hour and a half,' says Marten. 'I'll let you know the moment we get something.'

Jon nods. 'Zero thinks he's smarter than we are, like so many of these cocky internet activists. But we have the power, and more possibilities than they think. So use them,' he says, turning to leave.

The low afternoon sun picks out strands of hair, makes spectacles and earrings sparkle and casts sharp shadows over the sea of heads. These heads are streaming in all directions – slowly, hastily, with gritted teeth or relaxed expressions, chatting, laughing, talking and phoning.

There are red and green squares around the faces of passers-by. Bigger or smaller, depending on how far away the person is, they move along with the people, occasionally overlapping for a second, while others vanish and new ones appear: a psychedelic ballet of abstract patterns. Within seconds the red squares turn green.

'Wow, it's like tripping!' Vi cries. She moves her head slowly this way and that. New faces, new squares.

'I wanna go!' Bettany whines.

'In a minute,' Vi says. 'You can see it all on your phone anyway.'

'I wanna see for myself!' Bettany looks down again at her smartphone, where the glasses are transmitting everything in Vi's field of vision. The same view is shown on Sally's, Adam's and Edward's phones.

'Wink at someone,' Adam challenges Vi.

Vi's gaze alights on Bettany. She runs her fingers along the frame of the glasses. Within two seconds a caption and a few pictures appear beside her friend's face. To Vi they look as though they're floating in the air alongside Bettany's head.

Cowdry, Bettany
London
DOB: 25.06.1997
More >

'Cool!' Vi says with a laugh.

'Hang on!' Bettany calls out. She lets down her ponytail and combs her long dark hair in front of her face. 'How about now? Still recognize me?'

Bettany has confounded the facial recognition software for a second, but then an app for identifying body movements cuts in and projects her details on to the glasses again.

'Totally sci-fi!' Vi cries.

'Totally now!' Eddie reminds her.

'It's my turn now!' Bettany shouts.

'OK, OK.' Vi hands her the glasses and follows on her own smartphone what Bettany's seeing. Whereas the boxes around the other heads on Vi's screen turn green and vanish, one of them remains stubbornly red.

'What's up with him?' asks Bettany.

'Impossible to identify,' replies Adam. 'Keep an eye on him. Let's find out why.' On the spur of the moment he walks up to a slim man of about thirty with dark skin and hazel eyes with a slight yellow tinge to them. *A Bengali or maybe a Bangladeshi*, thinks Vi.

Adam speaks to him. 'Hello. Excuse me, but we're doing a survey . . .'

The man looks at him distrustfully. He doesn't stop until Adam stands in his path.

'May I ask you a few questions?'

The man says nothing, shakes his head and tries to keep walking.

Adam walks backwards in front of him. 'Would you mind telling me your name, sir?'

The man glances left and right, then speeds up.

Vi takes a quick look at her phone. The little box is still red.

'Sir?'

The man looks harassed and is now waving his arms around, trying to shoo Adam away like a bothersome fly, but Adam isn't at all intimidated.

'Sir, could it be you're an illegal immigrant in Britain?'

The man's eyes widen in alarm, he pauses and then darts past the youth who's accosting him.

'Sir!'

Adam watches him race away. The man glances back anxiously once more before melting into the throng of pedestrians.

'Bull's eye!' says Adam, laughing.

'Or the facial recognition wasn't working,' Eddie objects. 'Meaning you've just accused him for no reason.'

'Why wouldn't it be working?' says Adam.

'All a bit weird,' says Sally, seeking out Eddie's gaze.

The smartphones in their hands shriek like police sirens, and Vi almost drops hers in shock.

'Wow!' shouts Adam before whispering, 'Be quiet and don't give anything away.' Carefully he takes the glasses from Bettany, trying hard as he does so not to change the angle of the device, then puts them on.

'Hey!' Bettany protests.

Vi shushes her. She can already see from her mobile what triggered the alarm. One face is framed in blue. A beefy man is coming towards them, still maybe twenty feet or so away. He approaches at a swagger, shoulders rocking to and fro, his arms turned outwards like a gorilla and with the backs of his hands facing forwards, as though trying to make himself look taller and broader. There's a chunky gold chain gleaming around his neck.

Artist's impressions flash up beside the square:

Wanted
Lean, Trevor
London
DOB: 17.04.1988
Criminal record: burglary, theft, GBH
More >

'Shit,' Eddie hisses beside her. 'What do we do now?'

'Call the police, what do you think?' Adam says quietly. 'Don't attract his attention. Police hotline call,' he orders the glasses under his breath.

Vi can feel her pulse racing. She doesn't dare look at the guy, who's almost level with her now. She stares numbly at her mobile and even slants her body away from him. Adam continues to stare directly at the man, though, and so Vi's able to watch the entire scene unfold.

A phone symbol and the hotline number are just appearing before Adam's eyes. Lean glances about and looks Adam straight in the eye. Adam evades his gaze, but too late: Lean quickens his pace.

Via her smartphone Vi hears a woman's voice answer, introducing herself as So-and-so from the Metropolitan Police. Adam breathlessly explains whom he's spotted and where. He's following Lean at a distance, his eyes riveted to the man's back. Vi and the others march along fast to keep up with Adam, but Vi has a nasty feeling. This isn't fun any longer.

Londoners have long grown accustomed to the eyes in the sky observing events in the city's side streets and thoroughfares right around the clock. It's no different with this bunch of young people hurrying along Mare Street. They simply don't notice the many cameras that have been installed since the nineties, neither the one about a hundred yards behind them nor a second one three hundred yards further up the road. The footage travels across the city at something approaching the speed of light, and because no police force in the world can afford to post thirty thousand officers in front of thirty thousand screens to check the images from thirty thousand cameras, it's a modern computer program that does the work. If the software notices something strange, it raises the alarm and passes on the pictures. Either to a screen, or to an actual operator – in this case someone from the CCTV surveillance unit in Lambeth. In theory. This is one of the three command headquarters of London's Metropolitan Police. If someone from the CCTV surveillance unit sees suspicious pictures on their screen, they inform a team in the main room next door.

Dozens of uniform staff and plain-clothes police officers sit in this room in front of countless computer screens, taking emergency calls, assessing them, sending out operational teams if necessary and then coordinating them. The room is full of the hum and purr of their concentrated, whispering voices.

Gigantic banks of monitors stretch over their heads along the room's two side walls, showing constantly changing footage from surveillance cameras. Buildings, streets, wide shots and close-ups from various perspectives, passing cars and ambling or jostling pedestrians create a fragmented panorama of the city, a flickering panopticon, feeding a continually shifting kaleidoscope. It's enough to drive you mad if you're not used to it.

The operator receives Adam Denham's call over his headset, while simultaneously viewing the images from his colleague in the CCTV surveillance unit. The operator spots the incident straight away. One person's running along a busy street, and four others are chasing after him at some distance and with varying degrees of determination. The front runner must be Trevor Lean, as the caller identified him. The operator zooms in on footage from the camera the five of them are currently running towards. The peak of his cap obscures the fugitive's face. He's wearing a dark tracksuit. The people pursuing him are young – seventeen or eighteen years old, the operator reckons. The boy out in front is burly and wears glasses. The operator can't see a phone in his hand. What's he phoning with, then? The other boy's somewhat smaller and slighter in build, but looks more agile. The two girls are lagging some way behind.

'OK, lad, I've got you,' whispers the operator and says into the headset, 'Mr Denham, we can see you on CCTV. Don't take any risks.'

Meanwhile the running man has thrown his head back and is struggling for breath. The operator can make out his face under the peaked cap now, and takes advantage of this opportunity to save a picture. The quality's too poor for facial recognition, though.

'Run a check on this Trevor Lean,' he asks his neighbour to the right. His colleague opens the database on one of his monitors and enters the name. He obtains a face and some information. The operator squints across at the monitor. Trevor Lean is indeed wanted for a variety of offences including grievous bodily harm. The running man matches the artist's impressions.

'Can you hear me, Mr Denham?'

No response.

Someone needs help, in any case. Not to mention the public disturbance this pursuit is causing and which the operator must end before people start to panic. He informs nearby units via his headset: 'I have a chase on Mare Street, near the junction with Richmond Road. Several individuals, one of them apparently wanted by the police and probably dangerous.'

He immediately receives a reply from a patrol. 'On our way to the scene. ETA approximately two minutes.'

People step out of Lean's path. He casts a frantic glance over his shoulder at his pursuers.

'What are you doing, Adam?' asks the operator. 'We've got a visual on Lean. Let him run. Don't worry, we'll get him.'

Vi is running ten yards behind Adam and Eddie. Sally's beside her, totally out of breath, but they've lost Bettany. Vi can only manage intermittent peeks at her phone, which is showing the jerky pictures from Cyn's smart glasses.

Stop! Don't go any further!

Adam must see these blinking red words in his glasses too. So why's he still haring after the man? He'd never have dared do that before.

Vi has second thoughts and falls further behind. All of a sudden she sees Lean pull a metal object from the waistband of his tracksuit bottoms. Shock courses through her like a bolt of lightning. She looks at her smartphone. The transmission's blurred, but she can still clearly see a revolver.

'Adam—' she screams. 'He's got a gun!'

'Fuck!' the operator hisses and hammers the alarm button. 'Armed man in Mare Street!' he roars into the headset, calling his team together. His three colleagues at the neighbouring monitors hook up with him.

'Calling all units around Mare Street,' the operator calls. 'Armed man in the street. Heading for Richmond Road!'

On the screens the operator sees people leaping aside, flinging themselves to the ground, taking cover. He can't hear anything, but the pedestrians' panicked reactions are unequivocal: Lean has fired his gun.

'Armed shooter!' the operator warns the outside units. 'All available patrols to Mare Street at Richmond Road junction!'

Images from seven cameras flicker across his screen and those of his two neighbours. Police cars speed across three of them. Disappear from one monitor. Appear again on another. Smaller, bigger, in the opposite direction, from a different angle. It isn't easy to make sense of it.

The operator gives instructions to the patrol cars on their way to the scene. The first ones are almost there and communicate their positions. They reach Lean and screech to a halt a few yards away from him. Two men in uniform jump out of the car. Over his headset the operator hears them shout, 'Trevor Lean, stay right where you are – you're under arrest!' Onlookers watch in shock or run away.

Lean and the police officers raise their weapons. The operator hears shots and sees a woman officer fall to her knees in slow motion and then crumple forwards. Lean simultaneously topples backwards. As he hits the ground the gun rolls from his grip and he lies on his back, completely still, with his arms spreadeagled. A pool of blood spreads around his chest.

Several uniformed men rush forward with their guns levelled at Lean, kick his revolver away and check his pulse. Others tend to their injured colleague. The operator can't make out how seriously wounded she is, as three uniformed officers are bent over her. He concludes from the wild shouting in his headphones that the woman's unconscious. A few yards away two policemen are performing cardiac massage and mouth-to-mouth resuscitation, fighting for Lean's life. The operator feverishly scours the monitors for signs that uninvolved bystanders might have been hit.

'Where's the lad who was pursuing him?' he asks his colleagues. 'Where are the other boy and the two girls? I saw more casualties.'

Will Dekkert looks over the heads of his three co-workers gathered around his meeting table and out across the roofs of Brooklyn to the skyline of Lower Manhattan. At forty-five, Will's the oldest in the room, but he doesn't feel it. Others might notice the grey streaks in his hair and the first signs of wrinkles on his face, but he himself doesn't see them.

His gaze has just alighted on One World Trade Center when his view's spoiled by a blinking red light before his eyes.

Code 705, London GB

The other three people at the table sit up straight with perfect synchronization and roll their eyes behind their glasses as though on the brink of a collective epileptic fit.

47

'Put it up on the screen,' Will orders. 705 is one of the very few codes that alarm even him as Freemee's Vice-President for Marketing and Communications.

The live streams from two surveillance cameras light up a subdivided monitor covering the whole of one wall of his office. People are scattering in all directions and three individuals are left lying on the ground in their midst, one motionless, the other two writhing in pain.

'Mare Street, London, UK,' explains the superimposed caption at the bottom of the screen, also giving the names of the two shops streaming their footage directly on to the internet. Alongside the words is a map showing the Borough of Hackney. Purple triangles with small camera icons represent the fields of view of all the known private surveillance cameras in the neighbourhood; they have it almost completely covered. A host of red dots are moving around the streets. One of them is blinking. Will activates it with a sweep of his hand that's picked up by an invisible sensor on the video wall. The red dot opens up into a window with photos of a young man, along with a caption:

Freemee user:
Adam Denham, 18, London GB
Vital functions interrupted

'Fu—' Will bites back the swear word. With one economical flick of his fingers he sends a message to the entire department. 'The whole communications department to my office now,' he orders. 'We have our first Code 705.'

A good twenty members of staff have crowded together in front of the giant monitor in Will Dekkert's office. Various windows on the screen are showing footage from the Mare

Street surveillance cameras, some of it out of focus and of poor quality. Paramedics are pumping the casualties' chests while ambulance officers kneel beside them, holding up drips. Onlookers are as usual getting in the way, and police officers are running this way and that.

The London city map and personal details from Adam Denham's Freemee profile are superimposed on the screen.

'The Code 705 came in five minutes ago,' Will explains. He registers the shock on some faces. The images upset him too, but he's trying hard to set his emotions aside. 'Eighteen-year-old Adam Denham was shot in London after identifying a wanted criminal on the street with the aid of smart glasses. According to first reports, four other individuals were seriously injured in the shoot-out.'

He points to Adam Denham's Freemee profile, which resembles any other social media profile: portraits, pictures, messages, comments and all manner of diagrams and emoticons.

'We know everything there is to know about Adam. He's a registered Freemee user and a very active one too. He's collected all his measurable data on his account – from his smartphone, his computer, internet connection, and bank and loyalty cards. Add to that his smartwatch and sleep sensor, and we know his movement profile, his communication habits and his lifestyle functions. He also uses many of our lifestyle apps to improve himself.'

Will plays back the recordings from the moment Adam's glasses identify Lean. He opens the conversation with the police in a window below the video. Three other bars feature graph curves showing his pulse, walking pace and skin resistance.

'He used the smart glasses to stream the chase live to his Freemee account.'

49

The recording reaches the point where Lean shoots Adam. The shot itself is virtually inaudible, but the recording wobbles and then the screen is filled with blue sky.

'Our automatic tracking and analysis software raised the alarm when it registered the sudden end of Adam Denham's physical functions even though he was still wearing the sensor clock.'

Will turns to face the live pictures from the surveillance cameras. Two paramedics push a lifeless body on a stretcher into an ambulance.

'According to our software analysis, the medics will declare the boy dead at the scene.'

'Oh my God,' Alice Kinkaid gasps. 'That poor boy . . . his poor parents!' As Freemee's Director of Communications, she reports directly to Will and is in charge of the company's public relations work. She's smart, with a degree in Computer Science from Stanford and another in Law from Yale, and good-looking too – a former runner-up in the Miss Virginia pageant.

'He'll be the first person to die as a result of using smart glasses and Freemee's facial recognition software,' says Will. 'This story's going to cause a massive media storm. We have to do something.'

'A cynic might suggest repeating the whole thing,' replies Alice, having quickly regained her composure. 'Our membership figures have gone through the roof since Zero's Presidents' Day operation yesterday. People's curiosity is obviously stronger than their fear of forfeiting their privacy. The debate this accident's going to unleash will only drive them higher. Our programs are pretty accurate when it comes to predicting such things.'

'It's like after the massacre of schoolchildren in Newtown in late 2012,' remarks Pjotr, who's six foot six and has long straight hair, a Van Dyck beard and a paunch under his heavy metal T-shirt. He's Freemee's Head of Statistics. 'You'd be inclined to think that gun purchases would fall after a disaster like that, but instead they're skyrocketing.'

'Fantastic comparison,' Will says with a scowl. 'Anyone else feel like chipping in?'

'Let's leave cynicism out of it for a minute. We have communication plans tailored for tricky situations,' says Alice, glancing around. 'We know how to deal with this kind of thing. Expressing our sympathy to the families, pointing out the benefits of our applications, reminding people how to use them correctly, issuing warnings about misuse and distancing ourselves from it, and so on. Two days from now, at the latest, the traditional media will have dropped this topic and moved on to the next, and online media has a half-life of a few hours, anyway. At most. The important thing is to turn this to our advantage.' She tilts her head slightly to one side. Will can only stare at her as she continues unerringly. 'We will, for example, stress the advantages of our security apps. If Adam Denham had had a consumer version of pre-crime software, it would have notified him about the likelihood of Lean having a gun and using it. He might then never have put himself in that situation.'

'There'll be fresh debate about live facial recognition,' Will comments, 'and demands to roll it back to the earlier stage when it only recognized people in the user's circle of contacts.'

'We aren't the only providers,' Carl Montik interjects. Carl is one of Freemee's founders, the Chair of the Board and Head of Research, Development and Programming. He looks older than twenty-eight and has a compact and athletic physique. So far he has kept to the background, as usual. 'Since Meyes launched four months ago and refused to sell out as Face 2012 did to Facebook, there are now at least twenty-four different types of software on the market. By the way, the boy could just as well have seen that guy on some website and then recognized him in the street. They don't just put up wanted posters in police stations nowadays, they can be found online too. And let's not forget how many criminals have been caught this way.' He leans back, and a ray of light glints off his shaved head. 'To sum up the situation, neither the glasses nor facial recognition are to blame for what happened. Adam Denham ran after that stranger of his own accord. The app warned him several times to give up the chase.'

'So why didn't he stop then?' Alice asks.

Carl raises his eyebrows. 'Heightened adrenaline? We can't measure that yet, sadly, but I'm working on it.'

Alice shoots Will a quick glance, then at a barely perceptible sign from him she has the floor again. 'The real question isn't how we come through these discussions unharmed – they won't harm us, quite the opposite – but rather how we keep them bubbling away without people getting bored. As I said, a cynic would repeat the whole operation. But then again, we can't have someone dying every day, can we?'

'If only you knew,' Henry Emerald mumbles to himself. He's one of those men whose looks remain boyish long after their hair has turned white. His suit and shirt are tailormade, and his silk tie was handsewn in a mountain village in northern Italy. Daylight slants through the full-length wooden-framed, multi-paned French windows along the southern front of the building; the scene is reminiscent of a painting by Vermeer. Outside, an immaculate lawn, bordered on both sides by woods, slopes gently down to a lake over a mile away. The room is so spacious that an entire house could fit inside it – and a larger house at that than any of the other ninety on this Gilded Age estate. The modern screen standing on the heavy, dark desk looks like an exotic insect, in an interior preserved in its original state, dotted with valuable antiques. Henry Emerald leans back in the deep leather armchair as he waits for his online meeting, one hand cocked pensively under his chin. Code 705. They'd contemplated every possible scenario in advance, attributing codes to the most critical ones, and for each, according to its urgency, the names of the various executives to be notified. Code 705 is at the very top of the list: the death of a Freemee user, combined with a crime, facial recognition, smart glasses – and the experiment.

Carl Montik, sitting now in his own office, appears on the screen. He's wearing a pair of smart glasses via which he's conducting this conversation. Henry still prefers to talk via the screen of his laptop. Or in person. Being an investor in cutting-edge technologies doesn't mean he has to use them, with the notable exception of a secure connection and the latest encryption techniques, of course.

'What was wrong with the boy?' Henry asks.

Carl plays Adam Denham's Freemee profile and his photo gallery on Henry's screen. On the first photo Henry sees an overweight teenager with a haircut only his mother could have given him. Picture by picture, he metamorphoses into an attractive, confident-looking young adult. Below the photo gallery Henry sees the usual dashboard of symbols, graphics and tables. A shimmering white ball spins above it. At Freemee they call this the 'crystal ball' – their miracle weapon, their killer application. It's the secret of

Freemee's success, often copied but never even remotely equalled.

'From loser to Mr Cool in only six months,' Henry observes. 'Too cool.'

'Experiment level 7,' Carl says. 'The highest possible change in results.'

'The boy would never have followed that gangster before. I thought we had this under control?'

'He's the first in a month,' Carl argues. 'The number of unnatural deaths in the groups affected by the experiment has fallen to the average in the general population over the last 28.5 days. Adam Denham is an outlier. There was no way of predicting that he'd run into Lean. We're still vulnerable to accidents, like everyone else.'

'It should have been possible to predict his behaviour in such a situation,' argues Henry. 'The same as with the other trial individuals who overestimated themselves, became depressed or even went mad. Three thousand deaths – as many as on 9/11! This entire experiment is like sitting on a ticking bomb . . .'

'May I remind you that you were in favour of the experiment too,' Carl retorts, undaunted.

'If the public ever gets wind of what the algorithms have done, then Freemee's finished. We'll all be behind bars. And I'm talking about the best-case scenario.'

'The algorithms didn't do a thing. They didn't shoot Adam Denham,' Carl contradicts him. 'Nor any of the others. It was the individuals themselves who drove too fast or jumped off bridges.'

But your algorithms drove them to it, thinks Henry. *Although it is good to know what we're capable of.*

'Also, those three thousand cases are a drop in the ocean in the context of one hundred and seventy million Freemee

54

users,' Carl adds. 'Of the five million trial subjects, far fewer than one in a thousand have died.'

'Joszef spotted them,' Henry reminds him.

'Fortunately, otherwise we might have noticed them too late. But Joszef was a genius, and as Vice-President for Statistics and Strategy he had access to the relevant data, which we've since blocked. Anyone else would first have to extract that data from other sources, and then they'd have to study it very, very closely, think about it properly and know something about statistics.'

Henry isn't convinced. 'Why has the software marked out these two Londoners, Edward Brickle and Cynthia Bonsant? A school pupil and an old-fashioned journalist.'

'I know,' Carl admits through pursed lips. 'Common sense would suggest they're harmless, but luckily we don't need to rely on common sense. Data is unequivocal.'

Henry knows Carl trusts mountains of data more than human emotions and logic. Humans seek a reason for things – and often find the wrong one, from lack of information. They think their boss is in a bad mood because of a conversation the day before, when actually he had an argument with his wife that morning or simply slept badly. They just don't know *that*.

Often Carl doesn't find anything in the modern data mountains either, but why should he dig for causes when the algorithms offer him immediate solutions?

'The problem's like weedkiller, icing sugar and diesel,' says Carl. 'Each on its own is harmless, but in combination they're highly explosive.'

Carl opens Edward Brickle's profile.

'Edward was a good friend of Adam Denham's and a witness to his death. He's part of the experiment too. Level four. An average change in his results of about sixty per cent.'

'Which means he might have noticed Denham's rapid transformation,' Henry thinks aloud. 'So we can't rule out that he'll smell a rat.'

Carl nods. 'If he knew there was something to uncover, he'd almost certainly go looking for it.'

'Would he be capable of doing that?'

'Brickle's an IT whizz-kid, so unfortunately there's a good chance he'd find out. That's also down to Cynthia Bonsant's influence. They know each other well, and Brickle is also crazy about her daughter. Whenever he comes close to her, there's a clear change in his results: a quickening of the pulse, reduced skin resistance, etc.'

Carl calls up Cynthia Bonsant's dataset. 'She isn't a Freemee user, but there are enough publicly available data points for our needs. She works as a journalist, which is already bad. Always on the lookout for a story. She was a freelance investigative reporter before her daughter was born. Some of her scores are still much higher than her colleagues' average results: curiosity, persistence, truth, transparency, sense of duty, passion. This woman loves causing trouble – and getting into trouble. If she gets her teeth into something, then it takes a lot to make her let go. When I add inquisitive Bonsant to clever Brickle I get a 19.38 per cent probability that they'll discover the problem cases. That's far, far higher than anyone else to date.'

Henry feels a rising sense of unease. 'And your plan is?'

'I'll change the settings for Brickle and for Bonsant's daughter. She's on Freemee too. To judge by her results, she isn't in love with Eddie Brickle, but I can perhaps get her to distract Brickle so he doesn't get an itch to sniff around.'

He opens a page full of lines of code, of which Henry can make neither head nor tail. In double-quick time Carl changes a few, deletes others and adds some new ones.

'Their lifestyle apps will immediately start giving them tips to guide them in that direction without their noticing the changes in their settings,' he explains. 'I'm also raising the expectations levelled at them so the apps shower them with tasks in other areas that test them to their very limits. It can take a few days for the changes to bite, mind you. I'll also try to influence Cynthia Bonsant via her daughter, but in that regard my options are still limited.'

'It's high time we halted the experiment so you can delegate these minutiae to others,' Henry says reproachfully. 'These unpredictable events are impacting on your real responsibilities.'

'I know,' says Carl. 'I'll have the final results of the experiment in a fortnight, and the ones from the mayoral elections in Emmerstown four days from now. I can tell you already they're going to be sensational. Then we'll start the implementation phase.'

Henry terminates the connection. He can't leave Carl to handle this matter on his own. He makes a short call and summons the other relevant person to his estate. Henry decides to practise his exercises with focus and concentration until his guest arrives. He exits the room through the middle of the seven sets of double doors, stepping straight out on to the soft lawn.

Cyn leans back in her chair. Zero's latest video is playing on her monitor. This guy is slowly growing on her.

'Well, well, Mr President, that's what it's like to be watched all day when you'd rather be left in peace,' announces an indefinable voice with a peculiar lilting tone over the footage of the frantic bodyguards. The President's face appears on screen before, by means of sophisticated animation techniques, he morphs into the Secretary of the Interior and then into the heads of the FBI, CIA and NSA, as Zero continues his commentary. 'We paid the President a visit on vacation, at the cost of a few nice little machines. The video's online everywhere,' the voice says with a laugh. 'Enjoy *Zero's Presidents' Day* some more! We're going to stay incognito, though. Another thing: we believe we must destroy the data krakens.'

'The making-of,' Jeff says merrily. 'Zero posted it at noon today.'

'He's got a nerve,' Charly mutters. 'He must know the Yanks are hot on his tail. Have you seen the stock exchange over there? His little stunt sent shares absolutely plummeting.'

'American paranoia,' says Jeff.

Cyn still needs to get used to her neighbours at work and to the background noise in the engine room or 'newsfloor'. Jeff and Charly simply call out if they feel like it, even if Cyn's working on an article.

'At least that fits the piece I'm writing,' she mumbles.

'Why are you writing copy again?' says Anthony, looming behind her. Hands on hips, he peers at Cyn's screen. 'I want modern presentation – animated graphics, videos! What—'

Cyn's smartphone, old-fashioned earphones plugged in, starts to ring.

'Mobiles must be turned off on the newsfloor,' the editor-in-chief reminds her in a sergeant-major's bark.

Cyn switches it to silent. A picture of Vi pops up on screen. She's about to reject the call when Anthony generously signals that she's allowed to take it.

Before Cyn can say anything, she hears Vi sobbing into her ear. At first Cyn doesn't understand a thing Vi's saying; the only words she catches through the weeping are 'shot' and 'seriously injured'. Cyn feels panic coursing through every cell in her body. She clings to the armrest to control the trembling that's taken hold of her.

'Calm down, love.'

'I can't calm down!' Vi cries into the phone through her sobs. 'Adam . . . Adam's dead!'

Cyn feels the blood drain from her face. Adam – isn't he one of Eddie's friends? She croaks, 'What about you? Where are you?' Vi recounts all the details, still weeping, and Cyn says, 'I'm on my way.'

With shaking hands she puts down her mobile. Her heart's pounding in her chest. 'It seems my daughter's been caught up in a shoot-out. I've got to go right now.'

'A shoot-out?' Anthony asks excitedly. 'Where? Take your glasses with you and report on it – live, if you can! We'll put it up on our home page.'

Cyn pulls back a fist to punch him but stops herself at the last moment. She grabs her bag and her mobile and dashes out of the engine room.

Curious onlookers are jockeying for position along the tape stretched across Mare Street, and police officers are watching so no one can sneak their way on to the crime scene. There's the thrum of a helicopter circling overhead. Uniformed officials in high-vis jackets are scurrying around or questioning witnesses. Tears of relief well up in Cyn's eyes when she spots Vi among them. Next to her she recognizes Eddie, who's talking to a man in uniform. She works her way forward to a policewoman.

'You can't come any further,' the woman tells her.

Cyn points calmly at Vi. 'That's my daughter over there.' She holds out her press ID. The policewoman checks it and mumbles something into her radio. As soon as she receives an answer, she lifts up the tape and lets Cyn into the cordoned-off area.

Vi doesn't see her at first, but when she catches sight of her mother she closes her swollen eyes for a second and bites her lip. Cyn gives her a hug. For the first time in years Vi returns her embrace, and Cyn feels the pressure of her warm, trembling body. The policewoman who was talking to Vi waits patiently.

'I've got to finish this,' Vi says, letting go of her mum. Lowering her eyes, she confesses, 'The police confiscated your glasses.'

Her mother strokes her upper arm. 'Don't worry about that now.'

Cyn looks around as Vi resumes her interview with the policewoman. A little way off, some forensics officers in overalls are kneeling down, collecting evidence. Cyn walks towards them until someone in uniform blocks her path.

She explains why she's there. 'The dead boy was wearing a pair of glasses that belonged to me.'

'You'll get them back as soon as the forensics department has examined them,' the man says.

She hears a strange buzzing noise and realizes it's her smartphone vibrating in her handbag. The editor-in-chief.

'Is your daughter all right?' he asks.

'Yes.'

'Excellent! Glad to hear it. Anything to report from the scene? Are our competitors already there? You could put your glasses on and carry out a few interviews with the police and your daughter. We'll stream them live.'

'They're not working right now,' Cyn lies. 'I've got to go.' *There's going to be a right palaver when he finds out what really happened to the glasses*, she thinks.

She glances furtively around, searching for evidence and taking shots with her smartphone. She spots a few blood-stains. Lean's? Or Adam's?

She gulps. She wonders how Vi and her friends got caught up in this whole thing and how they're going to cope with what's happened here.

Vi's ready at last. 'I want to go home,' she says. Her voice betrays her exhaustion.

Eddie's questioning is over too. 'Hi, Cyn,' he says awkwardly. He and Vi have been close friends since nursery and go to the same school, although they're in different classes. Vi thinks of Eddie like a brother, but in recent months Cyn hasn't been quite so sure how he feels about her daughter.

Another girl joins them. Her blonde hair looks sweaty and her eyes are puffy from crying. Sally, Cyn remembers: she's been round to their flat a few times.

'I can't get through to my parents,' says Sally.

'You're all coming home with us,' Cyn says decisively.

Eddie peers at his smartphone and groans. 'No, I've got to go home. I've got things to do.'

Cyn glimpses a string of text messages on his screen. 'What do you mean you've got things to do?' she asks.

'I've got to study.'

'Study? Now? After all this?'

He holds up his mobile to show her.

You must go home to study, Edward.
Maths, physics, geography, saxophone.

'Who wrote that? Your mother?'

'My . . . phone.'

'Your phone? Don't be stupid! You're not going to let your phone tell you what to do! Come on, we're going.'

'But then my results will dip,' Eddie says.

'What kind of results?' Cyn enquires. 'Are you diabetic? Or do you have low blood pressure?'

'Forget it,' he says with a dismissive wave of his hand.

The first of Cyn's fellow journalists have now reached the police cordon and are asking for details of the incident. She recognizes a few of them, but they haven't spotted her yet. She forces Eddie and Vi to walk in the opposite direction, with Sally tagging along. As they leave she notices her daughter's also staring at a list of messages on her mobile display. When they reach an inconspicuous part of the police cordon, Cyn leads them under the tape and they melt into the crowd of bystanders.

Vi's touched by the fact that her mum hails a taxi for the trip home even though she can't really afford it. She, Eddie and Sally climb in the back.

As the car pulls off, Vi gives a faltering description of events: fooling around with the smart glasses, recognizing the criminal, Adam's call to the police. She has to fight back her tears and can barely continue.

Eddie and Sally call their mums, but Vi's thoughts keep circling around one image: the paramedic bending over Adam and declaring him dead, right there on the asphalt.

'We tried to stop Adam,' she says, 'but he just kept chasing after that man Lean.'

'He did that kind of thing a lot recently,' Sally remarks, sniffing. 'He couldn't be stopped.'

'He had a long way to catch up,' Vi says.

'What do you mean?' her mother asks.

'Adam was a total loser until a few months ago,' Sally says. 'Then all of a sudden he became really cool.'

'He probably wanted to record the police operation,' Eddie offers by way of explanation.

'But he ended up streaming his own death live on the internet instead,' groans Vi, feeling the tears welling up again. 'We could follow the whole thing on our smart-phones. If he shared it with the rest of the world, then it's probably made the news bulletins already.'

She can feel her mother's eyes boring into her. She averts her gaze and stares tensely out of the taxi window as London's grey streets flash past.

'Pull!' Henry shouts and fires. A hundred yards away the clay pigeon shatters. In place of his suit jacket he's now wearing a sleeveless, lightly padded vest with a leather patch on the right shoulder.

'Pull!'

The next pigeon explodes.

He sees the man he's expecting approach over the hill to the left of the shooting range. Henry removes his ear defenders and protective glasses, breaks the shotgun over the crook of his arm and greets the man with a curt nod.

Joaquim Proust used to be Henry's bodyguard, but he's now the head of a global security firm that he built up decades ago from Henry's personal security detail. He's a head taller than Henry, and his face has the angular patrician features of a former elite soldier from a good family.

Henry knows this estate, barely an hour by helicopter from Manhattan, offers complete privacy, although Joaquim must now review a number of potential scenarios and the existing precautions for his security in the wake of the Presidents' Day incident.

Joaquim is the only person Henry has fully initiated into the secrets of the Freemee project. He knew from the very outset that he'd need to use every means at his disposal to protect this particular investment. Freemee was bound to arouse greed and criticism from various quarters once certain people had grasped its potential. In order to guarantee Joaquim's loyalty, Henry's even given him a two per cent stake in Freemee that Carl knows nothing about. It also became necessary to tell Joaquim about the experiment because of the unexpected deaths no one was ever to find out about.

Joaquim comes straight to the point. 'I presume this is about Eddie Brickle, a friend of the deceased Adam Denham, and that British journalist.'

'Primarily, yes,' Henry replies. 'Your programs have got even me flustered. The two of them seem so harmless, but if the algorithms are right . . .'

'They're similar systems to the ones we've been using at EmerSec for several years to combat or predict crime and terrorism. You know how reliable they are. Carl is steering Brickle via Freemee. We're keeping a special eye on him, and we're working on Bonsant too.'

'I'm eager to avoid another Joszef case,' says Henry.

'We all are,' Joaquim answers. 'There's no need to intervene just yet. With Joszef we had to act immediately because the algorithms had calculated there was a ninety per cent chance he would talk. It's only around twenty per cent for Brickle and Bonsant.'

'What if they suss it out?'

'If they really do stumble across the three thousand deaths, we'll go through the usual steps, one after the other. First, distraction. Then, if that isn't enough, we'll offer them a stake in Freemee's equity to make them millionaires.'

'So we'll try to buy them off,' Henry summarizes.

'Yes. Elimination only becomes an option in an absolute emergency or if the conditions are perfect. There's always a risk of attracting attention.'

'Fine. Anyone else?'

'Not really. The guy in Toronto, the two in LA, two in Berlin and one in Sydney are all above three per cent. They speculate in their blogs and articles, but they're not presenting any facts. So they're no more dangerous than the usual conspiracy theorists. No one has gathered any presentable evidence. So far we haven't come across anyone who's even tried.'

Henry loads his gun. 'Good.'

He puts on his ear defenders and glasses, nods farewell to Joaquim, turns round and raises his shotgun. 'Pull!'

Cyn and the youngsters clear away the plates, which have a few lingering remnants of pasta sticking to them. The homely smell of spaghetti Bolognese is still wafting around the kitchen when the doorbell rings.

Annie Brickle almost crushes Cyn in her embrace and then rushes into the living room. Eddie smartly sidesteps his mother's anxious attempts to give him a hug. She's come straight from her job in a shop and gratefully accepts Cyn's offer of a quick drink. The two of them have been close ever since their kids made friends in the playground. Eddie's father left Annie two years after Vi's father left Cyn, when he ran off shortly after her birth. Good riddance, too.

Annie herds the young people back into the kitchen, plops down on to a chair and forces them to tell her everything from the very beginning. The three of them are more composed now than they were in the taxi. The initial shock has subsided, and Cyn senses that Vi and her friends are now in the grip of a combination of grief and anger.

65

Eddie leaves the talking to the girls and checks another message on his smartphone. What he reads appears to worry him. Soon afterwards Vi also interrupts her tale and glances critically at her phone. She starts tapping excitedly on it. The children's rude preoccupation with their mobiles at the expense of the conversation irritates Cyn. She's about to say something when her own phone rings, displaying the number of a journalist from a rival paper. Cyn steps out into the hallway to take the call.

'Your daughter was there!' he says after a quick greeting. 'How do you feel? Guilty?'

Actually she doesn't find this colleague so bad. Quite the opposite: if he didn't harp on so much about how happily married he is, she could really quite fancy him. But his question enrages her.

'Why should I feel guilty?' she snaps at him.

'Because of the kind of thing your daughter gets up to?'

'*What* kind of thing?'

'No comment, then?'

'None at all,' she replies and cuts the call. She casts her mind back to the crime scene. Did one of her colleagues spot her there after all? Or did the police give out Vi's name? She's just about to go back into the kitchen when the doorbell rings. She opens it, expecting to see Sally's mum, but instead of a woman there are two men standing outside, one of them holding a small video camera to his eye.

'Hi, Cynthia,' bleats the other man. 'Some scoop you got! Is your daughter here?'

'If you have any idea what your kid gets up to, that is,' hisses the guy with the camera. 'We'd like to speak to her.'

Cyn knows them both. They're reporters for two nasty tabloids. She pushes the door shut, but one of the two has stuck his foot in the gap.

'And with you too, while we're at it. Are you an uncaring mother, as Zero claims in his video about Adam Denham's death?'

An uncaring mother?

'What video?'

'She hasn't heard about it yet,' says the bloke with the camera.

'Obviously not,' bleats the other one like a billy goat.

'Well? Who wants to go first, mother or daughter?'

She slams the door with an audible 'Fuck off!' She gets a sliver of satisfaction from the cry of pain as the man extracts his foot from the doorway.

'Bloody vultures!' she hisses with her back against the door.

'Colleagues of yours,' she's reminded by Vi, who's gathered in the hallway with the others. 'You seriously believe that'll be enough to get rid of them?'

The men's voices can be heard outside, as can their fists banging on the door.

'Sh—' Cyn curses. 'They're going to lay siege to the house. And they're probably only the start. What video was that guy talking about?'

Eddie turns his smartphone so she can see the screen. 'This one, I guess.'

Zero's strange shape-shifting face roams through the footage of private surveillance cameras on Mare Street, as though reporting as events unfold.

'So it's finally happened,' Zero explains. 'Two people were shot dead today in London and several others seriously injured because a bored youth went on a manhunt.'

The backdrop freezes, but Zero keeps moving until he stops next to ... Adam Denham! 'He was using a fancy

67

pair of smart glasses to scan the people around him,' explains Zero as the scene switches to a pedestrian's perspective with passers-by streaming past on all sides. Cyn realizes this is the view through her glasses on Adam Denham's nose. Vi and Eddie appear in his field of vision!

'Shit!' Vi gasps. 'That's us.'

'And he was recording the whole thing on his Freemee profile,' Zero continues. 'Hey, parents – do you know what your child is up to?' he cries, as the face of a man in a peaked cap is framed by a blue square. A composite picture and some text pop up next to the coloured box:

Wanted
Lean, Trevor
London
DOB: 17.04.1988
Criminal record: burglary, theft, GBH
More >

'As bad luck would have it, the boy spots a wanted criminal. Without knowing anything more about him – whether he's merely accused of a crime, convicted or on the run – he makes it his business to pursue him. Much to his misfortune, for that discovery was to be his last.'

The video spools forwards until Lean pulls his gun and aims it at his pursuer. Mercifully the recording stops there.

'What turned this nice lad into a wannabe sheriff? A wish or desire to stand out? Well, he sure got what he wanted,' says Zero, having now slipped into the guise of an old man. In a sweet singsong he continues, 'But it's not fair to criticize the young man. After all, everyone out there is engaged in some kind of manhunt. Banks, credit card firms, supermarkets, car manufacturers, garment producers, everybody.

Some internet giants even refer to themselves as search engines.'

For a split second Cyn thinks she recognizes traces of Google's CEO in Zero's features, but he's already metamorphosed into the boss of Facebook.

'Facebook, the book of faces, is what another of those giants calls itself,' Zero explains, continuing his transformations. 'They've experienced many a problem and scandal, and yet still they've got billions of members. As toilet walls the world over know: Eat shit – millions of flies can't be wrong!' Zero pauses momentarily before thundering, 'So eat that shit – all of you! *You!* That's right, you – the person watching this video! You couldn't give a shit what they know about you or what they do with that knowledge . . . But nothing had better go wrong, because otherwise you'll moan, "How could this happen? How do they get away with it? I didn't know!" Wrong! You didn't *want* to know! As long as the internet companies offer you some ridiculous advantage, you're on board. The keyword is convenience. But how much longer are you going to put up with this? Fight back! You're not going to get me, you data oligarchs! My soul's not for sale . . . Another thing: I believe we must destroy the data krakens.'

Hey, parents – do you know what your child is up to?

Cyn feels her throat tighten. So that's what those two louts meant. The entire world knows it's her daughter in this video!

'Shit,' Eddie says, 'we're in a Zero video.'

'Watch your mouth, young man!' his mother warns him. 'Who is this Zero?'

'Mum!' Eddie groans.

Before anyone can tell Annie, Cyn's mobile rings again. She recognizes the number.

'Hi, Cynthia,' Anthony greets her. 'How's your daughter? What a story, eh! Have you written anything yet? Made a video? An interview with your daughter? A *Daily* exclusive?'

She says nothing and pushes the 'End' button.

I should write an article about your inappropriate reactions!

Eddie's and Sally's phones ring at almost exactly the same time.

'Don't answer,' Cyn warns them.

The hooligans outside bang on the door again and shout Cyn's name. She shrugs. 'I'm sorry. I do apologize for my colleagues.'

'No, I'm sorry,' says Vi, adding helplessly, 'that video . . . We had no idea this would happen.'

Cyn stops herself from commenting on the use of certain devices and applications, preferring to console Vi instead. 'None of us comes out of this very well. It'd be better if you went into the living room with the others.'

The kerfuffle outside the door is getting louder. Cyn thinks she can hear more voices, and a peek through the spyhole confirms her suspicions. 'Great. Now there are five of them.'

'Good grief,' gasps Eddie's mother. 'Have they got us cornered? How are we supposed to get past them? Can't you talk to them as a colleague?'

'Forget it – they want their story.'

Anthony's number appears again on Cyn's mobile display. She ignores it.

'Can we call the police?'

'If they hear I'm a journalist too, they'll just laugh themselves silly.'

'So we're stuck here?'

'Not necessarily,' remarks Eddie, who's bent over his smartphone, frantically tapping and swiping on it.

'Has one of your ActApps got some advice?' Sally asks him, fiddling around with her own device. 'Maybe there's even an ActApp for this specific situation. For public relations or something. Why didn't it warn us?'

'It just did,' replies Eddie. 'Why do you think it occurred to me?'

'Me too,' says Vi. 'It's even increased our results for high name recognition.'

'Sick!' Sally cries.

Cynthia hasn't a clue what Vi and her friends are going on about.

'What the hell are you doing?' asks Eddie's mother.

'Watch your mouth, young lady,' Eddie mocks her without looking up.

'Hey guys,' Vi interjects, 'we don't need an ActApp! They want a statement from us? They'll get one. Who needs journalists to make a statement nowadays?'

Great, thinks Cyn. *Now my own daughter's making me redundant.*

'So, this is what we're going to do,' Vi begins. As soon as she's explained her plan, they all take up positions next to the front door with their mobiles. The door chain is fastened to ensure that the door can open only a few inches.

At Vi's command, Cyn opens the door. The reporters outside call out wildly to them. All five people inside the flat poke their mobiles through the gap and start taking pictures.

Carl's mood pervades the meeting room like a bad smell. It's the second time Will has convened his team in one day.

'Now this bunch,' Carl says angrily as the final image of Zero's video is still glowing on the screen. 'They're annoying. Who do they think they are? Savonarola? Howard Beale? V?'

'Who's Savoranola?' Will hears someone whisper in front of the video wall. He motions to Alice to speak. He can always rely utterly on her professionalism in tricky situations like these.

'Let's consider the positive aspects of the operation,' Alice notes. 'Pjotr,' she says, handing the baton to the Head of Statistics.

'As predicted, reports from London over the past few hours have been very useful to us,' he explains. 'We're seeing huge growth in Western European markets in particular: the Newtown effect. The same is true of the condemnation from Zero – we even have precise figures to demonstrate it.' He projects a graphic with some brightly coloured curves on it. 'There's a clear correlation between the increasing number of people watching Zero's videos and the rise in our user figures. Both of those numbers have exploded since Zero's Presidents' Day operation. We've gained over eleven million new users in the past twenty-four hours! We've never achieved that through our own marketing campaigns. Put plainly, Zero's videos that are critical of Freemee have brought people flocking to us.'

'They mention us too, do they?' Carl asks indignantly. 'What are they moaning about?'

'The human rating agency, the possibilities for influencing people's behaviour, the usual stuff.'

'They criticize us, and it works to our advantage?' asks Carl.

'The Newtown effect again,' says Alice.

'It's a good thing they don't know,' says Will with a chuckle, 'or else they'd stop.'

'Or perhaps they don't care.'

'Mind you, Zero's popularity will soon fizzle out if they don't follow it up with something equally spectacular.' Pjotr presents another curve, which rises very steeply but then dips again just as fast. 'Future developments will probably look like this.'

'Too bad,' says Will. 'Zero's popularity will decline, and if fewer and fewer people watch Zero's videos, that'll reduce its positive impact for us too.'

'That's true,' Alice confirms. 'We should make sure that Zero stays as popular as possible.' She leaves the others some time to process this thought before adding, 'I might have a suggestion.'

'Zero thinks we're evil, and yet you want to encourage him?' asks Carl.

'You saw Pjotr's statistics,' she says.

Carl nods. 'Fine. How do you want to go about it?'

'The hysterical reports about Zero highlight something: people are fascinated by manhunts! Even more so when the hunted individual divides opinion. Remember the hunt for Edward Snowden? The slow drip of reports. The guessing game about where might grant him asylum and what would happen next. You'd have been forgiven for thinking that a screenwriter was scripting his escape.'

'That'll only work for a few days at most,' Will objects.

'We can keep interest simmering along nicely and then turn up the heat at regular intervals,' counters Alice. 'It's the same principle behind every series.'

She fiddles with her mobile and projects a film poster on to the wall of monitors: *The Fugitive*.

'An old film from the nineties, based on an even older TV series from the sixties. If any of you can remember what TV is.' This earns a gentle ripple of laughter. Will suddenly feels old.

'Both the series and the film are about a doctor who's wanted for murdering his wife, even though he's innocent. The public stayed loyal to the original TV series for four years. Four years! Just to watch a guy on the run!' Alice continues.

'You want to stage a similar story in the digital age?' Will asks in disbelief.

'We have the perfect ingredients. The world's most powerful politician is furiously searching for Zero, and at the same time there's a lot of sympathy for Zero in his battle against global surveillance.'

'A price on Zero's head or heads?' Will enquires.

'Probably heads,' says Alice. 'No one knows how many people are behind Zero.'

'Overwhelming force hunts underdog,' Will contemplates, increasingly tempted by Alice's idea. 'A successful recipe in *Enemy of the State*, *The Running Man* and *V for Vendetta*.'

'And many other films,' Alice adds. 'This hunt will be incredibly controversial! Data protection activists and privacy junkies around the world howl in outrage, soon joined by politicians of all stripes. What publicity! Some people will start hunting for Zero, others will back him or them. The duel between the hunters and the hunted will become a showdown between two world views. It'll make for awesome drama – and yet it's real life!'

'But if even the FBI can't find Zero . . .'

'We don't need to find him. It's all about the hunt! The longer it lasts, the better it is for us! It just has to be high profile.'

'There's just one snag,' Will interjects. 'A hunt like that would make us unpopular with many people. People's sympathies are always with the underdog.'

'That depends on how we spin it,' says Alice. 'Lots of people here in the States think that Chelsea Manning and Edward Snowden are traitors. But that's not what we're about. All we want to do is raise Zero's profile, because he drives users into our arms. But you're right, of course: we have to get someone else to organize the chase.'

'Who?' Will asks. He looks from one face to another for suggestions.

No one answers. Carl alone taps on his lips with his index finger as though he's seriously contemplating the matter. Finally he says, 'Give me a minute to make some slight adjustments to one of our search algorithms.'

He sits down at Will's desk with his tablet and starts to type at great speed.

'Let's see who's best suited to the job,' he says. 'We need the right medium and a suitable individual. He or she must work internationally, our target groups must be able to identify with them over the coming months and they must be good communicators. The more famous the better. The person must also be available and have a good reason to look for Zero.'

'Is that a yes?' asks Alice.

Will isn't sure if Carl is treating Alice's proposal seriously. He'd have taken a more conventional path himself, but he's tempted to give her a freer rein. The woman has potential, that's for sure.

Carl is still hunched obsessively over his tablet. 'There,' he says eventually, making an exaggerated swipe with his finger to complete his work before looking up at the group. 'I've got someone.'

Cyn adores the photo of her fellow journalists outside her front door. The way they gape greedily as they point their cameras and microphones like guns at her mobile! Cyn is also astounded by the audacity with which her daughter posts the picture on her online profiles after tagging it with a caption in a large font.

Rest in peace, Adam?

It's only a few hours since our friend Adam Denham was violently killed before our eyes. We extend our sincerest condolences to his family. We too mourn him from the bottom of our hearts. Sadly, the tabloid press respect neither grief nor privacy. We ask them to leave the dead in peace and the living to their tears. Please share this message with your friends so that together we can send a strong signal to so-called journalists and their employers.

Vi has added the names of the reporters and the media they work for. Cyn is amazed at how skilfully and quickly Vi and Eddie have put the post together.

Everyone's a reporter now.

'Less than fifteen minutes online and it's already got over a thousand Likes, Faves, Yeahs and positive comments on social media,' Vi observes with satisfaction. 'And it's been shared more than seven hundred times already!'

'Same thing on mine,' reports Eddie.

'Mine too,' says Sally.

'Come on, Mum. You share it too,' Vi encourages Cyn.

Yet Cyn's reluctant to publish the message on her small number of accounts. They were supposed to be left in peace by the media, as Vi demanded in her statement. They were supposed to be left alone with their grief and their thoughts. The journalists may not have got any doorstep or phone interviews, but they've still managed to coax a statement from Vi and the others. Is she the only one to whom this feels like a defeat?

Her mobile's buzzing again. For a change, it isn't Anthony's number that appears; he's already rung her a thousand times. Cyn recognizes the first few digits as those of a major TV channel. She hesitates for a second, then takes the call. She knows the woman on the other end of the line a little. The woman announces that she's seen Vi's photo and message and asks if Vi would like to appear on a talk show about privacy and social media that evening; Cyn can come along too. It'd be useful to discuss a parent's role, especially in light of Zero's video. Ah, so this woman's seen it already. Cyn politely declines the invitation.

Vi peers through the spyhole. 'Let's hope this works.'

'Maybe I can find another ActApp to help us with the next steps,' says Eddie, swiping his smartphone screen.

'Hey, can you please tell me precisely what sort of help you're expecting from your mobile phone?' Cyn asks harshly. 'It's not a lifestyle guru.'

'Yeah, I'd like to know too,' Annie joins in.

Eddie and Vi exchange a glance Cyn has seen many, many times since they were small. Caught in the act! it says. It's followed by some secret deliberations: Is there any point denying it? Forget it, she won't leave us in peace now.

Correct: she won't.

'You know, mobiles have become pretty handy,' Vi replies. She's dreaded this day. There are a few things her mother won't get – or want to get – and she's now going to have to explain them. The best plan is to reveal as little as possible. She just hopes smart alec Eddie won't butt in.

'ActApps are Freemee's individual lifestyle apps for many areas of life, from diet to sport and maths,' he's already spouting. 'It's not much different from having a coach or private tutor or a clever friend. As you can see, they work brilliantly! How do you think Vi got such good marks recently?'

'Great, Eddie. Thanks a lot!' Vi chunters. 'Maybe because I studied hard?' *What an idiot!* She glares at him to shut him up, but Eddie won't stop.

'But why did you start studying? And so efficiently too.'

'Well, what about you?' Vi counters. 'So your good marks just came out of the blue, did they?'

'This is all gobbledegook to me,' Cyn says. 'So have your smartphones started tutoring you? Now that would be the first really useful thing they've ever done.'

'That's right! Great, isn't it?' Vi confirms. She glances quickly at her mobile, which has alerted her to another call. It's a good thing she switched it to silent.

'Viola!' her mother warns her as Vi rejects the call. 'Don't change the subject, OK? How does it work? These apps don't even know you. How are they supposed to give you personalized advice?' She pauses. 'Good Lord! Have they stolen your data?'

Eddie looks warily at his mother, who is all ears, before continuing with a sigh. 'No, it's nothing to do with data theft. I've turned the tables on them by collecting my own data, and it works much more efficiently than previous data thieves. A few providers, most of them from the quantified self movement, have recently launched that kind of product.'

'The what?'

Vi can tell from the way her mother sucks in her breath that this news is sticking in her craw.

'That's what they call people who observe themselves as closely as possible and measure everything, even their food intake and physical performance. It's a growing trend.'

'What they used to call hypochondriacs,' Cyn shoots back.

'Why?' says Eddie. 'It's a very simple way of improving your life. Fitness, diet, health checks, education – all via the app. But you can also include data from other sources: social media, mobile phone, credit and loyalty cards, even the satnav in your car. That way everything's in one place and you can access it with your mobile. Freemee and other companies have developed systems that allow you to upload your data continuously to your account.' He shows her the small screen strapped to his wrist. 'It also takes into account the data from my smartwatch. It measures my steps, my pulse, skin resistance, where I hang out, my sleep.'

'Quantified self . . .'

'You even record your pulse and your footsteps?' Eddie's mother gasps disbelievingly. This is obviously news to her.

'Yes, Mum,' answers Eddie, rolling his eyes. 'It's just an improved version of the heart-rate monitors many joggers have been using for years, only I wear my smartwatch all the time. I can see my results live on my display. It shows me if I'm getting enough exercise, if I have a balanced lifestyle—'

'I don't need a watch to tell me that,' Cyn objects.

'But this way I get far better information about myself than any snoop could ever steal and collate. And I can do myself what only huge companies have been able to do until now: by collecting, analysing and interpreting data I can calculate my future opportunities and risks and turn them to my advantage. Why should only banks, supermarkets, mail-order firms and clothing brands know my prospects? I'm the one who needs the information most, right?'

'That's absolutely right,' Cyn admits.

'But Freemee didn't stop at data analysis and predictions,' Vi explains. 'It doesn't only help us to *calculate* opportunities and risks, but also to make the most of the opportunities and avoid the risks, which improves our lives. You want that too, Mum, don't you?'

Before Cyn can object, Eddie continues, 'That's why they worked with psychologists, sociologists and other specialists to develop lots of small lifestyle apps – so-called Action Applications, abbreviated to ActApps – which make appropriate recommendations for different areas of your life.'

'And you listen to them?' Cyn asks, flabbergasted. 'You too, Vi?'

'Yes,' Vi admits. 'And as you can see, it works. You could register too, by the way. I've heard that their dating apps are much, much better than traditional ones.'

Her mother ignores this jibe. 'When did you start using them?'

'About nine or ten months ago,' Vi says with a shrug. This interrogation will soon be over, hopefully.

Cyn immediately realizes that this was shortly before Vi's transformation kicked in. 'Adam too?' she asks in an off-hand tone.

'Of course,' Sally interjects.

'So *they* were responsible for turning him from a wimp into Captain Fantastic?'

'Possibly,' Vi replies. 'He wanted to be cooler, and the apps probably helped. The same way a psychiatrist or a coach or a friend would have helped him.'

'They seem to have overshot the mark,' observes Cyn, although she immediately wishes she could take back her words.

'Great choice of words, Mum. Respect.'

'I'm sorry. We're all a bit shaken up, I guess,' she says.

Her phone blinks with a text from Charly: 'Boss in a right tizz. Get in touch.'

It was only to be expected, but he must understand it's impossible to write an objective report when you're personally involved. Still, she's going to be in very hot water tomorrow. She pushes the thought to the back of her mind.

'Now I see why the apps know so much about you,' she says. 'Because you feed them your data. But surely they can only give you approximate and general advice. How can they tailor it to an individual person?'

Vi shrugs her shoulders. 'No idea. The main thing is it works.'

'Everything's changing so fast in this field,' Eddie lectures her cockily, 'but virtually no one knows about it.'

Like me, for example, thinks Cyn, shooting Annie a quick sideways glance.

'What did it use to be like and what's changing?' she enquires, although Eddie's tone is rubbing her up the wrong way.

Vi rolls her eyes, but Eddie refuses to be put off. 'For years and years computer programs were simply calculators. You fed them as much information as possible, and they came up with some results. It was basically one gigantic, and largely unsuccessful, exercise in storing and retrieving information.'

Much to Cyn's irritation Eddie's eyes keep wandering to his smartphone during his explanations, and again and again he swipes the touchscreen with his thumbs. Checking his messages does nothing to stem the stream of words, though.

'Then they developed a totally new kind of program. What they call "machine learning" means that computers don't just calculate any more, they learn by themselves. Put simply, they test one of two options and measure the outcome. If it's positive, they keep doing it in the future; if it's negative, they try the other option. It's like a kid touching a hot stove: it learns from its mistakes. Unlike humans, though, this doesn't take them years but mere fractions of a second. By doing this they work out their own rules and assumptions which then help them assert themselves in their environment. Depending on which environment you use the program in, it'll develop different strategies and produce the results it needs to succeed. You may well have heard that a computer can beat chess grandmasters, and a human now has no chance at *Jeopardy!*'

Cyn nods, although the idea unsettles her.

'You mean these ActApps get to know me the same way people do? By approaching me in a particular way and then working out from my reaction if they were wrong or right?'

'Basically, yes. And through data analysis techniques that identify patterns and correlations, at some stage they know you better than you know yourself.'

'You're a dab hand at unsettling people,' she says tersely. She tries to digest what Eddie has just told her. 'How far does it go? Does it affect every area of our lives? Can the programmer still comprehend how the software comes to its decisions?'

'It depends. There are more and more types of app where nobody can.'

'You mean no one knows any longer why, for example, the app recommended shooting down a suspicious airliner or ordered drones to assassinate suspected terrorists? So an intelligence chief might actually say before the US Senate, "We don't know. No human knows."'

'He wouldn't say that,' retorts Eddie, 'although he probably should.'

Cyn's head is spinning. She'd really like to check out of this world, but that's no longer possible.

'The comments on our post are going wild,' Vi states after a satisfied look at her mobile. 'Virtually all of them support us.'

'Then hopefully we'll soon be rid of those people outside,' Eddie sighs.

Cyn decides not to bombard him with any more questions and to do her own research later. Her inner resistance to everything she's heard is extremely strong. She doesn't want to believe that reality has far outstripped the science fiction stories of her childhood – without her even noticing! Yet she has to admit these lifestyle apps do seem to work. In any case, they've had a very positive impact on Vi. She's still sceptical, though. There's something fishy about this whole affair, even if she can't pin down exactly what it is. She has the impression that amid their enthusiasm for these lifestyle apps, the kids aren't coming completely clean to her.

Her phone buzzes again and she answers it tetchily.

'Are we going to get our report at long last?' he yells at her.

'Definitely not now.'

'That's refusal to work,' he spits down the line. 'You're fired! The only reason for you to come in tomorrow morning is to fetch your P45 and your belongings!'

Cyn hangs up on him. She has more important things than the *Daily* on her mind right now.

It's gone quiet outside. Cyn tugs gently at one of the kitchen curtains. She can't see any of her pushy colleagues in the light of the streetlamps or the gathering dark. She wonders anxiously whether Anthony meant his angry outburst. She can't afford to get sacked. She feels a hint of panic.

Eddie's fiddling with his smartphone. 'Over a hundred thousand Yeahs, Likes and other signs of approval,' he reports. 'Shared and retweeted over four thousand times. First reports in various media.'

Cyn feels divided. A photo and a few lines of copy: these eighteen-year-olds use them as instinctively and as clinically as the experienced reporters they've just beaten at their own game and driven away.

'I think we can go now,' says Eddie's mother, adding to Sally, 'We'll take you home.'

As they troop out, Cyn's eyes alight on Vi's mobile on the kitchen table.

Give them a big hug goodbye, Viola. It'll do you all good. Edward in particular needs one.

That's the phone's advice. Cyn shudders. How does the electronic adviser know Eddie and Sally are leaving?

Cyn watches as Vi hugs Sally goodbye and gives Eddie an extra-long embrace. Her daughter's following the instructions on her phone.

When the others have left, Vi immediately pats her pockets for her smartphone, finds it in the kitchen, glances at it and then declares, 'I really should go and study now.'

'Are those lifestyle apps always so sensitive?' Cyn asks.

Vi holds up her phone for Cyn to read.

Forget maths for today. It's too late now anyway. I'll help you catch up in the next few days. Do some more physics. That'd be easiest and keep you busy.

It also gives a book title, the relevant pages and several links to websites.

'Not bad, but wouldn't it be better to get some rest?' Cyn remarks, still reeling from events and confused by the

84

message on Vi's mobile. 'You know, after all that's happened? Are you going to be able to cope? I mean your friend Adam—'

'Doing nothing won't bring him back,' Vi says. 'A bit of distraction is exactly what I need.'

Cyn wonders if Vi read that line on her mobile, but she doesn't want to nag her. 'All right. I'm here if you need anything.'

'Thanks, Mum.'

She hugs Vi, kisses her on the forehead and lets her go to her room. Cyn stands there in the hallway, staring at her daughter's closed door with the day's images flashing through her mind. Her smartphone vibrates in her pocket. Again. She rejects the call without so much as a glance at the device.

Four smartphones are ringing simultaneously on Anthony's desk. For hours now every caller has asked for information about Cynthia Bonsant and her daughter. His email inbox is overflowing, and steam is coming out of Anthony's ears. There are photos of the police at the crime scene everywhere, as well as pictures of Cyn and the teenagers taken by other journalists from outside the police cordon. Equally ubiquitous is the snapshot of Cynthia's surprised face through her half-open front door. Those photos appear as frequently now as the screenshots of Adam Denham's Freemee account when he identified Lean and the picture of Adam staring down the barrel of Lean's gun. Yet the *Daily* has had to fall back on agency photos despite their own employee's exclusive coverage at the scene and the fact that her daughter actually witnessed the crime. Adam Denham's death has already displaced Presidents' Day from the front-page headlines in Britain and other parts of Western Europe. Zero's video about it has been viewed tens of millions of times. Christ Almighty, if only Cyn were more cooperative the *Daily* could be leading the world in reporting on this incident!

Anthony isn't sure what angers him more – the missed opportunity or Cyn's refusal to work, which he takes as a personal affront. Who the hell does she think she is? She can clear her desk tomorrow!

Mel, the head of the advertising department, knocks on the plate-glass window through which Anthony surveys the newsfloor. Anthony waves him into his office.

'I need to have a word with you about a request I've received. Right now,' says Mel.

'Why right now? As if I didn't already have my hands full at the moment!'

'Because it's linked to the hype around Zero and our colleague Cynthia Bonsant.'

'She isn't our colleague any more. I've just sacked her.'

'You might want to rethink that.'

'Why?'

'Because a potential client is willing to spend four million pounds on a promotional campaign with us, but it's contingent on Cynthia doing the scheduled series of articles about Zero, albeit in a revised form.'

'Ever hear of the wall between advertising and news?' Anthony asks disparagingly.

Mel chuckles. 'That's a good one!'

Anthony laughs too. When he's composed himself again, he asks, 'Why Cynthia?'

'Because Adam Denham's death, her daughter and Zero's video have made her a household name.'

'Fifteen minutes of fame . . .'

'. . . which our client would like to prolong and use for their own purposes.'

'Are we talking about Jeff and Cynthia's series of articles or a promotional campaign?'

'It's one and the same thing.'

'I don't get it. Who's the client?'

'Sheeld, a well-financed start-up that develops privacy apps.'

Anthony pulls up the company's website. 'Sheeld,' he repeats as he skims through the uninformative introductory text on the home page.

'As in armour,' Mel explains. 'They don't want to place any ads, nor do they demand their name is mentioned.'

'This gets more and more mysterious. What do they hope to gain from our series?'

'According to what the guy told me, Zero's Presidents' Day operation has sent demand for privacy products through the roof. Since Sheeld is the leader in its particular sector, they automatically benefit the most from increased demand. So for them it's sufficient if people carry on talking about Zero, which is what our – revised – series with Cynthia is supposed to achieve.'

'Four million,' says Anthony. 'We could certainly do with the money. "Revised", you say. How? What's Cynthia meant to do?'

Cyn peeps through the crack in the door at her daughter, who's already asleep. Her breathing's quiet and regular. Softly Cyn pulls the door shut. This afternoon's events will haunt her for years.

She sits down at the kitchen table with her laptop. She's earned a glass of wine after a day like today, even if there's only a bottle of supermarket plonk in the cupboard. She pours herself a glass and takes a long swig.

She almost chokes when she spots the first headlines alongside her photo and coughs until tears come to her eyes.

She browses the reports with growing disbelief that her name is mentioned almost as often as Adam Denham's, even if it is less prominent and in smaller print.

Parents, do you know what your child is up to?

Her face seen through the crack in the front door has become a symbol of parental naivety. In her anger she considers posting some comments, but then decides to leave it be. Her email inbox is brimming with messages. Countless papers and broadcasters, both British and international, are asking her for a statement. Some of the messages are from worried friends who've been unable to get through to her by phone. Cyn types brief answers, thanking them for their concern.

The reports on the news pages quote outraged eyewitnesses, indignant politicians and excited commentators about smart glasses, facial recognition and whether they should be banned or at least kept in check. As usual, critics lament the fact that all the tens of thousands of CCTV cameras in London have once again failed to prevent a crime. The articles run through Adam Denham's life and his cosseted childhood and youth as the only child of a teacher and a bank clerk.

An only child! thinks Cyn with a lump in her throat.

Cyn can chart Adam's sudden metamorphosis from the recent photos illustrating the reports. It immediately reminds her of Vi's transformation and the peculiar tips on the youngsters' mobile phones. All of a sudden her well-mannered, very proper behaviour doesn't seem merely pleasant, but suspicious. Why, practically overnight, this conformist, obedient attitude after four years of constant defiance? She recalls that furtive exchange of looks with Eddie before the two of them reluctantly opened up about the lifestyle apps. *I hope she hasn't fallen into the clutches of some sect!* it suddenly occurs to Cyn. She has to find out who's giving her daughter advice and to whom Vi is listening. Wasn't it the same apps that turned Adam Denham from a scared little boy into a daredevil? Too much of a daredevil?

She goes on to Freemee's company website. The firm's mission is emblazoned across the home page in dark green letters:

> *Our overarching goal is to enable every person to develop their personal abilities to the full and, by doing so, nurture the peaceful, happy and mutually beneficial coexistence of all people everywhere in the world.*

Wow, there's ambition for you! Cyn scrolls down. A host of happy faces describe what they've already accomplished thanks to Freemee's ActApps: they've achieved better marks at school, learned to play the piano, found a partner, won back their digital privacy, earned some extra income, found a job . . .

Extra income?

She clicks on the accompanying video in which a cheerful young woman explains, 'Now I understand how Google and co. became the richest companies in the world. Ever since I started collecting my own data with Freemee, I've been earning hundreds of dollars per month – it's worth it, I can tell you! Start making the most of your own data today instead of letting yourself be spied on and exploited. Just register with Freemee, and you're away!'

Hundreds of dollars? Cyn scrambles to find her daughter's profile. It looks much like any other social media profile, but Vi has made lots of things public. Photo galleries trace her transformation in recent months. At the bottom Cyn finds a button marked 'Professional'. Sounds enticing . . . She clicks on it and discovers a kind of thermometer visual on which

Vi apparently boasts about how much of her data can be bought and in what level of detail. If Cyn's miserable attempts to interpret what she sees are correct, then her daughter's peddling her entire data portfolio!

How does this work? What are these kids up to? A quick check of Eddie's and Sally's profiles reveals that both of them are doing exactly the same. Cyn stares at the monitor in total astonishment. Half the world is up in arms about data theft and surveillance scandals, while these kids are out there flogging their most personal information! That's why the two of them baulked at revealing any more . . . This confirms her impression that there's something suspect going on. *Just you wait, young lady. Tomorrow morning the honeymoon's over! You've got some explaining to do . . .*

Eddie sits under the covers in his pyjamas with his laptop on his knees. The screen's cold glow is the only source of light in the room, suffusing his face and hands with a bluish gleam. He can't sleep. As soon as he closes his eyes, the images of the past day pour into his mind. That look in Adam's eye. His disbelieving expression as he turns towards Eddie and crumples to the ground, as though an invisible wall had stopped him in his tracks, as though an alien had sucked all the bones out of him.

Eddie opens his eyes wide to try to escape that look. He's still ashamed that he hesitated at first before rushing over to Adam's lifeless body . . . Even if his reaction was a pure reflex he couldn't control, reflexes can still be wrong, cowardly and weak.

However hard he washes his hands, he can't remove the feel of the warm blood pouring from Adam's chest as he tried to stem the bleeding. His invisibly tainted hands tremble above the keys and the trackpad.

His gaze wanders over Adam's Freemee profile, which the company converted into a memorial site within hours of Adam's death. There are countless comments expressing grief and horror. How on earth could this happen? Some people blame the glasses or facial recognition, but that's obviously ludicrous. The glasses had even warned Adam and told him to stop. The real question is why he didn't obey them. Otherwise, this past year, he'd always taken ActApps' advice to heart. He'd changed his clothes and his haircut, fed the fitness apps with personal data and, as a result, begun to play rugby because it suited his build and challenged his previously anxious disposition. On Adam's Freemee profile Eddie finds a host of tables and photos, which his friend used to record his progress: better results for fitness, stamina and strength; pictures of him jogging with a transmitter belt; selfies with tensed biceps or six-pack. Two months ago he'd been selected for the school team, and there are photos of that too. He'd also suddenly become a hit with the girls after years of being taunted as a virgin. Adam grinning. New duds, new hairstyle, a chick on each arm. Adam with a girl, then a different one, then a third one.

The ActApps had helped make Adam cool. As Cyn had said earlier: from a wimp to Captain Fantastic. He also recalls Cyn's next words: *They seem to have overshot the mark*. And Vi's stinging rebuke: *Great choice of words, Mum*.

That's Vi for you. Funny, quick-witted, clever, brave . . . and, since she stopped applying that black make-up, really good-looking. She's changed a lot over the past few months as well. He'd like her to be here right now. He doesn't really know when it happened. They've known each other for ever and were always like brother and sister, but then a few weeks ago – boom! He's afraid it's only him, though. He hasn't said anything to her yet. He's been using a relationship ActApp for a few days now – it gives him good advice but counsels him to be patient.

He stumbles across a photo of her and Adam in the latter's picture gallery. They're laughing at the camera. Adam has one arm tight around her, and Eddie spots Vi's fingers on his far hip: she's hugging him back. He feels a twinge of jealousy. No, there wasn't anything going on between them, even though they did have quite a bit in common, not least their remarkable and simultaneous transformation. And they both loved that.

Eddie has changed too, albeit far less than Adam or Vi. Still, everybody is constantly changing at their age, some a little more, some a little less. He finds the lifestyle apps useful too, as all his mates do. Very few parents seem capable of giving any useful advice. All they do is complain that their kids spend hours and hours on their mobiles and computers, despite lounging in front of the telly themselves the whole time. OK, Cyn doesn't, as far as he knows. But that didn't stop Vi from bitching about her mum for years. If truth be told, Eddie secretly had far more sympathy for Cyn than for her ghoulish daughter. It's interesting she doesn't make such snide remarks about her daughter's transformation as Adam's mum did. It seems fine by her. Vi's still alive, too, thank God! But his best friend is dead.

Out of nowhere, anger overwhelms him. Anger at the criminal who shot Adam in cold blood. At least he got his just deserts – an eye for an eye. But that doesn't bring Adam back. He'll never see him again. They'll never go on another pub crawl together, drowning their sorrows or celebrating their successes, chatting through the night, programming and gaming, listening to music and doing all the other stupid things you do with your best friends. Eddie can feel tears in his eyes. He's angry with Adam too. Why was he crazy enough to run after the criminal, even though all the red warning lights were blinking?

Haven't the ActApps overshot the mark?

Great choice of words, Mum.

Maybe not, thinks Eddie. *But still* . . . He gets up, goes over to the window and stares out into the dark night. By the city's dim glow he can make out a few wretched bushes in the small garden at the back of the house.

The idea of it, though . . . Could it happen? Might they have pushed Adam until he lost control? No way. On the other hand, they have pushed Adam, Vi, Eddie and many of their friends towards other things. Better marks, better career prospects, better guidance regarding their plans for the future and their particular talents, better health, better sleep and many other achievements. However, they often set Eddie real challenges, pushing him to the limit, at sport or in his studies, practising the saxophone, and dealing with his mother, his teachers or nasty classmates. Sometimes he got annoyed or enraged and wanted to give up, but he always managed in the end. They always helped – and what a brilliant feeling it was to expand his horizons, accomplish new things and achieve things he'd never thought possible. The ActApps had never pushed *him* over the edge. Is that what they did to Adam? Why blame the ActApps? All kinds of urges could have been driving Adam.

But what if? Oh crap. You always decide yourself what you're going to do. Eddie notices he's clutching the window-sill and relaxes his fingers. He starts pacing up and down his tiny room, three strides and then back, but this only makes him more agitated.

If you followed this thought through to its logical conclusion, then Adam could not be the sole victim. Freemee's ActApps might have made a lot of users more self-confident,

93

like Adam. In fact, that was their purpose. Not *overly* self-confident, though. But might they not also have had the opposite effect, even inadvertently? Despair, depression or even suicide because people had failed to achieve their goals or were overworked? It sounds far-fetched. Self-help software users should really be happier and more successful – some statistics somewhere must reflect that. Happier, more successful people are healthier and less likely to commit suicide. Does that show up in the mortality rates? He may even be able to find the figures on Freemee: after all, hundreds of millions of people publish their data on the platform.

Eddie types in a few search terms. The only result is a general statistic about Freemee accounts that have been converted into memorial sites after the user's death. Eddie compares the figures with the mortality rates in Great Britain, the USA and other European countries, which can be easily found online. There are no obvious discrepancies.

A small window containing a Freemee message pops up.

You should go to bed now, Eddie, if you want to be in shape tomorrow.

Yeah, yeah, you're beginning to sound like my mother.
He shuts the computer and goes to the kitchen for a snack. He really shouldn't eat at this time of the evening: it's bad for your digestion, sleep and fitness. But these are exceptional circumstances, and even the ActApps and their clever tips can take a hike! His mother keeps crisps, biscuits and chocolate bars in a cupboard alongside other food like pasta and flour. His gaze comes to rest on a small paper bag with a picture of potatoes on it, and the cogs start whirring in his brain. He peers inside and finds several potatoes of a similar size.

He rushes back to his room and opens his laptop again.

Shouldn't the number of Freemee users who died of unnatural causes actually be lower than in the general population? That's not what the Freemee data shows, though. There are several possible reasons for this, Eddie thinks, noting his ideas in a Word document:

- In both cases, the figures are insufficiently precise.
- Freemee is not so effective that its impact in this area can be statistically proven.
- Freemee hasn't been around for long enough to have a recognizable effect on statistics.
- Or else it's the same as a bag of potatoes.

A two-kilo pack may contain twenty potatoes of approximately equivalent size, or three very large ones and ten small ones. The point is that all he knows until he has looked in the bag is that it contains two kilos. It's the same with the mortality rates.

But what could work against there being fewer dead? Eddie ponders this question long and hard, but only one reason comes to mind: maybe there were fewer casualties in certain Freemee user groups, and more in others.

He searches the Freemee database using some new keywords and gets an interesting answer: 'No information about the causes of death will be disclosed out of respect for the deceased.'

So all Eddie discovers is that a certain number of Freemee users have died. However, he can't find out who these dead people were, where they lived or when and how they died, and he'd need this information in order to prove his theory. He can't peek inside the bag of potatoes. He's irritated he can't go any further with this. *I must be able to find this information somewhere online*, he thinks. *But it'll probably be a slog. There's no point in searching on my own – there's just too much data – but a little search script ought to be able to sift through the open data portals and other sources.* He glances at the time. Three o'clock!

Three thousand miles to the west, Joaquim Proust's glasses have been sounding the alarm for some minutes now.

'Leave it, kid,' Carl whispers to himself. The automatic tracking and alarm systems alerted him to Edward's search a few minutes ago. To begin with, Carl merely taps his fingertips along the top of the desk, starting in the bottom left-hand corner, an unconscious, obsessive impulse, but as his fingers move systematically right and then back, row by row, until they end up on the left again, he monitors Edward's search through the prototype data lenses Freemee's developed in partnership with the Institute of Technology and which are destined to replace smart glasses within a few years. The dim lights and muted noise of the city reach him from outside, and the night skyline of Manhattan shimmers in the distance. His fingers encounter a box containing a test device; he's growing increasingly tense. When Eddie continues his investigations, Carl begins to tidy the objects on his desk with a nervous precision he isn't fully aware of. He places and lays them in orderly lines by size: the lamp, the smart-glasses case, the tablet, printouts and other items, leaving exactly the same distance between each object, making small adjustments here and there, then beginning the entire process all over again. The software had calculated a 17.8 per cent probability. There was a 17.8 per cent chance that young Edward Brickle from London would be a thorn in their side. There was an 82.2

per cent probability that he'd cause nobody any trouble, neither them nor himself. Yet Brickle has chosen the 17.8 per cent option. Carl hates it when people buck the normal trend, when they act unpredictably and bring uncertainty into his world. The lamp is too far to the right, the pile of papers is slightly askew. A little push, and it's fine now.

Brickle's search entries show he's on the right track. Eddie pauses for a second, and Carl finally notices the strange arrangement on his desk. This only makes him angrier with the boy. Suddenly Carl is that two-year-old boy again who almost went deaf from an ear infection. Afterwards he could hear voices with the help of hearing aids – words reached his ears, and his brain formed them into sentences and lent them meaning – but he still didn't understand people. It was as though people didn't mean what they said. Neither his gift for maths, which saw him proclaimed a prodigy, nor the fact he sold his first home-made computer app at the age of twelve were of any use. Others remained as suspicious of him as he was of them. He soon came to terms with the fact that people regarded him as an arrogant maverick. He taught himself techniques to interpret basic messages from the facial expressions and gestures of people around him. It was like mathematics. Arched eyebrows signalled scepticism or bewilderment. He even produced an index of expressions, gestures and behaviours for his own use so he might compare and comprehend them. Then, one day, that girl turned up in class. The teacher assigned her a desk in the front row and treated her differently to all her classmates. She didn't say much and if she did, she stuck to facts and soon gained a reputation for arrogance, like him. One day someone said, 'You and Carl are a perfect match.' They'd hardly exchanged a word up to that point. It would most likely have stayed that way if the girl hadn't come up to him one morning and asked, 'Have you got Asperger's too?'

'I'm Carl Montik,' he replied, puzzled, and he still sees some of Forrest Gump in his reaction when he thinks back to it. He looked the term up when he got home.

The very first lines of the description were a revelation, and an hour later he was a new person. One talk with his parents, one test with a specialist doctor later, and everything was suddenly much plainer. He has trouble apprehending and interpreting other people's emotions, and so he'd rather keep himself to himself. He knows he needs routine and order. Only when he's extremely agitated does he veer into frantic tidying activities to regain control of his bewildering emotions. As just now, he doesn't always realize he's doing it. He sits up abruptly and presses his palms down on the tabletop.

Brickle is clever enough and he's an able programmer. He's capable of writing a search program in a few days that will let him scour the internet for the necessary data. That's how much time Carl has to stop him by diverting his interests towards other topics. Not long. Freemee's a powerful tool, but not a quick one. It can't achieve radical change in a few hours – it takes days or, more likely, weeks and months. So Carl has to buy himself some time by other means.

He opens the boy's account via a secret back door and adjusts a few settings so the ActApps will keep him on an even tighter rein. The kid has always followed Freemee's recommendations until now.

Keep it up! thinks Carl. *It's in your own best interests.*

He's done all he can with Eddie for now. That leaves the boy's friend's mother, the busybody journalist. She needs a little assistance to carry out the assignment Alice has devised for her. He doesn't need a search program to find a suitable person this time. He uses his glasses to call a contact he thinks would be right for this job. He's currently on holiday in Europe and so it's the middle of the night for him, but the man answers quickly and his voice doesn't sound at all sleepy.

'Miss me so much you have to ring me up at this time of night?' Carl's contact says with an audible grin. 'Or is it merely urgent?'

Erben's fingers stroke the misted cocktail glass. He loves the feel of the cold moisture on his skin as he first draws a few lines on the glass before gradually wiping away the condensation, a finger's breadth at a time, until he can see through the contents from the outside too. The clink of glasses, the clatter of cutlery on crockery, voices of all pitches and music mingle to form a dense blanket of sound in this exclusive Washington, DC club, making eavesdropping an impossible task.

Outwardly relaxed, Erben Pennicott stands at the bar, waving to someone in one corner, then noticing something elsewhere. He knows practically everyone in the room, and they all know him. The members are handpicked, so Erben doesn't need a bodyguard. He's conscious that his presence here after Zero's Presidents' Day sends a signal, as does his choice of companion, who's now taken a seat beside him at the bar. No big deal, his presence says. It also strengthens the other man's position – and Erben still has many plans for him. First, though, they have a few things to discuss.

'The President wants to know if Zero's new video provides any clues as to the perpetrators,' says Erben. He hates this topic: he regards paying any further attention to these activists as a waste of time. 'They demonstrate, we legislate,' a German politician once trenchantly put it. Presidents' Day had given them their fifteen minutes of international

99

fame, an instant of gratification and self-satisfaction for the powerless. Erben would shut down the case if only the President himself were not so boundlessly vain and so personally stung. Especially as public interest is already flagging. No dead? No terrorists? Next story, please. Yet Erben must ask the question, at the very least.

'Not yet,' Jonathan Stem explains. 'The wireless cards in the drones were our main hope until now, but they haven't given us any leads. Our investigations of the digital tracks have turned up some preliminary trends, but we're nowhere near to identifying any real individuals.'

'We've created the most powerful surveillance system in the history of the world, turned the entire planet into a panopticon, and yet we're incapable of finding these idiots?'

Jon's eyebrows offer a twitch of regret. 'The fact we're *able* to see and hear everything doesn't mean we actually see and hear it. You know the system's weaknesses. Vast amounts of data just vanish into the bellies of the machines.'

'You know how important this is to the President.' Jon nods. 'But actually, that's not what I'm here to talk about,' Erben continues. 'It's in the past. Now, Freemee: what do you know about it?'

'A successful web start-up for individualized data collection and analysis. They keep that up and they'll be a big gun one day.'

Erben stares coldly at Jon and allows the noise of the club to invade their conversation for a second to be sure that what he says next blends into it seamlessly and is for Jon's ears only: 'We need control of that company.'

Jon's gaze is almost as inscrutable as Erben's, and yet the chief of staff knows exactly what the other man is thinking. Jon's smart, hard-working and loyal and he gets things done, but he thinks that visions are something you need to see a doctor about. So he doesn't see what Freemee can do for them. Can do for *him*, Erben Pennicott. And for Jonathan Stem too, if he's up for it. If he gets it. Right now, he's desperately trying to figure out what lies behind Erben's request.

'*We?*' asks Jon.

This, Erben knows, is a diversionary tactic to buy some thinking time.

'You. Me. The President. You understand.'

He has to mention the President to stir Jon's loyalty of course, even though the Commander-in-Chief has nothing to do with this. Nothing whatsoever – just the opposite, in fact. 'One condition complicates our task. Another makes it easier.'

'They cancel each other out.'

'The crucial thing is that our control stays undetected,' Erben insists. 'That's what makes this a tough proposition. Outwardly nothing changes. The management team stays in place for the time being, especially Carl Montik. He's Freemee's superbrain. The investors should continue to see a profit. Officially they include about a dozen venture capital firms, although not all their real owners are known. It makes no difference. They mustn't find out about this.'

Much to Erben's pleasure, Jon drops his guard for a split second and is unable to disguise his confusion.

'In fact, that's what makes the operation easier: all we really need is control of Carl Montik. He's the one who designed and planned the system. He developed and wrote the basic algorithms. He coordinates and commands the programmers.'

Erben realizes from Jon's now limited facial expressions that he's beginning to grasp the stakes. 'We need a line to Montik,' he goes on. 'A direct line. A stable line. A secret line. Something he depends on, without question. Find a way – whatever it takes. And the sooner, the better.'

LotsofZs: Bit of a rush job. The kids shouldn't have been exposed like that.

ArchieT: All their own fault. Streaming a person's death live like that!

Submarine: And the mother?

ArchieT: There's the clincher: you're always complicit in this interconnected world.

Snowman: I'm going to check out for the rest of the evening. Bye!

Wednesday

Time for bed, Eddie. Here are a few great tips for getting to sleep.

It's the second time the ActApps have told Eddie off. They're getting on his nerves. They can't know everything either. How are they supposed to give the right tips in exceptional circumstances like these? His best friend is dead. Murdered. How often does that happen in Britain, in this kind of environment? Not often enough for the apps to draw the optimal conclusions and make recommendations, of that Eddie is certain. All they notice is that it's nearly morning and he's still awake. Maybe they made the same kind of mistake with Adam too?

Eddie opens his Freemee account and turns off the lifestyle apps. No more helpful tips until further notice. It won't be good for his data results, but he has to concentrate now. For a second he feels odd and a little lost when he realizes he's silenced his digital adviser, if only temporarily, and is now completely on his own. Alone.

He goes back to his coding, feeling more alert than ever. He has to go on to specialist forums a few times to ask for assistance. He requires as many open data sources as possible where he might be able to find the information he's looking for. He can't look for it by himself, of course: the software has to find it. That means he needs to build in semantic capabilities so it can extract information from text. Eddie has some basic experience here, but he scours various forums for additional tips and tools. He also uses Wolfram Alpha. He has to build in quality assurance loops, connect the data in a meaningful way and get up to speed on some statistical details.

Finally leaning back, satisfied but exhausted by all the work he's done, he realizes there's no point in going to bed now. Never mind, he'll freshen up for the day ahead by taking a cold shower. He bangs the return key to send off his search program. He ruffles his hair and, as he closes everything down, spies his Freemee account in a window of his browser, its advisory feature turned off. He'd have to log in to reactivate it. He doesn't want to see the ActApps' criticism of his sleepless night. That can wait until after his shower.

'You're selling yourself!' her mother shouts indignantly.

She was bound to find out sooner or later, Vi thinks. As cool as a cucumber, she spreads butter on her toast and answers, 'Rather me than somebody else. Try to be realistic about this. I'm not selling myself, I'm selling my data. So what? They've been ripping us off for years – and *you're* still being conned! You give away thousands of pounds' worth of data every year in exchange for your free email address and a search engine. Nobody's getting such a complete data set from me for nothing. I collect it myself, and far more than the data thieves could ever pinch from me. That's why my data is worth more than the info the data dealers have.'

'You've got one of those too,' says Cyn, pointing at Vi's wrist.

'A smartwatch. Wearable tech.'

'Those devices must cost a fortune.'

'Not that much. This one costs about eighty pounds.'

'What? Call that "not that much"?'

'Calm down. It didn't cost me anything actually. Freemee gives me so-called Frees for my data. They're like bonus points I can spend online when I want to buy something. Not just with Freemee, but elsewhere on the internet too.' She bites into her toast, then continues. 'It's not an expense, anyway. It's an investment. It makes my data packet more comprehensive, more precise and more valuable.' She laughs. 'By the way, adults can have Frees transferred to their account as cash.'

'That's . . . That's . . .'

'Pretty brilliant, I know,' Vi says.

'How many Frees do you get on average, say?'

Oh dear.

'It depends on the amount of data retrieved. I got about two hundred and forty Frees last month.'

'How much is that worth?'

'About a hundred and sixty pounds,' Vi says as casually as she can to play down the sum. Of course it doesn't work.

'A hundred and sixty pounds?' Her mother stresses each syllable and her face is a picture of astonishment. 'You don't need pocket money any longer!'

'*What* pocket money? A few measly quid a month.' She immediately regrets those words when she sees Cyn's expression. 'Sorry, that was mean.' She knows how her mother scrimps and saves each month to give her even that modest allowance.

'How do they calculate the amount?'

'It's all on their home page. Basically it's the sum I have to spend each year, on food, household items, clothes, leisure activities – and as a young adult I'm an important influencer on my parents in their purchasing decisions – minus various handling costs with Freemee and the data buyers, minus their profit, other expenses and so on . . . Just think how much you spend on food every month. Supermarket chains are desperate for your cash.'

'Have you ever wondered what they do with your data?' Cyn asks, controlling herself. 'You've lost all privacy.'

'Privacy!' Vi laughs. 'May I remind you about your fellow journalists yesterday? Or the blanket surveillance of London and many other parts of this country? Not to mention all the spying by the intelligence services? Google, Facebook and all the other data collectors? Privacy!' she says again, laughing louder this time. 'Ever since I was a kid, Mum, I've known that there are cameras everywhere, that there's a log of every time we pay with our credit and loyalty cards, that our smartphones record and pass on our every movement, along with our friends' addresses and phone numbers, that the secret services, banks, supermarkets and even our coffee machines keep character profiles of us.' She shrugs. 'It's just the way we've grown up. Mobile phones and the internet were born before we were. *Your* generation crafted this world for us, so don't you get all worked up about it.'

'*My* generation? I still lock my diary with a padlock.'

'What's in it that's so special?' Vi says, grinning. 'Don't you have any friends you can talk to about stuff?'

'Yes, but not with everyone else listening in.'

Typical. Once again her mother has misunderstood her. A year ago this would have sent Vi up the wall, but the Act-Apps have taught her to be tolerant of dinosaurs. 'If everybody's picturing me anyway, I'd rather sketch the outline myself.' She sighs. 'The ancient Greeks got worked up about the not-so-ancient Greeks too, because they introduced writing! You're exactly the same.'

Vi notices that her mother is unconsciously crumbling her toast between her fingers. 'You could probably exploit your data even better than I can mine,' Vi says to tempt her. 'After all, you have far more possibilities than I do, with your credit card, your bank account and all your loyalty cards. You could always do with a little extra money. What's more, your data must be worth even more after today's headlines.'

'What headlines?'

'Don't tell me you haven't seen them?' She picks up her mobile, searches for the news and holds the screen up in front of Cyn's eyes.

Adam's picture is still at the top, but just below it are the snapshots of Cyn at the crime scene and through the crack in her front door.

'Her glasses,' a headline notes.

'The police revealed whose glasses Adam was wearing,' Vi explains. She looks up other websites. 'Hey, you've become pretty famous overnight. Your face is the symbol of all the parents who've never really taken an interest in how we interact with new technologies because they believe that elders always know better.'

'Let me have a look,' her mother demands, seizing the device from her. She goes pale as she runs her fingers over the touchscreen.

'Don't take it too much to heart,' Vi consoles her. 'Your fame boosts my score, so it's of some use at least. But maybe this will at last convince you to move with the times.' She takes her phone back. 'I'll send you an invitation. If you do consider joining, then do it via me – that way I get a bonus.'

This earns her another baffled look from Cyn.

'Welcome to the present day, Mum.'

*

Cyn's appointment with Anthony is causing her serious concern as she travels to the office. What is she to do if he really does sack her? In an effort to control her panic she directs her thoughts towards this morning's conversation with Vi. In her agitation after having discovered Vi's data sales yesterday evening, she'd curtailed taking a look at the company for herself.

Who's behind this firm? On the page with information about the management team she finds five faces. Will Dekkert, in his mid-forties, with the first streaks of grey in his close-cropped hair and three-day stubble, is Vice-President for Marketing and Communications. She always thought you had to be under thirty to become a dot-com billionaire. She learns from Dekkert's CV that he's not one of the company's founders, and neither is his fellow board member Kim Huang. Freemee was set up two years ago by three other people, all under thirty – Jenna Wojczewski, Carl Montik and Joszef Abberidan. She was right. This last guy is no longer involved; he must be pretty miffed given all the profits the company's presumably making. Cyn looks him up. She's always curious about this kind of human interest story. No, the third founder is no longer miffed. Joszef Abberidan, the former Vice-President for Statistics and Strategy, died in a car accident two months back. *Even billionaires die*, thinks Cyn.

She searches for further details about the company's history and comes across a whole range of articles. Boasting one hundred and seventy million users or more, Freemee appears to be the undisputed top dog of the fledgling market for personal data storage and use. Some people are already predicting that the firm will grow to the dimensions of Facebook or Google. But Cyn has been around the block often enough in the past few years to know that kind of prediction has been made about many companies and it was generally nothing but cleverly planted PR.

The usual continual murmur of her colleagues at work subsides appreciably for a moment as she enters the engine room. She pretends she hasn't noticed, draws herself up to her full height and walks over to her desk. Before she reaches it, however, she hears Anthony call loudly across the whole room, 'Cynthia, in my office!'

To get there she has to walk along the aisle between the desks with all her colleagues watching. Talk about running the gauntlet . . . Involuntarily she hunches her shoulders. Now she's really fearing for her job. No sooner has Anthony's office door closed behind her than the whispering outside resumes.

Anthony gestures silently to the chair on the opposite side of his desk. His other hand is toying with her glasses.

'The police brought these in this morning,' he explains with an innocent air. He studies her, waiting for an answer.

Let him play his little games. Cyn says nothing. She's already sufficiently racked with guilt for letting Vi borrow the glasses, but she feels none towards Anthony, this stuck-up twerp. If her daughter hadn't got hold of those glasses, Adam would never have chased the man. He'd still be alive. And it could so easily have been Vi.

'Very well,' says Anthony with a sigh. 'You used company property – and even let other people use it – for unauthorized purposes. That led to two people being killed and caused a huge public furore. The glasses manufacturer is threatening to sue us!'

Cyn has had enough. 'That's a sick joke! Who made it possible to use these apps in the first place? Those damn things! And now they're trying to shirk their responsibility?' She lowers her voice and pulls herself together. 'Which doesn't mean I don't accept my share of responsibility.'

Anthony shrugs. 'Let's drop the subject. What's more serious is that you refused to do your job.'

'I did *what*? My daughter was caught up in an emergency! She—'

'The boy you lent the glasses to is dead. Your daughter is unhurt. You could have filed a report without any bother, but instead you even allowed your daughter to vilify our entire profession.'

'Those vultures saw to that themselves with their unscrupulous behaviour! You're shooting the messenger rather than the people who are actually responsible! All my daughter did was to document and publish the whole incident. Today everyone's a reporter – to quote *you*.' Cyn is fuming now, but rage feels better than the mixture of guilt and existential angst festering in the pit of her stomach.

'Exactly,' Anthony retorts. 'Which is precisely why we don't need reporters like you any more. I've already spoken to the union reps. You've already received several disciplinary letters. For the aforementioned reasons, I could even sack you on the spot, with no severance payment.' He waves the spectacles around. 'Should the glasses manufacturer sue us, we naturally retain the right to take legal action against you.'

Cyn is close to tears. 'That would never hold up in court!' She can already see herself down at the jobcentre – a journalist in her forties with no experience in new media to speak of. No savings either. Living in London is simply too expensive for that. She'll never find another job in her field . . . How long will she be able to claim unemployment benefit? And after that?

As though muffled she hears Anthony say, 'Our lawyer sees things differently. I told you that you were on my list.'

Cyn would love to leap to her feet and leave the room, but her feet refuse to respond to her brain. She's so caught up in herself and her feelings that at first she doesn't understand what Anthony's saying.

'But I want to give you another chance.'

When the words finally penetrate her skull, she takes a deep breath to compose herself. She hopes Anthony will interpret this pause as a sign of her imperturbability. She detests the idea of revealing any weakness to this upstart.

'If anyone here is giving someone another chance, then that's me to you,' she says craning her neck loftily.

'That's very kind of you,' Anthony replies with a curled lip, 'but don't get carried away, Cyn. Well, let's give each other a second chance.'

She's suspicious of this sudden show of forgiveness but has no time to reflect on it as he immediately continues. 'I'd like you to do the series we discussed yesterday. You're now the worldwide face of parents who can't come to terms with the digital world.'

'Fantastic! What am I supposed to write? A column entitled "Parents, do you know what your children are up to?"'

Anthony falters and then bursts out laughing. 'That's good – it's excellent! No, I mean it.'

'Nice to know at least one person finds it funny.'

'It sounds as if it was a deliberate stunt to promote the series in advance,' Anthony says, grinning. 'Let's use your fame to your advantage.'

'Mine, or the *Daily*'s?'

'Both, for all I care.'

Cyn thinks this over for a second. 'There's enough material. I found out yesterday that kids flog their own data – for cash! We have to tell people. It's—'

'That's old hat,' says Anthony. 'You just weren't aware of it. It's a business model that returns the power over their own data to consumers. That kind of company is sprouting up all over the internet.'

'You can't expect me to keep up with every last trend,' Cyn answers cheekily.

'The important ones you can,' Anthony says coolly. 'Which is why it'd be better if other people mastermind these topics. We have to delve into them, make them more exciting, more controversial. We're journalists – investigative journalists!'

Especially you, thinks Cyn. *Please don't start bragging . . .*

'We aim to get to the bottom of things, uncover hidden facts. We can't just write about Zero – we have to find Zero and talk to him.'

'Why?'

'Because it's no longer enough just to inform our readers. We have to mobilize them!'

'Entertain them, you mean.' Anthony's words strike her as studied or perhaps even rehearsed in front of the mirror.

'What's wrong with people having fun while they learn?' he replies. 'Let's give our readers the chance to help us look for Zero – or help Zero. It doesn't matter which: the main thing is they take part because that gets them emotionally involved in the whole story.'

Cyn hasn't the foggiest idea what he's driving at. 'I bet the entire US secret service is after Zero, even if they won't admit it so as not to lose face. And you want us to jump on the bandwagon?'

'We're looking for Zero to talk to him, not arrest him.'

'And we have no hope of finding him,' says Cyn. 'We aren't properly equipped. You're only interested in a sham operation to sell a paper.'

'A paper that pays your salary,' Anthony reminds her, adding, 'If you still want one.'

Of course she does.

'We're looking for Zero. Full stop,' Anthony says firmly.

Zero's last video appears before Cyn's mind's eye. *Parents, do you know what your child is up to?* Her face has become indelibly associated with that phrase since last night. She must admit that Anthony's idea of tracking Zero down has a certain appeal, if only to expose Zero in the same way he did her.

'We'll start off with a reader survey to find out if they'd rather find Zero or support him,' Anthony explains. 'We'll report on our own investigations in as much detail as makes sense. Anyone who'd like to can join us. Or is free to sabotage us.'

'There might be a whole group behind Zero. Maybe a worldwide gang,' Cyn comments.

'That's possible.'

She's still torn. Between her anger at Anthony, because he has her where he wants her, and her ongoing financial dependence, that she has to keep jumping through hoops so she and Vi can get by. Between this being Anthony's idea and the fact that she could even turn this to her own advantage. She searches for reasons to turn down the proposal.

'We'd have to analyse the content of dozens of videos as well as the technology behind them. Follow online clues. I've no idea how to do that. Do Jeff, Charly, or our IT people? Who's supposed to handle that? Are they even capable of it? Not really.'

'We've brought in a specialist for all those things,' says Anthony, getting to his feet.

Anthony motions her to follow him into the meeting room behind his office. A man's working on his laptop at the large table in the cool, bare room. Cyn catches his eye and can suddenly hardly breathe: he's gorgeous!

'This is Chander.'

His family must come from the Indian subcontinent originally. She can't read his dark eyes, but she doesn't want to – she wants to sink into them. His skin glows with eternal summer and he's tamed his hair with copious amounts of oil. She reckons he must be in his late twenties, but she'll look him up on the internet at the first opportunity.

'Pleased to meet you,' says Chander, beaming at her and stretching out his long, slender fingers.

Not as much as I am to meet you! His handshake is as winning as his smile.

'Chander is our Q,' Anthony explains. 'He's a digital forensic scientist.'

He could just as easily pass for a film star, thinks Cyn. *This fabulous hunk was made for the romantic lead.*

'He's already worked for the FBI, Interpol, Europol and some of the world's largest companies,' Anthony continues.

Chander rolls his eyes and sketches a modest smile. 'Big words,' he says in a velvety voice. 'I prefer to keep to the background.'

'Chander sounds Indian,' Cyn says.

'My parents live in Mumbai,' he replies in the characteristic accent of an elite British university. 'I studied in Mumbai, Stanford and Oxford.'

So he's clever too.

Nodding at the laptop she says, 'Already hunt—' but has to break off in embarrassing fashion, because her voice has gone all squeaky. She clears her throat. Why this teenage behaviour? She has another try, and this time she sounds more composed. 'Already hunting for Zero?'

'I've told Chander everything he needs to know,' Anthony boasts.

Well, in that case, Cyn thinks. 'How does it look? Do we stand any chance of finding Zero?' she asks, angling her body towards Chander.

'Why not?' he replies. 'We may not have the same funding and networks as the NSA or the FBI, but we're more flexible and more creative.'

'Then we'd better not waste any more time,' says Anthony. He claps his hands again. 'Let's strike while the iron's hot. First we'll make a little video of the start of the operation.' He presses the glasses into Cyn's hand. 'Here, you're going to need these.'

Cyn almost hurls them on to the big table. 'You can't be serious! Yesterday those things—'

'Those things are part of your job from now on,' Anthony shoots back.

Cyn recalls the conversation with the youngsters. They didn't blame the glasses for Adam's death. To their mind they're simply a tool to be used. Whether for good or for bad is up to you. And yet . . .

'Do we maybe have one that hasn't . . .' she starts.

Anthony raises one eyebrow, then says, 'I think that's probably possible.'

He disappears into his office and quickly returns with two boxes. 'Here, take these. And if you're going to write about this stuff, have this too.' It looks like Vi's smartwatch.

'What do I need this for?'

'It's related to your subject. You don't want to report on something you know nothing about, do you?'

Anthony plans to feature in the video too, which is why he's booked make-up and styling in addition to the film crew. He rehearses his lines in a low whisper and strikes a pose in front of the mirror while a young woman powders his forehead and nose. He turns and tilts his head to check there are no unfortunate shiny patches of skin. Chander and Cyn are being prepared alongside him. The digital forensic scientist seems relaxed and keeps his eyes shut. Cyn, on the other hand, has a face like thunder.

'Do I really have to be in this video?' she asks. She usually excels at keeping herself out of the limelight.

'We're deliberately making this a three-person discussion so you're not on your own,' Anthony says.

'How selfless,' Cyn mutters.

He leaps cheerfully to his feet and drags Cyn and Chander in front of the camera. They stand against a green screen so Zero's videos can be edited into the background at a later stage. 'Please smile,' Anthony warns Cyn with a sideways glance.

'With his Presidents' Day operation Zero made some powerful enemies,' Anthony says, addressing the camera.

'And lots of friends too,' Cyn adds from beside him.

'That's right, Cynthia. Zero became a superstar overnight,' Anthony replies. 'Which is why we at the *Daily* would like to speak to Zero.'

'Especially me,' Cyn interjects with a tight smile.

'I can imagine.'

Chander steps into the picture, and a caption introduces him as an IT expert. 'That's why we've decided to look for Zero.'

'But how do we find him?' asks Anthony. 'Who is Zero? Why does he hide behind an ever-changing array of faces?'

'Is it caution, because the US intelligence services are hunting him?' wonders Cyn. *We have to provoke Zero to lure him into making a mistake*, Anthony had told them when he presented the script for the teaser. 'Maybe he's simply scared?'

'Even before this, he concealed his identity,' Chander points out.

'Well, I think Zero's hiding because he's as vain as a peacock,' Anthony chimes in. 'Because he wants to be a star. Once, only people who made it on to the silver screen were stars. Now every baby has its own YouTube channel!'

'It's Andy Warhol's prophecy: in the future everyone will be world-famous for fifteen minutes,' quotes Cyn.

'Absolutely. Except that's turned everything the other way up. If you make it on to the screen nowadays, you're one of multitudes. The thing about stars is that they stand out from the crowd. So now, to be different, you have to remain invisible!

'Which confronts Zero with a dilemma,' Anthony explains, 'because those invisible characters are vain, oh so vain! They can't bear to remain unknown, which is why they keep appearing and playing to the gallery: disguised, dressed up, masked.'

Behind them the end of one of Zero's videos rolls, showing a shifting face calling out, 'You can't catch me!'

'You can't catch me,' Anthony repeats. 'He doesn't want to be seen and yet he shows himself just the same. All flirtation and puffery.'

'Or caution?' Cyn suggests once again.

'Vain stars or cowardly activists: just who is Zero?' Anthony asks the camera. 'Vote! Help us find Zero or defend him, and win lots of fantastic prizes! Follow the *Daily* live!' He winks. 'See you soon. At the *Daily*! Are you going to be tuning in too, Zero?'

'Wonderful,' is Carl's laconic comment. 'The age of the attention economy has only just dawned, and you're killing it off already. The nameless are the latest stars? A hugely ambitious concept.'

'What would you know about it?' Alice replies. 'A tried and tested strategy. A mysterious masked figure has always been a proven formula for gaining attention – from *The Man in the Iron Mask* and Zorro to all those superheroes in their pyjamas.'

'Like that old Cree saying: "Only when the last face has been shown will we realize we can't eat attention." '

'Yes, that reminds me of that story by . . .' Alice begins a thought but doesn't complete it.

Carl turns to Will. 'I get it. The common man as archetype . . .'

'And Zero's fully aware of that,' Will confirms. 'Why do you think he always signs off his videos with a zero? He's been playing games since his very first appearance. It's a cleverly devised marketing strategy.'

'That makes Cynthia Bonsant and Anthony Heast "ones", right? But your idea for the commercial teaser – it was your idea, admit it – is a weird one,' says Carl. 'Zero might turn out to be someone who's already in the public eye.'

'That's one of the nice paradoxes about this story. It makes it all the more enticing,' Alice interjects. 'What's the secret behind it all? You can't prove someone doesn't exist.'

'Going to start a debate about identity now?' Will asks Carl. 'It's a promotional video, not a philosophical treatise.'

'No, but I'll be interested to see if this achieves your objective.'

'Me too,' Will says with a chuckle.

'Is this some joke?' asks Marten. 'The combined power of the US intelligence agencies is trained on catching this guy, and now these clowns say they're going after Zero? Well, good luck to them!'

'Heast has had a fairly eccentric career,' Luís explains. 'He took part in an early series of *Big Brother* in the UK while still a journalism student and made it through to the last three, no less. Next, he made a name for himself via a range of media outlets, even if he shone more by virtue of his appearances than his actual successes.'

'Cynthia Bonsant appeared in Zero's video yesterday,' a second man says. 'Previously she was best known for her reporting, but she's never addressed any of the topics that are her focus now. She wrote a lot of critically acclaimed magazine articles twenty years ago – interesting pieces on human rights and profile features, although not very commercial. She then experienced a bit of a hiccup in her career for personal reasons before ending up at the *Daily*.'

'And this odd couple is somehow supposed to be better than the world's most sophisticated intelligence and surveillance apparatus?' asks Marten. 'By complete fluke, maybe.'

'I think it's a pretty good idea to involve the public in the search,' offers the first technician.

'By the way, that Chander Argawal is of a totally different calibre,' says a third technician. 'He's an elite programmer and digital forensic scientist. He's worked for some of the biggest outfits around, including us. How did he get caught up with this crew?'

'Ask our buddies at the NSA,' Marten orders. 'Why else do they record every electronic interaction worldwide?'

One phone call later, they know that Argawal has been extra cautious.

'He uses encrypted communication channels even the NSA can't crack,' says the third technician. 'What he can't hide, though, are certain parts of his career. When and where he went to school, studied and worked, who he met there, metadata of some of his material, especially older ones before he learned to cover his tracks. Our friends are working on those bits.'

'Let me know what you find out,' says Marten, before immediately adding, 'In fact, it's no skin off our nose if someone like Argawal does work on this. It doesn't cost us anything to set an alarm just in case these amateur head-hunters do turn out to get lucky. You never know, they may even lead us to Zero.'

'And how do you intend to go about finding Zero?' Cyn asks Chander. They're sitting around a table in the *Daily*'s spacious staffroom with Anthony, Jeff, Charly, a young female web designer and an intern. Here too there are screens on every wall, blasting out news channels and web-sites. What's more, anyone who knows how to can use their smartphone as a remote control and switch to whatever content interests them.

'A combination of our own hunt and crowdsourcing,' Chander replies with his characteristic beaming smile.

Cyn is tempted to drag him straight into the nearest broom cupboard, but just repeats somewhat fatuously, 'Crowdsourcing?'

'We let *Daily* readers do the work,' Anthony says, chuckling. 'It's cheaper, gets better results if organized properly and is more fun for the participants than simply reading or watching the news.'

'Let me introduce Kimberly and Frances,' Jeff says, looking over at the two young women at the table. 'On Anthony's instructions, the two of them have already set up a chat room where visitors can share their ideas. Frances,' he says, pointing to the intern, 'will moderate it.'

'Search programs will scan all incoming messages for relevance, trustworthiness, bias for or against Zero and a few other factors,' Frances explains.

'Your video's doing really well, you know,' says Kimberly with the cool self-confidence of the young that Cyn knows so well from Vi, and that she'd never have shown at their age in a situation like this. 'It's only been up for about an hour, but we've already had several hundred comments.'

'And the best thing,' Frances adds, smiling at Anthony, 'is that they've come from seventeen different countries around the globe. The operation is having an international impact, exactly as Anthony wanted.'

'What kind of comments?' Cyn asks.

'A lot of crap,' says Frances with a chuckle, 'but some useful info too. Within minutes various people were researching the email and IP addresses used to register Zero's YouTube account and the Presidents' Day website. And obviously there's a great deal of protest and many declarations of sympathy. Some guys claiming to belong to Anonymous are threatening to attack the *Daily* if we actively continue our hunt.'

'Fantastic.' Anthony's ecstatic. 'That'll only generate even more publicity for us.'

'Your IT guys should be ready just in case Anonymous really does try to attack,' Chander warns him.

'We're already on it,' says Charly.

'So what exactly is your role?' Cyn asks Chander for a second time.

'Basically I'm doing the same as the people out there – scanning the internet with a range of special programs. I've got a few up my sleeve, but I'm not alone. I'd bet my life that a few really good hackers will join in soon, but I'm eager to see whose side they'll come in on. Probably Zero's, but a few may help us.'

'And what are you hoping to find?'

'Mistakes. You can use the TOR network or Virtual Private Networks, for example, to move around online undetected. The Onion Router directs your internet traffic through different servers to conceal your original IP address. You have to be careful, though. First, the intelligence services must have partially subverted it by now, and second, some types of data such as videos leave traces on your browser. Virtual Private Networks, or VPNs, can also mask your origin because you're routed via a foreign network. However, intelligence services and the FISC can force VPN providers in the US to hand over data.' He leans back. 'Zero described all this in his *Guerrilla Guide*. But still . . . Every anonymous internet user makes a mistake at some stage. In most cases it was long ago, before they really cared about anonymity, when they didn't know their way around or got distracted.'

'You mean, if I don't have any particular reason to hide or maybe think I'm not of enough interest to need to cover my tracks, I make the whopping mistake of not considering some unspecified "tomorrow" where things may be completely different . . .' Cyn thinks aloud. 'And that's how you nail them, by finding past trails they can no longer erase.'

'Exactly. There are so many ways to mess up.'

'You'll have to explain that to me in greater detail,' she says, attempting a smile.

'I'd love to,' he replies, his eyes twinkling.

'How about Zero's earlier videos?' Anthony cuts in.

'We'll have to take a closer look at them,' says Chander. 'We've already checked them for metadata, but Zero's carefully removed important information like the author, location, date when it was created, when the program was modified, and other things. Maybe we'll find something in the film snippets they've used, though.'

'And his message? I mean, that's what really matters,' says Cyn.

'People will know about that from watching the videos,' says Anthony. 'But you can write something about them if you like. If they're of any interest – they're nothing new.'

Maybe not for you, thinks Cyn. *But there were plenty of things that were new to me.*

Anthony gets up and walks over to the door. 'I've got to go. You'll handle this just fine!' He claps his hands and is gone.

'My daughter gathers and sells her own data,' Cyn bursts out.

The two young women shrug, and stare at her in astonishment.

'So what? So do I,' says Kimberly.

'Me too,' says Jeff. 'At last it's possible, and it's a nice little earner too. But if that kind of thing rankles you, then I have just the Zero video for you.'

'I love rankings!' declares the Olympic champion with a medal around his neck – and changes into a long-legged model on the catwalk. 'Who's the most beautiful, the fastest, the strongest, the cleverest, the richest?' She morphs into a guy ticking items off on a list. 'Rankings help to rate things. It's not just me, we all rate things,' says a City trader, placing a weight on a set of scales, 'constantly – both consciously and unconsciously. Ratings make life easier: they help you make decisions. You use them to choose your partner, your friends, your enemies and your phone. The more effectively you can rate things, the smarter your choices – and the better your life will be. You rate books, hotels, electrical appliances and online sellers, so you're always working with rankings.' And hey presto, the City trader's hurled into the pan of a gigantic set of scales. He fights his way up the side but slips down and slithers around the pan. 'But of course you are rated *too*. Advertising firms rate your purchasing power, your consumer behaviour and your brand preferences. Commercial credit agencies have been rating you for decades. No one will give you credit? The interest rate on your loan's too high, or your payment terms with an online seller are harsh? That's down to your credit rating. Banks and insurance firms rate you on the basis of your income, your neighbourhood, your car, your gender and many other metrics. One of the ways Google earns money is by knowing its users' results and selling this information to advertisers. Companies rate your web activity via your online reputation or e-score. Dating sites earn their dough by matching members with similar ranking. Some social networks only accept "beautiful people", with other members rating candidates' photos. In rating communities, members tell you how attractive, intelligent or horny they think you are. Most companies operate rating systems for their employees, from punching in to balanced scorecards and smartwatches. Forbes ranks the world's richest people. And now there's a new listing!' Pieces of paper rain down on the man in a tailcoat until he's buried under a heap. He emerges, spluttering and holding up one slip which he looks at with some amusement. 'You can now exploit your own data via a host of new services! Find out how much you're worth – yes, you there!

'So your data's available for one cent, whereas your neighbour's costs seven cents? Damn, does that mean I'm worth less than him? Well, if you really want to find out, look it up in a new little app called ManRank – it's an ingenious Freemee service that ranks everyone by the value of their data! And all based on results you publish yourself on Freemee and other platforms. Now we not only know the world's hundred wealthiest billionaires but also the billions of poor people who come after them: the Forbes list of the ninety-nine per cent. The days are gone when there were only rating agencies for companies and states. Here we have it: ManRank – the first rating agency for people!'

By now his tailcoat is a tattered mess, and his eyes and voice turn grave. '*But I don't have to exploit my data*, I hear you say. Well, then you don't make it into the rankings. Smart! But is it so smart? As any credit rating agency will tell you, there's only one rating worse than a rock-bottom one, and that's none at all! It doesn't matter if it's a loan, your job or your partner: better results give you better chances. No score means no chance.'

He tugs at his bowtie, his expression changes to a beaming smile and his tailcoat looks neater again. 'Fortunately, you can improve your results with the aid of all kinds of digital coaches who give you good advice. Doesn't it feel good to see yourself climbing the rankings? You'll do anything to stay there or rise even higher – because that increases your chances of a better job, a better partner, more success, money, power and love. "Nowadays people know the price of everything and the value of nothing," quipped Oscar Wilde. Well, the times are a-changing. Wilde would be agog. Nowadays we know the price of every value! Just ask Acxiom, or Google, Apple, Facebook ... or Freemee. Do you know your value? Another thing: I believe we must destroy the data krakens.'

'What are they talking about?' Cyn asks. 'A rating agency for people?'

Jeff goes to the ManRank website. 'It's been around for a few months. It's the largest one, a kind of development and summary of the original lists Zero mentioned. Over four billion people arranged by the value of their data!'

'That's—' she stammers in shock.

'—what collectors, salespeople and exploiters of data have been doing for ages. But now everyone can see it here. It's the democratization of rating, so to speak.'

'Democratization, my arse!' Cyn isn't sure if she really grasps the significance of the instrument, but something about it unsettles her more than at any moment in her life so far, with a few notable exceptions: her first period; the end of school; Viola's birth; Gary's disappearance; when her mother passed away. An intuitive realization that the world has changed.

'Want to see your results?'

Jeff has typed her name in before she can even react. A graph shows the evolution of Cyn's score like the volatile curve of a share price. In the middle it makes a huge leap and then continues to climb before reaching a plateau. At the end of the line, a number with many digits changes every second.

'You're currently ranked between 1,756,385,884 and 1,861, 305,718 out of more than four billion,' says Jeff.

That low! Vexed, Cyn calls herself to order. *Surely you don't take these ratings seriously?*

'See the rise since yesterday?' Jess moves the cursor along the line, and a window pops up featuring various terms such as fame, popularity and appeal. 'Your fame has shot up since the first photos of you appeared in the media. That also boosted your overall score, then Zero's video sent it rocketing. Before that, you were somewhere between three and four billion, in the lower middle of the rankings.'

'You can also compare your results with other people's,' Frances explains in a businesslike voice. 'Like on financial websites or stock trading software.'

She says this without any hint of irony, Cyn notices. 'But these are people, not shares,' she cries. 'The only thing missing is for people to be able to invest in me or bet on me, like on the stock market!'

'This is going to make you laugh then: several companies are actually working on that,' Jeff adds drily.

'So we've finally been incorporated into the capitalist system as a measurable quantity, a line on a graph. What's the sum of all the curves of everyone in Britain? All the Germans, every one-eyed Japanese person over sixty, childless women, Parisian men, children in Nigeria?'

'This has been going on for years, even decades, Cyn. Any number of companies categorize you – that's what Zero just explained in his video,' Jeff reminds her. 'The only difference is that now it's clearly displayed on a graph. Freemee and ManRank are merely the largest publicly available lists. There are challengers too. They have the data as it is – all they have to do is analyse and present it.'

It occurs to Cyn that Vi must know about this list too. *And it's a brilliant incentive for Freemee users to follow their ActApps' recommendations – the perfect rewards system!* A further realization sends a shiver down her spine: Google, Facebook and others filter information and can therefore influence people's behaviour, but ActApps give instructions for how to behave! That means that lifestyle app providers directly influence people's attitudes, and users freely decide to follow the advice in order to boost their results. This gives companies like Freemee amazing opportunities for manipulating people.

'Why am I even in there?' she asks, her voice on edge. 'I don't use any of those data analysis sites.'

'They still know enough about you to calculate a rating,' says Frances. 'Of course you'd be in a much better position if you collected your own data.'

'But what if I don't want to be on the list?'

'Then you can have your name removed,' says Jeff. 'There's an opt-out possibility. But what did Zero say before? There's only one rating worse than a rock-bottom one and that's no rating at all. You're literally worthless then.'

'Or suspicious,' adds Frances. 'Like people who don't have profiles on social media or don't use smart meters to measure their electricity consumption.'

'That's terrible!' Cyn blurts out.

'Absolutely,' says Frances. 'Who wants to be worthless?'

Cyn stares at her in disbelief.

'And who's number one?' asks Cyn when she regains her voice.

Jeff switches to list view, but the top-ranked names change too quickly to be read. He lowers the time period from 'continuous' to 'one week', and the new list displays static results. She doesn't recognize any of the names.

'Does it match the Forbes list?'

'No,' Kimberly replies. 'ManRank takes all kinds of other categories into account, not just wealth.'

'You can also view the detailed lists,' says Jeff. 'There's everything from wealth and influence to love, bravery and creativity. In that respect you're only half right about incorporation into the capitalist system, if at all. That's because other results contribute to your ranking, and every score is weighted in line with social attitudes. So love and peace can be highly appreciated and have a significant influence on the list – if people behave accordingly, that is.'

'They don't, though, do they?' Cyn whispers.

Jeff shrugs. 'That's the point: this measures and assesses acts, not chit-chat.'

'But there are over four billion people on this earth,' says Cyn.

'It's mainly people in developing countries without internet access or mobiles who are missing,' says Jeff. 'But their data is gradually being recorded too. Within a few years practically everyone will be online.'

Cyn shakes her head as she gazes at the advert. She's never before felt so conscious of being part of one gigantic system. And there's no escaping it.

'How are these results produced?'

'They're continually updated according to people's behaviour,' says Jeff. 'Should ambition or love or power become more important for a larger number of people and they behave accordingly, then the parameters change and those values have a greater effect on the overall score. The system's in a constant state of flux.'

He switches to the graphics. Cyn has to admit they're impressive. They look like permanently flickering, bright cobwebs, with more lines connecting billions of living dots into a giant organism. If she understands it correctly, this system shows the ever-changing relations between billions of people in real time! It's only now that she realizes what the large internet companies have been up to for years behind closed doors. One of the countless dots in that monstrous web of mutual bonds and dependencies is her, inextricably woven into the overall fabric like a tiny fly in a cobweb.

'I must write about this,' she declares.

'Lots of people already have. It'd be better to make a cool video instead,' Frances advises her. 'Although there are already some of those out there too.'

Cyn bites back a remark. Frances already sounds like Anthony. She asks everyone, 'Do you use these lifestyle apps too?'

'Of course I do,' says Jeff.

'So do we,' the young women agree.

'To increase your scores?' Cyn says, part question, part statement.

'Among other things, yeah,' says Jeff. 'ManRank gives you perfect guidance. You finally understand how society works.'

'You've just given me the topic for my first column,' says Cyn with a sigh.

'Waterfalls?' Jon asks impatiently. 'What is this?'

Everything on the technician's monitor is in flow. A wall tiled with dozens of small video screens shows close-up pictures of different combinations of water, spray and light.

'Take the plunge and relax,' the italicized headline reads.

The technician clicks on one of the videos and enlarges it until it fills the entire screen. Blue-green torrents, veiled in clouds of fine white spray, pour from top to bottom.

'The only thing we've turned up so far,' says Marten. 'A home page that helps you meditate by staring at recorded or live images of waterfalls.'

'And what's this got to do with Zero?' Jon doesn't like it when people waste his time, or when they're running ahead of him in their thoughts and don't come to the point.

'Our friends at the NSA have done some verification, including the email and IP addresses used to register Zero's YouTube account and the Presidents' Day operation home page. They're also checking a whole bunch of name variations and all the places on the web where those addresses and possible name variations appear, who they communicate with and so on,' Marten explains at a leisurely pace. 'Both addresses are disposable ones, and the IP addresses come from the TOR anonymous network. When Zero opened the YouTube account in 2010, TOR users still felt safe. During the session when Zero opened his YouTube account, he also logged into a totally normal news website from a different email address to participate in some of its chat-room discussions. Soon afterwards that email address appeared in esoteric forums, always with similar comments such as "Recently came across a page called *fall-in-meditation*. What do you reckon? Does it work?"'

Marten displays this message on to a second screen as he continues his explanation. 'A classic online ploy to get a website to go viral. None of this would have stood out if the programs hadn't immediately sounded the alarm because' – here the technician calls up a second similar message underneath the first one – 'another address was also promoting the waterfall: mucitponap89@sedjak.com. As anyone can tell, that's simply the Latin form of the other email address backwards. Don't ask me exactly how they know, but the guys from the NSA claim it belongs to a family of email addresses used by the same user or group of users as the panopticon address the Presidents' Day home page is registered to.'

'So what if Zero promotes esoteric websites in his free time? That fits. We've nothing more?' says Jon, arching his eyebrows.

'It's a start at least,' Marten replies. 'We're currently checking everyone who visits the site, although the number is into the hundreds of thousands now. It might be a kind of meeting place for Zero or maybe some of Zero's members met there.'

'How do we know there's more than one of them?'

'An operation like Presidents' Day could hardly be pulled off by one person working solo. Also, our NSA colleagues say that some behavioural traits of the email families we're investigating point to multiple users.'

Jon contemplates the screen-sized waterfall. Even though every pixel in the restless picture is moving, within seconds he begins to feel its relaxing effect.

'It's also noteworthy,' Marten explains in the meantime, 'that most people who look at the site haven't made any effort to re-route their traffic. Only a small percentage of visits are by anonymized IP addresses and we can barely trace those, if at all.'

Is this soporific website some kind of secret weapon? Jon wonders, tearing himself away from the glittering pictures. 'Who runs this site?'

'Another noteworthy element,' says Marten. 'It was also registered anonymously.'

'I'd do the same if I produced garbage like this,' says Jon and spins on his heel to leave. 'Call me when you've really got something.'

Her journey to the editorial office and then home again used to be a wonderful opportunity to switch off and let her mind wander. Since the advent of mobiles, the internet and smartphones, however, she's increasingly spent the time communicating and looking things up. No sooner is she down in the Underground today than she reaches for the new glasses Anthony gave her. She hesitates for a second before putting them on. It's strange she has fewer reservations simply because it's a different pair from the ones Adam was wearing.

She doesn't want to spy on any of her fellow passengers today. It's just that it's far easier to do research with the glasses than using her smartphone. She returns to the ManRank website and reads the FAQs. She needs some information for her article. She clicks on the page and enters Vi's name. Cyn is surprised to find that Vi is highly ranked, between 575,946,335 and 493,551,091. Cyn also spots Vi's friends Sally, Brenda and Bettany, as well as a former friend, Ashley, who has the same goth look in her profile portrait as Vi sported for so many years. Cyn feels a moment's irritation without knowing exactly why, then carries on searching. She finds a few of her own friends. The highest-ranked person she knows is an acquaintance who owns a specialist technology company – he's at number 8,500,000. The lowest ranked is a colleague of hers who's hovering around the 2.3 billion mark. Anthony! She naturally checks Anthony. Chander Argawal is up in the four millions. Jeff comes in just above Vi, as do Cyn's young colleagues Kimberly and Frances.

All young people look for advice from those little apps. If she's going to write about them, does she have to try them out herself? Cyn feels an intense reluctance to do so. Is it an older person's dislike for anything new? Ancient Greeks against young Greeks, as Vi put it? She swore she'd never be that way . . .

She tentatively clicks on Vi's invitation and opens the Freemee home page. A video starts to play alongside some introductory text to the sound of welcoming music.

'Hi, Cynthia. Nice of you to pay us a visit! Find out more about Freemee and how you can make life more pleasurable!'

Cut to an alarm clock showing six o'clock in the morning. A woman of Cyn's age hops out of bed and stretches, a broad smile on her face. A caption reads: 'What's your idea of a better day? Waking up after a good night's sleep? Try our Sweet Dreams ActApp.'

A slim young woman tosses a bowl of crisp lettuce leaves, and Cyn wonders why these dishes always look so good and yet she never feels like eating them. 'Want to eat something tasty *and* really healthy? Take a look at the EatWell Act-App. You'll be amazed at what it has to offer!'

Next, the woman is out jogging. She looks happier than Cyn has ever felt running – the rare times she gets out, that is. It'd be nice if someone could motivate her one day.

'Want to keep fit? Our Fit ActApps have some great ideas for you and they'll even teach you the right technique to make it fun at last!' It's as though the film-makers have read her mind.

'Want to give your professional life a boost? We have just the thing for you – Career ActApp!' The same woman comes striding out of a shoe shop carrying two full bags. 'Or maybe you'd like to earn a bit extra on the side? Find out how your own data can make you money. No obligation, though – after all, it's your data and yours alone!'

OK, OK, that's enough! These marketing types have the knack of wrapping you around their little finger.

She studies the commercials, the explanatory videos and articles about the ActApps. Critical though she is, the cheerful, happy people in them bear no resemblance to saleswomen on TV shopping channels: they come across as authentic. There are countless other positive testimonials

134

on YouTube. Can a company like Freemee really be making all of this up?

Cyn is forced to admit to herself that the worst thing would be if the ActApps actually work as advertised: she'd have to abandon her scepticism! Also, if she's honest, there's something incredibly alluring about the thought of being more successful at work and in love. Her current strategies haven't brought her much success in either so far.

She's in two minds but clicks on the 'Sign Up' button. A registration form appears. First name, second name . . . Everything's already filled in.

Should she really do this? She knows precisely what she's scared of: that once she's part of it she'll be trapped, of her own accord, either out of convenience or conviction. She reasons with herself: this is purely for research. She can stop at any time if it doesn't work out or if she gets cold feet.

The sign-up process is quick and pleasantly simple. Free-mee already has all the necessary details anyway, and so she only has to agree to the terms and conditions and approve her registration.

Again she hesitates. As usual, the terms and conditions comprise an endless litany of small print. Even studying it closely, the legal mumbo-jumbo makes no sense to her, and even if she did understand it and had concerns – if she doesn't accept them, she can't use the service. *So what the hell.* 'OK,' she whispers.

'Welcome to a world of new possibilities, Cynthia! You can now complete your details in your account. We've already collected the available information for you. Don't be surprised, there's an awful lot of it!'

Cyn is indeed amazed at how much of her personal information Freemee has stored and classified according to subject. Her address, email addresses (private and professional), phone numbers including her mobile: it's all there. OK, that was only to be expected. Lots of stores and supermarkets where she shops or has shopped at least once; how she travels and when and how frequently; her browsing history. The deeper she goes, the more appalled she is by everything that's out there about her. Practically every article she's ever written, even the ones that only appeared in print. Credit ratings. Her present location. Modern analysis software, a short caption explains, can recognize a person carrying a mobile from their gait, to the point of being able to draw up a fairly detailed personality profile. Cyn skim-reads it. It's pretty accurate in most areas. *But not all*, she thinks.

'We'd love to know more about you, Cynthia. The main goal of these questionnaires is to match your perception of yourself with your behaviour – the situations in which you judge your behaviour accurately, as well as those in which you incorrectly perceive your words and actions without knowing it.'

Do I really want to know every time I fool myself? Cyn asks herself.

It's easier to answer the questions on the touchscreen of her smartphone than using the glasses. As on other portals, she starts to tap on the boxes next to simple multiple-choice questions. She notices that she answers some questions differently than she would normally do. *What do you most like to do when you get home from work? Carry on working, do sport, watch television, cook dinner . . .* She thinks hard about what she's really like, what she actually wants, loves and does. Is her perception of herself already changing? Has Freemee already started to manipulate her personality? She makes some mental notes for her article.

Her glasses remind her to change trains. Cyn pauses her filling in of the forms and disembarks from the train.

*

'Welcome, Ms Bonsant,' whispers Carl as the lift heads up to the forty-eighth floor. The predictions about her curiosity are proving accurate, and this has the advantage that Carl can now set about influencing her. It clearly works with her daughter, even if the younger Bonsant was selected, like all the other test subjects, by Carl's software for the experiment, which also adjusted the results. There's no way Carl would have been able to work through millions of hand-picked subjects. He only does that with individual and especially sensitive cases like Cynthia Bonsant. He's going to sedate her as much as he can. He'll have to be careful, mind you. Bonsant will remain suspicious. He taps on the arm of his glasses, blinks to open her newly created account and dives into the lines of code among which he feels so at home.

Having reached his destination, he steps out of the lift and finishes off his work in the foyer before proceeding. This floor is the administrative heart of Henry's empire. The tasteful, unpretentious decor calls to mind an updated version of a venerable European private bank, with none of the pragmatic nouveau-riche ostentation of their American counterparts. The same lady has presided in the antechamber to Henry's office for the last thirty-five years. Carl doesn't come up here very often. It's not unusual for him to pay visits to investors, but as Henry officially owns only a small stake in Freemee, they restrict their meetings here to the odd occasion.

Carl finds Henry's office modest in view of the man's enormous wealth. He is however impressed every time by the view over Midtown and Central Park. As always, Henry's clothes and hair are impeccably styled. He sets aside the documents he was studying when Carl entered.

Paper – how very twentieth-century! It still amazes Carl that Henry was so quick to recognize Freemee's potential.

Henry guides him over to a group of leather armchairs in one corner. A carafe of water and two tumblers are standing on a glass table. The coasters feature hunting scenes and catch Carl's eye. Something about them unsettles him.

'The experiment is drawing to a close,' Henry explains with little by way of preliminaries. 'The next stage presents a security risk, especially in the initial phase once you've told your fellow board members the news. Your programs have kept an eye on them and guided them very well so far, but I do not wish to take any gambles. Freemee is an incredibly powerful tool but also somewhat sluggish – and it will lose some of its effect on anyone aware of its power. In such situations, we must be able to react swiftly and in an extremely targeted fashion. Also, we must finally relieve you of all the operational trivia. I have therefore taken the liberty of arranging a little backup. As you know, my group owns an international security company. Its boss and a small team know precisely what they need to in order to do their job. No more.'

At an invisible sign, the door opens to admit a towering man in his mid-sixties with the aura of an Ironman athlete and the buzz cut of a former soldier.

'May I present Joaquim Proust. Joaquim, this is Carl Montik, the super-brain behind Freemee.'

Proust's smile is meant to be winning, Carl presumes, as they shake hands.

'My idea is that Joaquim's team will, in future, take on special security assignments for Freemee that your customary, established security system cannot and may not officially provide. This will include such matters as comprehensive surveillance of certain critics, but also – at least in the coming months – increased oversight of your fellow board members until we are able to ensure their loyalty under the altered circumstances. You can leave everything to him, starting now. Joaquim receives the same alerts from the programs as you and I do, and he can act accordingly. I'm asking you to immediately deactivate your notifications for Codes 703 to 708 so you can fully concentrate on your core tasks.'

'I'd like nothing better,' says Carl. At last he can use his time more efficiently again. He does have one question, though. 'What if we cannot secure their loyalty? If journalists want to publish damaging stories? Like this British woman, for example.'

'You've already dealt with Cynthia Bonsant, I see.' Proust's soft voice is in surprising contrast to his appearance. 'Let's hope it works. In principle, we work in a similar way to Freemee – pre-emptively and constructively. This basically involves identifying dangerous situations in advance. One example: your fellow board members are intensive Freemee users. Most of the time the software knows where they are and with whom. It can also predict behaviour with a high degree of probability. Freemee signals unusual behaviour such as removing sensor devices for any lengthy period. During that time other automatic systems take over, including a now close-meshed net of private surveillance cameras and modern facial recognition, geolocation for vehicles, miniature drones and other devices. If none of these prove effective, then we have our human operatives. For instance, if a board member meets people suspected of breaches of secrecy or we overhear clear conversations, we can intervene with temporary distraction, irritation and other techniques. That gives us the chance to talk privately with the colleague later on.'

Carl's amused at the care Proust is taking to paint total surveillance in appealing terms.

'Our procedure is the same with prying individuals,' the security professional continues. 'Henry told me about the newest intrusions in London. We'll also assume responsibility for them.'

Carl knows who he means: Edward Brickle, the IT whizz-kid. 'I don't like it,' he says. 'But I can see it's necessary.'

Henry and Proust exchange glances.

'We'll only resort to these measures for as long as necessary,' says Henry.

Now Carl realizes what's odd about the coasters. With a couple of flicks of his hand, he stands them up on edge on the square table before getting to his feet and giving a sharp farewell nod in Henry and Joaquim's direction.

After changing trains, Cyn continues to answer Freemee's questions, although she leaves some large gaps – she can fill the rest in later. She's just got to the end of the questionnaire when her glasses again urge her to change trains. As she's walking along the connecting Underground tunnel, Freemee thanks her via the glasses. She's just reached the next platform when she reads: 'Why not boost your results! Thanks to our DataSub App you can now even get hold of data that only others could collect about you before. This data is completely secure and belongs to you alone, until you decide to release it for others to utilize.'

A list of all the relevant companies appears. Cyn's scarcely surprised to learn that Freemee knows her bank, her loyalty cards, social media accounts, mobile phone and internet providers, and mobile devices. A bold headline is emblazoned across the top of the list:

Find out what companies know about you – and more!

Blinking 'OK' and 'Info' buttons next to the name of every firm and function invite her to click on them. She wrestles with her conscience. *Find out what companies know about you – and more!*

She boards the next train and examines the list once again. Well, she's not very concerned about the data generated from her Facebook account. There isn't much there: she seldom logs in.

OK.

It's a similar story with the data from her mobile. And the loyalty cards? It's her data, after all. Why should it only belong to others?

OK. OK. OK.

The bank. Hmm, maybe that's not so good.

'Your credit score is slightly below average,' reads a caption that flashes up before her eyes, as though Freemee can read her thoughts. 'Optimizing your money management can improve it. Freemee's MoneyManager ActApp can give you a hand, and you don't have to publish your data.'

The creepiness factor: isn't that what Jeff called it? But somehow she no longer finds it quite so spooky. Nothing surprises her any more.

The glasses signal that she's reached her destination. Her index finger hovers briefly over the button before she presses OK.

'Thank you, Cynthia. We'll start retrieving the data straight away. You'll receive forms from some of the companies in the next few hours. Sign them and you will immediately start to get a constant stream of your data. As soon as you send back the signed forms, your data will be uploaded to your Freemee account.'

She can't believe what she's done. She puts away her smartphone and leaves it there for the rest of her way home.

The sun has already set, and the street is hatched with shadows. A warm breeze caresses her face and ruffles her hair. What a strange day!

On the walk home she runs through the events so she can arrange them into an article in her head.

No sooner has she stepped through the door and kicked off her shoes than her glasses inform her, 'You have not yet completed your Freemee registration process. Would you like to continue, Cynthia?'

Cynthia slumps into a chair.

'OK.' If she must.

Freemee wants to know if she wears body trackers. Her thoughts turn to her handbag and the smartwatch Anthony slapped on her desk that morning.

No thanks. She'd rather do without a sensor device to begin with. With her current status Freemee calculates maximum revenues of two hundred and twenty Frees or one hundred and thirty-two pounds per month! She's already deep into exploitation mode.

'Improve your results! Record your physical data and your account's current monthly score will rise to three hundred and thirty Frees or one hundred and ninety-eight pounds.'

Nearly seventy pounds more for wearing a watch? A tempting offer. Cyn recalls the happy woman shopping for shoes in the video. *Don't let them trick you!* she reminds herself. *You're just writing a report. Or are you? You can try the watch later.* She refuses, although it isn't easy, as she mentally notes for her article.

Yet Freemee still has more in its locker. Next they offer her individual sensors for the home, to be placed in the fridge, on the coffee machine, in bed, on medicine bottles and anywhere else they can measure people's behaviour. So they can remind you to take your pills or that you've already drunk four cups of coffee today. They cost something, but not much, and can be paid for with loaned Frees. Obviously. She puts this off until later as well. What she's really curious about, she has to confess, is the crystal ball – a glimpse into her future. She doesn't believe in it, of course not, or only to the extent she believes in horoscopes: she'll gladly trust a positive forecast, but she won't take a negative one seriously. Definitely not.

As she runs the cursor over the ball, a caption appears. 'Hi, Cyn! You're using the free version of our crystal ball, but that doesn't incorporate all the ball's possibilities. Would you like to use the complete version? It costs 7 Frees or £4 per month.'

What was I expecting? she thinks, disillusioned. She'll make do with the free version for the moment, although she knows full well this isn't free of charge either.

After she's clicked 'No', a little cartoon figure warns her via a speech bubble: 'Your data profile is still only partially complete, Cynthia. Its accuracy for analysis is 67%.'

Who cares, she thinks. *This way I can more readily disregard the results if they don't suit me.*

She clicks on the ball. It spins and bursts open, releasing a horde of small cartoon Cynthias. Each is wearing a T-shirt of a different colour marked with a word such as Health, Career, Love, Wealth and Leisure – just like a horoscope!

'Suggestion: You always wanted to learn the saxophone. Start today: it's easy with FreeSax,' the 'Leisure' Cyn announces in a speech bubble with a blinking gold saxophone beneath it.

Only her very best friends know of this wish, she thinks, somewhat startled. Yet other people obviously do too.

Whatever. She doesn't have any free time anyway. *So let's ask the ball what it has to say about 'Love'.* She clicks on 'Love' Cynthia's red T-shirt. A transparent male cartoon character like a passing ghost appears beside it. The Cynthia figure says in a speech bubble, 'You have a 13% chance of finding a new partner in the next twelve months.'

Great. She might as well become a nun right now ... Both numbers are highlighted in colour. Above them a blinking pink caption reads: 'Improve your chances with the relevant ActApps! Choose one of our Love ActApps!'

Cyn sees a row of symbols representing the various Love ActApps apparently best suited to her needs. Some of the apps are free; for others she'd need to fork out up to twenty pounds. Per month! Payment by Freemee data or data advance possible. The cheapest in the top ten cost ten Frees or seven pounds per month.

Wow!

All of them offer a thirty-day test version, however. Cyn can also sort the list by price. As she's about to click on the corresponding menu, a small pop-up appears: 'WARNING! The ActApps are ranked specifically for you, Cynthia. We recommend you use one of the ranked ActApps. N.B. Maybe you wonder why there aren't any of the customer ratings you usually find in this kind of list. Freemee suggests a personalized ActApp list for every customer. Something that works for someone else may not work for you, Cynthia, which makes customer ActApp ratings meaningless.'

She thinks about this for a second, then clicks 'Cancel'. Her head's bursting with impressions and she needs time to digest them. She removes the glasses.

Eddie's sitting in his bedroom with his laptop. He looks pale and is sweating. *How does the line in that film go? Just because you're paranoid doesn't mean they aren't after you?* Nobody's after him, but if the figures produced by his little search program on the screen in front of him are correct, then they're more than enough to make him paranoid.

Has he made a mistake somewhere? In his interpretation? In the script? These are only preliminary findings. Where might the mistake lie? Can he read the numbers differently? There must be a reasonable explanation for the discrepancies. Freemee must have identified them too: statistics are its core business.

Eddie has disabled his ActApps so they don't keep chastising him. Doing without them isn't easy. His attention keeps wandering. His results are going to sink even further. Not good. The thought sets him a little on edge.

What if he hasn't made an error? What if his suspicions are correct? The consequences would be . . .

Eddie leans back, his head swirling with suppositions. He stands up and looks out of the window at the bushes in the twilight and up at the dark blue London sky. *Until he's certain . . .* He glances at the smartwatch on his wrist and fiddles with the clasp. He opens it. He lays the smartwatch on the windowsill and cups his hand over it for a second.

Caught in two minds, he goes back to his laptop, opens his Freemee account and suspends his data collection subscription. A dialogue box asks if he's sure he wants to do this.

OK.

'Don't forget to reactivate your account again soon, Eddie,' Freemee reminds him. 'Would you mind briefly telling us why you're suspending your subscription?'

- I'm not satisfied with the advice from the ActApps
- I haven't achieved my goals in spite of using Freemee

- I'm worried about privacy
- Other reasons

Eddie doesn't answer. No, he's not going to cancel his registration just yet. But he does have to check. If he's made a mistake he'll reactivate his subscription, but until he's sure . . . First he has to read through the script, line by line. Where might the error in his reasoning lie? Or maybe it's a simple coding error? He opens the file and starts to read.

'Watch out, little boy,' whispers Joaquim as he looks through his glasses three thousand miles to the west. 'You're on thin ice. Very thin ice.'

'I think's it great you signed up to Freemee, Mum,' Vi says to her mother as she comes in and puts down two bags of shopping on the table. 'Were you that stung by Zero's words about ignorant parents?'

'Yes,' Cyn says, laughing. 'So stung I'm going to write about it.'

'Oh no!'

'I only signed up for research purposes.'

''Course you did!' Vi grins. 'By the way, I saw your teaser. Pretty mediocre.'

'It wasn't my idea, but this story has at least kept me in a job for a while.'

Vi has bought lots of healthy things, and they make dinner together in the kitchen.

'Have you heard of ManRank?' Cyn asks in passing as she serves salad on to two plates.

'Yeah,' Vi replies and sits down at the table.

'Your old friend Ashley has a similar score to you despite still being a goth. Doesn't that seem odd to you?'

Vi shrugs. 'Are you cross because I listened to the Act-Apps rather than you?'

'No, why would I be? I'm just interested in how ActApps make recommendations that improve your results.'

'No idea. The software figures it out. Watch the Freemee videos. They explain everything. It must work a bit like Google when it optimizes my searches for me, or Facebook with my timeline.'

'Fabulous examples. And who guarantees that Google is really filtering your search according to your personal preferences and not its own?'

Vi looks at her in bewilderment. She stabs a piece of tomato with her fork. 'Well, Google – who else?'

'Exactly. Who else?'

'Jesus, Mum! Are you paranoid or what? This discussion is as old as the hills! What's wrong with you lot? Has something terrible happened?' asks Vi. 'Has Google or Facebook or Freemee brainwashed me? No. So lay off, will you?'

'The first sign of brainwashing is that the subject doesn't notice it.'

'So how do you do your research, eh? Not with Google by any chance?'

'Touché. But you do admit Freemee has changed you?'

'No, Mum. I changed myself. Freemee just helped me. And it works. I get better marks at school. The two of us get along. Well, as long as you don't start conversations like this one, anyway. I eat more healthily. I have more friends and nicer ones than before. I feel a lot better than I used to and I'm delighted about that. Aren't you? What's your problem?'

Yes, what is my problem actually, Cyn wonders.

'By the way,' says Vi, 'I'm going over to Sally's afterwards to study and stay the night.'

A year ago this would have worried Cyn, but now she merely says, 'OK. But just explain something to me . . . What happened back then? Did you look into the crystal ball?'

'No,' Vi says. 'My marks were low. I just asked how I could improve them. The ActApps gave me a load of tips and immediately calculated what the results would be.'

Cyn remembers days when Vi would come back from school and hole up in her room without a word. She obviously wasn't well, and Cyn couldn't pull her daughter out of the hole by herself. Yet that isn't the same as a low score.

'What recommendations did you get?' she enquires. 'Ones you were happy to follow from the very start?'

'Some I did, some less so and others not at all. It's really simple actually. Marks are important when you're a pupil like me. The ActApp explained that however well I did, if I kept dressing like a goth, most teachers would mark me a grade or two lower than my classmates.'

Cyn lays down her fork. 'So good marks were more important to you than your identity?'

'Oh, come on! What identity? Yesterday I was a goth, today I'm not. So? Your generation were the same. Look at Madonna – a new identity every year.'

Cyn has no comeback to this.

'I got a different hairstyle, took out a couple of earrings and changed my make-up. That boosted my score.'

'The teachers immediately gave you better marks?'

'No, Freemee did the scoring. Assessing photos of me, measuring my physical performance.'

'You could have cheated by changing your hairstyle and piercings on only a few photos and uploading those.'

'And then one of my friends uploads a photo with spiky hair and piercings and exposes me?'

'Don't you find that strange? That you're afraid of being exposed? That means you didn't actually want to behave like that, but felt you were being policed.'

'Oh, Mum, please! I don't feel as if I'm being policed! Except by you, perhaps, but that's got better too. I think you're seeing monsters where there are none.'

'But how could Ashley stay a goth if the teachers find it so annoying?'

Vi shrugs again. 'No idea.' She starts to clear the table. They haven't eaten much.

'Haven't you and Ashley ever talked about it? About the kind of tips you receive, and the advice she gets from her ActApps? Why they're so different?'

'No.'

'She must have been surprised to see you change.'

'We weren't seeing so much of each other at the time and then one day we stopped meeting altogether. You know how it is. People change. Friends drift apart. Does it bother you that Freemee encourages variety?'

Cyn has snuggled up on the sofa. Vi went off to Sally's after dinner. Cyn would have rather spent the evening with her, like old times, but that's nonsense: her daughter's a grown-up now. Also, she has more than enough to keep her busy.

Her email account is overflowing with requests, comments and nasty insults. After reading a few, she deletes all the messages from senders she doesn't recognize. She isn't in the mood for being hassled by strangers.

She mulls over what she should write about ManRank and has a go at putting it into words, but she can't quite find the right angle. She has a look at the *Daily*'s chat room about the search for Zero. Debate is raging, even this late at night. She soon loses track. The original discussions have split into new ones, which have then further subdivided. Some of the threads are technical and she can't understand a word – she doesn't even have a clue what they're about. Other threads interest her more because she can follow their contents. She gets hooked on one about what Zero wants to achieve and whether his goals are legitimate or not. She reads the statements and finds that most of them approve of Zero's critique. *They sound like me in my discussions with Vi*, she thinks. It strikes her how fearful and old-fashioned these arguments often sound. Like back when her parents cautioned her against the dangers of television and a Walkman. Square eyes. Dumbing down. Isolation. None of those things happened and yet she feels greater kinship with the critics than with the advocates. *Am I looking for a discussion*, she wonders, *or just confirmation of my own negative attitude?*

'You can't hear yourself speak,' says Jon, gesturing towards the darkness and the din of the crickets and cicadas.

'Good,' Erben replies. 'Then nobody else will hear you either.'

He doesn't really need to worry about that. Once a day at least, he has his property by the Potomac checked by several independent security firms. He bought the villa with the sweeping grounds before the move to Washington so his children could grow up surrounded by greenery. They're already fast asleep, as are Jon's two little ones, and their wives are whispering and laughing over a bottle of French wine at the other end of the veranda. They've draped their jackets over their shoulders against the cool evening air seeping off the woods and meadows. The dark outline of an ancient oak tree looms up in the moonlight from the spacious lawn before them, and the ribbon of the Milky Way stretches out above their heads.

Erben wipes some of the condensation from his Martini glass with his index finger. 'Waterfalls,' he mutters with a shake of his head. 'Pathetic. Maybe we should cut the NSA's budget if that's all they can find.'

Jon shakes his head too before raising his glass to Erben. 'Thanks again for inviting us.'

'We always love having you and Samantha to stay,' replies Erben.

'Henry Emerald,' says Jon.

Erben's gaze wanders up in the direction of the stars. 'What about him?'

'You know him?'

'Of course. How could I not? Emerald's one of the two hundred richest men in the country, owns countless stakes in all kinds of companies, from energy and software to security, and is an important backer of the President. What about him?'

'You recently mentioned we should get control of Carl Montik because you need to have control of Freemee.'

'What's Emerald got to do with that?'

'He has a stake in the company. Four per cent.'

'He can't have much influence over Montik.'

'Not officially,' Jon replies, taking a sip of his brandy. 'We've taken a closer look at the investment structure. Over forty different investors hold shares in Freemee. Most of them are based offshore and keep the circumstances of their ownership a secret.'

'So far, so normal.' Erben's eyes track the path of a shooting star.

'We've dug a bit deeper. Using the means at our disposal.'

'Which I don't wish to know anything more about. What did you come up with?'

'Fifty-one per cent is in the hands of the Freemee founders or their heirs.'

'Heirs?'

'One of the founders died a couple of months back in a car accident. He left behind a partner and their two kids.'

'And the remaining forty-nine per cent? Minus the four that belong to Emerald.'

'They belong to Emerald too.'

Erben wipes the remaining moisture from his glass. 'Isn't Emerald a major government contractor? EmerSec, his security firm, receives billions from us, right?'

'Yep. A reliable partner and has been for decades.'

Erben drains his drink in one. The ice cubes clink against the glass as he sets it down on the cast-iron table.

Two thirty in the morning! Cyn should have gone to sleep long ago, but her thoughts have been revolving obsessively around the events of the last thirty-six hours, hoovering up more and more articles and comments.

For a bit of relaxation she opens her dating site account. Three new messages, but none to her liking. She sighs. Chander's to her liking, even though he's quite a few years younger than her – or maybe for that precise reason. She could do with a nice little fling. The last one was so long ago.

She browses the internet, looking for traces of him. The Google entries confirm Anthony's pronouncements about Chander's professional experience. There are far fewer details about his private life. Does he have a girlfriend? She clicks on his social media profiles, one by one, but he's barred access to every single one to anyone but friends. She can go no further.

What if she asked one of the Love ActApps Vi's praised so highly? She picks up the glasses and calls up the list of

Freemee's suggestions. A free thirty-day trial. The first Act-App on the list doesn't have a contrived name like Lovematch or Datequeen. It's called Peggy, as though it were her best friend.

She hesitates. What on earth is she doing? Yet she's intrigued to find out how these supposedly tailor-made apps work. She checks one more time that the free thirty-day offer contains no unwelcome financial conditions, then activates Peggy. It feels damn peculiar.

The next moment, a transparent woman of Cyn's age is standing in her cramped living room. She's attractive, blonde and slim, like a sales assistant in a fashionable boutique.

'Hi, Cynthia,' she says in a voice that reminds Cyn of her satnav, looks around and, signalling to the armchair next to the sofa, asks, 'May I sit on the sofa or in the armchair?'

Cyn struggles to form any words, not only because the animation is so perfect but also because the ghost can find her way around the living room. The glasses must be filming and incorporating the location into the software live! She ought to turn it off right now.

'Delighted to meet you,' Peggy continues, smiling at her.

What the hell. 'Please take a seat,' Cyn manages to say, gesturing to the armchair. She doesn't want Peggy to come too close. She catches herself gazing at Peggy's projection – her hair, facial features, body and shoes – as though it were a real person sitting opposite her.

'How can I help you, Cynthia?'

She has to remind herself that she's speaking to a computer program. Somehow this feels less embarrassing than talking to a real-life woman about her downright adolescent feelings. *This is only research*, she tells herself. *Let's see what this Peggy's got to say for herself.*

'Chander Argawal,' she says before she can have any second thoughts. 'I like him. What can I do about it?'

'This Chander?' asks Peggy, beaming a picture of the young Indian into the space in front of Cyn.

'Yes.'

'Interesting guy. Good-looking too,' says Peggy. 'I can see why you like him, Cynthia.'

All this makes Cyn's flesh crawl, even if the artificial voice does undermine the illusion that she's speaking with a real person. *Be a bit more nonchalant about it*, she tells herself. *See the whole thing as a game.*

'The more I know about you, the better my tips will be,' Peggy continues. 'Physical factors play a crucial role in interpersonal matters. A sensor device would be very useful to ascertain more about them, Cynthia. Would you like to use one?'

Peggy shows Cyn the list she saw when she registered. It includes the smartwatch that's still in her bag. She hesitates, then heaves herself off the sofa with a grunt, gropes her way out into the hallway where her bag's lying on the small cabinet and takes out the watch. It's made of some kind of plastic and has a small display. *Data handcuffs!* thinks Cyn. Still, her curiosity urges her to try them out. What's the worst that can happen? Unlike handcuffs she can take the watch off at any time. And it makes no difference now: if she's going to do this, she has to go the whole hog. It's not for real. She needs more information anyway, so she must go through with this. She puts on the watch as she makes her way back into the living room.

The glasses ask her if the device should record data and save it to Freemee. All she has to do is agree and her current pulse, her movements, steps, skin resistance and other results Cyn knows nothing about start streaming into her data account. *This is all so weird!*

'Your data score has just gone up by twenty-one per cent,' an announcement informs her.

'Fantastic!' Peggy exclaims. 'That was quick! Just a few more seconds ... OK then,' she explains after the designated period of time. 'What can I say about you and Chander? The man is twelve years younger than you.'

I know that, thinks Cyn. *Mind you, what does Cyborg Peggy know about human attraction?*

'In any case, you're far more likely to be interested in an affair with him than the other way around.'

To ensure that Cyn grasps this unfortunate, although not unexpected situation quickly and easily, Peggy's designers have made Chander and her into two simple figures who are, quite literally, not very close to each other. Chander's glowing a cool blue colour on the left-hand edge of her field of vision, while Cyn is a warm red on the right.

'Chander's levels of desire for you show up as low as twenty per cent,' says Peggy, pointing to the blue figure. 'Not so bad.'

Exactly. Not so bad!

'Would you like to know more about the underlying statistics?' asks Peggy. 'Or go straight to solutions?'

That's what you call a friend! Cyn can't help grinning. No ranting and raving about men in general or even about this one in particular. Peggy just rolls up her sleeves and gets on with suggesting solutions. She does want to test Peggy a bit, though. After all, she's only the free version. 'Summarize the reasons for me,' she requests. 'In a nutshell, if you can.'

'I'm not familiar with the reasons or the causes,' Peggy lectures her. 'I work with statistics. My findings are exclusively based on a comparison of a large quantity of other people's data. I don't know *why* situations are as they are, I just know that they are so.'

'Then give me a summary of your findings,' Cyn orders her.

'Age difference is a relatively minor obstacle to potential relationships of this kind. What's more problematic is the large discrepancy between your social backgrounds' – the Cyn and Chander figures move even further apart, and Cyn wonders what exactly 'social backgrounds' is supposed to mean here. Peggy needs to hone her terminology. 'The common cultural foundations of comparable couplings don't look so promising.'

Cultural foundations: another of those terms. 'Couplings' is even worse. *Is Peggy doing this on purpose?*

'He's attracted to intelligent women, though.'

'Thanks for the compliment.'

'Some of the biological results complicate matters,' Peggy remarks. 'He literally can't stand the smell of you. But there are ways of dealing with that.' Cyn can't believe her ears – or, rather, the bones behind the ears to which Peggy's voice is being transmitted. 'His previous girlfriends were all of a different type from you. Tall, slim, blonde and feminine.'

She feels a slight twinge of female jealousy. Still, all exes, she reflects. She's enraged by Peggy's conclusion that this man isn't for her. It felt very different when Chander gave her a smouldering look in the meeting room earlier. *I'm going to prove you wrong! You're only a program! What do you know about emotions?*

'So what do you recommend?'

'Eat less meat – or better, none at all – and more vegetables.'

That's to alter the biological factors, Cyn presumes. *To deal with the smell factor. Not stupid. Well, either not stupid, or else completely barmy.*

Peggy has a bunch of other, similarly reasonable pieces of advice in her repertoire. Cyn hears her out. She should go vegetarian, contort herself at yoga, go to classical concerts and try out specific role-playing exercises on the computer. Peggy also recommends some soaps and perfumes with a specific type of fragrance. If she follows this advice, she can increase the likelihood of Chander being inclined to have an affair with her from twenty per cent to fifty. Not bad.

Peggy would also like to comment on Cyn's outfit, but the virtual blonde complains somewhat indignantly that she has too little data to work with. 'It'd help me if you filmed yourself in front of the mirror,' she explains.

'No way!'

'OK, I respect that. We'll make do with what we've got. Incidentally, Chander won't mind that scar you keep hidden.'

A flashback of her accident threatens to overwhelm Cyn for a moment. Tongues of fire. Pain. Several weeks in hospital. Her self-consciousness and anger at being so disfigured.

She hasn't told Freemee about it, so how does Peggy know? She found the saxophone thing harmless, but this! Creepy. Seriously creepy. She feels like cancelling this experiment, turning off all her devices, all the surveillance cameras and whatever else is out there poking around in her personal business. But she knows she can't. She could take off the smartwatch and log out of Freemee. And then? She can't escape the complete exposure of her daily life. She can only play the game, and be smarter when it really counts.

ArchieT: Vain! Us?

LotsofZs: Good description of you, is it? ;-)

ArchieT: Did you see that newspaper editor? All modesty aside, I'll show him who's vain!

Thursday

Jeff and Frances intercept Cyn the next morning as she walks into the engine room, feeling a little fatigued.

'We've got the first results from our readers,' Jeff tells her excitedly.

Together they enter the meeting room that Anthony has designated as both Chander's office and the operations centre for the hunt for Zero.

'Good morning,' Chander greets her with a radiant smile, as if she were the only one in the room. Chander, the man who wouldn't mind her scar. Gary did.

She hasn't yet taken off the glasses after her journey on the Tube. She activates Peggy with a whispered command as Chander asks how she is. Her blonde adviser doesn't appear this time, but her voice keeps feeding the bone behind her ear with tips on posture as well as the odd phrase and cue. She's turned Peggy's settings up too high and finds she can't concentrate on Chander. *This is what being schizophrenic must feel like*, she thinks.

'Yes, thanks, I'm, um, fine,' she stammers. 'Back in a second.'

This is never going to work. In the toilets, she sets Peggy to only give tips with an eighty per cent likelihood of success. When she returns, Chander, Jeff and Frances have gathered in front of a screen.

'Ah, you're back,' says Chander. That smile again!

'Yes. Something exciting going on?'

Peggy speaks to Cyn only occasionally now, and her advice blends almost naturally into her stream of consciousness. She can now devote herself fully to her conversation with Chander, but he's absorbed in his work.

'Readers have figured out what program Zero used to animate his videos,' Chander explains. '3DWhizz. Here, you can see an entry from checkmax89. He gives a few examples to back up his analysis.'

Jeff calls the relevant entry up on screen. There's a string of comments below it. 'In the continuing discussion, more and more users either challenge or confirm this supposition and give additional examples.'

'How many people use this program?' Cyn asks.

'Millions of people worldwide,' says Chander.

'Oh well, rules out a few billion at least,' Cyn says tartly.

'Take Chander's work seriously!' Peggy remonstrates inside her head. *Wow, she can even analyse semantics!* She's right, of course. He wouldn't be the first man to run a mile as a result of Cyn's sarcasm.

'But surely you're smart enough to draw a few conclusions?' she continues, addressing Chander. *Sycophant*, she thinks as he answers.

'In combination with Zero's patterns of speech, for instance, yes. It's high-level stuff, and they can't reproduce that quality electronically yet. Someone is speaking these texts and only afterwards are they put through various electronic filters. Which means that the speaker or speakers have a perfect command of English.'

'Can people out there also recognize that?'

'We'll see,' says Chander. 'Maybe someone's hacked into the company and the register of every 3DWhizz client is now floating around the internet somewhere.'

'Nothing's turned up yet, though,' says Jeff, 'so we'll most likely have to search for it ourselves. Let's get to work.'

For the next few hours Cyn concentrates on her article about ManRank and looks at reactions when the initial videos emerged four months ago and how these have changed over time. Whereas the usual critics protested vehemently at first and proclaimed the final decline of Western civilization, the series quickly found a huge number of online followers. She realizes they regarded it as bringing order to a chaotic and incomprehensible world. She still has a few unresolved questions, though, and thinks they could be a wonderful excuse for a conversation with Chander. She consults Peggy.

'Chander loves talking about the internet and technological innovations, even in his free time,' Peggy says. Cyn doesn't see much of a thrill in that just now, but she decides to turn his superior knowledge in this field to her advantage. 'His other interests at the moment are creative cookery and sport, especially an Indian martial art called *kalarippayat*.'

Good to know, thinks Cyn, even though the whole appeal of talking to a member of the opposite sex once consisted of finding out precisely those kinds of titbits.

Chander's sitting in the meeting room. He's gazing slightly madly into his glasses and intermittently typing on his tablet.

'Have you got a minute?' she asks.

Flashing her one of his fabulous smiles, he invites her to sit down with him. 'What's up?'

'I can't get one comment from the Zero video out of my head. How can I be sure Google and Co.'s results really show what I'm looking for, and not what the people operating the search engines want to show me? How do I know ActApp recommendations really are in my best interests, and not in the best interests of the ActApp programmers?'

'There's a simple answer to that: you can never be sure until you've seen the underlying algorithms.'

Cyn nods. That's what she thought.

'Search engines are always accused of manipulating results,' Chander explains. 'That's why the EU even went as far as threatening Google with a fine running into billions of euros. But the question is more where the manipulation begins.'

Cyn looks helplessly at him, urging him to go into more detail.

'All software is underpinned by its programmers' basic assumptions about how the world works. Those assumptions – for example, if the person's an advocate of non-cooperative or cooperative game theory – feed into the program itself. That means that the program ultimately replicates its author's world view. If different people with different intentions write the program, then it'll be a different program, producing different results, however slight. Is that manipulation?'

Cyn merely arches her eyebrows by way of answer.

'Also, search engines personalize the search,' Chander says, continuing his lecture. 'You and I will get completely different results if we each enter Zero or another term into Google. Is that manipulation? What criteria do the programs use to personalize their search?

'Search engines do sometimes deliberately influence results, though, for example when it comes to pornography or hate crimes. Or if they do business in dictatorships or monarchies in the Gulf. They'll remove from the index links to insults aimed at potentates or monarchs because they're forbidden by law. Those are just a few examples. In short, there's no such thing as a neutral search result, and the same is true of most results and recommendations online. That's why we talk not about freedom of information, but filtering of information. None of it's truly neutral. Why would it be? The internet isn't a new world, it's simply an addition to our existing one. People use it to trick and cheat, dissimulate, divulge and expose, manipulate and intrigue, worship and ridicule, hate and love, just like anywhere else.' He shrugs his shoulders. 'Just involving far more people and at much greater speeds than before. Making use of a service on the internet is like asking a taxi driver in an unknown city to take you to a good hotel. In the best-case scenario, he does exactly that. In the second best, he takes you to one he thinks is good, although unfortunately his standards aren't the same as yours. And in most, he takes you to his cousin's hotel.' He grins. 'But what's your point?'

Peggy encourages Cyn to react to his joke, but she's too lost in her thoughts to flirt right now. 'By filtering information all these companies influence our opinions and our actions,' she observes.

Chander pulls a face. 'You're a journalist. Mistrust is an occupational hazard.'

'A loss of trust isn't an occupational hazard, it's our new culture,' Cyn counters pensively.

'Welcome to paranoia!' he says, laughing.

'I rest my case!'

'Of course these companies influence our opinions and our actions, whether they intend to or not. That may even be the key point. Do they want that level of influence? And if so, how do they want to use it? And the next question is: Do users know *how* they're likely to be influenced?'

'But—'

'What's that?' He interrupts her, pointing to a sequence of images playing in a thumbnail preview. *New video!* it says. 'Looks like—'

'Zero,' Cyn and Chander cry in unison.

Anthony comes charging into the room with Jeff in hot pursuit. 'Zero's posted a new video!'

'We saw,' says Chander. 'Directly on our site!'

'Can you find out where it came from?' Anthony asks Chander.

'Already on it.' His fingers scamper across his tablet keyboard.

Jeff has opened the video on full-screen mode. Cyn freezes. She's grinning out at herself from Zero's video, explaining: 'Someone else is hunting me now.' Her face and voice morph into Anthony's. 'Yes, well, I don't really care. Our friends should really be paying a visit to some totally different people, such as Takisha Washington. Takisha lives in Philadelphia. She's a mother of two and works at a branch of Barner's, a regional supermarket chain.'

Zero's pacing up and down in front of said store, disguised as an overweight man in a Hawaiian shirt. 'Sadly, Barner's hasn't been doing so well in recent years. A few weeks ago they had to "let go" a few people, as the euphemism goes. Twenty per cent of their total staff! So the question for Barner's was, who should go?'

Anthony's fidgeting beside Chander. 'So? Found anything?'

'It takes longer than that.'

Cyn continues to follow the video attentively to see if she can spot any clues.

'Barner's has an in-house staff appraisal system which evaluates a range of criteria. Unfortunately it turned out that almost ninety per cent of staff met the criteria.'

As in his earlier videos, Zero's moving through real-life surroundings, but he appears less and less frequently as his tale progresses. Cyn notices that the video's taking a different path from previous ones. The footage reminds her of TV reports that reconstruct real-life scenes with a voice-over commentary by the newsreader. Forms, supermarket branches with customers, library footage of staff meetings . . . Just as labour-intensive as Zero's usual animations and film montages, but less sensationalist.

'I've got a server,' whispers Chander without getting up. 'In Germany. Must be a re-router.'

Cyn focuses on the curvaceous black woman who's now appeared on screen. She's wearing a flowery dress and standing in front of a rubbish bin. The caption gives her name as Takisha Washington.

'I worked in that store for seven years. Barner's administrative centre was right upstairs from us,' she explains in a thick American drawl.

'Who did the interview?' Anthony asks. He instructs Jeff and Frances to find Takisha Washington as quickly as possible.

'I'd just come off duty,' Takisha continues, 'and I had to throw something in the trash. That's when I found this list.' She holds up a bunch of crumpled papers to the camera. 'Y'all know what this is. Somebody from HR threw the printout in the trash instead of puttin' it through the shredder. Cain't have thought nothin' of it.'

'A server in Brazil,' Chander interjects. 'Zero's covered his trail – or laid a false one.'

'I takes a good look at this list and I sees my name on it too. I think, "That's weird." Look at this.' Washington points to the table of names with several long columns of numbers.

'Got her!' cries Jeff.

Anthony's already standing behind him, staring at the screen.

'Takisha Washington. Look, that's her face. With contact details and all.'

Anthony's already tapping on his smartphone. Cyn's having trouble concentrating on the video, but they have to be quick now.

'I knew they were gonna fire people and I told myself that list could have something to do with it. So to be safe I took it home.'

The video switches back to TV report mode. The film-maker might be able to give them some clues about Zero. They've got to talk to Takisha Washington.

'A few days after they fired me, I got a letter from my credit card company.' Takisha's dark fingers with bright-red nails pull a letter from an envelope. 'They done reduced my coverage to zero. I had to pay off most of my debts right away. Huh? I just lost my job! How was I s'posed to pay my debts? No chance. My credit score went down when I was fired, and I had to pay to keep them from blockin' my card. What was I gonna do? I had to send my rent money, and me with two kids in school. They daddies don't pay a goddam cent. So I had to sell my car. Great!' Now she's standing in front of a dented car door. A man's hand counts bills into hers. 'Next thing I know, my landlord calls. Says he's worried I ain't gonna make rent. He right. I took any job I could get. Many I didn't get because I ain't got no car no more. My credit card been blocked for a long time, and the credit card company was threatenin' to sue me.'

'No way!' whispers Chander alongside Cyn, and he isn't talking about Takisha's story. His fingers are flitting across the touchscreen even faster than before. She's dying to hear what he's found, but one of them has to keep track of Takisha's tale.

'Two months later my landlord kicked me out. There I was, out on the street with two kids.' Takisha's in a street in a run-down American suburb. 'No job. No credit. No car. No home. Friends took me in, but only for two weeks. I found the list again when I was packin'. I'd totally forgotten about it. I was about to throw it out, but then I got on the bus to my old supermarket and showed the list to one of the women in HR. First she got all red and asked me where did I get it from, and then she said the document wasn't nothin'. That it belonged to the company and I should give it to her. I said no way. I got a lawyer. He knew what it meant. The columns in the list showed the grades from the different assessment systems Barner's used – Barner's Human Resources, the company's internal evaluation system for its workers, a sub-system called Barner's Social for social aspects, and then ManRank. The lawyer told me it was some new kind of internet appraisal system. I ain't never heard of it. He said I had a chance. Not because they'd used ManRank, but because they never told me they was usin' it. But even if I had a chance, I'd lost everything I goddam owned! D'you know what it's like bein' out on the streets? That's where I ended up because of that shitty list! Can you imagine that shit? I mean, I've heard of people losin' their jobs because they posted something dumb on Facebook, or not gettin' a loan or a job because of fifteen-year-old notifications of a foreclosure sale of they house on Google. Damn, they so many things you gotta look out for nowadays!'

'Yeah, so many things,' repeats Zero, dressed as a sad-faced clown. 'Fired because of ManRank, Freemee's public rating agency for people. The first case we've ever heard about. This was Zero almost live from Philadelphia. And now for our normal ending.' Zero waves his arms like a conductor: 'Another thing: I believe we must destroy the data krakens.'

'Fuck!' shouts Carl, his voice almost cracking as he launches into a tirade. 'This story is going to be all over the headlines, up and down the land! Fucking Miss Washington is going to be telling her story on every goddam prime-time talk show in the nation! The first supporters' pages are popping up on social media, even on our website! This is a fucking disaster!'

Will lets him rage. He knows there's no hope of getting through to Carl when he's in this kind of funk.

'You're wrong,' Alice retorts, unperturbed. 'The hunt for Zero has hardly even begun, and Zero has already got everybody talking about us.'

'As the first rating agency for people!'

'As the first public—'

'As if that mattered.'

'It does,' she says, displaying a graph. 'You can follow here, live, how new memberships ballooned during the report. Not to mention interest from corporate clients.' She laughs. 'Customer services are swamped with requests. If we put the right spin on this, public opinion will mainly turn against Barner's because they didn't notify their staff.'

Carl nervously arranges a small vase, some pens and a smartphone until they're in a neat line on the meeting table.

'You're probably right,' he admits. 'Still, Zero's come up with a catchy slogan – "the rating agency for people" – which could do us long-term damage.'

'Public . . .'

'If you like.' He tinkers with a pen that to Will's eyes already looked perfectly parallel to the others.

'No, that's the major difference. Zero has done us a huge favour by saying that. It means we can stick to our story: Freemee makes public the things others seek to hide.'

'And as a result people get fired.'

'Barner's is responsible for that, not Freemee,' retorts Alice.

'That sounds like pointing the finger!' He has to align another pen. Will feels an overwhelming urge to mess all the items up.

'Good Lord, we have a hit on our hands! Enjoy it! This story's a massive scoop! Half the world's journalists want to know who's behind Zero, and they've joined the hunt. Our idea's working.'

Will's glasses signal the arrival of a new message. He skims through it while listening to Carl's response with half an ear. The next moment, however, he's lost any interest in what Carl is saying.

'The *Daily*'s about to broadcast a live interview with Takisha Washington.'

'Oh my God,' Carl groans.

Will goes to the British newspaper's home page and switches the stream to the wall monitor.

'Thank you for your willingness to talk to us, Miss Washington,' says Anthony, flashing her what he believes to be his most appealing smile. The broadcast hasn't started yet.

Less than an hour has passed since Zero's video went online. Takisha Washington is in a different dress from the one she was wearing in the video, although this one is also flowery. She's positioned herself in front of a good-quality camera and made sure the lighting is decent.

'We'll crop the video differently for the recording so only Washington is in shot,' Anthony orders quietly. He stares anxiously at the screen in front of him. 'Over a million viewers,' he whispers. 'This is amazing!'

They've hurriedly set up a makeshift live studio in the engine room. Cyn's sitting with Anthony and Chander at one table, while Jeff, Frances and Charly are on red alert nearby. All of them are wearing smart glasses. Five cameras are trained on them from a variety of angles. The newsfloor can be seen in the background, complete with editors working at long tables. The giant wall of monitors serves as a backdrop to the whole set-up.

'Did you find anything?' Anthony asks Chander, who nods absentmindedly, hunched over his computer.

Cyn takes a sip of water. She's nervous. Viewers all over the world can see her on their computer screens, mobiles and glasses.

'OK,' Anthony says to her, 'we're about to go live. Almost live. There's a ninety-second buffer, just in case there are broadcasting problems or we get mixed up or something else occurs that requires a quick response. So we can be totally relaxed.'

Yeah, I'm really going to be totally relaxed with a million people watching me and absolutely no training, is the thought racing through Cyn's mind. The footage of Takisha Washington is going to be beamed directly to her glasses. Anthony wants two co-presenters, an arrangement he knows from television news and which is similar to the set-up for their teaser.

'Everyone ready?' Anthony asks.

Nods all round.

Anthony gives the signal and leads in. 'Miss Washington, welcome to the *Daily*'s live studio. We're very grateful for your time. Tell us how you first came into contact with Zero.'

'So one day this guy calls to interview me,' answers Takisha Washington in a slightly rasping voice. 'He asks me to tell him my story and says he wants to post it on his blog and video channel.'

'How did he know what had happened to you?' asks Cyn.

'I posted it on Facebook, but hardly nobody reacted until that phone call.'

Cyn realizes she's finding this interview easier than she expected. Her nervousness is diminishing, and she's fully focused on the interviewee. 'And then you met him. A man?'

'Yeah, it was a man.'

'What was his name?'

'He said he called Don Endress.'

'Did you check him out before you met up? Take a look at the blog where he was going to post your story, I mean.'

'For sure. The blog he mentioned did exist. It looked totally OK.'

'And then he came over to interview you.'

'Sure did.'

'What did he look like?'

Takisha Washington holds a smartphone up to the camera. Cyn can see a snapshot of a man's face on the touchscreen. 'Like this.'

'Brilliant!' cries Anthony. 'You got a photo of him. Can you give us a better view?'

Takisha holds her mobile even closer to the camera.

Chander has saved a still and sends it through facial recognition software. They have a ninety-second headstart on the rest of the world.

Identify

'That's great. So this man talked to you?'

'Yeah.'
'And what did he ask you first?'

Kosak, Alvin
Cincinnati, USA
DOB: 12.10.1964
Height: 5' 11"

Cyn doesn't catch the other details because Anthony whispers, 'You carry on!'

Anthony and Jeff give each other a sign and instruct their glasses to make some calls. Anthony is waving his arms around furiously. Jeff and Frances are also trying to make contact with Alvin Kosak.

'He asked me how I felt about the whole thing,' replies Takisha.

'How did you feel? It can't have been easy for you—'

'I felt terrible! Cheated.'

Cyn hears Anthony whispering excitedly beside her. 'Alvin Kosak?'

She has to focus on her own interview, which is no easy task because she's desperate to hear what the others have uncovered. Anthony's having an agitated, half-audible conversation with Charly and a technician.

'And then you told him your story,' she continues. Alvin Kosak's identity will have been published online by now. She doesn't catch what Washington says next because Anthony murmurs to her, 'We have two and a half million viewers! And we have Alvin Kosak on the line. He's willing to join us live!'

She looks at him, wide-eyed. 'What do I do now?' she whispers.

'Improvise,' Anthony hisses. 'Tell her we've got a surprise for our viewers and that Alvin Kosak is our new live guest.'

She follows his instructions. Takisha Washington doesn't seem surprised – she's the phlegmatic type. On her glasses Cyn now has a split-screen with Alvin Kosak appearing next to Takisha. His smartphone camera distorts his face unflatteringly.

'Ladies and gentlemen,' Cyn announces, mimicking the TV presenters she's seen. 'This is Alvin Kosak, the man who interviewed Takisha Washington under the pseudonym Don Endress. Alvin Kosak, are you Zero?'

Kosak furrows his brow. 'Me? No, I have nothing to do with Zero. Apart from that he – or should I say they? ... anyway, somebody called me ... Hi, Miss Washington!'

'Where did Zero call you from?' asks Cyn.

'How should I know?'

Chander is typing like crazy on his tablet next to her, while Anthony talks quietly to Takisha Washington and her lawyers.

'Why did Zero call you?'

'He wanted me to tell him my story?'

'*Your* story?'

'Yeah. We spoke a few times, the last time two days before I spoke to Miss Washington. Zero told me back then that the media would soon be in touch.'

Cyn falters for a second before enquiring, 'The media? Zero knew the media would call you?'

'He told me they would.'

Cyn peers uncertainly at Anthony. He hunches his shoulders, clueless, and motions for her to carry on.

'What ... what else did he say?'

'That I should fly to Philadelphia to meet Miss Washington and do the interview. Zero wired me money for the flight and a fee. I also received an email containing an online address where I was to upload the film. And he told me to call myself Don Endress.'

'And you just did as he told you?'

'I didn't have anything else to do, and I could sure use the money. Also, he said I'd be famous nationwide and would soon find a job. I didn't believe that bit, but what did I have to lose?'

She decides to trust her instincts. Kosak isn't a particularly charismatic interviewee, but something about his story has set her antennae twitching. 'A new job? So you lost your job too?'

'Yeah, that's why Zero contacted me. He must have read my old blog. Probably the only person who did.'

Even as Kosak is talking, Cyn grasps his plan. 'And he told you we'd ring you?!'

Zero had counted on Kosak being identified by whichever media outlet he planned to send the video to. He probably sent him to Takisha Washington on purpose so they'd find him.

'He said I should also tell you my story. That way more people were likely to see it.'

Anthony grins and nods appreciatively. He holds up his right hand and splays all five fingers, forming the word 'millions' with his lips and opening his eyes wide. Cyn understands. They now have five million viewers. The news is spreading like wildfire. Anthony triumphantly clenches his fist. She casts one final glance at him. Should she continue? He nods.

'Then please tell us your story.'

'Well, I had this vintage store in Cincinnati. Nice stuff, nothing cheap. I sold only the best brands – Prada, Gucci and the others, all barely worn.'

'A second-hand store where the well-off could sell their clothes when they needed cash?' she enquires.

'No. These people didn't need cash, they needed space in their closet for items from the next summer or winter collection.' He scratches his nose. 'And I prefer the word "vintage". We weren't some small-time outfit reeking of dust, unwashed clothes and mothballs, see?'

She does see, even if she can't even afford designer clothing from a vintage store.

'Business was good,' Kosak continues. 'Very good. We had lots of customers, but then . . .' Kosak's face, with its slightly yellowish tinge and dark circles under his eyes, is now very close to the camera. 'A year back I noticed customers were staying away. At first I thought, OK, this sometimes happens, but they'll be back after Thanksgiving. Christmas was always the biggest time of the year for me too. But they didn't come. My takings slumped. In mid-December I started to panic . . .'

Cyn is having trouble concentrating on Kosak. She wishes he'd put down his smartphone so the picture didn't wobble so much, but she doesn't want to interrupt him now.

'I had a popular Facebook site for the store and a blog and I tweeted, with several thousand followers and a good amount of interaction. I also had a pretty big database of regular customers and sent out mails every day. But none of that helped. None of it! My takings were down seventy per cent on the previous year. That's enough to drive any store to its knees. Maybe I've got competition somewhere, I thought. I did some advertising and organized some offers. I reduced my prices, but even that didn't work. Some days I was the only person in the store.'

The picture goes out of focus for a while, then he continues to talk. 'A week before Christmas I ran into one of my former regular customers in the street. I asked him straight out how he was doing. He beat around the bush, saying he'd moved away and didn't come back to the neighbourhood very often. I saw other old customers. All of them mentioned various reasons why they hadn't been in for a while, but they promised to drop in again soon. Nobody came. In the spring I was forced to close. It was all over. My situation since is similar to Miss Washington's. My credit score fell off a cliff, I had to move into a one-room apartment and who knows how long I'll be able to afford that. Soon I may have to sleep in my car.'

He sniffles. 'I thought I must have done something wrong until one night I happened to meet one of my old regular customers in a bar. We got chatting and drinking – the ancient Romans knew all about these things, *in vino veritas* and all that, even if we were on the beer. Eventually I told him I'd had to shut down the store. I asked him straight out why he'd stayed away. He pussyfooted around for a while, but then he came out with it. He was using this new program called Freemee and he sounded pretty excited about it.'

'I knew it!' groans Carl.

'I'd heard about it,' Kosak continues, as his face is displayed in its full unattractive glory on the monitor wall in Will's office, 'but I'd never really taken the trouble to find out more.'

'Well, you should've,' mutters Carl.

'He basically told me the program gave him tips about how to improve his lifestyle . . .'

Carl rearranges the pens without taking his eyes off the screen.

'. . . make more dough, have better luck with women. He sounded as if his goal was to be Mr Universe. He was totally convinced by the whole thing. Sounded more like a cult to me.'

'A cult!' Carl gives a sarcastic laugh. 'We don't need gurus, slogans or psycho-terror!' He scrutinizes the line-up on the table and pushes the vase a fraction of an inch to the left. 'Structures,' he mumbles. 'That's what matters. People only need structures.'

'In any case, at some point the program advised him not to buy any more second-hand clothes or past collections, as they'd have a negative effect on his results. Other people would think he couldn't afford the latest collection and needed to save money. *His results* – like something in a lab. Somehow they've replaced what reputation or image used to be. That's why he didn't come to my vintage store any longer – because my goods were bad for his results! I wasn't expecting such a bullshit explanation.'

Kosak's face turns blurry. 'Hang on,' he says, 'I've got to put the device down somewhere. My arm's about to drop off.'

'What more has he got to say?' Carl asks, annoyed. 'We get the message! Refuse to go along with new technology and you fall flat on your face. Splat! Nobody but yourself to blame.'

The picture has stabilized now, and Kosak continues. 'Next morning I thought, I've got nothing to lose by checking. So I called a few of my old customers, chatted to them, you know, and asked in passing what they thought about Freemee. After a bit of humming and hawing, some of them confessed they'd stopped coming to my store for the same reason as the guy the night before. Because that shitty program had advised them to buy new products rather than vintage clothes! You see? They let themselves be fucking brainwashed!'

'Just the opposite,' comments Carl. 'They finally began to use their brains.'

'Yeah, they're crazy!' Takisha Washington interjects, and the two of them embark on a series of mutual commiserations and curses against modern technology, which Anthony brings to a swift conclusion when he notices the audience figures are falling. They say goodbye to the two of them for the time being and end the broadcast.

'That was so cool!' he cheers afterwards. 'Many a TV show is looking enviously at our ratings right now!'

'While you were having fun, I was working and analysing Zero's video,' says Chander. 'I don't know why, but this time they made a crucial mistake.'

'This shit has got to stop!' Carl rages. 'The *Daily* is screwing everything up, goddammit!'

Will doesn't try to stop him. He knows the storm will soon blow over. When Carl has vented his anger Will says, 'It's no big deal. We've got plans for precisely this scenario in our bottom drawer.'

'I bet there's nothing but chewing gum in your bottom drawer. The most important things are all on servers!'

'You're right,' Will says to appease him, 'but there were bound to be reports like this sooner or later. We discussed it, remember.'

'Yeah, yeah,' Carl agrees. 'But it's still annoying people don't understand that all ActApps do is nudge completely normal social processes.'

'That's what we're here for,' Will reassures him. 'To explain that to people. To highlight the opportunities they provide. That junk dealer's business would have gone to the wall anyway, sooner or later, when vintage goes out of fashion again.'

'He wasn't even on Freemee!' Carl objects.

'There you go. With the right tools he could have both foreseen and avoided bankruptcy. That's how we'll sell the story. Look to the future! Exploit your potential! Think long-term! Improve your prospects! At long last you have the tools – with Freemee!'

'Still, Zero's done more than enough damage. We should put some specialists on him, not these bunglers!'

'It's all about the hunt,' Will reminds him.

'No,' Carl counters, arranging the pens around the vase with nimble fingers. 'Now it's about finding him.'

'Just let us get on with our public relations work. Look at the numbers and you'll see this was just the beginning.'

'I *am* looking at the numbers,' Carl retorts, 'and they show a mass of imponderables.'

'That's the nature of the beast,' says Will, 'but probability's on our side.'

'Then keep it that way,' replies Carl before getting up and leaving the room.

'Well!' she urges Chander. 'What have you found?'

He shares the info from his glasses so Cyn and Anthony can see what he's feeding into the devices. Cyn's a little disappointed: nothing but tables and series of numbers and letters. Peggy, now reactivated, advises her to give Chander an appreciative smile. *Oh, all right then.*

'Every file, such as Zero's videos for example, contains what is known as metadata,' he begins. 'Metadata has advantages and disadvantages. One advantage is that you find a variety of information in it, for instance the software used to create a file, the software's licence code maybe, the date it was created, and so on. The disadvantage is it usually gets lost when the files are converted into different video formats. What's more, this metadata can be deleted or manipulated, so even if we can find it, we can't necessarily trust it. I scanned Zero's videos for metadata right from the outset of our research. It had been systematically deleted. Until today, that is. For whatever reason, Zero appears to have forgotten to do so in the Washington video.'

'Maybe it was intentional,' Cyn interjects, 'and the data has been manipulated.' *You should praise his work first. You can express an opinion afterwards*, Peggy rebukes her. Cyn frowns. She's supposed to play the dumb female?

'It's possible,' Chander admits, 'but I don't believe so. The metadata gives a lot away here. First, the software used to create the video. It really is called 3DWhizz – the readers were right – and is produced by the US firm 3D Wonder Vision. Second, I found the licence number under which the software copy Zero used is registered. And third, the metadata also contained the MAC address – a specific ID number for the computer running that copy.'

And where does that leave us? Cyn bites her tongue. With Peggy's reminder ringing in her ear, she shoots Chander an admiring smile and says, 'That's amazing!'

He rewards her with a grin.

'And how exactly does that help us?' she asks, her knees like jelly. *Yuck!* But Chander seems to take the bait.

'That, my dear, could well tell us who uses the software copy,' he explains considerately. 'And if the data wasn't manipulated and the computer wasn't stolen, then it might just be a member of Zero.'

'I'm still not clear how you can figure out all that from a few figures and numbers.'

'Very simple.'

Very simple. *Yeah, sure.* Cyn readies herself for a very simple explanation from an IT specialist, knowing she won't understand a word.

'I looked on online forums for any potential weaknesses in 3DWhizz. I found some. Like most software, there's the occasional spot where it's shoddily or oddly written. There's one weakness that might be useful to us, because you have to register the licence number online with the manufacturer before you can use it. And you can only use it on a maximum of two devices after registering.' Cyn nods. She had to register her printer at home. For free customer support, supposedly. 'That's how the manufacturer guards against pirate copies and illegal use. During the registration process, however, its behaviour is somewhat unusual for software of this kind. It checks the user's local IP address before this goes through any possible re-routers and sends it to 3D Wonder Vision. The company most probably does this to find out more about its users, even if they're trying to conceal their IP address and origin. So when someone registers their copy of 3DWhizz, the manufacturer knows not only that they've done so but also roughly where the user did it. Which means that 3D Wonder Vision knows the IP address to which the software copy Zero uses was registered.'

'That's nice for Wonder Vision,' observes Anthony. 'But how far does it get us?'

'A long way if we're smart enough. We're going to do a bit of social engineering.'

'Social what?'

'3D Wonder Vision is based in the States,' Chander explains, smiling at Cyn. 'I'll go ahead and call them!'

Chander hooks up Cyn, Jeff and Anthony so they can listen in on the conversation. After only one ring a bland male voice answers and rattles out a formulaic greeting.

A call centre somewhere, Cyn thinks. *India, judging by the speaker's accent.*

'Hi,' Chander responds, every bit as friendly. 'I've got a huge favour to ask. Some time ago I registered to use 3DWhizz. Now I need the invoice for my tax return and I seem to have mislaid it. Could you help me out and send me a copy, please?'

Before the other guy can say a word, Chander continues, 'You'll obviously need the licence number of my copy of 3DWhizz,' then reads out the number he found in the meta-data of Zero's video. 'My email address has changed since, though,' he explains and provides an email address he's just set up, an alphabet soup that provides no clues to a real name.

This can't be the first time the call-centre worker has been confronted with an invoice request or a change of email address. Without any fuss he cheerfully says, 'There, I've found you. Ah, Mr Tuttle, you're a loyal user of our software.'

Tuttle? Cyn notes excitedly. *We have a name!*

'And your invoice – it's on its way. Is there anything else I can do for you?'

Chander checks his inbox. The message with the attached invoice is already there. He scans the document and smiles. 'No, that's all, thanks. Have a nice day.'

'You too,' purrs the man, wherever he may be.

Chander hangs up.

'A name! We have a name!' Anthony cries with huge enthusiasm.

Cyn is stunned. That was really easy. Social engineering. She expected some technical wizardry when she heard the word 'engineering'. Not a bit of it. Just trickery and decep-tion: profoundly human techniques. She likes it.

'No security questions? Nothing?' she asks.

'What for?' he answers. 'Who apart from the software user will know the licence number? It's like when you have a question about your phone bill and they ask you for your customer reference.'

'I see! And Zero's name and address are on the bill!' Cyn responds excitedly.

'They're surely not careless enough to register the software under their real name.'

She runs an eye over the document. 'Archibald Tuttle,' she says. 'Now where have I heard that name before?'

'From a film,' Chander says, grinning. '*Brazil*. Tuttle's a renegade in a surveillance state: a cute in joke.'

'So what makes you so satisfied about this bill?'

'Give me a few more minutes.'

While Chander's still researching the 3D Wonder Vision bill, Cyn, Jeff and the others are swamped with incoming phone calls.

The phone symbol lights up on Cyn's glasses again. She takes the call. The woman on the other end claims to be from a television channel whose name she doesn't catch. She sounds hysterical, like a saleswoman on a shopping channel. She's been following the *Daily*'s reports and would like to invite Cyn to a talk show in three days' time. Cyn enquires again after the name of the station.

NBC.

'The US broadcaster?' she asks, nettled. Her glasses now feed her information about the woman on the other end of the line. She really is a producer at the American network – but in New York. 'I didn't know you produced talk shows in the UK as well.'

'We don't,' the woman answers, bewildered. 'I'd like to bring you over to New York.'

Cyn doesn't ask again; she's understood. The woman on the other side of the Pond says that the show's planned topic is 'Does big data turn us into puppets?'

'NBC want me to appear on a talk show,' she whispers to Anthony.

'You?' Anthony pulls a face, squeezes out a smile and says, 'Great!' before turning his attention back to his own caller.

'In New York,' she adds.

The smile dies on Anthony's lips. 'Does she know *I'm* editor-in-chief of the *Daily*?'

'No idea. What do you think?' says Cyn. 'Should I—'

'If you don't want to, then I'll gladly sacrifice myself,' he answers graciously.

Cyn passes on the suggestion.

'No, we want you,' the woman replies firmly. 'You handled that interview brilliantly. Your daughter was also part of that live chase for the criminal and there when Adam Denham died. And we need a woman on the panel,' she adds curtly.

'They want me,' she tells Anthony.

Anthony's expression darkens for a second before he eventually gives her a double thumbs-up. 'Well, poppet, you've just made your debut in front of five million viewers,' he hisses at her, 'and the talk shows are already on the line! You must have done something right. Say yes, of course! It's brilliant PR for us. Ask who the other guests are.'

A sociology professor, the editor-in-chief of a renowned US daily newspaper and, if possible, Takisha Washington, Alvin Kosak and Freemee's Vice-President for Marketing and Communications, the producer replies when Cyn puts the question to her.

'Oh,' is all Cyn can think to say to this. The guy from Freemee is bound not to pull his punches. For one awful moment she wonders how much he knows about her. *Peggy?* She holds her head in her hands. Peggy's a computer program, and you can look into a program. What if the Freemee guy exposes her in front of a large audience? That's nonsense. He won't have an eye on every single one of their millions of users, and even if he did, he wouldn't admit it. After all, Freemee's trademark is that she alone owns her data, as long as she doesn't publish it.

Anthony urges her to accept at last.

All right, mate! Give me a second to think! Unlike you I've never been on TV before. If she's honest, she feels flattered. Even if she's just appeared in a live stream in front of five million people, she's still a kid from the TV generation. Television is still a bigger deal than the internet, and she's been invited to appear on a talk show on one of the major US networks. She'd be lying if she said she hasn't always secretly dreamed of this. What's more, she's never been to New York before.

'OK, I'll come.'

She deactivates Peggy with two taps of her fingers on the spectacle arms. *You can never be too sure*, she thinks.

'OK, folks,' Chander calls. 'Time-out – we've got something!'

Anthony finishes his conversation and Cyn stops fielding calls. The technicians will have to deal with them on their own for a while.

'Have we got Zero?' Anthony asks.

'That would be too good to be true,' Chander replies. 'No. But there was something almost as valuable as a name on that bill.'

'Don't keep us in suspense,' Cyn chides him, 'or else . . .'

Chander gives her a mischievous look, then says, 'On the bill was the IP address from which the user registered the 3DWhizz copy.'

'Aha. So we know where Zero lives?'

'Not completely, unfortunately. The IP address belongs to a Wi-Fi network provided to their patrons by several cafés on a square in Vienna.'

'Vienna. Can I use the Wi-Fi to go online if I'm in one of those cafés?'

'That's right. As in most coffee shops.'

'So whoever registered this copy of 3DWhizz was sitting in one of those Viennese cafés as they were doing it?'

'That's right.'

'But when was that? Zero's been using the software for a long time, right?'

'Only for the past two years with this copy.'

'The guy might only ever have been to that place once!' Cyn objects.

'That's why I looked into something. As I said, the metadata in Zero's video not only gave away the software and the licence number, but also the MAC address of the computer from which the video was uploaded to the internet.'

'How does that help you?'

'The Wi-Fi networks in cafés are generally not very secure, and I was able to hack into the Viennese network in question relatively easily. Once inside, I only had to search the logs, i.e. the protocols. In them, for example, I found details of the MAC addresses of the devices that log on to the internet via this Wi-Fi network, when they do it and so on. You have three guesses at what I came across there.'

'The device to which the 3DWhizz copy was registered at the time,' Cyn infers.

'Exactly!' He beams at Cyn. 'Regularly, too. This computer logs in to the Wi-Fi network every few days. The owner's a regular. It fits too. There are lots of data privacy activists in Germany and Austria, so it's not unlikely that Zero members live there.'

'Might the number crop up elsewhere too?' Jeff interjects.

'Of course it can,' replies Chander. 'We'll put a search program on it right away.'

'Who says Zero isn't leading us on a wild goose chase?' Cyn asks.

'It's possible. MAC addresses can be manipulated. But I think it's pretty unlikely. The peculiar programming of the 3DWhizz registration process has been publicized in insider circles, but the news didn't cause much of a stir. After those articles 3D Wonder Vision took half a year to repair the bug. Both of those things happened after the licence in question was registered, meaning that the user didn't know about the error at the time. And if he's a film student or a designer and not a programmer, he still might not know.'

'Zero must have a few computer hotshots who've told him,' Jeff counters.

'But they're only human too and make the odd mistake, like today with the licence number. Or else they think they're out of reach.'

'So what does this mean for us now?' Cyn asks, thinking hard.

'We need to go to Vienna,' Anthony announces.

'But I'm supposed to go to New York!' cries Cyn.

'That's three days away,' Anthony argues. 'But if need be, Chander and I will take care of Vienna without you.'

'You're coming along?'

'Definitely! I'm not missing this.'

'I want to come too,' she says hastily. A trip to Vienna with Chander? She can't pass up this opportunity! 'You need me as your co-presenter.'

'Fine. We'll make a quick video announcing that we're on Zero's scent. Quick and dirty!' Anthony rubs his hands with glee.

'You're going to give everything away?' she asks.

'No,' says Anthony. 'We're not going to share this information with the public for the moment. We'll just mention that we're on to something. We've got to create some suspense.'

'I'd drop the video idea,' says Chander. 'Let sleeping dogs lie. We're going to need a lot of luck as it is. A few whizz-kids among our crowd of contributors will discover the metadata soon enough, and probably the bug in 3DWhizz too. The only question is whether they'll get to the IP address like we did. At some stage a program in 3DWhizz is going to raise the alarm when it receives too many enquiries. But if people discuss it in the *Daily*'s Zero forum, Zero might get wind of a weak spot. And the moment he does, he'll avoid that Wi-Fi network in Vienna like the plague.'

'Oh, all right,' says Anthony in a deflated voice.

'When do we leave?' asks Cyn. Chander gives her a quick glance, and she feels herself blush.

'First plane we can get on tomorrow morning,' says Anthony, checking his smartphone. 'I'll get someone to book the tickets straightaway. We'll meet at Heathrow at nine.'

'Interesting,' Luís says to Marten. 'Only a few minutes ago a caller asked for the bill for the initial registration. A service agent sent it to them.'

'Who?'

'A hidden email address. I can't figure out who's behind it or who called. He sent his call via several anonymization services.'

'So someone else has found the metadata and fooled 3D Wonder Vision's customer service.'

'Presumably.'

'We'll ask Interpol to cooperate. The Austrian police have to find this person.'

'We're proceeding with a second check on Archibald Tuttle.'

'What are the waterfalls up to?' Marten asks, only half in jest. They still don't have any better leads.

'There are three hundred and seventy-four in all,' says Luís, scrolling through the never-ending pictures of flowing water on his monitor. 'We can identify three hundred and twelve of them – at least, the site's community of visitors has, as well as putting up new ones all the time. They puzzle over the unknown ones. It's kind of a game on the website.'

He switches to a text document with, alongside it, a world map covered with red dots, most of which are clustered in cities. 'Most of the site's visitors don't anonymize: their IP addresses can be tracked and attributed. Only about five per cent go through anonymous networks like TOR or VPN. Our buddies at the NSA were even able to find some of those going through TOR, but their software hasn't detected any suspicious behaviour so far. Around one per cent came or come via VPN providers, and those are the ones we're working on. Two of the providers are based in the US. We've applied for FISA orders and National Security Letters to send to their operators. Once those are approved, they'll have to hand over the data, which may contain some clues.'

'OK,' says Marten. He thinks for a second and sighs. 'And our friends in Langley should send someone to Vienna too.'

Eddie stares at the screen, exhausted, his features drawn. He's checked the script again and again. His approach. His interpretations. He can't spot a single error. In the meantime, his search program has produced further results. They're similar to the ones yesterday. He therefore faces an immediate and essential question: does Freemee know about this problem? Maybe he should get in touch with them. He clicks on the company's contact page, but another thought immediately occurs to him. Who, if not them, is best placed to detect irregularities like these? Another fact sets Eddie's pulse racing. Supposedly out of respect for the deceased, Freemee is blocking the very data – and only this data – that would allow anyone who knows what they're doing to draw the same conclusions as Eddie has. Another thought rattles him. He could only find data for a small proportion of Freemee users, so he can't rule out the fact that this scenario might be on an altogether larger scale. The consequences would be terrifying!

Eddie tries to keep a cool head. However, he believes ever more fervently that Freemee is covering up a gigantic scandal. A terrible secret! *I watch too much stuff about conspiracy theories. There must be a completely different explanation.*

He doesn't know what to do with the results. He could tell Vi – after all, it was her complaints about her mother's nagging that put him on to this investigation in the first place. But he knows his IT stories don't impress Vi; they bore her.

As a journalist Cyn should be interested in them. The question is whether she'd understand what's involved. She's as ignorant of the most important cultural technology of the modern age as ninety-nine per cent of the population.

Or he could simply publish his findings and open them up for debate, either on his Freemee profile, which would be particularly cheeky, or on the other platforms he frequents. He feels too unsure of his facts for that, though. He'd rather discuss the numbers with a few experts first and ask them to verify them. He doesn't fancy embarrassing himself, or being sued for libel by Freemee and plunged into life-long bankruptcy.

His first step is to draft a short presentation. He can decide who to show it to later.

No one in the meeting room notices that Joaquim's eyes are trained not on the large monitor at the front, but on the secure phone directly under his nose, which he uses to send a message made up entirely of short numerical code. The man who receives it knows exactly what the message means. Joaquim turns his attention back to the speaker beside the monitor.

Snowman: Back in the headlines around the globe ^^

Peekaboo777: Sorry, what was that about vanity? ;-)

Nightowl: Maybe people finally have some idea of what data sovereignty means?

ArchieT: Even data sovereignty is just a business model.

Peekaboo777: All of us are just a business model.

Snowman: I'd rather be in the model business.

Friday

Eddie plugs in his earphones on his way to school. What he listens to is not what his mother would call music, but he has to concentrate now and he can do that best while listening to rap. His legs feel leaden and he has to drag himself to the Tube station. He hardly slept a wink. His mind tossed this way and that all night long, as did his exhausted body in his bed.

He reaches a decision. It's a little early to call people, but Eddie just has to talk to someone about his discoveries. He takes out his smartphone, turns the music down – and then puts it away again. He looks around for a phone box and to his amazement spots one next to the entrance to the Underground. He rings Cyn's home number from it.

After three rings she picks up. 'Eddie! This early? What's up? Do you want to speak to Vi?'

His heart skips a beat at the mention of Vi's name. He pulls himself together. 'No, I wanted to talk to you. As a journalist.'

'At this time of the morning? OK. Is it urgent? I'm just leaving for the airport.'

'Are you picking someone up?'

'No, I'm flying to Vienna.'

'Oh?'

'What did you want to talk about?'

'I've discovered something. You remember how, after Adam was killed, we talked about various things including Freemee?'

'I do, yes.'

'I might have a story, but it's too complicated to explain over the phone. I need to tell you in person.'

'Can it wait until I get back from Vienna? I'll only be there for a couple of days.'

That gives me time to check it through again, thinks Eddie. 'All right then. What are you doing in Vienna? Vi said something about New York.'

'I can't tell anyone yet. And New York isn't until the day after tomorrow, after I get back.'

'Well, enjoy your jetting around!'

Eddie turns his music back on and heads into the Tube station. On the crowded platform he turns the music up louder so he doesn't hear the noise of the other passengers so much. Someone barges into him. Eddie spins around angrily. A middle-aged man in tinted glasses and a hat is standing next to him.

'Good morning, Eddie.'

Eddie takes an irritated step backwards, bumping into someone behind him, and stops. He doesn't know this man whose voice cuts through the music.

'I'd like to talk to you,' the man says, pointing to the ear-phones.

'Who says *I* want to talk to *you*,' Eddie replies, stepping to one side. The platform's packed and he can barely move. The man is creepy, but Eddie isn't scared. He knows there are cameras everywhere and no one's seriously going to molest him under their gaze.

The man manages to force his way through to Eddie. Eddie can tell from his lips that the man's saying something as he smiles at him. Calmer now, Eddie gives in and turns down the music.

'What do you want?'

'To make you an offer. A once-in-a-lifetime offer.'

When the boy doesn't answer, he continues, 'I'm sorry, how rude of me. My name's William Bertrand and I work for a human resources company. I'm not one for long lead-ins. You're damn talented with computers. You could get some great jobs and earn a lot of money – a huge amount of money. I'd like to offer you one of those jobs.'

'Here?' asks Eddie, looking at the throng around him. 'Did you follow me here? What's the deal? I'm still at school.'

'You can carry on going to school. In New York, if you like.'

'Leave me alone. If you want something from me, send me a message or phone me, but please don't ambush me like this in the Tube.'

The train arrives, and the crowd starts to move forwards.

'I'll make myself clearer,' the man explains, getting into the carriage close behind Eddie. 'You've found out something very important and worth a great deal of money. To *you*.'

Eddie's pulse starts to race. *Is the man talking about what he thinks he's talking about?* He says nothing, trying hard to keep calm, and lets the other man make the next move. He'd dearly like to press 'Record' on his smartphone. He searches for it, but realizes it's too loud down here in the Underground.

'You know what I'm talking about,' says Bertrand.

Eddie's heart is really pounding now and sweat's running from every pore. Even though he did his best to keep his

195

work confidential, they've watched him and followed him, and now one of them is right here in front of him! Only hours after he made his discovery! *Shitting hell!*

Despite his rising panic he makes sure his voice sounds very calm as he replies, 'I've no idea. Please tell me.'

Bertrand smiles. 'We're offering you twenty million dollars, payable here and now, if you promise to keep your findings to yourself,' he says so quietly that only Eddie can hear him. 'Plus an amazing job in New York. If you want it. Because you'll never have to work in your entire life.'

Eddie clings hard to the overhead strap as his knees give way under him. He's struggling for breath.

Bertrand studies him, grinning. 'A tidy sum, don't you think?'

Eddie pulls a face. Money. As if that's what he was after!

'So . . . so it's true,' he finally stammers.

Bertrand doesn't answer.

Eddie feels sweat trickling down behind his ears. His scalp is itching. He runs his tongue nervously over his lips. A trembling starts somewhere deep inside him and grows until he can hardly control it.

'You're . . . trying to buy me off.'

'We're trying to secure your talent and know-how,' Bertrand replies.

'I don't know what to say.'

'Yes. Just say yes – to a wonderful future.'

To his even greater embarrassment, Eddie's eyes fill with tears. He's finding the situation completely overwhelming. 'And what if I don't want to?'

'Then we'll raise our offer,' Bertrand replies, his tone still amiable.

The next station is announced over the loudspeakers.

'To over twenty million?' Eddie asks in disbelief.

'Name a figure.'

Eddie's stomach is doing somersaults. This is a completely surreal situation. He's standing in a crammed Underground carriage alongside a stranger who's whispering absurd proposals. *Fuck!* he swears inside his head. *Me and my bloody curiosity!*

The carriage comes to a halt, and people stream out.

'You have to change here,' Bertrand reminds him.

Eddie has trouble following this instruction. His legs don't want to obey him. Bertrand sticks to his side. They advance along the platform with the crowd as the train clatters into the tunnel and disappears.

'How can you be sure I'll keep my side of the bargain?' asks Eddie.

'You're an honest person. But then you know that yourself. Look at your Freemee profile if you don't believe me. Your data is pretty clear.'

'I'd lose that honesty if I accepted your offer,' Eddie remarks.

'No,' Bertrand contradicts him. 'You'd be honest with us.'

They travel up the escalator in silence. Eddie doesn't have to look for the way to the Circle Line; as usual, he automatically makes the correct turn. He takes a deep breath. 'Fifty million pounds.' Will the guy take him up on this?

Bertrand screws up his eyes. 'All right,' he says. 'So we have your word?'

'Yes,' Eddie replies, adding with a grimace, 'I'm on your radar, anyway. Always and everywhere.'

On the monitor, Joaquim calmly watches the feed from the glasses of the man who goes by the name of Bertrand. The two screens next to it display the analysis of the sensors in Eddie's smartphone and the small microphone disguised as a button on Bertrand's jacket. What a shame they learned only that Eddie had called Cynthia Bonsant and not the contents of their conversation. They should have bugged Bonsant's flat after all. Her landline. That's too bad for Cynthia Bonsant.

The undulating curves and lines on the screens jump and jolt, and warning lights start to blink. The first software capable of detecting if someone is telling the truth by their voice was developed shortly after the turn of the millennium. It's been continually improving ever since and has long been part of the security services' standard apparatus. It produces excellent results when used in conjunction with data regarding other physical responses, even when the subjects know they're being tested. The old-fashioned lie detectors familiar from old spy films are like Stone Age axes by comparison. Freemee applies these techniques to its dating ActApps with great success. They tell Joaquim there's an eight per cent chance that Eddie's lying.

'He's lying,' says Joaquim and wonders if the boy really thinks he can escape, despite how lucid he is about the situation.

Three thousand miles to the east, the man who goes by the name of Bertrand hears Joaquim's code word via his earphone and understands what he has to do.

Cyn is so worked up on the way to the airport that she's unable to concentrate on her glasses. Staring out of the train window, she realizes this is the first time she's left these islands in eight years. That was on an ultra-cheap last-minute package holiday to southern Spain, a treat for herself and Vi. It's the only time Vi's ever been on a plane, and Cyn's last until now. Her laptop and a sports bag containing clothes for two days are in the overhead luggage rack. She rummages nervously in her handbag, checking for her passport, wallet and smartphone. She resists the temptation to call Vi again to see if everything's OK. Of course she's OK. What could possibly go wrong? Her daughter's in class, so she couldn't answer anyway.

Anthony's assistant took care of Cyn's online check-in last night. She doesn't have any luggage to drop off, so after arriving at the airport she goes straight through security. She meets up with Chander and Anthony on the far side. She feels herself tense up when Chander looks at her and realizes that she misses Peggy's advice. She feels as insecure as though her satnav had conked out while she was driving through an unfamiliar city. However, she'd rather leave her new girlfriend be until after her TV show appearance with the Freemee board member.

'So, ready for an adventure?' says Chander, beaming at her.

'Too right!'

'May I take your heavy bag off you?'

What a gentleman.

'Thank you.' He places the misshapen lump on top of his small wheeled suitcase. 'You have even less luggage than I do,' she observes.

'I've already dropped off the rest,' he explains.

Anthony issues a brusque greeting, then turns away and continues a phone conversation via his glasses.

'We still have time for a coffee,' says Chander. They sit down on a couple of bar stools in the nearest café and place their order. Anthony's still on the phone.

Cyn has to say something to take her mind off how nervous she feels. 'How's the discussion in the *Daily*'s chat room going?'

'Sync with my glasses,' Chander suggests, and she does so. As her view aligns with his, he explains, 'Other people obviously soon discovered the metadata, followed by the bug in 3DWhizz, although that topic only featured in a sub-discussion. Most users weren't interested. Probably too technical for them.'

'But the IP address in Vienna isn't mentioned anywhere,' Cyn remarks after a quick scan. She glances at him. 'Zero was possibly warned.'

'Possibly, but not necessarily. It all depends on how closely they're following the discussions. After all, there are thousands of comments. We only know about this because we're clear on what we're looking for.'

They make for their boarding gate. Anthony's still talking on the phone as Chander removes his glasses. There's a twinkle in his eye. 'I've got to go to New York because of Zero and some other matters,' he says. 'I think I'm going to fly straight there after Vienna. Do you know the city?'

Cyn feels herself blush. 'No, I've never been there before.'

'Then I'll show you around,' he says cheerfully. 'You'll see what a great place it is! Maybe you can add on a couple of days.'

'I'll see if that's possible.' *Nice work, Peggy*, she thinks excitedly.

Once inside the plane, they fight their way to their seats.

'Economy. What a drag!' Anthony moans. 'But what can you do, eh? The owners are clamping down on expenses.'

The men invite Cyn to take the window seat, with Chander sitting in the middle of the row of three. Anthony continues to talk into his phone until a flight attendant tells him to switch it off at long last. *Pompous arse*. He pushes the glasses crossly up on to his forehead and stares grimly at the heads of the people in the row in front, drumming his fingers on the armrests. The aircraft accelerates and takes off. Cyn gazes out of the window as they're tilted back in their seats during the few silent minutes of ascent. The ground recedes further and further below them.

'What do we do if we find Zero?' she whispers as they enter the clouds and the view is lost in fog.

'Interview him, what else?' Anthony replies just as quietly.

'Or her,' Cyn adds. 'There may be women involved.'

'Or her.'

'What if they don't want to talk to us?'

'We'll film them and post the video. Live.'

'But . . . they're wanted by the US authorities!'

'*They're* not going to do anything if the public's watching.'

'You can count me out right now,' Cyn hisses. 'Interviews, yes. Extradition, no.'

'All right, all right,' Anthony agrees. 'Everything will depend on the circumstances anyhow.'

Their conversation is interrupted by the pilot's announcement about the duration of their flight and the weather in Vienna. Cloudy with sunny intervals. After that, for the umpteenth time they scour Zero's videos for telltale signs on Anthony's laptop. The content, particularly of some of the older videos, has been updated or has proved prophetic.

'Data is not just the new oil, as a common metaphor would have it,' a smudgy face explains from under a dirty helmet. 'In many sectors it has long since replaced traditional cash as a currency. Some companies such as Cyclins, Freemee and BitValU have recently begun to innovate and make data the cornerstone of their business model.' Zero impersonates Liza Minnelli in *Cabaret*, dancing as he sings 'Frees Make The World Go Around'. 'Just you wait: someone soon is going to start paying or charging you interest on your data. There'll be data inflation and deflation, sophisticated financial products and speculation bubbles, which will one day burst . . .'

'This stuff gives me the creeps,' says Cyn. 'Shouldn't we keep at least a shred of our privacy intact?'

'Oh, Cyn,' Anthony says pityingly. 'Sooner or later we'll all have to come to terms with the fact that the world knows such and such about us. Besides, it's always been the same. I grew up in this tiny Sussex village where everyone knew everyone, knew who disappeared behind the nearest bramble patch with whom, who was an alcoholic, sick or impotent, and about any skulduggery going on. It's simply that the village has gone global now.'

'You could get your head around the old village.'

'It wasn't any more pleasant, though. Or any kinder. Woe betide you if you didn't play along, go to church on Sunday, attend the local fire brigade fete or join the school governors. Anonymity? Privacy? No chance! Village life can be tough for outsiders.'

'You can move away from a village. City air is liberating. Why did you come to London?'

'Maybe because all you can do out there is become a shepherd or an alcoholic,' says Anthony. 'Or both.'

'You can't move out of the global village.'

'Is that what you want?'

'I like having a place where I can't be disturbed.'

'I've nothing to hide,' says Anthony jovially.

'How dull!' she shoots back, relishing the startled look on Anthony's face. Next to her, Chander grins.

'How much do you earn actually?' she asks.

'What business is that of yours?' Anthony asks back.

'How much do you earn?'

'I, um . . .' Anthony grunts evasively.

'See! What does your dick look like?'

'Come on, out with it!' Chander says, chuckling.

'I know what you're driving at,' Anthony says with an indulgent smile.

'She sure got you there, old boy,' Chander taunts him.

'People got by just fine without any privacy until some crafty lawyer invented it a hundred years ago,' Anthony says, trying to maintain a semblance of dignity.

'He didn't invent it. He just enshrined it in law,' Cyn objects.

'Laws come and go, and so does privacy.'

Eyes big and small peer into Cyn's nostrils and mouth and every orifice, busily trying to worm their way even further inside. They writhe and whisper to one another, twisting their pupils in all directions. Cyn feels dizzy at the sight of them.

'Wake up,' says Chander, giving her a gentle nudge. 'We'll be there any minute.'

It takes her a second to recover her bearings, and then the aircraft lands none too softly on the runway. Welcome to Vienna.

The sky is cloudy as they leave the plane, but the air is pleasantly warm. A taxi takes them to their hotel, which is in a charming part of the old town near where they hope to track down their suspect. Cyn would love to see more of the city, but work comes first. They go to their rooms to freshen up and by the time they come down again, Chander's waiting in the lobby with three small rucksacks he's prepared.

'What's inside?' Anthony asks.

'You'll soon see,' Chander replies. 'For the moment let's just go.'

They walk through alleys lined with old houses until a broad square opens out before them with magnificent historical buildings on all sides. They pass through an archway into the enormous courtyard of a baroque precinct containing what the signs identify as two modern-art museums, several open-air cafés and some bright plastic benches on which hundreds of people are relaxing in the sunshine. Tourists stroll past, as children cavort and locals push their bikes across the plaza. Cyn feels as though she's stumbled into a country fete shorn of its stands. *I hope we don't have to search for our suspect in this crowd*, she thinks.

'This is the museum quarter,' Chander explains. 'There are some smaller courtyards besides this one, two museums, six cafés and various other amenities. The person we're looking for logged on to the neighbourhood's public Wi-Fi network.'

'This is absolutely hopeless!' groans Anthony. 'How the hell are we ever going to find someone here?'

'It's easier than you think,' Chander answers, making for a futuristic-looking snack bar. 'But let's get something to eat first.'

'It's strange you can't buy a Vienna sausage in Vienna,' Anthony remarks. He orders some exotic-sounding charcuterie, while Chander and Cyn opt for salad. They sit down on a wide bench freshly vacated by a group of teenagers. There's plenty of room for the three of them.

'Basically we'll replicate what they do to locate mobile phones,' Chander explains between mouthfuls. 'We'll connect to the Wi-Fi and wait until the computer we're looking for logs on. We'll then know he's nearby and the next thing we do is triangulate him.'

'Sounds like strangulate,' says Cyn.

'That's what'll happen to him ultimately,' says Chander with a chuckle. 'You can open your rucksacks now.'

Inside hers Cyn finds a laptop, a stick-shaped object she doesn't recognize and a cylindrical Pringles tin. There aren't any crisps, though: the tin is empty. Anthony unpacks similar gear from his bag.

'We've got computers in case it's better not to use our glasses. And these sticks work like directional microphones,' Chander tells them. 'They allow us to split up and try to pinpoint the signal from the suspect computer. Once we've detected it we just need to see where our rays intersect, and that's where he'll be sitting.'

'Directional microphones?' says Cyn. 'Isn't that a bit conspicuous?'

'No, because that's what the tins are for. We hide the antennae inside them. They're lined with aluminium to increase their effectiveness. You simply lay the tin down on one of these tables or funny benches and rotate it slowly, as if you're fiddling with it out of pure boredom. No one will ever realize it's an antenna.'

Cyn pushes the stick completely inside the tin and lays it on its side in front of her. It's true that nobody will notice. James Bond meets MacGyver. She can't believe she's doing this. She glances surreptitiously around her. Not one person in this hive of activity is paying the slightest attention to them.

'How high-tech!' she says.

'Not at all,' says Chander. 'The kind of nerdy toy you can pick up in any decent electronics shop.'

'Is this legal?' she asks.

'Isn't that beside the point?' he replies. 'Come on. Let's give them a spin. The devices are already configured, so all

205

you have to do is switch them on.' Cyn and Anthony follow his instructions.

'Our suspect usually comes here every couple of days. He was last here two days ago. Maybe he's here today. If not, then there's a pretty good chance we'll run into him tomorrow. Whichever way, we can start practising triangulation now.'

Chander has fitted the laptops with software designed to map their search. Their current locations are shown by three red dots on satellite images from an online mapping service. Transparent red bands indicate the directional antennae's radio waves. Chander explains the on-screen displays to them. They turn their antennae slightly and watch the changes on-screen.

Next, they spread out across the courtyard. Cyn makes her way through clusters of tourists. She finds some space at one end of the flight of steps in front of the grey museum towering over half of the courtyard, a little apart from the groups of young people dotted across the entire width of the staircase. Anthony sits down on the far side of the square in the shade of the white-fronted museum. Chander takes up a position between them on a bench near the archway.

The tin concealing the directional antenna is lying next to Cyn. The three of them keep in touch via their glasses and smartphones.

'Everyone ready?' asks Chander. The others give the green light, and Chander describes how he's logging into the network to see if the licence number of the device they're looking for appears. It doesn't seem to be active right now.

'He can't be here,' he observes. 'So we'd better practise a bit before he arrives.'

Chander chooses a MAC address at random and starts the location procedure. Cyn also begins to rotate her tin.

Within a few minutes they have their target triangle on three girls sitting at a café table, tapping on their smartphones.

'One of them's using our practice device,' says Chander, 'but we can't know for sure which one because they're too close together.'

He announces a different MAC address, and within two minutes they've identified a bearded man with a laptop sitting on one of the benches.

Cyn's impressed. Her fingers fiddle idly with the tin as she follows the comings and goings around the square. The heat of the sun and the warmth of the steps are making her drowsy. She leans back against the museum wall and closes her eyes for a second.

She only realizes she must have dozed off when she's startled by Chander's voice.

'Can you hear me?'

'Loud and clear,' Anthony replies.

'Me too,' Cyn confirms, still in a daze.

'Good, then begin location. I've already tuned your antennae to the relevant MAC address.'

So Chander's traced their suspect online, and she slept through the whole thing? Slowly she revolves the crisp tin. On her screen the red beam sweeps the courtyard. Chander's ray is the first to locate the signal from the suspect device. He locks on to it. Their target must be sitting somewhere on this line. Cyn crosses her red line with Chander's, and Anthony does likewise. She carefully rotates her antenna until her laptop beeps. Anthony's device also raises the alarm a split second later.

'We've got him!' she hears him cry.

She feverishly searches for the spot marked on the satellite images. It must be somewhere in the middle of the square. Cyn's eyes roam feverishly over the large benches. A lanky young man wearing jeans and a T-shirt and, like so many others here, a peaked cap and sunglasses is reclining on one of them. He has a small laptop on his knees.

'The guy in the blue cap and shades?' Anthony asks.

'Yes,' Chander confirms.

Young people are lolling, chatting, on the loungers to the man's left and right, and some of them are playing with their computers and smartphones. A typical, everyday scene.

'I'm going to try and get inside his computer,' Chander says. 'Maybe we'll learn something.'

'You can do that?' Cyn asks incredulously.

'As long as it isn't encrypted.'

Cyn zooms in on the unknown man with her glasses. This inbuilt digital lens is another practical feature of the device. Although the man is at least thirty yards from her, she feels as though she could almost touch him. He has a thick, dark moustache and his cheeks are unshaven. He's concentrating yet seems relaxed. He raises his eyes from time to time, but looks deep in thought when he does this. He certainly isn't glancing nervously around him. The man feels safe. The sunglasses rule out using facial recognition software on him.

'I'm pretty sure he's our man,' she hears Chander say.

'What did you find on his computer?' Anthony asks.

'Nothing,' Chander replies. 'He's secured it remarkably well. Not something your average man in the street would do, so that's already suspicious. If I could hack into it – and I'm not sure I could – it'd take me hours or even days. This guy knows what he's doing.'

'Should I go over and speak to him?' asks Cyn. 'About an interview?'

'We're going online,' Anthony announces.

'What?' she protests, bewildered. 'But we just talked about—'

'The situation's changed,' Anthony cuts her off.

'He'll notice!'

'Possibly, but then we'll get a reaction from him. There are three of us and one of him,' counters Anthony. 'He can't escape. It's the show that counts! You're supposed to be reporting on a chase. No one ever mentioned finding anyone.'

What the hell!

Cyn zooms in on Anthony. He's talking to someone via his glasses before saying loudly enough for Chander and her to hear, 'I'm streaming the view through my glasses to the *Daily*. You can hook up with me if you want. London's taking over the reins.'

Cyn refuses to do that, but watches, speechless, as she's caught up in a live international broadcast. Via a pair of glasses and a smartphone.

'Those morons really are going live!' Jon rages.

'This ain't going to make things any easier,' mumbles Marten.

Up till now they've been following the scene purely through the camera glasses of the four CIA men on the ground. They identified the guy shortly before Heast's band of comedians did, when the Austrians didn't react swiftly and thoroughly enough to American calls for administrative assistance.

'We can't afford another embarrassment like Presidents' Day,' Jon says.

'No one apart from us knows we're on the ground,' Marten answers.

Over live pictures of a square full of people, Heast runs through the whole story, from 3DWhizz and licence numbers to the metadata that led them to Vienna. The camera in Heast's glasses pans across the square. The footage is similar to that relayed by the CIA agents. What's this idiot doing? Why is he publicly broadcasting his manhunt and potentially alerting his target? The agents are getting restless too. Langley's notified them of the live stream so they're aware the square is now the focus of worldwide attention.

'Can't you cut off his power?' one of them asks. 'He's going to wreck everything.'

'Can we?' asks Jon, turning to Marten and Luís.

'In theory, yes,' says Luís, 'but not immediately. Anyway, that's not up to us but to the CIA. They have to do what they consider necessary. We can only watch.'

Marten is following the broadcast with growing exasperation. It's killing him that he can't operate the camera himself. Heast is filming the hunt for Zero like some third-rate thriller director. He's indulging a penchant for distraction to build suspense. Lots of distraction.

'If he keeps on like this, everybody will soon stop watching anyway,' Jon groans.

Marten's practised eye recognizes, however, that Heast is unable to control his subconscious and is giving himself away. Again and again his camera lingers on a particular spot for a few fractions of a second. Right in the centre of the shot Marten spies the same guy with the laptop, dark blue baseball cap and shades that the CIA agents have identified.

'We can only hope that Zero hasn't installed the same alarm to the *Daily* as we have,' he sighs.

'How long are we going to sit around doing nothing?' Cyn asks Chander.

While Anthony tries to whip things up with his hysterical scene-setting, Chander's young suspect continues to type calmly on his laptop. He betrays no sign of nervousness or fear. Cyn wonders if they have the wrong man in their sights.

On her screen she follows the images that Anthony's broadcasting to the *Daily*'s website. She even sees herself for an instant as the camera sweeps the square. At that very moment a window opens on her screen, and in it she sees the *Daily*'s live stream! Did Anthony make that happen? Unlike the footage on the *Daily* website, however, pairs of animated eyes are flitting around the square, peeking over people's shoulders, sniffing them, even peering down a girl's blouse, before hurrying on. A caption is superimposed on this footage.

> Watch out! If you're in the Museum Quarter at the moment, you're being watched and your image is being streamed live online! Anyone ask your permission? Are you going to put up with this? This is the man responsible – Anthony Heast, editor-in-chief of the *Daily*, a British newspaper. Tell him to stop!

'Oh shit!' she hears Chander exclaim, as a close-up of Anthony standing on the other side of the square appears in the window!

The text switches from English to German, and surprised expressions appear on the faces of people around them who are working on their laptops or fiddling around on their smartphones. Several curious people turn to look.

'The bastard's taken over the Wi-Fi network,' Chander's voice hisses from Cyn's glasses. 'Anyone currently logged on to it will see this on their screen!'

Various groups on the square start to fidget as the text now changes into Italian on Cyn's screen. More and more heads turn in Anthony's direction. Others start whispering to one another and pulling phones, tablets and laptops from their bags and pockets. Anthony himself is now glancing around nervously.

Cease transmission, thinks Cyn.

There's a growing commotion. The first few people stand up and make for Anthony. He hastily shoves the tin with the antenna into his rucksack. People are now streaming towards him from all parts of the square. Some of them are shouting.

'Can you do anything, Chander?' Anthony asks, his voice stressed now.

Cyn is torn. Anthony brought this upon himself, but she wouldn't want to be in his shoes. From hunter to hunted. She can see the pictures from Anthony's glasses. A horde of glowering youths has stopped right in front of him.

'Stop broadcasting!' Chander urges Anthony.

The whole square is in upheaval now. At least three hundred people have got to their feet and coalesced into a human mass that's beginning to encircle the *Daily*'s editor-in-chief.

Anthony points frantically at the man in the peaked cap in the middle of the square. 'He's the one you should get! He's potentially wanted in several countries!'

Yet Cyn can see nothing but enraged faces through Anthony's glasses. Her boss brings his broadcast to a swift end, and the stream goes dead on her computer. Zero's coverage also disappears for a second, but is soon replaced by other pictures.

'The bastard!' curses Chander. 'He's going through a user's webcam or one of the CCTV cameras here.'

The footage shows Anthony, encircled now by a mass of people that covers half the square. Cyn sees him making placating gestures and pointing to the screens of some devices they have brought with them, but they won't let him off that easily. His glasses are still transmitting sound so she can hear a series of furious comments and accusations in a variety of languages. Voices are raised as some call for the police to get involved. A few people are on their phones now. Others are filming her boss with their smartphones. One man, sporting a long beard, punches Anthony's rucksack. He raises his hands in self-defence.

'Cunning,' Marten remarks, as he follows the fracas around Heast through the glasses of two CIA men. Not all of the onlookers appear aggressive: some are obviously merely curious.

'A smart riposte by Zero, if it was him,' Jon acknowledges.

'I don't understand why these people are so cross,' Luís replies. 'A social media stream on the Museum Quarter's website provides continuous updates about visitors with photos, videos and whatnot. So why all the outrage about this particular report?'

'How much longer will they need spooks like us if people are already spying on one another, ready to leap into action at any moment?' Marten asks no one in particular.

Away from the crowd around Heast, other people are standing and chatting in small groups. New visitors are pouring into the square through its various entrances, and most of them are soon caught up in the ongoing discussions. Marten spots the first uniforms arriving.

The only person paying absolutely no attention to events is the guy in the dark blue baseball cap, who casually snaps his laptop shut, slides it into a case and ambles away towards an exit. He doesn't choose the nearest exit, though, instead passing directly in front of the British journalist, who's so far remained seated on one of the steps and doesn't even notice him leave.

'She's let him get away,' Jon says, smirking. 'What an amateur.'

'How's Vienna fixed for cameras?' Marten asks Luís.

'Not good,' says his neighbour. 'We can get into the surveillance cameras in the subway, the trains and traffic control, but their coverage is far from comprehensive.'

'How do we get access to those cameras?'

Luís guffaws. 'Even Anonymous can hack into them. A few years back they published emails the Austrian police had sent to officers containing unencrypted passwords for the railroad cameras. A local police spokesperson explained it was only a test account, but, hey, you know how it is.'

Marten laughs inwardly. He does indeed. He doesn't need to worry how this might look, though. Four CIA agents are already following the suspect at varying distances.

Cyn observes the young man in the cap as he passes within a few yards of her. She hasn't taken her eyes off him for one second since the counter-attack began. Judging by Chander's curses, it's clear this commotion was all the young man's doing. *Respect.* She's impressed by his nonchalant manner and so she pretends not to notice him and lets him slip away.

'He's doing a runner,' Chander whispers unnecessarily. The noise of the happenings on the square easily covers their conversations. She's about to answer, when Anthony contacts them via his glasses.

'I can't get out of here,' he complains. 'I could actually do with some help now.'

'The police are on their way,' Chander says.

'Very funny.'

'I'm serious. They're already here. Don't worry, though – you haven't done anything illegal. Just stay friendly. We'll meet back at the hotel. Cyn and I will make sure we tail that guy. Right, Cyn?'

So she's forced to join in the hunt. Anthony will have to extract himself from this self-inflicted mess on his own.

'You can stream it,' Anthony adds.

'If the guy isn't wearing data lenses – and I'd bet against it, as so far only prototypes exist – then he doesn't know we're following him,' says Will. 'His shades are just normal glasses.'

'But his Zero chums must be watching and keeping him informed,' Alice says.

Will studies her lips, which keep moving as if she wanted to ward off fate by whispering silent prayers. *She's totally engrossed*, he thinks with some amusement.

It's still very early in the morning in New York as they sit staring at the huge wall of screens in Will's office. They can see only the back of the hunted man in the pictures Chander Argawal's camera is transmitting live to the *Daily* website. He's charting a course through a maze of small lanes and historic buildings of the kind you find only in Europe. He isn't bothering to comment on the action, as Anthony did. Bonsant doesn't appear to be broadcasting. The suspense is created by the jerky footage of the chase and whether the victim is aware of them or not, and if he'll manage to give them the slip.

'There,' says Alice, pointing to the monitor. The man pulls out a smartphone and raises it to his ear. The conversation is quick. He puts the phone away and continues on his way. 'Now we'll see,' she murmurs. 'Want to bet that was a warning signal?'

A *Daily* technician in London has clearly taken control of production. The coverage switches to Anthony, who's now reactivated his glasses. He's still surrounded by a crowd of people, joined now by two police officers in uniform. They're holding a conversation with him in fairly basic English. Will doesn't catch all of it. Anthony shows them the contents of his rucksack. Laptop. Pringles tin. Luckily for him, he'd managed to close it beforehand, and the police officers aren't suspicious because he made no mention of the antennae in his report. The picture wobbles, and suddenly we see Anthony's face. One of the police officers must have put on the glasses.

'Mr Bluecap's really giving them the run-around now,' says Alice.

Whoever is at the controls in London now switches cameras to Chander's glasses, showing a view of larger buildings and a tram running along the middle of the street. The man in the blue cap is making faster progress than before, repeatedly vanishing among the other pedestrians. His pursuers are maintaining a reasonable distance so as not to lose him.

Will follows the reactions on social media in parallel. Several hundred people from all over the world are already giving their view of events on Twitter and Freemee. *There's a clear majority of Bluecap fans*, thinks Will. Some send him messages of encouragement and warnings, while others insult his pursuers, quite a few of them in unrepeatable language, in some cases even going so far as to threaten them.

The tram stops, and Bluecap boards it. The pictures wobble again, turning blurry and pixelated. Chander's sprinting – Will can hear his frantic breathing. A brown hand jabs between the two closing doors and forces them apart. The carriage is full. Will seeks Bluecap in vain.

'Bluecap's in the front car,' says Alice.

Chander appears to have realized this too, since he pushes his way forwards through the other passengers. At the next stop he gets out and looks around to check. Cynthia Bonsant enters the picture and then disappears again. They get into the first carriage. Just as the doors are closing, someone gets out closer to the front. It's the young man in the baseball cap. The oldest trick in the book.

Again Chander has to stick his hand between the closing doors, push them open and jump out of the carriage. Now the warring parties are clear. From Chander's perspective Will and the others see the man standing about ten yards away, openly sizing up his adversary as the tram rumbles on its way, before turning round and running off.

'What's the point of this?' Cyn pants. Bloody hell, she's completely unfit! She's not going to be able to keep up this pace for very long. Luckily a city map flashes up on her glasses and shows her where she is. 'He won't lead us anywhere,' she says, gasping for air, 'and we're not allowed to arrest him.'

Chander doesn't reply. It's sensible of him, using the air to breathe rather than talk. They've run about two hundred yards, and her thighs are already aching. The man they're pursuing swerves around a cyclist and, after a quick glance, dashes across a junction despite the red light. Cars beep their horns and there's a screech of tyres. The laptop in his hand is slowing him down.

They're catching up. By the time they reach the junction, the lights have changed to green. Cyn can tell from the man's awkward gait that he too is short of breath. He's pulled back his shoulders and tilted his head slightly, and now he slackens his pace and looks round. She drops back, whereas Chander is steadily gaining on him. Then, to her surprise, two men run past her, as if they were also after the man in the cap. He glances over his shoulder just as a woman emerges from a building, right in front of him. They collide heavily and she's sent spinning, just about managing to catch hold of the wall to prevent herself from hitting the ground. Bluecap stumbles, falls and loses hold of the laptop in its case. Somewhat dazed, he clambers to his feet and looks around for the computer, which has slipped under a parked car. The woman yells furiously at him and he shouts something back.

Chander and the two men have almost caught up with him by now. He spots his pursuers, searches frenziedly for the laptop and spies it, but Chander's already upon him. He makes a grab for the man's face in an attempt to pull off his glasses and cap, but the man resists. After a brief tussle, Bluecap's able to fight his way free just before his other two pursuers reach them. He runs away with the two unidenti- fied men hot on his heels. Puffed out, Chander watches them go and then apologizes to the woman. As she goes on her way, he reaches into his rucksack and pulls something from it. Cyn has joined him. She's dripping with sweat.

Chander's holding a machine the size of a small mouse powered by two propellers. 'OK, time for a bit of airborne investigative journalism.' He tosses the device into the air and watches it soar up into the sky.

She glances at the smartphone in his other hand.

'The remote control,' he explains.

'Is that a drone?' she asks incredulously.

'Handy, don't you think? The sort of thing Zero used on Presidents' Day. And easy to control using this.'

'Where did you get it?' she asks.

'A kit,' says Chander. 'Easily available online or from all good hi-tech and toy shops.' He runs his thumb over his phone screen. The navigation symbols glow on top of the live images shot by the camera on the small flying object. The pictures on his mobile show the street they're standing in. Cyn can make out Chander and herself, seen from above. She thinks she spots Bluecap at the next junction, with the two pursuers lagging somewhat behind.

'Is that legal too?' asks Cyn.

'As long as we maintain visual contact with our fat bumblebee up there and don't film any individual people, then we're not doing anything your ordinary TV crew in a pedestrian zone wouldn't do.'

'Who are those two men?' Cyn asks.

'No idea.'

Airborne investigative journalism. The cynicism of it makes Cyn want to be sick. She should just stay where she is. This entire hunt is not to her liking.

'Could you retrieve the computer from under that car?' says Chander. 'We may find something interesting on it.'

'We can't just take it with us, though. It doesn't belong to us.'

'Should we leave it here? We could hand it in to the police, but we're going to take a look inside first.'

Cyn reluctantly bends down and fishes out the laptop from under the car with some difficulty.

Chander resumes his pursuit of the young man, his eyes glued to the smartphone in his hand. Cyn can barely make out anything on the screen; the street and the pavement seem to be swarming with ants, one of which is running, chased now by four others! Three figures suddenly block their path. The pursuers simply knock them to the ground, but it costs them precious time.

At least Cyn doesn't have to run any more. She trots sedately alongside Chander, the laptop tucked under her arm. *You're quite literally a hanger-on,* she thinks. *Really, what are you doing here?* She's not even sure why she suddenly has scruples about arresting this guy. Zero certainly had none when he denounced her before the eyes of the world in that video after Adam's death.

But four against one isn't fair! And she doesn't like the look of these unknown pursuers. *What's going on here?*

'He's on the phone again,' whispers Chander. 'I'd love to know who else is after him. Is someone already backing us up?'

'Or are they investigators, looking for him because of the incident on Presidents' Day?'

'He'd better get a move on if they are.'

If Cyn's perception is correct, then they're no longer in visual contact with their drone, which must be hovering over a side street. The images on Chander's smartphone keep jerking this way and that. Either he's not very practised at piloting drones or the little machine is sensitive to gusts of wind – or both.

'Shit! He's heading for the subway!' Chander curses, sprinting off.

Cyn can't locate a subway station anywhere and doesn't have much hope of catching up with Chander. He disappears around the nearest corner and by the time she reaches it, he's fifty yards ahead. The station is about three hundred yards further along the street. Cyn can make out at least half a dozen people running other than Chander. The young man has already vanished into the subway.

Chander pulls up at the top of the steps and taps hastily on his smartphone, then he ducks down and spins around.

Cyn realizes he's trying to catch the drone. He leaps up and down with outstretched arms, but it's no use. She stifles her laughter. Maybe she should broadcast the scene to the *Daily* live via her glasses, she thinks, but then all of a sudden she hears a menacing buzzing noise approaching.

'Duck!' roars Chander.

She feels a woosh, immediately followed by the drone smashing to pieces on the tarmac a few yards behind them.

'Shit!' He hurriedly gathers the pieces together and races down the steps into the station. She follows his lead, stowing away the laptop in her rucksack as she goes, which certainly doesn't make it any lighter.

'Did you find out who called the man to warn him?' Jon wants to know.

'No,' Luís answers. 'Prepaid cards. Non-assignable.'

Marten swears under his breath.

'Where's he heading?' he says, thinking out loud.

Wobbly, out-of-focus images flicker across the screen. They show the back of the man in the blue baseball cap from various distances. He runs out of the other end of the subway station, bursting out on to a busy street dotted with market stalls. He pauses for a second, allowing their men to gain on him, then he runs off across a car park. He disappears behind a railing and seems to climb down somewhere. When the CIA agents reach the spot, Marten catches sight of a concrete-lined riverbed down below between two roads.

'The Wien river,' announce his glasses. The agents clamber down a fixed ladder. The riverbed enters a tunnel, and the men plunge into the darkness. Their footsteps echo and their bodies cast long shadows on the wall until Marten can see nothing but silhouettes in the half-darkness. Their glasses aren't made for this level of light.

'Where's all this leading?' whispers Marten. 'Is this *The Third Man* or something?'

The *Daily* broadcasts similar pictures with only a few seconds' delay. They must come from the Indian and show the CIA agents already melting into the darkness. His camera's not good enough to adapt to the abrupt change in light conditions.

'At least no one can see what's happening down there,' says Jon.

'I hope not,' says Marten.

'You cannot be serious,' groans Cyn as Chander disappears into the tunnel. The cement-covered riverbed is about thirty feet wide, and she feels tiny between the walls towering above her on either side. Quite lost in the centre is a small watercourse perhaps a dozen feet wide and less than two feet deep.

A good three dozen individuals have now joined their pursuit of the stranger. She has no idea who they are or why they're after him. A horde of people stream into the hole beside her, and their echoing footsteps and voices mingle with the sound of gurgling water. All of them are wearing glasses – smart glasses, she presumes – or holding smartphones in their hands, probably filming. She stumbles into the half-darkness, swept along by the impetus of the throng, their small screens glowing like giant fireflies. She's surprised not to be plunged into total darkness. Far ahead she spots one overhead light and then another. It's just about bright enough for her to make out the silhouettes of the other pursuers, who are gradually leaving her behind. Drawing closer, she realizes the lamps are actually street grates through which a meagre amount of daylight is filtering.

Smaller sewers join the wide tunnel at regular intervals on both sides. She can't bear to imagine the kind of things that come floating down them. Fortunately the only smells so far are of damp and mould. A man overtakes her, then a second.

Someone bumps into her hard, sending her sprawling into the water. She hears her scream echoing and feels the ground beneath her hands and feet, but her face is submerged. The water isn't deep, but the bottom is slippery. She holds her breath, presses her lips together and manages to get enough purchase with her knees and palms to be able to crawl to the side, but her head is forced back underwater. She lashes out, trying desperately to get rid of the weight on the back of her neck. Water floods into her nose and mouth. She grabs hold of something that feels like an arm and clings to it, hoping it will pull her out. Instead, a fist seizes her wrist and tears it away. Something is now bearing down on her back. Her arms and legs thrash the water in panic as she gradually slides across the greasy concrete bottom. Someone seems to be lying on top of her with their entire body to keep her head underwater! She has to breathe! She's sorely tempted to open her mouth wide and fill her bursting lungs. She knows she's going to lose consciousness within seconds.

Vi's face appears in front of her, trying to tell her something. With all her remaining strength, Cyn throws herself to one side, but the weight on her back doesn't move, pressing her even more violently against the bottom and dragging her stomach, chest, thighs and knees across it. She can no longer tell up from down. There's a sudden brightness before her eyes. Her muscles relax. She'll be able to breathe now. Deep and long. She no longer feels any weight; she's floating, flying. That song. Violins, piano, flutes and a soft male voice singing of windmills. She's gliding over a flower-filled summer meadow, silhouetted against the late afternoon sun, like in a romantic film from the seventies. Soft, white, floating seeds and glowing insects accompany her silently into paradise.

Marten can see nothing but gloom. Their agents and other broadcasters are hurrying through a subterranean hall complete with columns, stairs, jetties and various entrances and exits – that's as much as he can tell, because the cameras in the glasses are not designed for these conditions, and the transmission breaks off with increasing frequency.

'Goddam, it looks like one of those labyrinths by Escher,' says Jon.

'We'll never catch this guy if he knows his way around down there,' Marten prophesies.

In addition to their agents there are at least two dozen other people wandering around in the murk, and more keep appearing from the tunnels.

'Who are all these people?' asks Jon. 'Other intelligence services looking for Zero who've neglected to coordinate their operations with us?'

'They look more like amateur hunters to me. Maybe they want to take advantage of his newfound fame,' says Marten. 'Or otherwise they're supporters of Zero, trying to stop his pursuers.'

The *Daily*'s coverage is no better, flickering on screen in fits and starts and interspersed with long periods of darkness. It's difficult to make out anything specific among the silhouettes and shadows.

The wearers of the glasses come to a maze of stairways. *The herd instinct*, thinks Marten. Everyone's running after everybody else, although it's clear no one can see the fugitive any more. It doesn't look good. 'Play the scene where the young man loses his laptop again,' Jon requests.

Luís has saved all the footage and he jumps to the scene in the *Daily*'s coverage where the man's computer slides under a car.

'Our people just ran straight past it!' Jon groans.

It's impossible to tell from the wobbly images that follow if the Indian or the reporter picks up the computer.

'Have they got it or not?'

In any case, the man runs off without his laptop. At least the guys in Langley have noted the incident and sent an agent back to the scene. Yet he can't find the laptop when he reaches the spot.

'Those people from the *Daily* won't have missed an opportunity like that,' says Marten.

'Maybe a passer-by came across it,' comments Luís.

They're going to have to return to this later. Lights glint on Marten's split-screen. Only two pairs of glasses are relaying now. Through the roar of water and the poor-quality recording they hear voices arguing. There's a scuffle, dimly illuminated by the light from a few smartphones.

'What's going on?' asks Jon. 'Have they caught him?'

'Sounds more like an argument between different groups of pursuers,' says Marten.

Two of their agents are wrestling with other unidentified people.

'Get a grip, guys. You may be sweating in a stinking central European sewer,' Jon says heatedly, 'but the whole world is watching!'

'That's not him!' says Alice.

Will can't see anything except shadows running around frantically and fingers pointing in different directions to a soundtrack of truncated shouts and their echoes.

'Well, you've sure got your advertising,' Carl says behind them. He's entered the room unseen and walks over to Will and Alice. For a few seconds there's nothing but a jumble of shadows on screen, accompanied by unintelligible sounds. 'Who are all these people?'

'Look like wannabe sleuths to me,' says Will. '*Daily* copycats, except they don't have any reception down there.'

'Brilliant,' grumbles Carl. 'Now we've got *The Running Man* in real life.'

Will switches his glasses over to the *Daily*'s social media feeds and projects the images on to the wall. New comments appear both there and on the newspaper's website every single second.

'Tens of thousands of comments since they started broadcasting!' he says, hoping to convince Carl. 'Most of them are encouraging the guy on the run. Several TV stations have latched on to the pictures, and countless websites are running live blogs.'

'Reminds me of the frenzied hunt for the Boston Marathon bombers in 2013,' says Alice. 'Local residents and people elsewhere in the world spent hours tweeting, blogging and reporting online, posting mobile recordings of night-time shoot-outs in Watertown, unscrambling police radio messages, discussing and, above all, spreading what turned out to be false rumours and mistaken pictures of possible suspects for hours.' She shudders. 'I still don't want to imagine what that digital mob would have done if any of those people really had fallen into their hands during that time.'

'Some people thought it spelled the final demise of the traditional media and their reporting,' says Will.

'Or a modern version of Ovid's Fama,' Alice contradicts him.

Will could feel very satisfied, but instead he registers an unpleasant sensation welling up inside him. *Something about this just isn't right*, he thinks, but he can't yet figure out what it is.

'I can't see the person they were following,' Alice observes. 'I think they've lost him. Thank goodness.'

'Why?' Carl asks, screwing up his eyes.

She looks at him with annoyance. 'Well, otherwise our promotion would be over already.'

The punch in the stomach brings tears to Cyn's eyes. She's hanging upside down with her belly over a beam or something. Coughing and choking, she spews out a torrent of water. Another blow to her midriff. Another torrent of water. She fights for air, wheezes, spits, vomits and almost coughs her guts up alongside another spurt of water, as two powerful arms close around her body and lower her to the ground. She gradually comes to on her hands and knees. She's aware of the cold, wet stone of the sewer beneath her.

A hand rubs her back, and she recoils.

'Feeling better?' a man's voice asks quietly in strangely inflected English. 'Don't worry, I'm not going to hurt you. The guy who pushed you underwater ran off a little battered, I'd say.'

He whispers these words in an accent she can't place. She sits down and looks up. She recognizes the man they were pursuing by his moustache and baseball cap! He's removed his sunglasses down here in the dark.

'What's he got against you?' he asks. He's panting and looks tense.

Cyn just shakes her head. She doesn't have a clue. 'Where . . . where are the others?' she stammers.

'Heading in the wrong direction,' the man murmurs. She offers no resistance as he lifts her to her feet and pulls her into a narrow corridor from which he takes another two turnoffs before they come to a halt in a slightly wider spot. She can't make out many of his features in the dark – his head is silhouetted against a dim glow from behind, and a few barely perceptible rays glance off his cheekbones, nose and chin.

'Thank you,' Cyn stammers just as quietly. 'By the look of it, you saved my life. And after everything else we did today.' Her whole body is trembling.

He draws her further along the corridor. 'You may have saved *my* life actually. I should thank you. You weren't the only ones after me, but the others are a completely different calibre, maybe the US secret service. But for your coverage I wouldn't have noticed them. That shitty software – who'd have thought that 3DWhizz were so hungry for data! Come on.'

'Didn't you follow the threads about it on the *Daily*'s forums?' Cyn asks, stumbling along behind him.

'All of them? Impossible. Were there some?'

'Uh-huh.'

'Oh well, everything turned out OK. Again.'

They come to a spot where the corridor forks into two narrower tunnels. Glancing around nervously, he stretches out his hand. 'My computer, please.' When she doesn't immediately react, he adds, 'Though your diving adventure probably wrecked it.'

Cyn can now feel her rucksack straps cutting into her shoulders; she'd forgotten all about it until now. She takes it off and undoes the buckles. Its contents are as soaked as she is. She hands him the machine, realizing as she does so that she must have lost her glasses during her underwater struggle. The phone in the pocket of her trousers must be dead too.

'So are you Zero? Or involved with them?'

'We need to get going, before someone comes back. It's obvious I'm not the only one they're after. Follow me!'

Her legs still feel like jelly. Can she trust this man? He may have been the person who held her underwater. Does he really mean to guide her out of here?

He sets off, then notices she's hesitating and stops. Eventually she follows him, holding on to the cold, damp wall for support. He feels his way along the corridor until they reach a larger passageway. Cyn's wet clothes are sticking to her and she's beginning to feel chilled. *Maybe I'm in shock* is one of the few thoughts she can actually hold in her mind.

'I'll tell you something by way of a thank you,' says the shadow ahead of her, as he sets off again. 'So long as you promise not to tell anyone else, let alone say anything on the phone, via email or any other electronic technology.'

She gropes her way after him on full alert, even if he shows no sign of attacking her. She can't memorize their path, with all its turnoffs, anyway, so it would be pointless to run away. 'I promise,' she says. 'It wouldn't be my first off-the-record conversation.' His statement stirs her professional curiosity and simultaneously takes her mind off her fear.

'Anthony Heast and the *Daily* are organizing this hunt for Zero at the suggestion of a company called Sheeld. Sheeld is paying them millions, but Sheeld is just a screen. Not even your editor-in-chief or your advertising department know that.'

Millions. 'Who's behind Sheeld?'

'The money actually comes from Freemee.'

She trips. Something is squeaking between her feet. She gives a startled scream.

'Rats,' the man explains, stopping.

She freezes. The man grabs her by the arm and although she recoils, he pulls her hastily onwards.

'What? Why would Freemee do that?'

When he realizes she isn't resisting, he lets go of her without slackening his pace. His grasp has sharpened her senses again, but she still has trouble keeping up with him.

'Reports on Zero increase Freemee's user figures more than any other form of advertising.'

'Our search is advertising for Freemee?'

'Heast thinks it's advertising for Sheeld.'

'That's no better! How do you know all this?'

'I have my sources, but for their safety you must tell no one about this. No one! But I thought the information might help you even so.'

'It sure does!' She stumbles on and a thought takes shape in her head. 'This morning a friend wanted to tell me something about Freemee. It sounded important, but he didn't want to talk about it on the phone. Was that it?' She blunders into the man, who's stopped in front of her.

'No chance,' he says. 'Did he drop any hints?'

'No. So what did he want then?'

Her guide again continues on his way. 'No idea,' he says.

Cyn is so absorbed and indignant at the same time that she barely reacts when she hears more squeaking nearby. The young man climbs into a conduit barely wide enough for a single person, and she's suddenly overwhelmed by fresh fears and doubts.

'Will we soon be outside?' she asks in an unnaturally high-pitched voice.

'Two more minutes.'

She pushes her way after him between the damp walls.

'By the way, they chose the *Daily* because you work there. They explicitly asked for you to report on this search.'

'*Me*?' She has to pause again. 'But why?'

'You were selected. By the software. As the most suitable person for their purposes at the time.'

'That's rubbish.'

'It's what I know,' he replies.

So that's why Anthony didn't sack her. They come to a wider passageway at the end of which Cyn is relieved to see daylight.

'You can get out there,' says her companion.

'And you?'

'I'll take a different route,' he says, turning back into the darkness.

'Where . . . how . . . can I contact you?' she calls after him.

But he's gone. The splashing of his footsteps fades until all she can hear is the burble of water from somewhere in the distance.

'We need that computer,' says Jon, reaching for the phone. 'We'll have to use unofficial channels for the time being.' He dials the number of a liaison officer at Interpol and gives a brief description of events in Vienna.

'Zero's members are wanted for forming a criminal organization and suspected terrorism,' he explains. 'We need police officers in Vienna to act immediately on an international arrest warrant. The first lead to the suspect is a computer that's probably to be found with one of three individuals who appear to have taken possession of it.' He provides the names and hotel address of Heast, Argawal and Bonsant. 'We'll send the official paperwork later, but action must be taken quickly.'

'I don't know how much I can do for you,' answers the officer on the other end of the line. 'Without an official order—'

'I told you I'll send it soon, goddammit! But this is urgent!'

'You know what our international colleagues are li—'

'I do, but this isn't the first time we've had to act fast.'

'Some of the Europeans aren't so keen on us at the moment.'

'They'll be even less keen on us when they feel the full force of our displeasure! Make that clear to them!' he shouts, slamming down the receiver.

Hopefully the guys at the CIA will help them out this time after making a mess of everything else. He drums his fingers furiously on the tabletop.

'Morons!' he roars.

Interest in the *Daily*'s live streaming has waned, as the producers in London have realized. Their coverage repeatedly switches back to Anthony Heast, who's keeping watch over several Austrian police vans and reporting on how officers are trying to bring the subterranean pandemonium under control. A dirt-smeared man clambers blinking out of a hole in the ground and is immediately greeted by several police officers, who lead him away to one of the vans. They take down his details and release him.

There's an incoming call on Jon's secure line. Erben.

'The President had nothing better to do than watch events unfold in Vienna. Were we part of that?'

Jon clears his throat. 'Yes.'

'Was it successful?'

'No news yet. Langley's on the scene.'

'I hope this wasn't our second humiliation in a few days.' Erben hangs up without saying goodbye. The call still very much on his mind, Jon puts the phone down. Nothing new on the screens.

'Fuck!' he says. 'If that young guy was Zero, then he got away . . . And it's those idiots from the *Daily* who are to blame! This will *not* happen again! I'm going to put our British colleagues on to them.' He snaps angrily at Luís, 'Have you found out anything out about this Archibald Tuttle?'

'No.'

'Have we got *anything* else at all?'

'We've sent out FISA orders to two VPN operators here in the US to get them to hand over their user data. Along with a National Security Letter forbidding them even to talk about it.'

'We keep doing that,' Jon remarks tartly. 'Is it going to move things forwards?'

Luís stays cool. 'We'll soon see.'

Light shines from under an old door made of wooden planks. Finding a cold cast-iron handle, Cyn presses down on it and the door creaks open. She enters a room resembling an ancient cellar and sees another door a few yards ahead. She hears a distant hum of voices. She peers cautiously through the crack between the next door and its frame. A brightly lit corridor with a wooden floor and posters advertising events on the walls. An elderly lady comes down the stairs and disappears through a doorway off the corridor. Cyn slips out. The voices grow louder; it sounds to her as though she's in a café. The door through which the woman disappeared is decorated with an old-fashioned metal figure of a woman in a long dress. A door opposite bears a metal man in a tailcoat. Zero must have left her in some restaurant toilets! What a joker. She strides cheerfully into the women's toilets but notes that her reflection in the mirror offers little cause for celebration. She also notices now that she reeks from the sewers. She's cleaning herself up as best she can at the washbasin when the woman from earlier steps out of one of the cubicles. She shrinks back in disgust at the sight of Cyn.

Cyn makes sure she gets out of there quickly. She'd give anything to be invisible as she works her way through the packed barrel-vaulted cellar restaurant with its rustic furniture and upbeat musicians, but the boisterous guests, most of them elderly, pay her no attention. She steps out into the open air, into a narrow lane lined with old houses. It's getting dark. Now she has to find her hotel. She knows the name and address, but she'll never be able to find her way there without her phone and glasses. She obviously doesn't have a physical map of the city on her, and in any case it would be sodden.

She glances down at herself. People must think she's homeless, and although she has money, she can't take a taxi in this state, as none would let her inside. She has no choice: she's going to have to ask someone for directions.

She approaches an elderly woman, who skilfully dodges her, staring determinedly off to one side. Her next two attempts prove no more successful. The first person to stop is a young man with a beard and dreadlocks he's painstakingly gathered into a ponytail. He eyes her suspiciously but does listen. She notes the relief on his face when she merely asks for directions rather than begging for money. He readily describes the route to her in decent English but maintains a clear distance. *Jesus, I must stink*, thinks Cyn. She checks twice to make sure she'll be able to remember the way, as it won't be easy to find a second person inclined to speak to her. The young man even asks if she needs help, but she says no and thank you and then sets off. She keeps her head down as she scuttles through the streets, which are busy on this fine summer's evening. If people catch sight of her in time, they give her a wide berth, while others simply accelerate past her.

Cyn feels tired in every fibre of her being. The afternoon's images pitch and tumble inside her head. Once again she can feel the pressure on the nape of her neck, holding her under the water, almost drowning her. It costs her an enormous effort to hold back the tears and conceal her trembling.

Twenty minutes later, the receptionist doesn't want to let her into the hotel. She's on the verge of either exploding or collapsing. With her last remaining strength, she asks the woman to call Chander's or Anthony's room. She hopes they're in. She has no idea how the hunt finished and where the two of them might be. The receptionist makes the call.

Two minutes later Anthony comes charging into the lobby. 'My God, you look awful! What happened?'

'I'll tell you later, but first I need a bath.'

'Too right! Chander looked the same way. Did you have to go down into the sewers?'

'You were partying in the square,' she replies, pressing the rucksack into his hand. His mobile announces itself with a rock 'n' roll ringtone as he gingerly takes her bag with the very tips of his fingers.

Cyn locks herself in her room, but has second thoughts about the bath. She's spent enough time lying in water today for her liking, so instead she has the longest shower of her life.

An hour later she meets up with Anthony and Chander in the bar. The two of them are sitting in the hotel courtyard, staring at their laptops through their smart glasses, while delicious aromas of roasting meat waft over from a large barbecue. They both enquire anxiously after her welfare.

She could do with a stiff drink, so she orders a cocktail containing a lot of gin and several other ingredients. Then she tells her story, hesitantly at first, but finally coming to the description of the moment when she was nearly drowned.

'Someone pushed you under?' Flustered, Anthony drains his almost untouched beer in one long swig.

'And then the guy in the baseball cap rescued you?' asks Chander, one eyebrow raised.

'Claimed to have, anyway,' says Anthony. 'He might have been the one who pushed you under in the first place. To get the computer back or take revenge for the chase. We must go to the police!'

'I have no proof whatsoever.' She turns around, bends her head forwards to show them the back of her neck and pushes the sleeve of her blouse up to her elbow. 'Can you see anything? Marks? Bruises?'

'No,' they answer after a brief examination.

'Exactly. So going to the police would be pretty pointless,' Cyn says and is about to resume her tale when Anthony looks away and accepts a call via his glasses. He takes a few steps off to one side to be able to talk without being disturbed.

'This has been going on for hours,' Chander explains, glancing at Anthony. 'The hunt for the man suspected of being Zero has caused a bit of a stir. All kinds of media outlets keep ringing him. But how do you feel after what you've been through?' he asks sympathetically. 'Can I do anything for you?'

You could take me in your arms, thinks Cyn, but all she says is, 'Thanks, that's very kind of you. I can manage.'

Anthony comes back. 'So what are we going to do? Go to the police?'

'Forget it,' says Cyn.

'You didn't finish your story,' he insists. 'What happened next? Did he just leave? Did you talk?'

Cyn studies him and then says, 'No. He wanted his laptop back.'

'And you . . .? Shit.'

'It was ruined anyway, if Cyn was underwater,' says Chander.

'Who the hell were those other people following him?' asks Cyn to change the subject.

'The crowd is looking into it right now,' Anthony explains excitedly, holding up his tablet so that a surprised Cyn can see the *Daily*'s Zero page. 'Hundreds of thousands of people around the world are taking part in the discussion! They are mainly amateur reporters and hobby hunters keen to join our search. They've posted their live streams on their social media accounts.'

'That's sick,' Cyn snorts.

'Not all of them, though,' says Chander. 'The crowd's already found that out too.'

'It's crazy how excited people are getting about this!' Anthony's enthusiasm is relentless. 'By comparing recordings in the public domain, they've worked out for example that eight of the pursuers started chasing the young man in the Museum Quarter, but five of them were streaming live.' He scrambles to find the relevant clips to illustrate his explanations. 'Other hunters have now posted images of those five. Unfortunately their pictures aren't really sharp enough to do any facial recognition, and anyway, they're wearing tinted glasses and caps. People out there are already talking about the weird make of glasses they're wearing! It looks as if their glasses have built-in mechanisms to dazzle facial recognition programs as well as other features to impede identification. People are now searching for other physical characteristics such as moles or tattoos. It's incredible! Some people reckon they've detected similarities between two of them and blokes in previous cases who turned out to be CIA agents!'

'People love that kind of conspiracy theory,' Cyn remarks sceptically. Yet she's reminded of the words of the young man as he pulled her out of the water, about there being a completely different calibre of people after him.

'It isn't so far-fetched,' says Chander. 'The chances that we really were chasing a member of Zero are high. We came to Vienna especially, so why wouldn't the intelligence services?'

'So he was right,' Cyn says pensively. She feels cold.

'What do you mean?' Chander enquires.

CIA. Sheeld. Freemee. For one second she wishes that Anthony was far away and she could confide in Chander, but then she gets a grip on herself. 'It was us who set the secret service on Zero's trail,' she says.

'I think they got there without us.'

'Zero posted that video with Kosak and Washington because of us. And made the mistake that put us on his scent, and the others too.'

'I think he'd have posted it soon, regardless of us,' says Chander.

'I don't like it,' Cyn states, shaking her head. 'How do we separate the wheat from the chaff in a gale of rumours like this?'

'People will do that themselves sooner or later,' says Chander. 'As the forum moderator, Frances is trying to help them.'

'We've got another two interns working on it now,' says Anthony. 'Talented though she is, Frances can't cope on her own any more. Jeff is overseeing the whole thing and Charly's carrying out further research. We're trending! We have hundreds of millions of hits from around the world! It's high time you made another appearance, Cyn.'

Behind Cyn's thousand-yard stare, the memories of her afternoon underground are stirring. Hunting the stranger; more and more people pouring into the sewers, like rats. She knocks back her cocktail.

'OK,' she says. 'Take us live, then. I'll report on my time in those tunnels. Quick and dirty, to use your oh-so-elegant expression.'

'Here?' Anthony asks, vexed.

She looks around. 'What's the problem? It's a lovely backdrop.'

'OK,' Anthony agrees. He whispers a few instructions and then they're live. He looks Cyn straight in the eye.

'Hi everyone, this is Anthony Heast from the *Daily* again. I'm sitting here with our reporter Cynthia Bonsant, who today followed Zero deep into the sewers of Vienna. What can you tell us about the situation down there, Cynthia?'

Cynthia gives the camera a smile before she starts to speak. 'It was shit, Anthony.' She finds his shocked expression very amusing. 'We chased a person who has done nothing wrong except snoop on the world's greatest surveillance state, the same way it and its minions snoop on us every minute of every day. I'd like to apologize to Zero and will no longer be any part of this. What we're doing is disgusting! It's the others we should be hunting. From now on, you can search for Zero without me.'

Anthony looks stunned, but then his expression changes as he whispers something, presumably some instructions to the editorial team in London. He takes off his glasses and carefully puts them away.

'You have to!' he barks. 'Remember our agreement.'

'I don't have to do anything,' she says. 'I told you back in the plane that I will not go along with things like this.'

Just then a young woman in hotel livery appears beside her. 'Are you Miss Cynthia Bonsant?' she asks, and when Cynthia answers yes, the hotel employee says, 'Your daughter would like you to ring her back. It sounded very urgent.'

My mobile! she thinks. *Vi can't reach me.*

Cyn uses the phone in her room to call Vi's mobile. Her daughter picks up immediately and before she can ask what's wrong, Vi croaks, 'Eddie's dead.'

She stares out of the window at the stucco decorations on the house front opposite. She must have misheard. 'You said Eddie's dead?' she checks.

'Yes.'

She sinks on to the edge of the bed. 'My God!' she stammers. Eddie . . . Poor Vi! Her second friend in a matter of days! 'How are you? Oh, my poor darling!'

She's overcome with uncontrollable shaking. Vi splutters something and starts to cry. Cyn feels distraught at not being able to take her daughter in her arms. What on earth can she do?

Her mind turns to Annie. If it wasn't for Eddie, she'd have sent Vi over to her place. She's now shaking so hard she can barely keep hold of the receiver. Her eyes dart to the clock.

'I'll fly home first thing tomorrow morning, darling,' she announces. She pulls herself together, despite feeling like bursting into tears too. 'I'll call Gwen. Maybe you can sleep over at hers.'

'No need,' Vi sniffs. 'I can manage.'

'I spoke to him on the phone just this morning,' Cyn recalls. In her mind's eye she can see Eddie's face as he sat at their kitchen table after Adam Denham died. None of this can really be happening.

'It must have happened just afterwards,' says Vi.

Cyn notices a catch in her voice. 'Do you know how?' she asks cautiously.

'He fell on to the tracks in the Underground.'

'Fell?!'

'The police say the platform was very crowded. It was morning rush hour. They're still assessing the footage from the CCTV cameras.'

Memories of her experience in the sewers come flooding back. All of a sudden, Cyn's body is drained of all sensation. 'Poor Annie! Have you spoken to her? How is she?'

There's silence on the other end of the line until Vi eventually says, 'I haven't managed to get through. She'll be a total wreck.'

They console each other for a few more minutes and then hang up with the mutual assurance that they'll talk again later.

After the conversation Cyn sits on the bed, completely numb. The trembling takes hold of her once more. She doesn't know if she can muster the strength to call Annie, but then realizes she no longer knows her friend's number by heart. It was in her phone – and her phone drowned in the sewers today. As did she.

Eddie's dead. A murder attempt on her too, for that's what it was. Or mere coincidence? *Welcome to paranoia, Cyn!*

She struggles down to the foyer on wobbly legs. A receptionist finds Annie's number on the internet, notes it on a piece of paper and hands it to her. She takes it like a robot and traipses back upstairs to her room.

Annie Brickle doesn't answer the phone, even at her fifth attempt.

She picks at her dinner, making up for her lack of appetite by knocking back glass after glass of wine. She's told the others of Eddie's demise. The news has stopped Anthony from arguing with her about refusing to cooperate any further with the hunt for Zero. Besides, he's continuously on the phone when he's not following developments on the *Daily* website simultaneously on his glasses, smartphone and tablet. Every few minutes he brandishes a new message about the manhunt under their noses. The operation has certainly attracted interest from around the globe. Cyn is conscious that Anthony's impossible behaviour does take her mind off her troubles, despite her public withdrawal from the search for Zero. This realization almost makes her feel emotional. Must be the booze.

With Anthony's approval Chander books three tickets for a flight tomorrow morning. 'We can't accomplish any more here in any case,' says Anthony. 'Book me into business class.'

After another phone call he announces, 'I'm meant to have a discussion with the presenter of the evening news on Austrian public television. It starts in an hour. I've got to go.'

No sooner has he left than Chander takes her hand and gives it a squeeze. Cyn's fighting back the tears, and the alcohol is making her vision slightly blurry too.

'That bad?' he says compassionately.

'Everything was too much for me today.'

He gives her a hug and leads her over to the bar. 'You need another drink.'

'I'm already tipsy.'

'You're allowed a little more today.' He orders two more cocktails, and she doesn't object. He asks her about Eddie, so she tells him.

'He rang me this morning – just imagine.'

'You've already told me,' he reminds her gently.

She downs the cocktail in one. It shakes her up a bit, but she orders another. Her brain is gradually turning to mush.

'And he didn't say what he wanted to tell you?' Chander asks.

She considers this again. 'I don't know, no . . .' She shakes her head, and it feels like a ripe cabbage on a very flimsy stalk. *I must stop after this one*, she thinks, as the barman sets down the second cocktail in front of her. A shiver runs through her when Chander's hand softly, soothingly caresses her back. She doesn't stop him.

He changes the subject. He tells her about previous visits to Vienna and other trips. He's well travelled. His stories reach her ears as if from a great distance and as if she were underwater. She abruptly interrupts him and borrows his smartphone to ring Vi. As she retreats to a quiet corner of the bar, she notes she can no longer walk in a straight line.

Her daughter's voice sounds more composed than during their first conversation. Cyn has to pay attention not to slur her words too much.

'What are you up to?' she asks.

'This and that,' answers Vi. 'Chatting online, calling people.'

Cyn can imagine what about.

'How about you?'

'Drowning my sorrows,' she admits.

'Good idea.'

'I haven't been able to get through to Annie yet,' she says.

'Nor have I,' says Vi.

'I land at noon tomorrow. We'll see each other very soon,' Cyn adds. They say goodnight, and Cyn tries Annie's number one last time. She doesn't even get through to her voicemail.

Luckily the place is so full now that it's impossible for Cyn to take the most direct route back to the bar and so her slaloming gait is less obvious. She straightens herself up a few times on the way. She makes it over to her colleague without barging into anyone.

He enquires sensitively about her conversation with Vi. She doesn't feel like holding back any longer and it all comes spilling out. The alcohol makes the situation seem less tragic than it really is.

'Are you still going to New York?' he asks.

'I don't know yet,' she says. She'll have to see Vi and Annie before deciding. After the young man's claims down in the tunnels earlier today, she feels almost duty-bound to go. She must find out what's behind all this.

'I need to go to bed,' she announces after some time. She doesn't dare contemplate the headache she'll have tomorrow morning.

'I'll walk you upstairs,' Chander says, putting his arm around her shoulders.

Their rooms are adjacent. Two men are waiting outside Chander's door. One of them shows his police credentials and several warrants. 'We've come to get the laptop you picked up earlier today. It's confiscated.'

Cyn is suddenly sober as a judge, and her fear comes flooding back.

Chander doesn't bother to examine the man's papers. 'We don't have it,' he answers, opening the door to his room. 'You're welcome to come inside and search everywhere. Likewise in my colleague's room.'

Cyn nods. 'I lost it in the sewers,' she explains. 'It fell in the water. Look in my room if you don't believe me.'

The two police officers exchange sceptical glances, then enter Chander's room. They rummage around under the sofa cushions, in the cupboards, in and under the bed. It only takes them a couple of minutes and they then repeat the procedure in Cyn's room.

'And Mr Heast?'

'He's at the television station,' Chander answers. 'You'll have to wait for him or ask at reception for a key. But it won't do you any good: we don't have the computer. Unfortunately.'

The two officers offer a brusque goodbye and turn to go.

'Important guests,' remarks Chander as soon as the policemen have left. He puts one hand on the small of Cyn's back and guides her gently but decisively into his room. He points to his glasses. 'They gave me a brief presentation about those guys. Austrian police, my foot. According to publicly available information they work for the Viennese subsidiary of an American firm. A front for the CIA, if you ask me,' he explains, as he goes into the bathroom and searches for something in his toiletry bag. 'It's quite possible that one of their lot took part in the hunt this afternoon.'

He hands her a painkiller and fills a glass with water. 'Here, take this. Just in case.'

She can feel the effects of the alcohol returning, even stronger than before. Her tongue is heavy in her mouth. 'They can't have been happy about our live streaming.'

'You can bet your life on that.'

Great. So now I'm on a US blacklist, Cyn silently swears, swallowing down the tablet. Chander takes the glass from her. His hand brushes her fingers, and for a second they stand there indecisively, facing each other.

'Feeling OK?' he says soothingly, running his fingers down her arm.

'Yes,' she says, holding his gaze. She can feel the warmth of his breath, then his lips as Chander gently embraces her. She hesitates for a second. Then she returns his kiss.

ArchieT: Shit, that was close!

Nightowl: Everything OK?

ArchieT: Yep. In Berlin for a while.

LotsofZs: Saved by those idiots from the *Daily*.

Submarine: Where else have we made fuck-ups like with 3DWhizz?

LotsofZs: One word: metadata.

Snowman: Sorry!

ArchieT: What are we going to do with Bonsant?

Saturday

Cyn wakes up with a throbbing head in spite of Chander's prophylactic painkiller the night before. The surrounding scents tell her she isn't in her own room. She opens her eyes but the piercing pain in her brain quickly makes her shut them again. She remembers having had a lot to drink. And she remembers Chander. She reaches out to one side and touches his body. He's asleep right next to her. Apart from her head, her body feels very nice. She savours this feeling for a few minutes as she listens to his regular breathing. As she carefully tries to move into a more comfortable position, she becomes aware of the scar. The scar! Instinctively she lays her hand over the spot, extricates herself as quietly as possible from the sheets and gathers her belongings, which are scattered halfway across the room. She steals into the bathroom, hurriedly gets dressed and haphazardly arranges her hair. Then she tiptoes back to the bed and gives Chander a peck on the lips. He stirs into half waking, and she whispers, 'See you later.' His eyelids flutter drowsily and he stretches a hand out towards her, but she's already at the doorway and a second later has disappeared through it.

Back in her room, she takes a shower. The warm water does her head good, but soon the previous day's events force their way back into her thoughts. Almost being drowned.

She's suddenly gasping for breath. She stumbles out of the shower and stands in front of the mirror, fighting for air. Not a pretty sight. Still trembling, she wraps herself in the bathrobe. She combs her hair, leans back against the wall and stares at the mirror. Her bathrobe slips, exposing her scar. She pulls the robe shut again, and her thoughts turn to Eddie. *Are there any connections here? Welcome to paranoia.* She pulls herself together, runs her fingers through her hair once more and rubs cream into the scar, recalling the sensations on her skin last night. For a moment she longs for Chander.

In the taxi to the airport Anthony feels obliged to describe his TV appearance again. It only lasted for two minutes, but boy, was he brilliant! Not only that, he made it on to television before Cyn to talk about the search for Zero, as befits an editor-in-chief! He didn't get round to giving them all the details of his appearance over breakfast. He's brought with him the hotel's Austrian and international newspapers, all of them featuring reports on the incident in Vienna. With photos. To the sound of loud rustling, he shows every single article to the others, who are sitting in the back of the cab.

'We're pretty big stars now,' he drones on, 'and the *Daily* has taken a giant leap in terms of international prominence and online hits. This trip's been worthwhile for that alone.'

'Zero's prominence has leaped even further,' Chander remarks. 'After all, we're the ones who've been conned.'

'Because you can't control your drone properly!' Anthony says with a snigger.

'Because we did a live stream. Otherwise we might have our interview by now,' Cyn objects.

'Or else the CIA would have him in its clutches,' Anthony snaps back. 'What on earth is wrong with you? You weren't being serious yesterday, were you? About not wanting to look for Zero any longer?'

'Deadly serious,' Cyn answers.

'Let's discuss it calmly back in London,' he says, fobbing her off and leafing through to the newspaper's business pages.

'I can't make it into the office this afternoon,' she says in a funereal voice. 'I have to look after my daughter and a dead boy's mother.'

He'd completely forgotten about it! 'That's fine,' he says without looking up from the share prices. Having swiftly skimmed through them, he puts the paper down and activates his glasses as Chander blurts out, 'I've just received an alert. Anonymous is recruiting people for an attack on the *Daily* after yesterday's operation.'

What's he talking about?

'Recruiting people for an attack?' Anthony frowns. 'What kind of attack?'

'You should warn your IT department immediately. Unless, that is, they've already installed an alarm against this.'

'What the hell?' Anthony says indignantly. 'How's it supposed to work? I thought Anonymous worked covertly, as the name suggests.'

'Anonymous, not covert. This is a typical approach for Anonymous. They post videos on YouTube from anonymized accounts, tweet and so on, then everyone can take part. All you have to do is download a small piece of free software from the internet on to your computer or on to certain websites. Those are then used to carry out denial-of-service attacks and the like.'

'Swamping our website with a deluge of questions until it crashes and can no longer be accessed?' Anthony enquires.

'Yep.'

'OK, we can't let that happen. Can we fend them off?'

'To a degree, as long as we start immediately.'

'I'll call Jeff right away,' says Anthony, mumbling, 'Bastards!'

While Anthony has an animated conversation via his glasses with the technicians in London, and Chander chips in with some judicious comments, Cyn stares out of the window at the scenery sliding past. As they drive along the motorway, the city's outskirts give way to industrial zones and fields. She thinks of Annie and Eddie. And Vi. For a moment she feels her knee brush against Chander's and she presses her lower leg against his with extreme caution, ready to pull it away if Anthony were to look round. Briefly returning the pressure, Chander turns to her and smiles, then focuses once more on his conversation.

She looks out of the window again. What's she going to say to Annie? A flock of starlings is coalescing into a living cloud over the fields, but the taxi has already sped past it.

Anthony gets out of the taxi and pays, holding simultaneous conversations with the driver and his glasses. After the baggage drop-off and security checks, he tells them, 'I need to go to the lounge and work.'

'See you love birds later,' he adds with a dirty chuckle and is gone.

Cyn is red to the roots of her hair. Chander simply smiles at her and shrugs. 'Let's grab a coffee.'

As they come into the immigration hall at Heathrow, several officials block their path and say, 'Please come with us.'

Even before Cyn can ask a question, two female officers have separated her from the men. 'You're suspected of supporting terrorism,' one of them explains. Cyn freezes midstep. The two officers push her rudely on.

'You must be confusing me with someone else,' she says, feverishly contemplating what this might mean. Those men from yesterday evening come to mind. She recalls the scandal in the summer of 2013 when the partner of an American journalist was held at the airport for nine hours. Harsh hands on her back force her forwards.

'You can explain that to the detectives,' one of the officers says.

They show her into a bare room. In the middle are a plain table and two chairs, with a bed along one wall. One of the officers takes Cyn's handbag away before she can object and empties its contents on to the table.

'Get undressed,' the other commands.

'Sorry?!'

'Strip search.'

'Why?!' Cyn's beginning to panic. She thinks back to the attack the day before, and her fear of dying underwater hits her again.

'You have no right to do this!'

'Oh yes, we do,' the woman retorts, adding in an irritated voice, 'Don't make this any harder than necessary for your sake and ours. You just take off your clothes for a moment, we search you and soon it'll all be over.'

Cyn looks around. She spots two small cameras at ceiling level in the corners. 'And you're filming this?'

'Those are the rules. For our safety.'

'*Yours?*'

'Madam?' the woman says again with a commanding gesture.

Cyn tries to calm herself down. She's starting to realize the point of this whole show. Harassment. Intimidation.

'No,' she says, crossing her arms in front of her chest.

The woman sighs and takes a step towards her.

'Don't you touch me!' Cyn declares as firmly as she can muster in the situation. Pointing to the cameras, she says, 'They're filming this. You just admitted it.'

The woman pauses and lowers her arms. She steps back. She waits.

Cyn doesn't have a clue what these people are allowed to do. They stand there for what feels like several minutes, even though Cyn knows the whole scene lasts only a few seconds.

'OK,' the woman says at last, pointing to one of the chairs. 'Sit down.' She turns away and opens the door.

A small triumph, Cyn thinks. *Or a pyrrhic victory?* She chooses the other chair. Mind games. But she has trouble suppressing the shaking that washes over her like a fever. With jelly-like knees, the few steps to the chair are akin to several miles. *I'm not going to show any weakness in front of you!*

Another woman and a man enter the room, both in plain clothes. They introduce themselves by rank and name, but Cyn's in such a state she immediately forgets this information.

'We're questioning you in relation to the Terrorism Act 2015,' the woman explains.

'I'm a journalist,' says Cyn. 'I demand to see a lawyer.'

'This isn't a TV series,' the man replies coolly. 'You can choose to cooperate with us or not.'

'There's nothing to cooperate over,' Cyn shoots back angrily. 'I'm just doing my job.'

'And we're doing ours. Where's the young man's laptop? You picked it up in Vienna and took it with you.'

'And then stuffed it up my arse to smuggle it into this country?! Are you mad? I lost it in the sewers during the hunt.' She can feel her anger at this gratuitous interrogation goading her to contradict them. 'But then you must know that. You must have viewed all the images that people have posted online, and probably the footage from surveillance cameras in Vienna. So you will have noted that I emerged from the sewers without a laptop.'

The man inspects the items on the table from her hand-bag. He picks up her mobile phone and says, 'We're confiscating this.'

'Fine,' she says with a chuckle. 'It's dead anyway.'

'She had no other electronic devices on her?' he asks the women in uniform.

'No, sir.'

His partner turns to Cyn. 'Your actions yesterday helped a suspected terrorist to escape.'

'That's nonsense, and you know it. I neither helped Zero nor, going by everything we know about him, is he a terrorist – even if he was involved in the Presidents' Day operation.'

By now Cyn is hopping mad. She has to keep herself in check so she doesn't raise her voice. 'And now if you would kindly let me go! A friend of mine died yesterday, and I have to go and see his mother.'

'You might have to spend the next forty-eight hours here,' the man explains. 'That's how long we're allowed to detain you.'

For the next hour they keep asking her the same questions, but she sticks stubbornly to her story. They threaten her; they try to intimidate her. At some point she's so annoyed that she falls silent and refuses to say another word.

Shortly afterwards a man enters the room and whispers something to the two detectives. They glower at Cyn, and the woman snaps, 'You may go.'

Cyn puts everything back into her bag, apart from the mobile, which she leaves on the table.

Anthony and Chander are waiting outside for her. They too have been questioned.

'You haven't heard the last of this!' Anthony shouts angrily over his shoulder at the officers, but Cyn can't be bothered to discuss the matter. More important things await her.

Eventually they get their luggage back. She can tell immediately that someone's been messing with her sports bag: the person hasn't even bothered to zip it shut properly.

Anthony and Chander go straight to the office to press ahead with fending off the Anonymous attack. Cyn's daughter is waiting for her.

She arrives home to find Vi pale and agitated. Cyn has held her tears back thus far, but now the dam breaks. She takes her daughter in her arms. For several minutes they stand sobbing in the hallway until Cyn regains her composure first.

Over a cup of tea Vi updates her mother on the investigation. 'The police say it was an accident.'

Cyn can't help expressing her doubts. 'Eddie rang me shortly before I flew to Vienna,' she tells Vi. 'He wanted to tell me something. Did he mention anything to you?'

Vi shakes her head. 'No. I've no idea what he wanted. Maybe . . . No.'

'Spit it out!'

'I think Eddie had had a crush on me for some time,' Vi says falteringly.

'And you?'

'I liked Eddie, but only as a friend.'

'You think he wanted to talk to me about it?'

Vi shrugs. 'Just a hunch.'

Maybe that was all Eddie wanted, Cyn thinks hopefully. *But then why would he mention Freemee?*

She tries her luck with Annie Brickle again from the landline. Someone picks up, and she feels sick to her stomach. She hardly recognizes Annie's voice, and her own cracks as she stammers, 'I'm so sorry, Annie. Should I come round? I can be there in forty-five minutes.'

'That . . . would be nice,' Eddie's mother sobs.

'See you in a bit.'

'Want to come along?' she asks her daughter.

Vi shakes her head.

'Better not.'

'I understand. No problem.'

Cyn takes a taxi. She feels safer that way. She hasn't told Vi anything about the Viennese underworld. She doesn't want to worry her daughter unnecessarily.

Annie opens the door and looks every bit as broken as her voice sounded on the phone. Cyn gives her a hug and wordlessly leads her to the kitchen.

With trembling hands Annie has a go at making some tea until Cyn takes the kettle from her and pours the hot water into the pot.

Meanwhile Annie talks haltingly and not always coherently. 'It was an accident, the police say, due to the crush on the platform. The camera recordings don't show anything clearly. Witnesses didn't notice anything. They say nobody's to blame.' She sits down and stares straight ahead. The delicate lines of tears shine damply on her cheeks, trickling down to her chin.

Cyn places a cup on the table in front of Annie. *I'd like to see those videos*, she thinks. *Mind you . . . 'like' is the wrong word*. She forces back the suspicion that has latched on to her brain like a tick and is steadily growing.

'He was so looking forward to learning to drive,' Annie says in a lifeless voice.

Cyn says nothing, sipping at her hot drink. For a few minutes neither of them speaks. Cyn listens to the sounds of the kitchen and the noises out in the street. She can see Eddie there in front of her, at the playground with Vi, the pensive young boy with those big brown eyes who was always more cautious at play than her daughter. His timid smile and how it blossomed during puberty into an attractive laugh. It hadn't escaped her that his feelings for Vi seemed to have changed in recent months.

'What do I do now?' asks Annie, her lips quivering.

Cyn stands up and hugs her from behind, the trembling of Annie's frame transmitted to her own. She stands there for what seems like for ever until Annie's body is once more still.

'I'm sorry,' sniffs Annie, wiping the tears from her face and sitting up straight.

'There's no need to apologize,' Cyn replies gently. She's reminded again of her last conversation with Eddie and wonders if she should tell Annie.

'He . . .' Annie begins, then falters before continuing. 'The police say he phoned you before he died.'

'He did,' she answers with a lump in her throat. 'It must have been shortly beforehand.'

'That was the last time he spoke to anyone. What . . . did he say?'

She tries to recall his precise words, but she can't. 'He wanted to tell me something. About a company. I don't know what. He said he might have a story for me. Do you know anything about it?'

'A story?' Annie looks at her helplessly. 'What kind of story? No.' Absentmindedly she smooths her dress and tidies her hair.

Cyn sympathizes with Annie. Meaningless last words, and not to his mother.

'Do you ... Do you know what he was busy doing recently, by any chance?'

Annie shrugs. 'What else? He was spending night after night on his computer, as he often did.'

Cyn hesitates, but then she asks the question anyway. 'Is his laptop here?'

Without a word Annie leads her to Eddie's room. It looks as if he'll be getting home any minute. There are posters of rappers on the door and the wall unit, and the smell of a boy's bedroom. Annie lingers in the doorway; she obviously can't bring herself to enter the room. Cyn steps gingerly over the threshold. The laptop's on the desk, closed. *An accident, after all?* thinks Cyn. If someone did murder him because of a story he wanted to tell Cyn about, wouldn't that person have got hold of Eddie's laptop?

Just because you believe you were attacked doesn't necessarily mean the same thing happened to Eddie, she tells herself. *You're making links between the two events because they took place on the same day, but they probably have nothing to do with each other.*

She prises the laptop open and presses the Start button.

'He wanted a pair of those glasses,' Annie says dully. 'Like the ones that other boy had.'

'They all want them,' Cyn replies.

A window pops up on the screen with a request for the password.

'Do you know the password?' asks Cyn.

Annie silently shakes her head.

Cyn snaps the computer shut again and rests her fingers on top of it. 'I—' she begins, but breaks off. She tries again. 'May I . . . take it with me? You'll get it back, of course.'

'It's encrypted. What use is it to me?'

Cyn tucks the laptop under her arm and leaves Eddie's room. 'When—?' she tries to ask, but she can't pronounce the words because of what feels like a golf ball stuck in her throat.

Annie knows what she was going to say. 'I don't know yet,' she replies. 'In the coming days.'

Cyn gives her another hug. 'Have you got someone to be with you?'

'Yes, thanks. My sister should be here any minute.'

'I . . . I have to leave town tomorrow morning, but you can ring me any time.' *I'll need a new mobile!* it occurs to her. 'I'll be back in a few days.'

'It's OK. Mali and Ben and a few others will be around. Thanks for coming.'

'Come here, Marten!' Luís calls across several rooms.

Marten leaves his glass cube and hurries over to the technicians. On one of Luís's screens he sees the home page with the waterfalls on it. The monitor next to it is full of text.

'This has just come in from the NSA,' says Luís, pointing to a list of email and IP addresses along with a great deal of other confusing information.

'While checking the visitors to the waterfalls, they came across an IP address used to send mails from addresses including DaBettaThrillCU@ . . .'

'The better thrill, see you?' says Marten, reading the mis-spelled abbreviation, but at the same moment he grasps what it really is. 'An anagram of Archibald Tuttle.'

'That's right,' says Luís. 'Our buddies kept digging for a while and after a few blind alleys they established a link to the Tuttle in Vienna. Good ole Archie's indiscretions while registering with 3DWhizz weren't the only ones he made when he was younger. However, DaBettaThrillCU, aka Archibald Tuttle, only visited the waterfalls once, in 2010, shortly after it went online. Never again. I don't think that one time was a coincidence, though.'

'You mean, you think there's something else behind it?'

'Yes. I just haven't got a . . . What did you just say?'

'You think there's something else behind it,' Marten repeats.

'You're a genius!'

'I know. Now tell me why.'

'If you're a genius, you should know.'

'What did I say?'

'"There's something else behind it." Remember that scene in *Jurassic Park* where the kids hide behind the waterfall?'

'Yeah.'

'There's an even better example in the Tintin comic book *Prisoners of the Sun*—'

'Never read it.'

'Tintin finds the secret entrance to the Aztec sun temple behind a waterfall.'

'Action films and comics. We might need to talk about your cultural education sometime.'

'Yours too, if you've never heard of *Prisoners of the Sun*.'

Marten laughs. 'So what's hidden behind these water-falls? It's a website.' He makes a show of peering behind the monitors. 'Nothing back here,' he says. 'Nothing but wires.'

'That's where my education comes in handy,' says Luís. 'OK, this is me putting one and one together. Did you see the film *Contact* when it came out?'

'Jodie Foster meets aliens.'

'Remember when Jodie Foster and her blind colleague hear a second signal emerging through electrostatic noise?'

'Adolf Hitler's opening speech at the 1936 Olympic Games. You mean—'

Luís nods.

'Steganography.' Marten's turned serious all of a sudden. As a boy he'd enjoyed writing secret messages with lemon juice that could only be read when you held the piece of paper over a candle and the dried juice turned brown. Knowing how to hide messages in a totally harmless-looking medium is one of the basic techniques of warfare, whether practised by the intelligence services, freedom fighters, guerrillas or terrorists. 'But why would someone hide secret messages in these waterfalls of all places?'

'There are two reasons why they're the perfect hiding-place and medium,' Luís explains. 'For technical purposes you need a moving picture, and I mean completely moving: no pixel is allowed to stay the same during the critical period. Otherwise that would be the Achilles heel by which you could intercept the message. But I'll spare you the technical details. Waterfalls are ideal in close-up. Everything is constantly in motion. Second, they look harmless, so they don't raise any suspicions. Who would ever imagine that an esoteric website conceals a hidden communications platform for internet activists?'

'And how can you tell that's what it really is?'

'I can't. That's what makes the idea so brilliant. So long as they don't make a mistake, it's simply a page with waterfall videos and streams. We can't even determine if there really are messages hidden inside there, let alone read them.'

Marten ponders what Luís has just said. 'They've made mistakes before,' he eventually remarks. 'Everyone makes mistakes. That's your theory. Do you think it makes sense to pursue it?'

'As you say: everyone makes mistakes. And if anybody can find them, it's us – us and our friends from the other agencies.'

'Let's do it!'

'Two friends dead in the same week,' Vi says. Despite her tone, she strikes her mother as being relatively calm.

They're sitting at the kitchen table, eating Vi's home-made macaroni cheese. Neither of them has much of an appetite and they only half clear their plates. Cyn feels completely torn. As a mother she's worried about Vi, as a friend she'd like to be there for Annie and yet she is desperate to go to New York where she'll meet the vice-president of Freemee and where the company has its headquarters. Should she tell him that a young man who'd wanted to talk to her about Freemee has died – what's more only a few hours before someone tried to murder her? She's also longing to find out more about the claims made by the stranger in the sewers of Vienna.

Welcome to paranoia!

'When do you have to leave tomorrow?' Vi asks.

'I don't know if I really ought to take that plane,' Cyn answers. 'I should really go to New York for another reason I can't explain to you right now, but I'd actually rather stay with you two and miss the TV programme.'

'I'll manage, if that's what you mean,' says Vi.

'I feel guilty.'

'I'm eighteen, Mum.'

She's an adult.

'I know. You can ring me whenever you want.'

'On which phone?'

She's also a smart cookie. Cyn goes to her room and comes back with the slip of paper on which she's noted the numbers. 'Here, this is the hotel in New York. This is my new mobile. The *Daily* has got me one, and they're bringing it to the airport tomorrow.'

'Is one of them coming with you?'

'Yes, the younger one – Chander,' she says as casually as she can.

Vi nods absently as she takes the piece of paper and studies the numbers.

'I need to leave here at ten,' Cyn says.

'Then we can have breakfast together,' says Vi, still staring at the list of phone numbers. 'This is mad,' she whispers, then a little louder, 'Don't you think?'

If you only knew how mad, she thinks. 'Yes.'

The doorbell rings. Cyn's and Vi's eyes meet.

'Are you expecting anyone?' asks Cyn.

'No.'

Cyn goes out into the hallway and asks over the intercom who's there.

'A parcel for Cynthia Bonsant,' a female voice replies.

At this time of day? It's just after eight o'clock. Cynthia presses the button for the front door downstairs, then waits and peers through the spyhole. A minute later a female bike courier appears in the entrance, carrying a parcel the size of a shoebox. From the kitchen Cyn hears the sounds of Vi clearing the table. She hesitates when the courier knocks, but then opens the door.

'Who's it from?' asks Cyn. The woman shrugs and presses the box into her hands. It's covered in plain wrapping paper.

It's unmarked except for their address. She turns it this way and that until she finds a large oval drawn in felt-tip pen on the narrow side. It looks like an 'O'. Above it, in small, careful block capitals, it says, 'Best regards.'

The courier proffers the electronic receipt pad. Cyn signs, steps back inside her flat and closes the door. She carries the parcel into the kitchen and puts it down on the table.

'What is it?' Vi asks.

'No idea.'

' "Best regards",' Vi reads out. ' "O".' She glances at her mother. ' "O" as in "o",' she says slowly, 'or "o" as in zero?'

'Don't be stupid.'

'It might be a bomb,' says Vi. 'That lot have every reason to be mad at you.'

'I've made a public apology and have abandoned the hunt,' Cyn reminds her. Also, the guy in the sewers really didn't strike her as the bomb-sending type. Her daughter doesn't know that, however. 'It might just be someone playing a stupid prank.'

She slides a fingernail under a fold in the packaging and rips it open. She does feel a little queasy. The paper comes off easily and she notes that it's got a metallic coating on the inside. A plain brown cardboard box comes into view. She pauses before saying, 'Go to your room.'

'You must be nuts!' cries Vi. 'If you really think there's something dangerous in there, then don't open it!'

'It isn't dangerous.'

'Then I can stay.'

Before Cyn can stop her, Vi lifts the lid. Cyn tries to clamp her hands over the top of the box, but it's already open. Inside is a see-through plastic box the size of a cigarette packet containing a circuit board and other small bits of technical gear. Her heart misses a beat. This is exactly what bombs look like in films. Next to it is a folded sheet of paper. There seems to be some kind of keyboard underneath the plastic circuit-board box.

Nothing is ticking or winking. Vi unfolds the sheet so Cyn can read it too.

Dear Cynthia Bonsant,

The circumstances of our meeting weren't so nice, but your announcement that you were quitting the hunt for us was. Here's the answer to your last question, just in case you feel like doing more than quitting. We're curious to see your next step.

Sincerely yours,
Zero

Cyn and Vi stare at each other, speechless.

'What question?' Vi asks, immediately continuing, 'Do you think this is genuine?' Without waiting for an answer, she reads on.

Inside this box you will find a preconfigured Raspberry Pi minicomputer, a small keyboard and a few cables. Use the cables to connect the Pi to the keyboard and your TV set, as shown in the sketch below. The device will immediately log on to a free Wi-Fi network nearby. Memorize your username in the dialog box. Don't write it down. Don't let anyone you don't trust 110% touch the computer. Do not take it abroad with you (baggage control!). Hide it in a safe place when you're not using it. In an emergency destroy the SD card (see sketch).

'Shit!' Vi whispers. 'A link to Zero.'

'You really think so? I have so many questions!'

'Well, now you can ask them.' Vi's already disappeared into the living room with the box. Two minutes later she's connected the Pi to the keyboard and the TV. A chaotic muddle of moving, rushing images appear on the screen, covering it like tiles on a wall. Everything appears to be moving. There doesn't seem to be a single still spot.

'What's that?' she asks.

'No idea,' replies Vi.

'It reminds me of white noise. Surf. Hey, that bit looks like water flowing! Are they waterfalls?'

A white window of the kind Cyn is familiar with from her email software pops up out of the flickering recordings.

Hi Cynthia!

This is a secure platform. Nice conversation we had. Apology accepted. And thanks again for yesterday.

'What do they mean?' asks Vi.

'Never you mind,' whispers Cyn. 'It looks like it really is Zero.'

Cyn excitedly grabs the keyboard from Vi. As she starts to type, a username appears above the text.

Guext: What did you tell me down there?

'What is this? Guext? Is that now your username?' asks Vi with some irritation just as the answer arrives.

Jakinta0046: Is that a test? Background and funding of the hunt for Zero.

Cyn slumps back on the sofa. 'It really is Zero,' she whispers.

'This is all gobbledegook to me,' says Vi.

'It's better that way. I'll explain later. You should probably leave me alone for a while.'

Vi shoots her a hurt look, but Cyn defies her and nods
encouragingly until her daughter gets up, goes over to the
doorway, from where she can't see the screen, and stands
there with her arms folded.

Cyn starts to type. She has to find out what really
happened.

Guext: Down in the sewers I told you about a friend who
wanted to tell me something before I left London. Something about Freemee. He's died. An accident, shortly before
I was attacked in Vienna. That too would have looked like
an accident. A coincidence? Could it have been about the
hushed-up financing story?

Jakinta0046: No way. Must have been something else.

Guext: I have his computer. It's encrypted.

A pause.

Jakinta0046: Then we can't get into it for now. Can you
ask someone else?

Guext: Yes. Planned to do so tomorrow.

Jakinta0046: Let us know if there's anything else we can do
to help.

Guext: An interview with Zero ☺

Jakinta0046: What we need to say we say ourselves.
But maybe we can help you with your story. Tell us
when you have more. Next time you'll need a password. Enter one you can remember now. At least ten

characters, including numbers, upper- and lower-case
letters, and symbols.

Cyn has to give this some thought. The crucial part of their
dialogue has now slid out of the window.

Guext: Md18.Ablonde

Jakinta0046: OK.

'Md18.Ablonde?' asks Vi. Cyn looks up, startled. She was
so absorbed in her chat that she didn't see or hear Vi coming nearer.

'I told you—' she lashes out, but Vi interrupts her: 'You
wouldn't have come up with it if not for me.'

Cyn purses her lips and relents. ' "My daughter", your
age and your hair colour.'

'Is that secure enough?' Vi says sceptically.

'Got anything better?'

Vi shakes her head. 'Ask them what the background pictures are for?'

Cyn types in the question.

Jakinta0046: Camouflage. Talk again soon.

For a few seconds they stare silently at the screen, but the
only things moving are the noisy images.

'Where do we hide that thing?' asks Vi.

'I don't feel happy with it in the flat,' Cyn answers, her
mind going back to her interrogation at the airport. 'We've
just been in contact with wanted terrorists.'

She removes the lens-sized SD card from the Raspberry
Pi, as shown in the sketch, pulls out the cable and packs
everything except for the card into the box.

'In the extractor hood above the cooker,' says Vi. 'It doesn't work anyway.'

'Good idea.'

Back in the kitchen, Vi removes the filter from the hood in a few quick movements, pushes the box into the hole and then snaps the filter back into place. Cyn puts the SD card in a small dish containing keys, fobs, pens and other stuff in the hall.

'Hidden in plain sight,' she says. 'Like in that Edgar Allan Poe story. And don't you dare touch it!'

Cyn checks the door locks one last time before going to bed. She packs enough clothes for four days and a smart outfit for the talk show into the only battered suitcase she owns. Can she really leave Vi on her own right now? Should she worry even more because of that little box? She remembers how her daughter opened the parcel and plugged in the device. *She's braver than me*, thinks Cyn. *Why should I worry? She knows less than I do. And that's how it must stay.*

She takes her laptop to bed with her and finally gets round to swotting up on Sheeld. It's a little-known start-up, but she can't discover any link to Freemee via its staff or any common investors. She can't get to sleep. Too much has happened in the past few days, and too much of it she doesn't understand.

Nightowl: Do you trust Bonsant?

Snowman: Because of her investigation, you mean?

ArchieT: I wonder what the boy found out about Freemee?

Peekaboo777: No idea.

Sunday

The next morning Cyn forces herself to get out of bed. Her eyes are all puffed up. The only thing Vi wants to talk about over breakfast is her mother's chat with Zero and the forthcoming talk show on NBC.

'What are you going to say?'

'Depends what they ask.'

The idea of the talk show makes her feel slightly uncomfortable. The other guests will certainly be experienced panel guests. Will she even get a word in edgeways?

'You're so lucky to be going to New York!' Vi raves.

'We'll make it there together one day. And I'll make sure I'm not working,' says Cyn.

'Speaking of work, I need to revise some French. I've got my exam tomorrow.' With those words she disappears into her room, and Cyn gets ready for her trip.

'I'll get in touch as soon as I arrive,' she assures Vi when they say goodbye.

'You'll be fine,' says Vi, sensing her mother's mounting anxiety.

Chander is waiting for Cyn at check-in an hour later. She feels her heartbeat speed up. As always, he looks bright-eyed and bushy-tailed, and he gives her one of those radiant smiles in greeting. He asks considerately how she is, and how Vi and Annie are too.

Cyn feels herself relax in his presence. *You're mad*, she thinks. *He's twelve years younger than you. You have no idea where he'll be headed when his work for the* Daily *is finished. Whatever . . .*

For now she reveals nothing about her conversation with Zero. She doesn't actually quite know herself how she should deal with the situation.

'How bad was the Anonymous attack?' she asks.

'We sustained only light injuries. Anthony's IT crew are up to the job.'

They drop off their bags, Cyn keeping only a small rucksack as hand luggage. At the sight of the officials at security, the mixture of fear and rage that she'd felt the previous day during her questioning floods her veins once more. They don't pay much attention to her, though.

'Another hour until boarding,' says Chander, glancing at the clock. 'Come on, let's go and have a coffee over there!'

In the café Chander hands Cyn her new smartphone and a glasses case. 'With regards from Anthony. You need to take better care of them this time, he says. Also, the company will pay international rate for your days in New York.'

'I want nothing more to do with his hunt for Zero. Hasn't he understood that yet?'

Chander laughs. 'You've known your boss for longer than I have.'

She hesitates for a second and looks around in all directions. 'I've got something for you too.' She opens the rucksack, pulls out the laptop and puts it on the table. 'This belonged to Eddie.' She flips it open and turns it on. 'I told you we spoke on the phone shortly before he died. It sounded important.'

'Where did you get it?' asks Chander. *This is how he looks when he's concentrating particularly hard,* she thinks. *Peggy was right: he's totally focused whenever talk turns to computers.*

'From his mother.'

'He's encrypted the hard drive,' Chander notes when the window with the password field appears on screen.

'Can you hack into it?'

'Is this the way you journalists always go about things?'

'If necessary.'

Chander examines the device. 'I'll have to try it out. It could take a while, though. I probably won't be able to start it up.'

'Give it a go. Please. I have to know what really happened.'

He takes out his own laptop. 'Was he handy with computers?'

'As far as I know, yes.'

'Good. Because such people like to think of themselves as being particularly smart and so they make the most elementary mistakes. We'll take the easy route first. If the password was short and simple enough, we might even get inside.'

'Can you start by trying out some specific variations?'

'Sure. Any ideas?'

'Anything relating to Viola.'

'Your daughter?'

'I think he was besotted with her.'

Five minutes later, all Eddie's data is laid out before their eyes.

'Spot on!' Chander says in appreciation. 'What are we looking for?'

'What was he working on last? Something unrelated to school, gaming or music.'

'Half an hour till boarding,' he observes. 'We'll have lots of time during the flight.'

'But we don't have anything to do now either,' she insists.

His fingers skip across the keyboard and trackpad until finally he says, 'People make mistakes. They always make mistakes. But this one here is especially interesting.'

He points to a folder on the screen. 'Someone tried to delete this one, and not just by putting it in the Recycle bin. Delete it properly. And I suspect that someone wasn't Eddie.'

'Who then?'

'Someone who got remote access to his computer. I might be able to find out who it was, but only when we get to New York.'

'What's in the folder? Can you open the files?'

'Scripts for software, tables. And a video.'

'Let's have a look.'

The sight of Eddie makes Cyn choke up. He looks pale and bleary-eyed. She recognizes his poster-covered bedroom wall in the background.

'Until less than a year ago, Adam Denham was a shy boy,' Eddie says to the camera. 'But then he began using Freemee ActApps and soon turned into an attractive, cocky young man. Too cocky? A few days ago he died in a shoot-out as he was chasing a wanted criminal. Shortly afterwards someone planted a strange idea in my head: might Freemee's ActApps be to blame?'

Cyn breaks into a sweat. Does he mean her?

'Crazy idea,' whispers Chander.

'Rubbish, I thought, because if so, the people Freemee emboldened must be dying all the time. So I examined the relevant data.' Eddie displays a bar chart as he continues to speak. 'I compared the mortality rate among Freemee users and non-users. The findings are unequivocal. Since Freemee was launched two years ago, the number of deceased Free-mee users is no different from the number of comparable non-users—'

'Well, everything's fine then,' says Chander. 'What's he driving at?'

'But if Freemee truly does have a positive effect on our lives, then there should actually be *fewer* accidents, suicides or similar causes of death. The mortality rate among Free-mee users should fall, but it doesn't. I considered that there might be several reasons for that.'

Eddie puts up a list. 'First, in neither case have the figures been recorded accurately enough. Second, Freemee is not as effective as claimed, although it might be asking too much to ask it to prevent fatalities. Third, the difference is too small to be statistically noticeable. Fourth, you can't see it because it's like this bag of potatoes.'

'Clever lad,' comments Chander, as Eddie reappears and holds up a bag of potatoes to the camera. 'There are four pounds of potatoes in here. Those are the mortality rates we know about. What we don't know, however, is how they're configured. Applied to these potatoes that means: are there lots of potatoes of the same size in here, or several large ones and a few small ones? Or, returning to deaths, lots of natural ones and a few unnatural ones? I decided to refine my search – to open the bag of potatoes, in other words – and search for unnatural causes of loss of life among Freemee users. The Adam Denham kind. Accidents. Suicides. Murders. To determine the number of large and small potatoes. However, Freemee provides no figures about the cause of death. Out of respect for the dead, they say.'

Eddie continues speaking, staring straight into the camera. 'I could understand that, but equally I saw it as a challenge. I wanted to know. It isn't so easy to get hold of that data, though. Luckily there are various innovative search engines like Wolfram Alpha and a whole load of open data projects – for official data that are available to all with no need to apply to a public agency.'

'Hmm, he's bitten off quite a lot there,' says Chander.

Cyn squints at the clock. Boarding is getting ever closer, but she can't tear herself away from the video. Chander seems mesmerized too.

'I wrote a search program and managed to gather sufficient information to get a good overview. Here are the results!'

At first Cyn can make out only a brightly coloured but unintelligible graph. She has no idea what Eddie's getting at.

'The number of unnatural forms of fatality didn't change significantly. So what do we learn from this?'

'That you have to examine them more closely,' whispers Chander.

A map of Europe and North America appears on the screen. On it are coloured patches ranging from yellow to dark red, as if the landmasses were flooded with lava.

'I carried out a search using additional criteria such as age, place of residence and so on. That's when things started to get interesting. For certain areas and groups, the number of suicides and accidents among Freemee users has risen noticeably over the past six months. Experts need to check this out!'

'Fuck!' Chander blurts out.

'I don't understand what he means.'

'Look at the graphs. This boy identified at least two groups of Freemee users with a significantly higher number of unnatural causes of death than among comparable non-users. One was in the San Francisco Bay Area, the other among German schoolkids, starting around seven months ago and rising to five to seven per cent above the average for the general population. You can't tell much from the overall number of casualties because plus and minus more or less cancel each other out. The same as in a bag of potatoes – it contains two kilos, regardless of whether they're big or small.'

Cyn glances at the nearest departures screen. 'Final call. We have to hurry!' Chander snaps the laptop shut and they run to their gate.

'It would appear that the number of cases of unnatural loss of life has regressed to the norm in the past couple of months. Something has changed. If his numbers are correct, that is,' Chander says quietly as they wait in line at the gate. 'I'd like to check them.'

'So his numbers can't be trusted?'

'You heard what he said at the end: he wanted to discuss his presentation with specialists. But he never got to do that.'

'Because he had an accident shortly after he tried to tell me about it.'

He gives her that look again.

Welcome to paranoia!

'I have to make a quick phone call,' she says.

'Me too,' says Chander.

Cyn hurriedly looks for Freemee's contact page on her smartphone. She dials the number, hoping that people in an ambitious start-up also work on Sunday mornings, and asks to speak to the Vice-President for Marketing and Communications, Will Dekkert. She explains who she is, and that she and Dekkert are scheduled to appear on a talk show together the following evening. She urgently needs to talk to him before her plane takes off. Right now. To her surprise the switchboard operator puts her through.

'The software flagged up this phone call?' asks Jonathan Stem. He plays back the conversation between Cynthia Bonsant and Will Dekkert.

'Yep. It contained some of the keywords we highlighted in the hunt for Zero,' Marten confirms, 'as well as the names of suspects or interested parties such as those people from the *Daily* in recent days.'

'You did the right thing by coming straight to me,' says Stem. His office is smaller than one might expect for a man in his position. The mahogany panelling looks classy, but it makes the room darker and more cramped. Two FBI agents Marten doesn't know have taken a seat beside him.

'What does our hunt for Zero have to do with Freemee?' asks Stem.

'Ours? Nothing. But maybe the *Daily*'s does.'

'I see. Their people should keep searching for Zero. You, on the other hand, must dig up any intelligence you can find on Cynthia Bonsant and Will Dekkert. You'll be answerable to Agent Dumbrost on your left: he's the team leader. Your two colleagues here and the rest of the team will check the contents of that phone call and either confirm or disprove it. Highest priority. Top secret. The team reports to me and only me. I want results before this woman touches down in New York, which means you have six hours, starting now.'

Marten is glad he doesn't have to grapple with the statistical stuff and only has to work on the two callers' backgrounds. A standard assignment. He didn't completely understand what the phone call was about. Dead people. But which deaths?

'OK, sir.'

Carl stares at Will for a few silent seconds.

'Interesting,' he says at last. 'Who have you told about this?'

'Only you,' says Will.

'And Alice?'

'No.'

'Any other members of staff?'

'No one.'

'This Bonsant is a desperate journalist whose best years are way behind her and who's in urgent need of a story. Don't talk to her again.'

'And if she digs in?'

'Put her off,' Carl snaps impatiently at him. 'Or trot out some PR bullshit about how we can make people's lives better but can't prevent death. Think something up. After all, that's your job.'

Will doesn't like the turn this conversation is taking.

'Did you change anything in the algorithms in the period mentioned?' he asks.

'We're constantly optimizing and expanding the algos, and you're fully aware of that.'

'So there's no way it can be connected?'

'Whose side are you on?' snorts Carl.

'Wow!' Will gasps.

'Freemee currently has one hundred and ninety-eight million enthusiastic users, and still rising steeply. We weren't able to support some of them with their problems quite as well as others over the past few months. They represent only a tiny fraction of the whole, but that mustn't prevent us from helping more and more people find happiness and success in their lives. The main thing is their future, not the past. That's what we have to focus on.'

Will clenches his jaw. He bites back a rejoinder.

Carl studies him with his inscrutable gaze. 'OK,' he says abruptly. He reaches for his glasses, which he removed at the start of their conversation. 'Kim, Jenna,' he says, giving the first names of their fellow board members. 'We have an important presentation this morning. Meeting in a half hour in the Bunker.'

NBC has splashed out on business class for Cyn. By the look of it, Chander can afford this luxury from his other sources of income, because there's no way the *Daily* paid for it.

'Nice to have you next to me,' Cyn says.

'I didn't want to miss out,' he says, putting his hand on her thigh.

She rests her head on his shoulder for a moment. 'This story is taking it out of me, Chander. I knew Eddie from way back, as a young boy . . . Forgive me if I'm not up to flirting.'

'I'll take your mind off it in New York,' he says with a laddish grin.

She has to smile, but her thoughts are still on the video. If Eddie's death really is linked to it, then there must be some truth to the story.

'So the series of fatalities began about seven months back and ended one or two months ago,' she recaps.

'Are you in paranoia land again?' asks Chander, stretching. 'You don't seriously believe that Freemee drove those people to an untimely end?'

'Not intentionally. Then again . . . Anyway, let's rule out such ideas from the start. Maybe it was some kind of digital accident. Immature crystal balls, improperly programmed ActApps, something like that. Big data's Chernobyl. It would be no surprise, given the way software is marketed nowadays – as a permanent beta version. We're no more than guinea pigs for developers.'

'The longer I think about it, the more sceptical I become,' Chander counters. 'The boy did some good research, but he didn't verify other potential causes of death – bad weather, long winters, cultural reasons, other causes of suicide or accidents.'

'You should still check the numbers.'

'I was hired to look for Zero. And besides, I can't concentrate very well with you around,' he teases her.

'If these numbers are correct, then they must be published!'

He sighs. 'Serious journalists like yourself need more. And anyway, who's interested in the internet as a topic? It's too abstract.'

'Hundreds of fatalities?'

'I'll bet you that even for the tabloids there's not enough meat on this bone. But then you know your colleagues better than I do.'

'You're right,' Cyn sighs. She takes his hand and strokes his long fingers. Suddenly she stops. In some hidden corner of her brain a memory awakens and takes shape as an idea. That paranoia again!

'Hey, who's in charge of all the statistics at Freemee?' she asks.

'Statisticians?' he says with a shrug. 'One of the most important jobs in a company like that.'

'One of Freemee's founders was a statistician. He died in an accident two months ago. Like Eddie,' she adds.

Chander pulls his hand away. 'For God's sake, Cyn! Not everything's connected!'

Doesn't he remember what happened to her only the day before yesterday in Vienna? Eddie's video scares her. The first thing she must do when she reaches New York is to ring Vi. *Vi!* Cyn thinks, panicking. *Is even she safe?*

'Bonsant is spooking the horses,' Henry remarks. 'From twenty per cent probability we're now at . . .?'

'We were at just under sixty,' Joaquim replies, 'shortly after Brickle's call to her. The opportunity in Vienna was convenient, which is why we didn't even attempt to speak to her. Unfortunately the freelancer we hired there at short notice was an incompetent jerk. We've now reached ninety per cent. We'll have to talk to her. We're unlikely to have a chance to enact the other option in the near future.'

'Carl's for forging ahead regardless, and will present the experiment and its results to his fellow board members today.'

'We will be paying them very special attention from now on,' says Joaquim. 'We're well prepared.'

They're sitting in Henry's office with its view of Central Park. It's drizzling outside. Raindrops trace lines on the windowpanes, and these lines converge to form small trickles. The upper floors of the tallest skyscrapers merge seamlessly into the unseasonal grey fog.

'Better than for Bonsant and Brickle, I hope. How did she get hold of the boy's information?'

'She had help from that Indian. He hacked into Brickle's hard drive and found the deleted folder.'

'Which hadn't been properly deleted. Sloppy work?'

Joaquim answers with a raised eyebrow. 'No.'

Henry has no choice but to believe him. He knows too little of the detail about these things, although he thinks he's heard that it's a simple task for a pro to delete something without a trace. Could such careless work have been intentional?

'What are we going to do about Bonsant? She can't be allowed to publish any of this. Even if the numbers are unsound, other people would start to drill down.'

'She lands in three hours. First she'll go to her hotel. And she'll want to get a statement from Will Dekkert, who'll refuse at first. As soon as the computer's available again, we'll delete the data for good, one hundred per cent, or else we'll steal it.'

'And then?'

'We've made plans to rub her out if she doesn't cooperate. Unlike in Vienna, we have a twelve-man team on standby. I hope we don't have to use it.'

'What do the crystal balls say?'

'It's highly likely that she'll meet Dekkert. Sadly the predictions of how he'll react after Montik's presentation are very imprecise. Freemee's analysis software can predict standard scenarios with great accuracy, but this is not a standard scenario. There's too little comparable statistical data available. The software does learn very quickly about an individual user's behaviour from what they're doing at a particular moment, but it doesn't produce findings until shortly afterwards.'

'Does that mean he might confirm all her assumptions and ultimately tell her even more? Do we want to let it get that far?'

'Dekkert's values pattern isn't equivocal. He's inclined to side with Freemee and his own financial interests, but he has other character traits that make him slightly unreliable. He'd probably be the best candidate to make her an offer.'

'If he's willing.'

'Carl also knows about the phone call. He'll talk to Dekkert. And of course from now on we'll always be nearby,' says Joaquim with a flicker of a smile to reassure Henry that the matter is in safe hands.

'I know you've got enough on your plate,' says Luís over the phone, 'but you've got to take a few minutes out for this. I think we've got a lead on Zero.'

Marten excuses himself from the colleagues with whom he's investigating the Bonsant–Dekkert case. A few minutes later he joins his staff two floors down, at the other end of the J. Edgar Hoover Building.

'We've received data from the two VPN providers in the US, and the NSA has assessed it. They've compared the IP addresses used to access the waterfalls with every person connected, however remotely, to this case. They came across an interesting link. Up until three years ago the waterfalls were visited from an IP address belonging to an internet café. That café is only two hundred yards from the then home of a woman who now works for Freemee.'

'Freemee again,' says Marten. 'It's an all-American company.'

'The woman's a US citizen too. So what?'

'We don't keep US citizens under surveillance,' Marten says drily.

They both laugh out loud.

'OK,' says Marten, when he's calmed down. 'Does the proximity of an internet café to the former residence of a US citizen employed by a successful start-up constitute sufficient grounds for suspicion?'

'We've run a background check. During her studies she focused on topics such as privacy and data protection – Zero's topics. Must have come in handy for her job at Freemee too.'

'Anything else?'

'She stopped using anonymous networks like TOR and VPN around three years ago.'

Marten arches his eyebrows. 'Now that's suspicious. I'll talk to Stem.'

'Why?' says Jon.

'Her online behaviour patterns changed suddenly about three years ago,' Marten explains. 'We assume she's been using separate devices since then – official ones that aren't anonymized and that we can therefore identify, and others she uses exclusively for anonymous communications.'

'Or else her circumstances have changed dramatically.'

'We've already checked that and they haven't, at least not at first sight. We're digging deeper. The change could be related to her becoming an activist back then. Incidentally the waterfalls went online shortly beforehand. Several elements fit together here.'

'But how do being an activist and working for a company like Freemee fit together? Anyone with even a passing interest in the company knows it has fingers in many pies too, even if slightly differently from the others.'

'Maybe for that very reason? Remember Edward Snowden. It's an even better fit if you consider her current position and look at what she seems to be in charge of right now.'

'Which is?'

'We have clear indications that Freemee boss Carl Montik is supporting the extremely prominent hunt for Zero organized by the *Daily*, a British newspaper. It can't be ruled out that for some reason Freemee cooked up this whole thing and maybe even financed it. We're investigating the cash flows right now. As Director of Communications, she would play a fairly major role in a campaign of this kind. If she's part of Zero, it makes sense, because then Freemee would be funding advertising for Zero.'

'Without realizing it, I presume.'

'Probably, but who knows?'

'OK,' says Jon. 'We'll apply for total surveillance. Trojans, phone-tap, bugs, tails, the whole caboodle.'

*

The Bunker is at the centre of the six-storey former soap factory into which Freemee moved only six months ago, but which the company has already outgrown. The walls are made of six-inch reinforced concrete with various weird and wonderful things built into them to make it impossible to eavesdrop from outside. All visitors to the Bunker must hand in their electronic devices before entering and then undergo a security check, including a body search.

Freemee's four board members – Carl, Kim Huang, Jenna Wojczewski and Will Dekkert – are the only people present.

Carl isn't partial to long preambles. 'OK, guys, I've got some good news and some bad news. I'll start with the good news. Almost ninety per cent of Freemee users are now following their ActApps' recommendations to increase the value of their data. To give you an example, there's a particular group of youngsters in every school – the influencers, the cool kids. Everyone wants to be part of this group. Thanks to our tools we know before they do which brands they're going to be wearing next. If someone wants to join the cool kids, an ActApp recommends that he or she dresses the same way – even before the cool kids show up at school in the same clothes.'

'So far, so familiar,' Jenna says. Will studies her. Has she lost weight? Her wrists and neck look unusually sinewy.

'So far, yes. A few months ago I took the liberty of initiating several experiments to optimize the program. For reasons that will soon become clear, I didn't inform anyone I'd done this. The results are so contentious that I'll only present them orally at first so as not to produce any superfluous documents.'

'Shit,' whispers Jenna.

It's also gradually dawning on Will what Carl's experiments might have involved.

'Aha,' says Carl, chuckling. 'I see from your faces that you can guess where this is leading. And you're right. I tested it on a small scale. Don't worry, the programmers I used don't know the purpose of the code conversions I instructed them to carry out.'

A horrible queasiness is brewing in Will's stomach.

'I included three million young people from several regions of the USA and Canada, Britain, Japan, Germany, France and Scandinavia in the program, all areas where we already have high numbers of users with very high-quality data. I used the example I mentioned before in the first trial: what happens if ActApps recommend brands to influencers and other youths who don't truly share their values? Would they buy those brands anyway, if they help them improve the value of their data? In short, I wanted to measure the influence of ActApps on these experimentees in situations where there was little or no apparent overlap between the individual's values and those of the brand. I therefore had programmers convert the algo codes accordingly. And what can I say? With the carrot of improving their data results dangling in front of their noses, the young people bought what the ActApps recommended.' He looks around proudly. 'Admittedly the whole set-up has its limitations. There must be a certain minimum overlap between the values of the person and those of the brand for them to go for it, but, depending on the individual, that intersection lies between twenty and thirty-five per cent.'

'Shit,' says Jenna. 'Does that mean teens will buy whatever the ActApps tell them to buy, whether they like it or not?'

'No,' Carl replies with a grin. 'The ActApps *tell* the youngsters *what* they like, and that's why they buy it.'

For a few seconds the room is completely silent. They first have to digest this news. Will's brain is working overtime. *Carl's manipulating people like puppets! If word of this gets out . . .*

'In the light of these positive results, I carried out further tests with a variety of products including various brands of shoes, sports goods, electronic appliances, games, study guides,' he continues. 'With a control group each time. The algos worked across the board.'

Shaking her head in disbelief, Jenna mutters, 'And people act contrary to their values because they want to improve their data results? How schizophrenic.'

Carl shrugs. 'No, they don't act contrary to them, they *change* them.'

'*You* change them.'

'I don't force anyone. That's just how people are. Every one of us changes our ideals over our lifetimes, some more so, some less. How often have you done things to score points with someone or to please them?'

Jenna nods reluctantly. *Carl got her there*, Will thinks.

'I tested it further and found out some amazing things. A change in an experimentee's ideals in one area often led to changes of behaviour in other areas I hadn't directly influenced. In a nutshell: we can make golfers out of skateboarders, thereby turning wannabe revolutionaries into perfect conformist sons-in-law – and vice versa. That even applies to people's political attitudes.'

Will groans.

'I can't believe it,' says Jenna.

'As I said, that's just how people are. You can calculate, predict and control virtually everything about them.'

'No, I can't believe you actually did this!'

'But the further development of the ActApps is a logical consequence of their design.'

'If anyone finds out about this, there'll be an outcry! Young people being used as guinea pigs!'

Once more, Carl laughs. 'I would of course have to test it on adults for verification.'

Will feels a stabbing pain shoot up his tense neck muscles to his head. He massages his temples. *Where does all of this lead?*

'What's wrong? This is no different than what advertising has been doing for decades – trying to influence our attitudes and our preferences. Major internet companies manipulate information by selecting what content they make available and how. That's how they influence people's behaviour. In my experiments, at least I got teens to use green products and buy organic food.'

And kill themselves, thinks Will. 'We influence people's actions far more directly through the ActApps,' he says.

'You could have run this past us in advance,' Kim accuses Carl.

'Could I?'

Kim says nothing. Will still holds back. Carl registers his silence, but makes no comment. 'Which brings us to the mayoral elections in Emmerstown,' he says instead.

'You didn't—' Jenna groans.

'I had to,' Carl says, grinning broadly. 'For Chrissake, why are you looking at me like that? Don't act as if you'd never thought about it. At the very least, in the past few minutes.'

'To be honest—' Jenna starts.

'See. Be glad I took these decisions out of your hands. You take care of the finances.' He notices that his fingers are drumming restlessly on the tabletop and presses his palms down flat on the surface. 'I take care of strategy and technology, and technology makes extraordinary things possible! Besides, big data and algorithms were the major factors in past election campaigns, only not many people realized. An algorithm doesn't stand outside your door prattling at you or press a leaflet into your hand in a shopping mall. It just tells the campaign manager where to send their flesh-and-blood election workers, and they can now do that down to the exact house number.

'Emmerstown was just the logical next step. A town of fifty thousand people in Massachusetts. The Democratic candidate had been mayor for the past eight years. The citizens were very satisfied with him. Half a year before the election, polls gave him a twenty-two-point lead over his Republican challenger and the two other candidates. I started to spin in the background six months ahead of the election.

'The conditions were tougher than in any of the other trials. I couldn't give our users any direct voting recommendations, because Freemee's bylaws state that we're apolitical. To keep it brief, just as I turned skateboarders into golfers, so I was able to turn the affiliation of Republicans, Democrats and the undecided by getting their ActApps to recommend products, brands and behaviour coinciding with the values of one of the independent candidates. Driven by a desire to increase their data scores, they followed their recommendations and began to alter their behaviour and opinions. What made it easier was that I didn't have to influence all voters. In this case I had to turn about thirty per cent of them, which is a lot. I could have gone easy on myself and simply turned Democrats into Republicans. That way I'd have needed only a twelve-percent swing. To everyone's surprise apart from mine, the alternative candidate won!' Carl laughs. 'I almost said *my* candidate.'

Will can hear the atoms buzzing around the Bunker. Carl has just been explaining that they're the new masters of the world.

'Was that the good or the bad news you mentioned at the start?' asks Jenna.

Everyone laughs. *As long as you can laugh,* Will thinks, *the situation isn't serious. Or a pessimist would say it's hopeless, but there aren't any pessimists in the room.*

'The bad news is quite simple, and it's for you,' Carl says, turning to Will.

'How do we sell this?' Will says, pre-empting Carl's explanation. 'It's going to be a tough nut to crack.'

'Exactly. It has huge potential. We can exert lasting influence over just about every area of people's lives – in the Western world at least. Not overnight, but all the more effectively for that.'

'With one crucial limitation,' Kim interjects. 'People mustn't find out about it. If the public finds out about that potential, our users will immediately lose trust and unsubscribe. It would mean the end of Freemee.'

'My calculations evaluate things a little differently,' Carl objects. 'People don't care, as long as they think the advantages outweigh the downsides. Have people stopped using Google, Facebook, Amazon, mobiles, credit, bank and loyalty cards, even though it must be obvious to everyone by now that they're all hoovering up data? In fact, it's the opposite: they have more clients than ever. It would be better, however, if people were kept in the dark. Anyway, our only possible clients are major corporations and large organizations with enough money to finance this kind of campaign. It goes without saying that we'll be able to charge them obscene amounts of money.'

Will can already see the figures spinning in Jenna's brain. 'That's a massive challenge,' he says.

'Maybe we should approach it from a completely different angle,' Kim suggests. 'I mean, what's the business model behind this?'

'I see what you're driving at,' says Carl. 'We can only influence and profit indirectly. We buy shares in a clothing brand and then push that brand. The shares go up. But of course it works both ways. Is that what you mean?'

'Something like that.'

'That's insider trading and it's illegal,' Jenna objects. 'They can lock you up for a very long time.'

'Oh dear, I hope nobody's going to take a closer look at the slide of two well-known consumer-goods brands I'll say no more about for the time being, or a few short positions that have earned someone I won't name a nine-figure profit.' He leans back smugly in his chair.

Without a word, Jenna lets her head sag forwards on to the tabletop.

'I have to agree with Jenna,' says Kim. 'That goes against Freemee's core values of transparency and autonomy. It'll damage the very heart of our brand. We shouldn't do this.'

Carl has such a fit of laughter he can barely utter his next words. 'Here we are, sitting in a bug-proof, windowless bunker, and he talks about transparency!' he snorts. He begins to gesticulate wildly. 'Transparency and autonomy, my ass! Where's the transparency at Freemee? Do the users know how the algorithms are written or how their results are calculated? They know nothing! And it doesn't interest them either – apart from a few serial bitchers – as long as it works!' He leaps to his feet and starts pacing around the table. 'And autonomy? In this interconnected world, having autonomy over your own life is an illusion! You can't enjoy the advantages of modern civilization without the other side of the coin, and that's us, the digital intermediaries and helmsmen!'

He adjusts an empty chair that's standing at a slant.

'Since as far back as 2007, machines have communicated with and via the internet more than humans. The digital world has penetrated every aspect of the real world – our phones and glasses, smartwatches and wearables, TVs, coffee machines and cars, our food, our clothes, floors, walls, water, air and our bodies. The digital world took over the real world long ago.'

He aligns two other chairs with the edge of the table.

'You can tell what happens to people outside this world by looking at any hillbilly or homeless person in the street. You're either in or out, on or off, one or zero. That's the essence of the digital world. There is no third option, and so it's also the essence of the entire world. There is no *a little bit*, no *maybe*, no *neither/nor*, no nuance.'

Two more chairs, and now all the empty chairs are evenly spaced and parallel to the table.

'Besides, that's the way most people organize their world: black–white, good–bad. As Jesus and President Bush both knew: "You're either with us, or against us." ' He waves his hand dismissively. 'So much for autonomy.'

Once he's seated again, Jenna cautiously asks, 'Have you finished venting your spleen, Professor? Good.'

Carl repeats his disparaging gesture.

'I think we should all let this sink in for a bit,' Jenna continues. 'It's too huge a subject to decide on here and now. Let's meet again tomorrow. That'll allow everyone to form an opinion between now and then.'

This restores Carl's good mood. 'Perfect!' he says, laughing. 'And by then we'll know who we're going to make the next president of the United States! And the future British prime minister and German chancellor while we're at it.'

'I'd like a word,' says Will, keeping Carl behind while Jenna and Kim leave the Bunker. 'Those mortality stats are correct, aren't they?'

Carl moves a chair a fraction of an inch. 'You'll have trouble proving any relation between Freemee and an individual death.'

'But the overall figures—'

'—aren't pretty of course, but there's no evidence.'

'But things would become a lot clearer if word gets out that you manipulated the algorithms.'

Carl stares at him. 'I didn't *manipulate* anything. All I did was adjust some of the settings. If word gets out, then we'll know who leaked it. One of us four.'

'How did the people die?' Will wants to know.

'For a variety of reasons,' Carl responds in the same tone of voice one might use when a recipe goes wrong. 'I was only able to analyse a few samples. Some users set the goals in their crystal balls too high, whereas ActApps overdid their tips for others, leading to over-confidence and reduced risk awareness and, in the second case, to frustration and even depression. With familiar consequences. In a few cases, there were false negatives and false positives, meaning wrong results from which the ActApps derived wrong recommendations. And some idiots thought they could feed the system false data and still use it. A classic case of "garbage in, garbage out" – fill the system with lousy data and you get lousy results. We probably exposed the largest group to exaggerated discrepancies in results. It was like prescribing schizophrenia to them. Most of those people just quit or switched to other ActApps. Only a handful couldn't deal with it.'

Although they're sitting in a secure bunker, Will quietly hisses, 'Quite a few handfuls, you mean! We're talking about hundreds of people!'

'Thousands, to be more precise. Your informer found only part of the data.'

'Thousands of people on Freemee's conscience.'

'No. Those people used Freemee and the ActApps of their own free will. They were the ones who drove their cars too fast or jumped off bridges; we neither had our foot on the pedal nor did we push them.'

'Why does the series of deaths come to a relatively abrupt end?'

'We tweaked the relevant parameters.'

'That's bureaucratic jargon.'

'Call it what you want. Language is your area of expertise.'

'How did you find out about the effect?'

Carl runs his tongue slowly over his lips as he stares at Will. 'Joszef drew my attention to it,' he answers. His lips stand out very red against the unchanging pallor of his face.

'Did he know about your experiments?'

'Not until then.'

'What did he say?'

'The same as you all. He was both revolted and fascinated by them. I think that's a normal reaction.'

'And then he died.'

'Goddammit!' Carl starts pacing around the table again, rearranging all the chairs as he goes. 'You don't get anywhere without experimenting! We'd still be living up in trees, hiding from lions and fighting hyenas for food if someone, some day, hadn't climbed back down again! Joszef and I were friends since university, and you know how few friends I have! You sit there whining as you pocket your seven-figure salaries, believing you're getting paid for your smart-ass ideas and your pretty faces! Well, fuck that! You have to dare and you have to get things done. An idea not put into practice is worthless! So is an ideal, come to think of it. You're accusing me? Look at yourself. You've organized a manhunt as a crappy promotional event! You think *that*'s OK? How else were we supposed to find out the limits of the ActApps? By testing them on fruit flies? You think I was glad when I discovered this?'

All the chairs are now standing to attention. 'I may not understand other people's feelings, but that doesn't mean I don't have any myself!'

He kicks one of the chairs violently, sending it flying into the wall. Will is startled. Carl pulls himself together, rights the chair and says, 'Sorry.' He places it back alongside the others and leans on it. Clings to it, Will notices.

'Do you grasp what we have our hands on here?' asks Carl. 'Tinkering with share prices or a mayoral election were necessary trial runs to probe the system's capacities and limits. Now we know they're almost limitless. We can make the world a better place! We're making people happier and more successful. We're helping them to live healthier lives, be greener and live with one another in peace.'

Or killing them.

'Inventors have been promising us the same thing about every new technological development for thousands of years,' Will reminds him. 'Anyway, who's *we*? *You* write the algorithms, or tell the programmers to. *You* help decide how the results are recorded, analysed and interpreted. And so *you* determine what health, happiness, success and peace mean – for hundreds of millions of people, perhaps billions soon. Without any oversight! Free will is turning into an illusion. *Your* algorithms are the new Ten Commandments, except no one knows they exist!'

'Will,' Carl sighs, his fingers scampering across the table-top, 'you don't have to prostrate yourself before me.'

'Don't get your hopes up,' Will says with a mirthless laugh.

'Somebody has always defined a society's values. Priests, philosophers, scientists, politicians, lawyers, bankers, businessmen.'

'But from past revolutions people have learned to define social values through inclusive debate. This is the Land of the Free, you may recall.'

'Don't be ridiculous! We've discussed freedom quite long enough for one day,' Carl hisses. 'Freemee does no more than replicate social dynamics and processes. How do we reach agreement on our common values? *This* is a new instrument for promoting your famous social dialogue. And a fairer one too, because practically everyone has access to it.'

'But its underlying rules were written by you, and no one but you knows what they are.'

'Yes, I wrote the algorithms. Or designed them at least. But I'm a product of my environment too and so it shapes them.'

'A wealthy, white, Western environment . . .'

'Which you're also part of, so be glad! The most successful, prosperous, healthy and happy society there has ever been!'

'A product of modern neo-liberalism, which sees everything as a commodity, even humans, a predictable part of the overall machine—'

'Are you turning all left-wing on me?' Carl says, his eyes wide and twinkling. 'Good heavens, Will, we aren't body-snatchers! We're not trying to produce soulless clones – quite the opposite! Freemee is here to help every individual achieve his or her full potential!'

'Says someone who acknowledges he has problems even understanding other people! I'm sorry to get personal, but it's pretty absurd that someone with psychological and social problems is writing the fundamental principles of human coexistence, don't you think?'

'Listening to you, I wonder if you're still committed to your job here. Make up your mind quickly because we've got a lot on our plate. You can earn more than you've ever dreamed, but if you don't want that, then I have to remind you of the strict non-disclosure agreement you signed.'

'You're not going to get rid of me that easily,' Will says, smiling.

'I knew it!' Carl pats him on the shoulder.

Will cannot recall Carl having ever made this jovial gesture before.

'Over a thousand,' Erben Pennicott repeats as he studies the printout. In line with protocol, Jon has given the data and captions codenames so unauthorized persons won't be able to interpret the figures and diagrams should the papers fall into the wrong hands.

He and Jonathan Stem are sitting in one of two rooms in the White House that various independent security firms sweep for bugs several times a day. They can talk here without any fear of eavesdroppers.

'They probably got the information from a boy they knew about,' explains Jon. 'He died in an accident a couple of days ago.'

'What a coincidence.'

'Probably not. We're still investigating it.' He adds, 'Our people have far more capabilities and data sources than an eighteen-year-old amateur does. The data and analysis were produced within two hours. You just have to be creative.'

'What do you make of the lists?'

'Our statisticians think the variations in unnatural deaths within specific groups diverge from the norm. The toughest task was defining the original groups. They're based less on classic social categories such as age, sex, sexual orientation, family status, place of residence or income than on clusters of values. That naturally makes it harder to figure out that there are concentrations in certain groups, since we don't know which values Freemee's algorithms assign to each individual. So far our analysis software has identified five, but there are probably more. Our people are working on it.'

'So these statistics show that for some reason the mortality rate was much higher in particular Freemee user groups.'

'Correct. We haven't yet found the cause.'

Erben wonders if Jon has grasped the full ramifications of these findings. 'There are likely to be several,' he says, thinking out loud. 'But Carl Montik will explain it to me in person. I assume our people can be trusted.'

'Of course.'

'Until further notice this matter is an absolute national priority and top secret. Under no circumstance must any of this go further than the team working on it or be leaked into the public domain. And that includes via the journalist, the Indian or anyone else.'

'Got it. By the way, we might have our first trail to Zero. Curiously enough, it also leads to Freemee.'

Jon gives Erben a quick summary. When he's gone, Erben uses the old-fashioned telephone on his desk to ring his secretary in the adjacent office. 'Book me a flight to New York, please.'

Next, he reaches for the secure mobile phone he always carries with him. It's been far too long since he last spoke to Henry Emerald.

They're still waiting to leave the aircraft when Cyn calls Vi. The sound of her daughter's voice dispels the accumulated tension of the past few hours.

'And you're sure Eddie didn't tell you what he wanted to talk to me about?' she asks loudly and clearly, just in case her mobile has been tapped.

'Nothing at all. I've told you that already,' Vi replies with a hint of irritation in her voice.

Did you lot hear that? Cyn thinks. *Paranoia.* To avoid worrying Vi any more, she changes the subject, chats a bit about her flight and then ends the call.

She's scared of the border controls. She can't guarantee she'll be able to hold it together if the Americans kick up the same stupid fuss as their British counterparts did yesterday. However, the immigration checks pass completely without incident. There's a man at the exit holding up a board with her name on it, as the TV channel had said there would be.

They get into the car. Half an hour later when Cyn catches sight of the Manhattan skyline for the first time, her smartwatch measures an acceleration in her pulse and increased perspiration. Can the device read her emotions too? Her excitement and joy? Her uncertainty and curiosity? How she would love Vi to be with her right now!

The Bedley Hotel, a functional seventies building that's been tarted up with a bit of modern design, is on the Lower East Side. At reception Cyn is presented with a welcome package from NBC containing all the necessary information and some thoughtful tips for shopping and going out. Her room is on the seventh floor, with a view of the courtyard, the backs of other buildings and a maze of fire escapes. Chander's booked his own room on the floor above. He's going to come down to meet her as soon as they've both freshened up.

Cyn puts her clothes away in the wardrobe and steps into the shower. As the water runs over her body, she still cannot shake the idea of Eddie's video from her mind. Still in her bathrobe, she saves the video from Eddie's laptop on to a memory stick and also records it on her own laptop. Using the latter, she then rigs up the secure VPN connection she must use to access her storage space on the *Daily*'s server. She enters her username and password, and backs up the video there as well. While it's uploading, she calls Jeff on his mobile.

'Where are you?' she asks.

'At the office.'

'On a Sunday evening?'

'Yeah. We're all doing round-the-clock weekend shifts because of the Anonymous attack. How about you? Already in New York?'

'I've just uploaded a video to my storage space,' she tells him. If someone's listening, there's nothing she can do about it. Never mind. Jeff has the video now too. 'I'll share it with you now. How do you do that again?'

He explains, and she follows his instructions.

'Can you have a look and tell me more about it? Maybe you can check the figures. It's from Eddie Brickle, the boy who was supposedly killed in an accident. But please treat it as confidential for the moment.'

'Consider it done. Bye!'

Next, she locks the memory stick in the safe in her room. She then rings Will Dekkert and is put through immediately. Dekkert asks politely how her journey went before asking, 'Do you have any plans for this evening? I'd like to meet you for dinner.'

This electrifies Cyn. Would Dekkert meet her if he wanted to rebut her questioning – and was easily able to? Thoughts ping around in her head. Is she going to be safe with him? She briefly considers inviting Chander along, but she'll obviously find out more one-on-one than if she comes accompanied.

'OK,' she says before she can have second thoughts. 'It's your town, so you tell me when and where.'

Quarter of an hour later Chander knocks on her door. 'Ready to head out?' he asks with a broad smile. 'Where do you want to go first? Times Square? Or Fifth Avenue?'

When Cyn tells him she has a dinner appointment with Will Dekkert, he puts on a hurt face but can easily understand why she'd prefer to meet the Freemee guy on her own.

'I can check the boy's data while you're out,' he suggests. 'Give me his laptop again.'

'Come in,' she says. She takes the memory stick on to which she's copied the video out of the safe and puts it in her handbag. She gives Chander the laptop and a kiss on the lips, then leaves.

She takes a cab to the appointed meeting place, peering out of the window on the way there at the skyscrapers, their tips out of sight. She feels a bit lost among the chasm-like streets. She's surprised to see a sign on the restaurant door forbidding data devices of any kind: smart glasses, smartwatches, sensors, smartphones.

She hands everything over to the young man in the coatroom, with the exception of her smartwatch. Worth a try. As she steps through the door into the dining room, the restaurant manager comes to meet her.

'I'm sorry, ma'am,' he says politely. 'You appear to have forgotten to hand in one of your devices.'

She acts all surprised and looks at her smartwatch. 'Oh dear! How did you notice?'

He points to the door frame. 'We have an inbuilt security gate, like the ones in airports.'

She takes her smartwatch back to the coatroom.

'Thank you, ma'am. You have a reservation?'

She gives Dekkert's name and glances around. The restaurant looks modern, chic and expensive. Half of the dinner guests could be models – well, for a mail-order catalogue at least. It's as if she's stepped into a time warp. No one here has a sensor or communication device on them – with the exception, perhaps, of a cutting-edge prototype, so small, invisible or unprecedented that it can be smuggled through the security gate without detection. She's learned from talking to Chander over the last few days that chips in stick-on tattoos are nothing new, though.

The restaurant manager leads her to the back of the premises, where the tables are further apart. She recognizes Will Dekkert sitting at one of the tables. He's smaller and slimmer than she expected, but he's pulsing with energy – or is it nervousness? – as he stands up and walks towards her.

'You've landed me in a bunch of trouble!' he says with the inimitable upbeat good humour with which only an American can turn an annoyance into a challenge. 'Please call me Will.'

'Cynthia. That's the first time I've ever seen one of those,' she says, pointing at the invisible gate behind her.

Will laughs. 'Most of the diners here work for some data collection company or other. You can't move in this city for surveillance cameras. Sometimes even we need a bit of peace and quiet.'

'Philistine,' Cyn teases him.

Next to the table a bottle cools in a bucket filled with ice cubes. A waiter serves them some sparkling wine. As they study the menu, Will kicks off the conversation with some harmless small talk about her journey and her first impressions of New York. Once they've ordered, however, he scrutinizes her more closely.

'Where did you get the figures you mentioned?' he exclaims.

'From a young man,' she replies. 'And a colleague explained them to me.' He doesn't need to know any more than that for now.

'Chander Argawal?' he asks, and before she can say anything, he adds, 'Naturally I read up on you.' Will takes a sip of his drink. 'May I ask you a question? Why don't you publish the figures? If they're correct you'd have a story that would blow the Washington-Kosak stuff and the hunt for Zero in Vienna out of the water.'

Why is he dithering like this? Cyn has the impression he wants to tell her something, but doesn't quite trust himself. She knows this feeling from some of her past interviews. She must give him time and then find his weak spot at the right moment.

'I'm no longer involved in the hunt for Zero,' she says to set things straight. 'And as for the figures, I need other people to check them. I would also like to give Freemee a chance to comment on them. As far as I can see, that's your responsibility.' She tries to meet Will's gaze. 'The question is whether you are going to tell me what you're *meant* to tell me or what you *want* to tell me.'

Will drains his glass and puts it down. He clasps his hands together in front of his mouth as if he were praying and trying to seal his lips with both index fingers at the same time. He shuts his eyes briefly then opens them again, takes his hands away from his face and lowers them slowly to the table, his fingers still interwoven. His knuckles are white.

'What would you do if the figures were correct?'

The clatter of crockery, the tinkle of cutlery, the clinking of glasses, the murmur of voices: so loud all of a sudden, so close.

Cyn expected to feel a sense of triumph – at her intuition, at having a major scoop – but she merely feels confused and so she keeps her guard up. The confession came so quickly.

'First of all, I'd want to know how it happened,' she says.

Will serves her and himself some more wine. He takes a deep breath, hesitates for a second and then launches into his tale. A tale of results set exaggeratedly high, over-ambitious ActApps and the ActApps' dubious analysis and recommendations. Until Joszef Abberidan showed up with the first statistics. After that, they changed the settings and the numbers fell.

'Abberidan,' she repeats. 'The man who died two months ago, shortly before the curve dipped again.'

'You're not thinking what I think you're thinking?'

'Just making a mental note.'

'Bravo!'

She can almost see his brain whirring in his skull.

'It was an accident,' Will explains. 'A car accident.'

'I know.'

'Joszef liked to drive too fast. It wasn't his first accident.'

She raises her eyebrows at this. She could choose to believe it, but she doesn't have to.

'The young man I got the data from also died in an accident,' she says. 'Two days ago. Just after he tried to tell me about this.'

'You can't be serious.'

'Yes, I am. He was a dear friend of mine.'

'I'm sorry to hear it,' Will replies, looking genuinely shocked – and slightly tipsy. 'But don't tell me you think there's a connection?'

Cyn doesn't tell him about the attack in the sewers of Vienna, for which she has no proof. Will would mark her down as paranoid if she did. 'I don't know,' she says instead.

The waiter brings their appetizers. Will orders another bottle of wine. She wonders if he always drinks this much.

'I've tried out a few ActApps,' she says. 'But I can't imagine they're really capable of driving people to the edge just by giving them a few tips.'

'The desire to improve your results can become an overwhelming urge. It stimulates your ambition and competitiveness. Some people have always lived very close to their limits and overstepped them in order to be somebody, to improve their image, their reputation, their qualifications . . . Our results are no more than a quantified illustration of those things. But we use other mechanisms too, and they tend to be more effective than the conventional tips.

'The principle of subconscious nudges, for instance. The idea came to prominence a few years ago. The best-known example is not really an appropriate subject for conversation over dinner.'

'I'm not squeamish,' Cyn answers. She points to her empty plate. 'Besides, I've finished my starter.'

'A few years ago they started to stick little pictures of flies in men's urinals. It reduced cleaning costs by an amazing eighty per cent, because men aim better.'

'Wow! So how does Freemee give these subconscious nudges?'

'In a thousand different ways. It starts with how the recommendations are formulated and ends with the different kinds of ActApps, their design and structure. To give you an example: you can tell people a hundred times how best to clean their teeth. It's more effective when we reward them for doing it properly. With Freemee it improves your results. All you need is an electric toothbrush connected to your account or you can install a sensor on your brush to do the same thing. People are even more driven by competition. Teeth-cleaning competitions.' He rolls his eyes. 'With your family or between friends. Also, of course, offer a glimpse of the future: you really want lots of gaps and rotten teeth? And so on. "Gamification" – incorporating elements of fun into activities. And of course we employ priming, framing and mere exposure, and either use heuristics or correct wrong or inappropriate ones; we eradicate cognitive illusions and base rate fallacy, anchor effects and so on; not to mention the entire psychological toolbox. It basically involves combining psychology, sociology and IT to automate thought and decision-making.' Will contemplates his wineglass, turning the stem in his fingers. 'Very, very effective,' he adds absently.

'A glimpse of the future . . . Don't the "crystal ball's" predictions take on new meaning the moment you hear them?' asks Cyn. She remembers how she reacted to Peggy's first forecast of her chances with Chander. 'Or even lose all their value? After all, we try to circumvent or prevent negative predictions from coming true.'

'Sure. It's a similar problem to the fact that people behave differently when they know they're being watched, as countless studies have demonstrated. If your home is equipped with a smart electricity meter, you save energy – not because you choose cheaper tariffs but because you know your supplier can check your electricity consumption at any time, and so you're much more conscious of how much you're using.'

'So the mere fact of keeping people under surveillance guarantees their subservience,' Cyn groans.

'That's right. The US should give Edward Snowden a medal rather than hunting him down,' Will jokes. 'Thanks to him we know that the NSA is monitoring each and every one of us. So every time we talk, the censor's scissors are snipping away in our heads.'

'Freemee is monitoring me as well.'

'No, Freemee works by people monitoring themselves. But the software generally takes account of those kinds of reactions and strategies,' Will retorts, 'and tailors its recommendations accordingly. It's not just that the apps can predict behaviour: they also predict the probability of being able to *influence* that behaviour.'

'Which means you know precisely whom you can manipulate with greater or lesser ease.'

'Whom, on which topics and at which moments. The programs know how to do that. It's very useful for marketing and also for elections. You can focus your energy and your budget on the people who are easiest to influence on a particular topic. That's how Barack Obama gained the decisive votes in the swing states to win a second term in office, for example.'

Cyn takes a long swig of wine to help her digest this information. 'So you admit to everything?' she asks. 'Why? It could spell the end of Freemee.'

'Not necessarily. After all, people still have their free will. They don't have to use Freemee and they don't have to follow the ActApps' recommendations. They were the ones who put themselves in harm's way and, in some cases, killed themselves.'

'That's what the arms and tobacco industries argue.'

Will throws up his arms in exasperation.

'So, again: why are you telling me all this? A guilty conscience? Trouble at work?'

'If anything, the former,' Will admits.

Cyn laughs. 'Or is it the wine?'

'It does help,' says Will.

The fact that Eddie was right makes Cyn feel somewhat crushed. Yet she feels the first stirrings of distrust and a spark of fear. Does she really want to know all these things? It's too late for softly-softly tactics, though. She requires proof.

'There's one thing I don't understand,' she says. 'Why are the deaths clustered in specific groups? I don't know anything about statistics, but if your explanation is correct, shouldn't they be spread equally across all Freemee users?'

Surprised, Will focuses fully on her again. 'I'm no statistician either,' he says, without taking his eyes off her.

Resting on her elbows, she leans across the table as far as she can. 'You have to talk about this,' she urges him quietly but insistently.

He continues to stare at her, as though he might find an answer in her face, then tosses back his wine, pours himself some more and empties his glass again.

'OK,' he says in a low voice.

Cyn has often experienced this same situation in inter-views. Will is on the point of making a confession. What else is he going to tell her? He's already owned up to every-thing. She mustn't rush him now.

'The fatalities were an accident too,' he says almost inau-dibly. And then Will explains, in a near whisper, about young people becoming skateboarders instead of golfers or the other way around, about mayoral elections and share prices and his recent conversation with Carl Montik, as the waiter clears their table and brings the main course and the next bottle of wine; then he takes her plate away again without her even noticing what she's eaten because she now realizes what happened to Adam and Eddie, and in the pit of her stomach she feels a mounting, barely controllable anxiety for Vi's well-being. When Will stops talking and the empty bottle is replaced by a third, the first thing Cyn does is draw a deep breath. For the second time in the space of a few days, she has the impression that a new age has just dawned. An irresistible trembling has taken hold of her. She presses the palms of her hands down on the table and tenses all her muscles to regain control of her body.

'This tool is powerful beyond our wildest dreams,' Will says gloomily.

'Our worst dreams . . .' She needs a good swig of wine now too. 'Why are you telling me all this?' she asks again.

He turns his wineglass in his fingers and contemplates the swirling liquid. 'I only found out today.'

So he says. Cyn is wary. 'How do I know you're not spin-ning me a line?'

He gives her a wry smile. 'Isn't it a paradox? We know more than ever about every single one of us, and yet less than ever about whom we can trust.'

'I need proof.'

'I don't have any. Not yet.'

'Can you get some? Are you *willing* to get some?'

Once more he raises his glass to his lips, but she puts her hand on his to stop him. Now she knows why he's been knocking it back all evening. The struggle between his corporate loyalty and his conscience is tearing him apart. *If* he's telling the truth.

Paranoia.

'Imagine there's an instrument that could make the world a better place,' says Will. 'Shouldn't we use it?'

'It depends on *who* wants to use it,' Cyn counters. 'Hitler? Pol Pot? Bin Laden? The Tea Party? Or just Carl Montik and Will Dekkert?'

'Thanks for the comparison.'

'You're welcome. Anyway, what does "better" mean? Freemee obviously has thousands of lives on its conscience. Do you want to carry on as before? Who says you're really going to make the world a "better" place, or if your better is the same as my "better"?' She takes a deep breath. 'I don't want Freemee, Google, Facebook and all the others to collect my data and, in return, generously offer me a few email services, maps, translations or friends. Or educate my kid. Educate millions of kids. I want to choose what I use and from whom. I—'

'Freemee doesn't steal. And as for the everything else, the users are to blame because they want everything for nothing. Development costs money, or alternatively that modern currency: data.'

'The result is there for all to see: data oligarchs, little better than the nineteenth-century robber barons. And we're at their mercy.'

'Nobody's forced to use the products.'

'Don't be ridiculous! Of course I am if I want to be part of modern life! You use Freemee too.'

'It wouldn't look good if the company's executives didn't use their own product.'

Cyn thinks for a moment. She needs to capture the high ground in this conversation. She still has one trump card left to play. 'Who actually guarantees that Carl Montik isn't manipulating you just like all the others?'

At first he just stares at her – *must be the wine*, she thinks; *he's had more than enough to drink* – then he laughs. 'That's a good one!'

His laughter doesn't sound genuine to Cyn's ear.

'I should rephrase my earlier question,' he says when he's regained his composure. 'If one views the deaths as unfortunate teething troubles that won't reoccur, what would Cynthia Bonsant do with an instrument like this?'

'How am I supposed to know? Look in my crystal ball,' she replies flippantly. 'Maybe I'd make the world a better place, as you suggested.' Now it's her turn to laugh. *How can she laugh at a time like this? It's the wine again.* 'And, at the same time make myself inordinately rich and powerful.'

'That's what's known as a win-win situation.'

'Except that I don't have that possibility,' she reminds him. 'You do.'

'And if you were offered that possibility?' asks Will.

She freezes.

'Is that why we're here? Are you supposed to make me an offer to keep my mouth shut?'

'Not really. Are you looking for one?'

Cyn knocks back the contents of her glass, playing for time. By the time she puts it down, she's made up her mind.

'What's driving her?'

Marten's standing close behind Luís, watching footage on his monitors from several CCTV cameras of passers-by walking through the Brooklyn evening.

'On her way home,' says Luís.

The two of them follow Alice Kinkaid along the busy street lined with bars and shops. The program that recognizes the woman by her gait and clothing switches automatically to the next camera. Alice disappears inside a 24-hour convenience store, and the software flips to the in-store cameras. Alice buys some drinks, snacks, bread and vegetables, pays and goes on her way.

'Why would she do this?' Marten wonders aloud. 'A clever, good-looking woman with a fine education and rosy career prospects.'

'Maybe for those very reasons,' says Luís.

Alice enters an apartment building and the view switches to the security cameras on the staircase. She takes the lift to the seventh floor.

'Chic,' says Luís.

'She can afford it,' Marten reckons.

Alice unlocks her apartment door, slips out of her shoes and carries her shopping into the kitchen.

'We have cameras in every room,' Luís explains. 'No blind spots.'

Fitting them was a piece of cake. Their men didn't even need to pretend to be electricians or plumbers. They simply waltzed in one day while Alice was at the office, worked without any interruption for an hour to install the devices and then left again. They made the most of the opportunity to sweep the apartment for any gadgets that Alice might be using for secret communications but found nothing.

Alice goes into the bathroom and begins to undress. Luís gives a low whistle.

'Behave yourself!' Marten orders, as Alice gets into the shower. They can see only her silhouette through the opaque plastic screen and hear the water running.

Luís reduces the image and drags it into the top left-hand corner of his screen.

'The programs will let us know as soon as she turns on an electronic device,' he says.

Carl knows that at least half his staff are still working on the floors below, even though it's almost 10 pm and Sunday to boot. He's ruminating over a few codes when his assistant rings through.

'There's someone from the FBI at the front desk who'd like to speak to you.'

Carl plays a picture from the CCTV camera in the lobby on his glasses. A stocky man in his mid-forties is waiting at the futuristic reception counter. Facial recognition confirms that the man is indeed a federal agent. Carl learns a lot about the man from the available data, but not what the man wants from him at this time of night. He asks for him to be shown up to his office.

He stands and waits for the agent. His assistant shows the plain-clothes police officer in and disappears again at a signal from her boss.

The man introduces himself and then says simply, 'I'm to give this to you.' With those words he hands Carl a smartphone.

Carl recognizes the secure official device. No sooner does he have it in his hand than it starts to vibrate.

'Take the call,' the FBI agent tells him.

He does as he's told. He's doesn't recognize the voice that speaks into his ear, but he does know the man.

'This is Erben Pennicott.'

Carl has met the chief of staff on a number of occasions, but only ever fleetingly. Their conversations were always superficial.

'I'd like to talk with you,' Pennicott explains.

It's taken you this long? Carl has been expecting this call for a while. The only thing that unnerves him is the timing, just as word of the experiment is threatening to get out. He acts naive. 'Sure. I'm very busy, but we—'

'Now. The man with the phone will bring you to me.'

Who does Pennicott think he is?

Carl's about to give a sharp retort, but Pennicott gets in first. 'It's about thousands of suspicious deaths among Freemee users.'

The FBI agent points to Carl's glasses, smartphone and smartwatch. 'You can leave those here.'

Carl feels a strong urge to argue about what he can and cannot do, but that would be wasting his intelligence on these people. The man isn't even on Freemee. So he does as he's bidden and follows the man out into the street.

A black limousine is double-parked in front of the Freemee building. The FBI agent opens the door for Carl. He slides into the back seat, while the other man takes the passenger seat.

'Where are we going?'

The man doesn't answer.

A few streets further on, they turn into an underground car park. On the third level below ground they park in a dimly lit space in a remote corner.

'Change of cars,' his companion explains.

There probably aren't any cameras down here, Carl thinks. Despite this strange manoeuvre, he isn't concerned that they might do something to him. They wouldn't go to such lengths if they were about to.

They switch to a beige car with tinted windows. The black limousine drives off through the dull light of the long subterranean car park. Two minutes later, the chauffeur of the new car drives them out on to the street. At the exit two cars are waiting ahead of them, and three other cars fall in behind them. Carl wonders if they're all part of this diversion tactic. For whose benefit? Anyone with an interest in the chief of staff's meetings.

His companions don't say a word during the drive from Brooklyn to Manhattan. They take the bridge. Carl doesn't look at the car headlights twinkling through the steel structure. He's coolly considering how Pennicott is going to handle this and how he should react. He's rehearsed this long-awaited conversation many times in his head. The fact that Pennicott knows about the experiment alters the starting position of course. There aren't so many possibilities.

The chauffeur drives them into the garage of the Ritz-Carlton. Carl presumes that the hotel also has a discreet area for VIPs, with no surveillance cameras, and is well versed in situations like this.

A lift takes him and the man with the phone up to the fortieth floor. The door slides noiselessly aside, revealing a lavishly furnished suite. The city skyline sparkles through the large windows. Facing them, Erben Pennicott sits on a voluptuous sofa, lit only by the subdued glow from two standard lamps. He's wearing slacks, a shirt with the top button undone and no tie.

At his side, as impeccably groomed and dressed as ever, sits Henry Emerald.

'It's very simple,' Henry begins. 'As you know, EmerSec has been a trustworthy partner of the US intelligence services for decades. When Erben contacted me today and suggested incorporating Freemee into the security architecture of the United States' – here he smiles – 'and of the Western world, I obviously regarded it as a great honour.'

Despite repeated invitations to take a seat in one of the velvet-upholstered armchairs, Carl remains standing. Having walked around the sofa, he is now behind the two men so they virtually have to crick their necks to look at him.

'This confirms just how seriously Freemee is already being taken,' Henry continues, managing to remain dignified even in this twisted sitting position. 'We are up there with the big boys.'

'We want to assign Freemee a special role,' Erben interjects, getting to his feet.

By now Carl is aware this involves more than the regular surveillance partnerships that other companies enter into, voluntarily or not, with the National Security Agency. Now they're in the game.

'What about the fatalities you mentioned?' he asks abrasively.

'Oh,' Erben says, dismissing the question. 'Let bygones be bygones. We want to talk about the future, and Freemee has a wonderful future ahead of it! Both of you will earn a lot of money – a ton of money. More than any person has ever earned before.'

Carl lets the chief of staff continue. Losing interest, he turns to face the panoramic windows and gazes out over the city. He can see Erben and Henry as dark silhouettes reflected in the glass.

'Henry here,' Erben says, gesturing towards the investor, 'confirmed what I'd guessed when I received the data.'

Erben gets up and walks around the end of the sofa. He's almost a head taller than Carl. He sits down nonchalantly on the back of the sofa, which brings him back to Carl's eye level.

'You've created an unbelievably powerful instrument,' he says with a nod of appreciation. 'Even more so if it continues to develop as successfully as it has until now. Four hundred million users by the end of the year, two billion in two years' time, according to the calculations. All very impressive!'

Carl stares at him.

'Henry and I both agree we can benefit from fabulous synergies between' – an expansive gesture with his right hand – 'the capacities of the state' – a gesture with his left hand – 'and Freemee's capabilities.' Stretching out his arms in the equivalent of an embrace, he brings his hands together as if to pray.

Henry nods in agreement.

'I don't know which capacities of the state you mean,' Carl replies coolly. 'If you mean you can read and listen in on every communication, then what's in it for you? Incidentally, we can do that too, the only difference being that people authorize us to do it; no, they explicitly ask us to do it! So they can know themselves better, receive better advice to live happier, more successful lives and, of course, increase the value of their data.'

'Our capacities to dig the dirt on bothersome individuals and neutralize them, for example,' says Erben. 'You are just as irritated by Zero's latest publications as we are.' He flashes Henry a meaningful glance. 'I'm also hearing, however, that our people are hot on Zero's scent. Curiously enough, it appears to lead to you.'

'To Freemee? That's absurd!'

'It has something to do with waterfalls—'

'Are you insinuating that I—?'

'God forbid, no! I'm not insinuating anything. It must be pure coincidence. I just mean to say that we too have our capabilities.'

'And now you want us to make you the next President of the United States,' Carl concludes. 'Isn't that right?'

Henry ends the ensuing momentary silence. 'Presidents have always been made, Carl. It's simply the means that change. It will be most advantageous for us to have a friend as president,' he points out.

'You're right.' Carl grins at Erben. 'Especially a president who's indebted to us.'

'You know, I think it's a win-win situation for us all,' Erben responds. 'And Freemee can carry on doing what it's already up to,' he adds, with a meaningful look.

'For all I care,' Carl says in a bored voice, 'there's a good chance the next president will be the last.'

Erben laughs indulgently. 'Maybe. Why elect another president, or any other politician for that matter, if in future we already know what people desire? Because a handful of people can channel that desire. And even if they can no longer cope – because the system has grown too complex – then everyone will know the people's ideals thanks to ManRank and other instruments like it. All that's needed is an administration that reads people's values and wishes on ManRank and then implements them. The administration will be made up of the people ManRank considers best suited to the task. The algorithms decide. The same is true of management in business, and ultimately in all jobs. And so forth. Man as a "thinking animal" will depose himself as "the crowning glory of creation". We will have to define anew what it means to be human.' He laughs. 'Or rather the programs will define it for us. Is that about it?'

'Something like that,' says Carl. He has to acknowledge that Pennicott is his equal. 'So why do you even want to be President?'

'Because I promised myself years ago that I would.'

'I see,' says Carl. 'Ticking off the list.' That, on the other hand, is pretty uninspiring. Maybe Pennicott isn't so good after all.

'And because we're not going to reach that point so quickly,' Erben adds, 'we'll elect a few more presidents in the traditional manner before we get there.'

'You've already informed your fellow board members, but you were intending to take some of your most trusted programmers into your confidence in the coming weeks,' Henry says, interrupting their dialogue. 'We'll use that opportunity to include a few of Erben's experts too so they can assist with developing the enhancements he'd like to see.'

'Assist, huh?' says Carl. 'And what are the new President's plans, if I may enquire? What are we to help him with? What values do you stand for?'

'What a question, especially coming from you,' Erben says with a chuckle. 'If anyone knew, it'd be you.'

'Touché,' says Carl, grinning. He pats himself down, as if searching for something. 'I can't ask it right now, unfortunately.'

'Sounds like he agreed,' Jon Stem observes in the adjoining suite, as the graphs show no asynchronous swings in Carl's voice analysis.

'Montik is a rational, calculating pragmatist,' says Joaquim Proust. 'Why would he ruin his life's work over such a trifle?'

'Because he lives by other values than Pennicott's?' Jon suggests.

'Of course you're right,' they hear Erben saying via the screen on which they're following events in the neighbouring room. 'It's all about results. It always is. And Freemee has demonstrated that better than anyone has ever done before. That's another great service they have provided to humankind.'

'He'll make a good president,' Joaquim notes. 'He really knows how to schmooze people!'

Joaquim shows Jon the pattern of values for both Erben and Carl. Erben may not be a Freemee user, but he's such a prominent public figure that Freemee's algorithms can draw up just as good a portrait of him.

'They look pretty similar. Both of their value clusters are grouped together in areas around recognition, vanity, self-assurance and the like,' Joaquim explains, as Erben offers Carl his hand on the other screen.

'I think we're going to get on well,' Erben says jovially as he and Carl shake hands.

A satisfied expression on his face, Henry Emerald joins them and places his hand on top of those of the two younger men. *His black suit makes him look like a vicar uniting a young couple for life*, Joaquim thinks.

When she gets back to the hotel, Cyn rings Chander and invites him round. Two minutes later he's there. She pulls him into her room and although he tries to throw his arms around her, she takes off his glasses, stretches out her hand and says, 'Give me your smartphone.'

Disconcerted, he hands her his devices, and she puts both hers and his under the duvet before dragging him into the bathroom.

'Aha,' he coos. 'A shower together?'

'Not now,' she says, turning on the tap and speaking under the cover of the running water.

When she's finished, she asks him, 'Can you check Dekkert's claims?'

Chander shakes his head. 'I can't verify that from publicly available data, especially as I don't know exactly what I'm looking for. Your information's far too imprecise. You'd find the material on Freemee, but only behind the paywall. You'd have to spend enormous amounts to gather the right data, and even then you'd have to know exactly what you were looking for. Drawing up the mortality rates was relatively simple in comparison. And even if you found the right stats,' he goes on, 'they wouldn't prove anything. Even if you could demonstrate the change in the algorithms, it remains normal behaviour for people acting on the recommendations of their ActApps. Which, incidentally, it is. Those people genuinely weren't compelled to do anything. To prove the changed behaviour of different groups you'd need access to the algorithms – the usual ones and the modified ones. Can we please turn that off?' he asks, pointing to the tap.

'Not while we're talking about this.'

'Then let's stop talking,' he says, grinning and slipping his hand under her blouse.

'No manipulation? Is that how you see it?'

'Differing treatment, no more,' he says with a shrug. 'Individualized. It's very common. Even a mother doesn't treat her children the same. She can't.'

'But the algorithms are meant to do just that!'

'Quite the opposite. They're meant to adapt to each of us individually.'

'But neither are they meant simply to reflect Carl Montik's ideas alone!'

'Why did Dekkert even tell you these stories if he can't back them up with evidence? Does he want you to publish them?'

'Without any proof I'd make myself a laughing stock – you said that yourself. Plus, I'd land myself in the most expensive libel case in history.'

'More than likely. Maybe that was the whole purpose of your meeting.'

'You mean . . . Dekkert made up those stories?'

'Welcome to paranoia!' Chander laughs. 'That's becoming our motto.'

'He confirmed the mortality rates. He even claims there were many others.'

'Any evidence?'

'No chance,' she has to admit. 'But then why did he—' She breaks off.

'Did he . . .?'

'Make me an offer,' she confesses hesitantly.

'An offer for what?'

'To join Freemee. We're meant to discuss it tomorrow at Freemee's offices.'

'Another feint?' Chander gives a wry smile. 'To see if you can be bought? If you accept, you'll destroy all your credibility should you ever publish anything negative about Freemee in the future.'

'Welcome to paranoia,' Cyn mutters under her breath.

'Don't get me wrong,' he says. 'I believe you. I just wonder about Will Dekkert's motives and objectives.'

'Me too.'

'And what about me? I also know about the deaths. Am I going to get an offer too? Or are you negotiating on my behalf and we'll get rich together?'

'You're coming with me.'

'If the offer's good enough, you might not get any more stupid ideas,' he says. His fingers are trying their luck again. 'Dekkert isn't wrong. Freemee can be used to encourage people to do a lot of good.'

'Probably true,' she counters. 'But a lot of bad too.'

'Why would anyone want to?' He takes her by the waist, pulls her towards him and gazes pensively at her. 'If what you heard is true – and I don't want to rule it out, because Freemee probably does offer such possibilities – then this is too big for you. Several sizes too big. Too big for any of us. We might just have glimpsed the future, and anyone who stands in its way is bound to lose out.'

'Like Eddie? Or Joszef Abberidan? Or like me, almost, in Vienna?'

'Welcome to—'

'Oh, stop it!'

Telling Chander everything has released some of her tension. The alcohol can now release its beneficial effects. She's dog-tired and can't think straight. She allows him to lead her out of the bathroom into her room and over to the bed. She lets him kiss her; it allows her to relax, which is exactly what she needs right now. She returns his kiss.

Teldif: Advisory platforms already exist in China too. Self-help, programmed on behalf of the Chinese Central Politburo!^

ArchieT: And here? Henry Emerald has shares in Freemee. EmerSec has been a major part of the military-industrial complex for decades.

Submarine: Think of Edward Snowden. He also got his info while working for a private company.

xxxhb67: The military-industrial complex has long since morphed into the military-information complex.

ArchieT: Has been since the ARPANET.

Submarine: So the Politburo programs the advice in China, the Kremlin in Russia and here it's the . . .

Snowman: Complexists.

Monday

Will's first move the next morning is to go to Carl's office. His boss is staring through his glasses at a tablet computer on his table. Will regularly works on two devices at a time now too.

'How was your dinner with Ms Bonsant?' Carl asks, glancing quickly up at him. 'You've got bags under your eyes.'

'Charming.'

'My great strength, as you know.'

'She's coming here at noon. With her colleague Argawal.'

'I saw it on the calendar.'

'Bunker,' Will says to Carl.

Carl's eyebrows twitch, but he stops working. They put down their devices at the entrance to the Bunker, as house rules require. They step inside the windowless room and close the door.

Will lets a few seconds pass before asking, 'What about me?' They stare and size each other up. 'Did you "adjust" my results too?'

'Will, Will, Will.' Carl smiles and shakes his head. 'Still got too much residual alcohol in your bloodstream? As you said yourself, I wrote the fundamentals for the algos you've long since adapted your behaviour to. What difference do gradual changes make?'

'Yesterday we stood almost on the edge of the cliff. Now we're a step closer. Due to that difference.'

'How funny! Remember, we improve the algos all the time.'

'*You* improve them. And they probably improve themselves by now too. I want to know if I'm a guinea pig. If you breed obedient board members.'

Carl looks him in the eye. 'No.'

'How can I be sure of that?'

'If you could read them, I'd give you the standard algorithms and the protocol of your data account to compare.'

'They're no use to me, as you know.'

'I can't help that you're all digitally illiterate. Well, you'll just have to trust me then.'

'How can I after what you told us?'

'For that very reason – *because* I told you. Instead of keeping it secret, re-programming you, forcing you out of the company and taking over the world.' That laugh again. 'I think you overestimate Freemee. This isn't some James Bond film with a supervillain. We have competitors working on similar models: the old major players have developed their first rival products. There's emerging competition between different systems, just as there should be in a free society.'

'The same competition as with operating systems, search engines and online traders? There's no genuine competition anywhere, just virtual monopolies.'

'Oh, come off it! Microsoft is a moribund giant, former superstars such as AOL and MySpace were toast within a few years, Facebook and Apple are already dinosaurs, and as for Google . . .'

'Are you trying to tell me you only give Freemee a few years?'

'I'm trying to tell you we are not going to be living in the kind of nightmarish future dictatorship under *Máximo Líder* Carl Montik you're imagining.' He laughs, and his face once more reverts to an emotionless mask Will is incapable of reading. 'I just want to offer people an amazing, life-enhancing tool! Are you on board?'

Who could say no to that?

'We'll put the same question to Ms Bonsant later,' Carl says. 'Even though her crystal ball suggests there's currently only an eighteen-point-six per cent chance that she'll say yes.' He stands up and fussily returns his chair to its former position. 'Oh, by the way,' he says as Will too gets to his feet and makes to leave the Bunker, 'maybe you should bring in some backup regarding marketing ideas, and let Alice Kinkaid in on our plans. She has to find out sooner or later.'

Marten and Luís watch Alice enter Freemee's headquarters. She's wearing a pair of beige trousers with a blazer and carrying a large handbag. A second window shows the view through her glasses.

'We're inside her smartphone, her glasses and her smartwatch,' says Luís.

'And her handbag?' Marten asks.

'As soon as she looks inside through her glasses,' says Luís.

They follow Alice's progress to her office via her glasses. On her way there she greets a few colleagues, occasionally stopping to exchange a few words.

'A very communicative lady,' Luís remarks.

'She *is* Director of Communications,' Marten mutters. 'I'd rather she made contact with her Zero mates instead of chattering to everyone.' His eyes feel as if someone's thrown sand in them, a long weekend at the office having taken its toll.

Alice has barely sat down at her desk when Will Dekkert calls her via her glasses.

'There's an urgent matter we have to discuss,' he says. 'When do you have time?'

Alice looks at her diary.

'I have meetings until twelve,' she says.

'OK,' says Will. 'Twelve. In the Bunker.'

Cyn and Chander are met by a wall of incipient New York summer heat as they step outside the hotel. Fortunately Will has sent a car for them. The driver ferries them through the streets, the car's interior chilled to frosty autumn temperatures while the air outside shimmers.

'Electric,' the chauffeur says in answer to her question.

Then she notices his hands aren't even on the steering wheel!

'It's a self-drive car,' he explains. 'A new prototype. Free-mee has a few in its fleet for testing. For now there's got to be someone at the wheel, for the insurance, but some day these goddam things are going to put me out of a job.' He points at the hordes of yellow cabs dominating the traffic. 'Those guys too.'

As so often in the past few days, Cyn feels as though she's been parachuted into one of those sci-fi films where the hero wakes after a long sleep to find him- or herself in an alien future. But in this case the future is already the present.

They drive east along the southern outskirts of China-town and on to the Brooklyn Bridge. Off to her right Cyn spots the Statue of Liberty, which she didn't see yesterday. What would Lady Liberty say to Freemee's business if she could speak?

Freemee is headquartered in what looks like a converted industrial building. Now the online firm's logo rides high over the entrance. A young man greets them and escorts them to one of the upper floors. A security guard awaits them outside the door of a conference room. He asks them for their tech appliances. Cyn reluctantly hands over her glasses, smartphone and watch. Chander surprisingly has two phones.

She notices that the meeting room has no windows.

'Secure,' he says in a whisper.

They don't need to wait for long. They have yet to sit down when Will and Carl Montik enter. They all introduce themselves, swap a few cordial remarks and the guests are offered something to drink.

Something about Carl Montik bothers Cyn. It's his eyes.

'You have to understand what Freemee is capable of,' Montik says, coming straight to the point. 'Our offer: you will each receive Freemee shares currently valued at thirty million dollars. Expected value a year from now: seventy million. Two years from now: one hundred and twenty. A conservative estimate. In exchange you will promise to keep absolutely silent about your findings.'

His directness surprises Cyn and impresses her at the same time. But she's not going to fall into his trap.

'I do indeed understand what Freemee is capable of,' she retorts. 'Driving people to their deaths.'

The corners of Carl's mouth twitch, as though a wasp has stung him.

'Teething problems,' he reluctantly replies. His hands are flat on the table, but his fingertips begin to tap nervously. 'Why are you being so negative? We've had that under control for ages. As you appear to know your statistics, you will also know that the mortality rate in other groups fell and is now down across the board. Freemee is good for people.'

'You want to make the world a better place with Freemee?'

'You think that's a bad thing?'

'If you're seeking to decide on your own what is good and what isn't—'

'Oh, please don't start that debate all over again,' Carl groans. 'What do you think I should do then?'

'Your tongue betrays you,' Cyn says snidely. ' "I." "What should *I* do?" See, you don't even include your co-founders and fellow board members, let alone Freemee users.'

Carl laughs heartily. He seems genuinely amused.

'You're creating a dictatorship,' she accuses him. 'Go ahead and laugh. I know it's a popular pastime, philosophizing about the post-democratic age. Quite a number of idiots are yearning for the return of strongmen.'

Her eyes flit briefly to Chander, who's completely detached from the conversation. *Why on earth did she bring him along? He's not being supportive in any way.* 'It's interesting, by the way, that people always talk about strongmen in this context. Whoever it may be, there's no such thing as a "good" dictatorship. The position of a dictator is always dangerous *per se*, no matter how good the person who occupies it. And in your case I'm not even sure that you're good.'

Carl is following her arguments with growing impatience, his hands lining up invisible objects on the empty table. 'You could be our Ethics Commissioner,' he blurts out, 'if you want a job to go with the money.' He turns to Will. 'Or do we have someone already?'

'Not directly,' says Will.

'So we need one! Would you like to be our Ethics Commissioner?' Carl asks, more and more excited by his own idea. 'An executive position. A board member, if you insist,' he adds when she doesn't respond. 'Vice-President for Ethics! Fantastic! Get involved instead of simply criticizing. We're offering you the chance to improve Freemee in the ways you think best!'

Cyn is caught off guard. Does he really mean this?

'You'll need a new job anyhow,' he says. 'Zero will soon be ancient history.'

This thought shocks her. 'Where did you hear that?'

'From the people who've practically caught him.'

Is this possible? She feels an urge to warn Zero. But she can't do that without the Raspberry Pi, and she doesn't want to get Vi caught up in this.

'So who is it?' she replies.

'You'll find out soon enough,' he says wearily and changes the subject. 'You see, we know some things went wrong in the past. But you also know we took corrective action immediately we found out. Our highest priority is to offer our users the best possible product.' He tries to put on a friendly expression. 'You're punchy, you're dogged and assertive, and that's why you're here today. We need people like you to improve Freemee and the lives of hundreds of millions of people around the world. Who knows, some day it could be billions! Actively help us to make the world a better place. That's what you want, isn't it? So why not with us?'

Cyn can sense he's pushed the right button for her. Her outrage at their attempts to bribe her is abating, and she's starting to consider how Freemee should change to live up to her standards.

'I'm still wondering whether the whole idea behind the software isn't perverse.' She casts her mind back to Vi, who's changed so much for the better. *Was it for the better?*

Her head says yes. But is that because she finds it easier to get on with Vi? *No, because Vi will have an easier life*, she tells herself. Vi has repeatedly stressed that she never felt any compulsion to change. But did she really do it of her own accord? Can Cyn be sure Vi wasn't forced into those changes? Manipulated? Her gut tells her there's something fishy about the whole thing, and she can generally trust her gut instinct, even though it keeps getting her into trouble.

'Have you manipulated my daughter?' she asks.

Disconcerted, Carl looks at her, then at Will, then back at her, before answering, 'Manipulated? No.'

Cyn uncertainly seeks Chander's gaze, then Will's, but neither of them reacts.

'Do you want more money?' asks Carl. 'Is that it?'

'Now, that would be a start,' Chander intervenes for the first time. 'Freemee's estimated to be worth a hundred million dollars already. Compared to that, thirty million is peanuts, not to say an insult.'

Carl stares at him for a second, then roars, 'Peanuts? For doing nothing? Are you out of your mind?'

Will clears his throat. Carl understands this signal and continues in more measured terms. 'These are reasonable sums. Think it over.' And with that he stands up.

Was that it? Cyn wonders, as Carl heads for the door. *The man will never make a diplomat.*

'Tonight, your Vice-President for Strategy and Communications and I are appearing on a talk show watched by several million viewers,' she says to no one in particular.

This gives Carl pause for thought. 'Television,' he says contemptuously, turning to face her. 'And what are you going to tell them? Something about statistics that no one will understand and which proves nothing? To an audience where half are convinced that Freemee is good and don't want to see someone running down their daily little helper? Will here will do what it takes. He's a brilliant salesman.'

'I could sow the seeds of doubt,' she counters.

'Why would you do that? You might deprive humanity of an amazing means of improving people's lives and tackling global problems in a lasting way. You wouldn't want that, would you?'

Cyn has no patience with this line of argument any longer, not least because she can't think of any other counter-arguments than the ones she's already used. 'You keep banging on about the same point: Freemee makes you more successful and happier. Why worry that they can control your life? So what if the state has its eye on you around the clock? In return it keeps you safe – at least until the next terror attack, which unfortunately it couldn't, or wouldn't, prevent.'

'Well, perhaps all these values you condemn and dismiss – success, happiness, security – are more important to ordinary people than the ones you highlight? Why shouldn't people decide for themselves?'

'Because in this case they don't decide for themselves!' Cyn is at the end of her tether. 'That's what I've been saying all along! They're manipulated, cheated and lied to by data oligarchs like you. You talk about freedom and a better world and yet all you're interested in is money! I'm just a share price to you. The billions of people gazing at their computers, tablets, smartphones and glasses all day are not actually your users – you're using them! They're your eyes on this monster, your remote controls for the billions of cells of the gigantic machine that's raking in cash for you!'

'Wow! That's a tirade straight out of Zero's playbook.'

'People's receptiveness to your arguments is a sign of how brainwashed they are!'

'Objection. People use products that make their lives easier. I'm not holding a pistol to anyone's head and ordering them to use Freemee. Neither are Google, Apple, Facebook, Amazon or the others. That isn't brainwashing. Don't you have a washing machine and a toilet at home? Do you still send news by snail mail? This is no different: it's called progress.'

Cyn realizes she's stumbled into the very same trap as during her discussions with Vi. The ageing mother who can't come to terms with the present: Plato complaining about writing for fear it'll lead to the death of thought. When did she lose her concentration?

'But it's up to you to shape this progress to your taste,' Carl says in a conciliatory voice. 'As Freemee's Vice-President for Ethics.' He opens the door. 'Our offer is on the table. Clearly you need to think it over. Let's meet again tomorrow.'

As he leaves the room, Carl takes back his glasses and smartphone. He wasn't required to hand over the lens in his eye, because it's of no use without a smartphone as its base station. However, he does slip the security guard the tiny recorder he was carrying. It immediately sends the voice file via a secure connection to a pre-programmed address.

Joaquim Proust is sitting in a booth equipped with various machines. He runs the data through speech analysis software. He'll have to wait a few minutes for the results. Too bad the Bunker was designed to be absolutely secure from eavesdroppers, so the programs couldn't carry out real-time analysis. He'd love to skim through the conversation right now to find out how it went and what the results are.

What he does receive now are live pictures from Carl's glasses as he and the Indian lag slightly behind Cynthia

Bonsant and Will. The two of them occupy all his attention.

'I for one am not going to be fobbed off with thirty million,' he hears Chander Argawal whisper to Carl. As if on some secret signal, Carl now turns his head so Joaquim can also get a good view of Chander's face through the glasses. 'And just in case you get any funny ideas, I've stored copies of the boy's video in secure places. If anything were to happen to me, they'll be published. You'd be finished.'

The voice analysis on Joaquim's screen shows the Indian's bluffing. *Feeble, Mr Argawal.*

'What is this bullshit?' Carl asks testily.

'Must I make myself even clearer?' Chander responds.

This Indian's never going to be satisfied, Joaquim thinks. *It's pointless negotiating with him. We need to find a solution for him – a permanent solution. Right now, before he can act on his empty threat.*

Joaquim would dearly like to know what Cynthia Bonsant and Will Dekkert are discussing, but Carl and Chander are too far behind them, and Will doesn't have his glasses on.

'Why didn't we talk about last night's conversa—' Cyn begins, but Will cuts her off.

'Because that wasn't today's topic.'

'Of course it was. Manip—'

'As we said,' he interrupts her again, 'think it over.'

'Does he really believe that with this offer he can b—'

'Carl has made you a serious proposition because he values your opinion,' he cuts in. 'We're already into the lead-management phase. So far only board members have been informed of the experiment, but I've now been asked to bring our Director of Communications into the loop.'

'Carl can give me jobs and take them away as he pleases? I'll tell you something: I've known for a while that Freemee wanted me on board for this hunt for Zero, and that's why you funded advertising in the *Daily*.'

'Who told you such nonsense?'

'Carl isn't the only one with sources. But I still don't understand: why me?'

Will walks alongside her in silence for a few seconds. 'Not even your editor-in-chief knows that Freemee's behind it,' Will says, more to himself. 'No one but a handful of people in this company do.'

'Who came up with the idea of the hunt for Zero, anyway?'

'Our Director of Communications, Alice Kinkaid.'

'Who you're supposed to bring in on the secret? Hmm. But why did I of all people need to be involved in the hunt?'

'A program selected you,' Will admits, 'according to a whole range of criteria.'

'*Me?* Don't be daft. Which program? Who wrote it and who defined the search criteria?'

'Carl,' he replies after a short pause.

She bursts out laughing. 'See what I mean?'

'I honestly have no idea,' he insists, but then falls to pondering again. 'I have to know who gave you that information.'

Cyn still doesn't know if she can trust him. Her brain is working overtime.

'Sorry,' she says.

Joaquim observes the little group with the utmost concentration as they walk along the hallway from the Bunker. Carl and the Indian have just caught up with Dekkert and the British lady.

'Give Carl's offer some thought,' Will says to her.

'Maybe I will,' Cynthia Bonsant replies.

Joaquim notes that there's something she isn't saying, but unfortunately he can't tell what it is. Neither does he know if she's decided to accept or turn down Carl's offer.

'Well?' Carl asks jovially from behind her. 'How do you plan to while away the hours until the talk show? A little shopping spree? That's something you'd certainly be able to afford in the future.'

Cyn glances at Will, but he doesn't react. They've reached the lobby.

'So we'll see each other this evening,' he says as they part.

'And we'll see each other tomorrow,' Carl adds.

'Hmm, we'll see about that,' Joaquim mutters.

'I don't get it!' Cyn rages as soon as they've left the building.

'That they're offering so little money?' asks Chander. 'It's insulting!'

The Freemee chauffeur opens the door of the self-driving limousine for them. Cyn declines his invitation.

'No thanks, we'll take a taxi.'

'What's up with you?' Chander says.

'They can't buy me,' she tells him, trying to hail one of the passing yellow cabs, but none stops. She continues walking and trying to flag one down. The heat is making beads of sweat stand out on her brow. Someone barges into her. She spins around angrily, but the man is already a good distance further on.

'Let's take the limo after all,' Chander urges her.

'Do you mean you want to accept?' she asks furiously.

'In any case it'd be more comfortable than walking in this heat.'

She keeps hailing taxis but now, with growing irritation, starts to look around. 'Where's the nearest subway station to here?'

'Let's. Take. The. Limo.'

'Take those things off now!' Before he can stop her, she removes his glasses. 'Put them away where they can't see or hear anything. I need to have a serious talk with you.'

Five hundred yards from the Freemee building, Joaquim's screen suddenly goes dark and the stream of sound from Chander's glasses falls silent.

He switches to one of the many surveillance cameras outside nearby stores that are live-streaming the view from their doors online. He can make out Chander and Cyn on two of the streams. Cyn is talking agitatedly to Chander while pulling her hand from his bag, where she must have stowed his glasses. *Damn*. The picture quality is too poor for lip-reading software to do its job.

'What do you mean you don't know?' she asks.

'Freemee are offering us a hell of a lot of money. We should at least give it some thought.'

'Money isn't everything.'

'But nor is it nothing. Just think what you could do with a sum of that size. Also, they'd have to offer us even more in future to keep us quiet,' Chander continues.

'You must be kidding,' she says, staring at him in disgust. 'You want to blackmail them?'

'No, I want to negotiate, and it doesn't only have to be about money. As Vice-President for Ethics you'd be in a position to push your interests.'

'Using those sorts of methods? Great!' She shakes her head. *It's too hot here.* 'Let's talk about it again later,' she says when a yellow cab stops at long last. She jumps inside and Chander slides on to the backseat next to her. She gives the driver their hotel address.

'What are they doing now?' asks Marten. He's watching events unfold from Alice Kinkaid's perspective on Luís's screen. He sees Will Dekkert remove his glasses and takes his smartphone from his trouser pocket before the picture becomes so blurred it's impossible to discern anything.

'They're going into the so-called Bunker, Freemee's secure room,' says Luís. 'This morning, that's where they agreed to meet.'

The screen goes dark, and Marten hears more muffled scraps of conversation, clinking and a roaring sound as someone obviously stores the devices somewhere.

'Maybe he'll finally tell her something she can immediately pass on to her Zero colleagues,' says Luís. 'You said he'd do that.'

'Where is it?' Cyn cries, staring at Eddie's laptop screen. She feels as though all the blood is draining out of her body. 'It was still there yesterday evening!'

'Are you sure you backed up the video properly?'

'Do you take me for an idiot?'

She rushes over to the safe and finds the memory stick she locked inside it the previous evening. She's about to push it into the laptop, but then asks Chander, 'Can a computer wipe a stick the moment you push it in?'

'You can in theory set it up to do that. Should I take a peek?'

'Please do!'

He sits down at the keyboard to explore the unfathomable depths of the hard drive. After a few minutes he tells her, 'Nothing there.'

'What about the video? You were able to claw it back before we boarded our flight.'

'They were more thorough this time.'

'Who are *they*?'

'Who do you think?'

'Damn! They broke in, didn't they? And I'm supposed to do business with these people?'

She clenches her fingers around the stick. 'I have to make a call,' she says, shooting him a glance that says she wants to be alone.

'I'll wait for you in my room. I desperately need a shower after chasing taxis as it is.'

'I won't be long,' she promises. 'I'll come up afterwards.'

'I'll leave the door on the latch,' he says with a smile and goes out.

She hurries over to the phone and dials a number. Jeff picks up immediately.

'Cyn, that video—'

'I've got lots more, Jeff!' she hisses. 'We have to—'

'Cyn?'

It isn't Jeff's voice.

'It's me, Anthony,' announces the editor-in-chief. 'What the hell is going on? Some kid makes absurd claims and you want to publish them? Do you intend to ruin the *Daily*? Freemee's going to sue us to kingdom come if we publish this. If they get even a whiff we're investigating this, we'll face a landslide of libel claims and much more besides!'

'But we have to—'

'Jeff will see what he can do, but it's going to take time and we've got a lot on our hands.'

'I've got a lot more—'

'What? Facts? Documents? Evidence?'

Cyn bites her lip. 'I'll get you them.'

'We'll take this further when you do. But I don't want to hear another word about it until then. Focus on coming through this TV show intact!'

Dialling tone. *Cowardly git!* She storms out. Chander has got to help her.

Henry's face appears in front of Joaquim. He's long since ceased wondering whether the images of the man he's talking to are authentic or not. A small app reliably tells him during a conversation, by means of a few simple symbols, if people are broadcasting real, touched-up or fake images of themselves. In the same way, the voice analysis software updates him constantly on whether the person he's talking to is speaking candidly with him or concealing secrets.

The picture of Henry's face is artificially produced. Joaquim's surprised because Henry generally gives digital devices a wide berth.

'What are the results of the analysis?' asks Henry.

Joaquim peers at the data in another corner of his glasses. 'Chander Argawal is genuinely willing to accept Carl's offer, but he wants more. The character composite we've been able to establish from the available data shows that no sum we give him now will change that. Sooner or later, he'll come back for more. He'll never be satisfied.'

'He'll blackmail us,' says Henry.

'There's a ninety-nine per cent chance of that.'

'So, sadly, we'll never come to any arrangement with him. How about the English woman?'

'She thinks it's beneath her. Argawal will try to change her mind, but he won't succeed. She will reveal Eddie Brickle's findings.'

'You were always good at solving problems,' is all Henry says.

Joaquim knows what this means. 'And we will solve this one quickly,' he says.

He ends the connection and opens a new one. He can only speak to this next person over the sort of secure device used by senior politicians, CEOs and intelligence agencies. Joaquim utters the code words associated with one of a number of pre-arranged plans.

He leans back tensely in his chair. He can be sure his people will deal with this matter efficiently, but there's always a residual risk. As in any other line of business.

Chander has left his room door open as promised. His clothes are lying on the bed, and she can hear the shower running in the bathroom.

A glint of light draws her eyes to Chander's bag. It's coming from the glasses. One lens is poking out of the bag and appears to be staring at her. It might be a coincidence of course, but for a second the lens looks gigantic. Knees trembling, she tiptoes around the bed and approaches the smart glasses from behind. First she pushes the glasses back into the outside pocket so they won't see anything if they're broadcasting, then she hastily opens the flap of the bag's main compartment where Chander keeps his two smartphones. Neither is password-secured! To quote Chander: IT people often think they're so smart they make the most elementary mistakes. Picking one up with each hand, she checks if they're connected to the glasses. She discovers that the device she's holding in her right hand is streaming images from the glasses. That doesn't necessarily mean anything. Maybe she's just being paranoid. She's still thinking it over when the new-message symbol blinks.

Didn't she once say that curiosity is her occupational risk? Vi accused her of being tactless. No matter, she can't resist it. She has a glance towards the bathroom before reading the message.

From: Carl Montik
Call me!

Other bubbles indicate that Chander's been communicating with Carl Montik for days! She hastily skims through the contents of the messages. She almost drops the phone. Their conversation is about her, and Eddie's video! Until yesterday their exchanges all involved her. He sent his first message after he met Cyn at the *Daily*.

Met Bonsant today.
Older than I thought ☺

Numbly, she pushes the phones back into the bag and shuts the flap.

A suspicion hits her like a punch in the solar plexus. Chander was never on Zero's trail, only ever on hers! His affections weren't born of passion: they were a cool and calculated part of his assignment. But why?

Her face is reflected in the large mirror on the wall opposite and she sees her grimace of despair change into a tight-lipped scowl. It makes her look old – *older than he thought*.

The shower's still running in the bathroom. She can't stand it in here a moment longer.

She runs to the door, but just as she gets there, there's a knock and a call of 'Room service!' She hesitates. There's no spyhole in the door. Has Chander ordered something?

She opens the door a couple of inches and glimpses a bellhop in livery outside. She opens the door further, but then catches sight of four other figures hugging the walls, so slams it shut again. She hears someone fiddling with the electronic lock. She rushes over to the window, from where the fire escape leads down into the courtyard or up on to the roof. She pushes up the window.

'What are you doing?' Chander's emerged from the bathroom.

She doesn't reply. She doesn't even look at him properly, taking in his stunned expression only out of the corner of her eye as she climbs through the half-open window on to the metal grille. The courtyard is small, dark and clammy with trapped heat. She tries to close the window behind her, but it gets stuck, leaving a small crack.

She's already heading down the first few steps when she sees the door of the room burst open. Chander, who's rummaging in his bag, spins round. Several people charge into the room, two of them overpower him and three others set to work on the window. Cyn hears their voices and odd words such as 'courtyard', 'down', 'catch' and 'trap', but her whole attention is focused on the iron staircase, which rattles as she gallops down, taking two steps at a time.

Chander's room is on the eighth floor. She's two storeys lower already. Someone's bound to be waiting for her at the bottom, though. She can't see anyone yet, but they'll get there any moment now. Images of film chases flash through her mind. Another floor, while thoughts scramble through her head as frantically as her feet down the steps. She feels the hot metal of the banister on her hand. Her pursuers' feet clang on the fire escape above her. She can't risk glancing up to check how many of them there are. Next floor. There's a half-open window. Without a second thought she pulls it open, wriggles through it, pushes it shut and locks it, then dashes past the room's bewildered occupants to the door.

For a fraction of a second she wonders if she should try to lose them by hiding in the bathroom and hoping the guests don't give her away as she waits for her pursuers to rush through the room and out into the hallway. Too risky. She flings the door open, steps into the corridor and slams it behind her.

She looks around feverishly. The men chasing her must have seen where she went. Maybe the locked window will hold them up for a few seconds. Maybe they'll simply break it. They'll surely inform their colleagues about her change in direction. Which way are they going to come? In the lift? Up the stairs? She's bound to run into them if she goes that way. She has a tiny sliver of a chance with the lift – if it comes in time and no one's waiting for her at the bottom. The lobby's always pretty busy, though, as Cyn recalls. Will she be safe there? For precious seconds at least?

She runs over to the lifts. Of the four two are heading up, one's coming down and one has stopped. She bangs on the button and prays. A door opens in front of her. The lift is empty. She jumps in and presses the button for reception. The doors slide shut.

Out of breath and bathed in sweat, she tries to order her thoughts. In less than thirty seconds the doors will open at the ground floor. If she needs any further confirmation that Eddie's death, and probably that of Joszef Abberidan too, were no coincidence, then now she has it. Although . . . she believes Carl Montik and Chander quite capable of stealing the video from her computer, but would they be capable of murder? No, she can't imagine that. Why did Chander even bother retrieving the video at the airport if someone had already deleted it? Might he not be in cahoots with Freemee after all? Or was he unaware of the experiment? What is his real mission? To keep an eye on her and distract her? Is he simply using her to make his fortune? Why was she attacked? Why was there no second attempt but an offer instead?

A sudden suspicion makes her stomach churn. Freemee now knows her pretty well thanks to her self-assessments via her smartwatch and glasses and their data collection. She's voluntarily handed over her own data. *All because of Peggy. No,* she corrects herself, *all because of Chander.* There's a bitter taste in her mouth like bile. She swallows as her thoughts continue to race headlong. Was it her results that persuaded Will to meet her? Is that why Carl made her an offer? Because Freemee's software sensed a chance she might accept? Would she ever have accepted? She did consider it for a second!

Kiss my arse!

Joaquim's glasses show flashing information from Cynthia's devices, and small numbers indicate the swiftly diminishing altitude as she travels down in the lift.

'She's taking the lift down,' he hisses into the microphone on the glasses. 'Hurry up! And remember the hotel has cameras trained on the lift entrances and the lobby. So no unusual behaviour, no running, don't group together and don't let yourselves be identified!'

Cyn's knees almost buckle when the lift comes to a stop. The doors grate as they slowly slide open. A bunch of seven people is waiting outside, led by an old black lady wearing large glasses. Next to her stands a family with two kids, and a young couple, he in shorts, she in a dress. Beyond them at least thirty people are criss-crossing the lobby, waiting at reception or standing around in small groups. Those waiting for the lift step aside to let her through. She quickly checks for any suspicious-looking characters in the lift area and has some doubts about two men in suits and one in jeans.

She ought to tell the man at the reception desk what's happened, but there are five people waiting in line. Besides, the two men in suits continue to look dodgy. She changes her mind and strides towards the exit. Twice she glances over her shoulder, but no one's following her.

The heat outside envelops her, but most people are walking fast in spite of it. She'd dearly love to have a cap and dark glasses – not against the sunlight but because of the public and private surveillance cameras that will soon signal her presence. She wends her way through a stream of pedestrians to the next junction.

A homeless woman is begging in front of the building on the corner. Cyn bends down quickly as if she's going to put some money in the woman's cardboard cup, but instead she pulls off her smartwatch and slides it on to the woman's wrist before she can protest.

'A present for you,' she says. 'Wear it a bit before you sell it.'

'You can't escape us that easily,' Joaquim whispers to himself.

The online footage from the coffee shop's CCTV camera doesn't reveal what Cyn gave the beggar, but the momentary interruption of Cyn's smartwatch readings, along with the subsequent change in pulse rate and other information including the localization details, tell him that a different person is now wearing it.

He barks this information to his men. What was the team leader thinking by not posting anyone in the lobby and ordering everyone into the courtyard instead? However, the guys are bound to put a real shift on now to make amends.

'The rules for inside the hotel are even more essential out in the street,' he reminds the team leader. 'Keep a low profile so the Domain Awareness System doesn't spot you. One pursuer at most on Bonsant's direct route. I've got my eye on her and I'll give you further instructions.'

Cyn's waiting in a cluster of people at the traffic lights on the corner. She's just slipping her smart glasses into a young man's messenger bag, when she spies the glow of a smartphone and decides to try her luck. She carefully pulls it out of the bag. Cupping it in one hand, she tests the screen with her fingertips. No code. She slides it into her trouser pocket so no one can see it. When the pedestrian light turns green, she presses her own smartphone into a girl's hand.

'Here, have this,' she says and walks across the road, paying no heed to the girl's calls.

Nice try, Joaquim thinks. Ms Bonsant must have seen *Enemy of the State*.

He doesn't lose track of her, though, thanks to practically unbroken online streaming from store and company CCTV cameras in this part of Manhattan, even if the poor-quality images from many cheap or outdated devices complicate matters a bit. The members of his pursuit team notify him that they're following Bonsant at various distances. Pointless information: he can see exactly where they are.

'We're not a mom and pop's police department any more,' said Michael Bloomberg, the mayor of New York City, as he presented the New York Police Department's new Domain Awareness System, and the Real Time Crime Center in Lower Manhattan does indeed resemble a scene from a futuristic film rather than your run-of-the-mill police headquarters. Dozens of police officers in dark suits sending information to their colleagues on the beat from their monitors lined up in front of a thirty-foot video wall. At the press of a button, their computers spit out details they would once have spent hours, days and even months scouring the archives for, without any guarantee of success. What is more, state-of-the-art software compiles and analyses incalculable amounts of data from thousands of crime files and parole reports, millions of personal documents, detailed city maps, satellite images and address directories, emergency calls, footage from thousands of surveillance cameras, the number plate of every car crossing into and leaving Manhattan, and much more besides.

Within seconds of an incoming 911 call from a female manager at the Bedley Hotel to report a casualty with serious head wounds, the Domain Awareness System has produced aerial photos and street maps of that part of the Lower East Side, supported by pictures from all the surveillance cameras within a five-hundred-yard radius beginning thirty seconds before the emergency call was made. Further data pops up even as these first tapes are being sent out.

The caller doesn't know how long the male victim has been lying in the hotel room, but according to initial reports it cannot have been more than a matter of minutes. As a result, the RTCC officials call up footage of nearby surveillance cameras to see if they can spot any suspicious incidents in the aforementioned thirty seconds.

The caller is a level-headed woman who makes her report in a composed voice. The room in which the victim was found was booked in the name of a man called Chander Argawal. No sooner is his name mentioned than several lights in the centre start flashing, and the air prickles with suspense.

'Possible link to terrorist activities!' announces a standard warning emblazoned across the large video wall.

Within seconds the police officers have access to comprehensive information about the IT specialist including his CV, employers' names, pictures, videos and media reports. They see he's a US citizen who only arrived at JFK the previous afternoon on a flight from London and has attracted attention in recent days in relation to the hunt for internet activists suspected of terrorism. The head of the RTCC immediately notifies the NYPD's Counter-Terrorism Unit.

Richard Straiten receives this information via his glasses. He is one of the first NYPD homicide detectives who have been asked to test them. As the notification flashes up, his colleague starts up the patrol car and sends it bounding out of the car park towards the Bedley Hotel.

Blood is pounding in Cyn's ears. She keeps looking round. She suddenly thinks she can make out a disturbance among pedestrians in front of a block of houses at the next crossroads. She can't see anything in particular, but starts to run, turns off at the next junction and then slackens her pace again. There are even more people here! She must get off the streets.

She spots a typical souvenir store up ahead. Scarves, T-shirts, sunglasses and baseball caps hang from racks out on the pavement. She grabs a cap and the nearest pair of glasses, puts them on and is quickly on her way again. She's halfway down the block when she hears someone shouting. She glances over her shoulder and spots a woman, presumably the shop assistant, who's shaking her fist but shows no sign of chasing her. Cyn nevertheless speeds up into a trot.

When she reaches the next junction, she turns around quickly. The woman has gone, but there's a man craning his neck way back up the street. He could be looking at anyone.

For safety's sake she keeps running, glancing back briefly every few yards, and then darts around the next corner. A hundred yards ahead of her she spots the sign for a subway station.

'She's wearing a green baseball cap and brown shades,' Joaquim tells his team. 'She's just entering Grand Street subway station by the southern exit.' He switches to the subway CCTV cameras. He has access to their footage too, even though he ought not to.

Joaquim paces up and down in his office. He's tense. He checks with his glasses to see if there are any Freemee users on the subway, maybe even some with active smart glasses. A moment later the statistics pop up before him. As in many other things, New Yorkers are also Freemee world-beaters. Of the roughly three million people who travel around Manhattan every day, twenty-two per cent already use Freemee, representing six hundred and sixty thousand people, no less. Just under half of them own a pair of smart glasses. So there's a very good chance, in an area as small as Manhattan, that one of them is presently at Grand Street station and might see and identify Cynthia Bonsant.

But it's too early to send users a message on their devices. Freemee can't do that until there's a plausible witness statement from the Bedley Hotel or the police linking Cynthia Bonsant to a murder case. Joaquim will have to wait at the very least for that first report.

The British woman stops and leans against a wall with her back to the cameras. Joaquim can't see what she takes from her trouser pocket or what she's doing because her body's in the way. She raises a hand to her ear. What's she holding in her hand? A different phone? Where did she get hold of it? Whose is it? Who's she talking to?

*

Vi is sitting eating a sandwich for dinner and chatting with her friends on her laptop. She doesn't recognize the number, which has a foreign dialling code.

'Hello?'

'Listen, darling, don't ask me any questions right now, just do as I say,' her mother orders, her voice choppy and agitated. Vi can hear a hubbub of conversation, a roar and footsteps in the background.

'Remember the night before last, the surprise. Use it and write something. You'll find a yellow Post-it note with a message on it in the left-hand drawer of the living-room cupboard. There's another one, pink this time, in the bits-and-bobs drawer in the kitchen with two scribbled lines on it. Type it in. They need to check it. Have you got all that?'

That wasn't so complicated. Vi is already off searching for the piece of paper. She finds it. On the yellow Post-it is an email address at the *Daily*. The lines on the pink slip appear to be a username and a password. But why's her mother being so cryptic? 'I think so. But what—'

'We don't need the pieces of paper any more after you've finished! Something else: write a short message to go with it. I've been told they're hot on their heels, especially where I am right now.'

'OK. Even if I don't have a clue what you're talking about.'

'That's good, believe me. Take care! I love you.'

That's the end of the call. Vi stares helplessly at her phone and the two pieces of paper.

'Which phone's she using?' Marten asks.

'Just checking,' says Luís.

'What are they talking about?'

'I'm guessing the kid's supposed to get in touch with someone.'

'Who?'

'No idea. The newspaper, maybe?'

'But then why doesn't her mother call them directly? And why's she speaking in riddles?'

'The cellphone belongs to a guy called Jesús Dominguez, a New Yorker. I'll have it analysed. Maybe she just stole it from him.'

'Can we get a fix on it?'

'It'll take a little while, but yes.'

'Are we inside the daughter's laptop to get her communications?'

'Yeah. We went in a few hours ago as a precaution. Same with her smartphone.'

With a few typed orders Luís magics up several windows on his screen.

'This is Viola Bonsant's laptop. It's on, but she's not using it.'

'Maybe we should ask our British friends to pay the young lady a visit,' Marten says, reaching for the phone.

Vi has the Pi ready to go. The waterfalls and the dialogue window appear on the TV screen. She nervously logs in, using the username and the password as agreed during Saturday's session. It doesn't escape her as she does this that she's contacting wanted terrorists. Was that why her mother sounded so odd on the phone? So frantic? Vi writes the message, as Cyn told her.

peekaboo777: Message received. Who is this? It isn't Cyn.

Guext: That doesn't matter, does it? What matters is you get the info.

353

Nothing happens in the window for a few seconds. Vi is on the point of logging out, when peekaboo777 writes:

Viola?

Her face goes bright red. She's about to break off the connection when the next words appear.

OK. We'll look into it.

—Session closed—

She sits there in the living room. Her heart is beating furiously. What did her mother mean by not needing the pieces of paper any more? Is she supposed to destroy them? This whole thing is freaking her out. She flushes the two Post-its down the toilet, just to be sure.

Cyn scrambles down a long corridor in the subterranean neon light. The air is hot and sticky, and she's finding it hard to breathe. She doesn't remove her sunglasses, but she's not the only one wearing them down here. Eavesdroppers could well find out the number of the stolen phone following her call to Vi and localize it. Get rid of it! She chucks it in a bin and makes a silent apology to its owner. She comes to the ticket barriers, digs a few coins out of her pockets and slots them into the machine, which churns out a ticket for her. She hears a train come rumbling into the station. She and dozens of others shove their way into one of the carriages. Pressing her face against the glass, she scours the platform for potential pursuers, but doesn't spot anyone hurrying or peering around suspiciously.

She leans back and stares at her fellow passengers' faces. Most of them have a fine sheen of sweat on their skin. She instinctively reaches to activate her glasses to find out more about the young black guy facing her. He's studying her through his own glasses. Are they smart glasses? She can't tell.

She hopes she's thrown her pursuers off her scent for the time being. Even if they can get their hands on some cars, they won't travel any faster in Manhattan's dense traffic than she will on the subway.

She considers her next move. Should she fight her way through to NBC or go to the police instead? She doubts they'll understand, let alone believe her. She's lost all trust in the security services since her terrible treatment by those border guards in London. If someone had told her that two weeks ago, she'd have thought they were nuts.

She feels for the memory stick in her pocket, then runs through her next few moves in her mind. If at all possible, she needs access to a computer and the internet; if not, she'll fight her way through to NBC.

The train's brakes screech as it enters the next station. It's so full there's no way she can check every person waiting on the platform. Her eyes scan the crowd in the hope that she'll instinctively pick up any suspicious signs. The glasses and their facial recognition function would be worth their weight in gold right now! If, that is, she could get reception down here. And if they wouldn't immediately give away her position.

Uniformed police officers are just cordoning off the street when Detective Richard Straiten arrives at the hotel. The lights of the ambulance flash red through the blue of the patrol cars' beacons. With a squeal of tyres, Straiten's partner pulls into a row of cars outside the hotel entrance.

A critical response vehicle races in from the opposite direction, and heavily armed members of a Hercules team jump out, guns at the ready. Some of them secure the entrance to the hotel while others stream into the building. Outside in the street, shaken bystanders cower against the walls or pull out their smartphones and start filming.

Straiten shows his badge, and he and his partner walk into the lobby. A good dozen police are already gathered there among a few civilians and the hotel employees. They all look tense but calm. Straiten hears more patrol cars pull up outside. The place will be teeming with officers in a few minutes. Straiten asks to be directed to the manager who put through the emergency call. The tall, slim Latina is waiting for him at the reception desk along with a female police officer and another woman in hotel livery. The manager introduces her colleague as the person who found the victim. A guest alerted the chambermaid to screams issuing from a room with an open door.

'I found a man lying unconscious on the floor. There was blood pouring from his head. Beside him was a blood-spattered laptop. I informed the manager immediately.'

'Who was the guest who drew your attention to it?' Straiten asks. 'Is he down here now or in his room?'

Neither the maid nor the manager can answer this question. The man hasn't been in touch again. Straiten asks for footage taken by the hotel's CCTV cameras.

'We only have them here in the lobby and in the lifts,' the manager explains. 'Not in the hallways.'

Straiten curses under his breath. 'Can you get through to the person who booked the room?'

'No. I can't rule out that the victim booked it himself. I couldn't identify him because he was lying on his front and his face was too much of a mess.'

No, they hadn't noticed anything strange about the guest since his arrival. 'But now you ask, I can remember a different event reported by some other guests just before the body was discovered. They claim that a woman climbed into their room through a window from the fire escape, but then went straight out through the door. That was a couple of floors down from the scene, though. Sadly there aren't any pictures of that incident either, because we don't have any cameras in the hallways and courtyard.'

'Maybe she took the lift afterwards,' Straiten says. 'Please compile all the video footage for that period of time.'

He asks a few more questions before going up to the room where some paramedics and a doctor are just wheeling the man away on a stretcher. Straiten can't see his face properly due to the oxygen mask and the copious bleeding. He goes back down to the lobby. In the meantime the manager has called up the surveillance videos on a computer in her office.

'I've looked through them a bit already,' she tells him, pointing to an image of a middle-aged woman getting into a lift. 'A few seconds after the complaint by the guests on the fourth floor, this woman took the elevator down from that floor to the lobby.'

'What about the other elevators?'

'They were in use. One coming up stops at the fourth floor a few seconds later, but the woman was gone by then.' She plays the footage of a lift with five people in it. Two men get out at the fourth floor. The camera has only filmed their backs. 'Nobody else takes the lift from that floor in the next few minutes,' the woman says. She calls up the images of the woman again. 'Her face is easy to identify. I took the liberty of running it through facial recognition software.'

Oh, just go ahead and do our job, why don't you? Straiten thinks grimly, but says politely, 'Thank you. That's very helpful.'

'And I found out something quite interesting,' the manager continues, clearly flattered. 'She's also a hotel guest: Cynthia Bonsant, a British journalist. NBC booked the room for her.'

'What, the TV channel?'

'They have a block booking and send us people on a regular basis. Talk-show guests and the like.'

An alarm bell rings inside Straiten's head – journalist! TV channel! They always make a mountain out of a molehill and spin events to fit their story. This investigation is going to take place amid a glare of publicity. Straiten and his colleagues will have to consider their every move with great care. No slip-ups.

'Our register shows that Ms Bonsant checked in at the same time as the man in whose room the victim was found.'

'Chander Argawal,' Straiten notes. 'Now *that* is interesting.'

By running one finger over the stem of his glasses he makes contact with the Real Time Crime Center. 'Cynthia Bonsant,' he says to the colleague whose image pops up in front of his eyes. 'I want everything you've got on her.'

Vi's just returned from the bathroom when a Freemee alert pops up on her computer screen.

Your score has just risen by five per cent!
More >

Something must have happened. Still shaken by the conversation with her mother, she clicks on the message.

Your mother Cynthia Bonsant's reputation just rose significantly. That benefits you too, Viola. More >

The talk show! Vi thinks. She'd totally forgotten about it. But wasn't it later? It's about half past three in the afternoon in New York. She clicks on 'More'. A window opens on her screen, showing several columns of messages from various different social media platforms. They come so thick and fast that she has trouble following the content. She manages to read a few, like snapshots.

Wow, what's going on? Tons of police and emergency lights at Bedley Hotel #NYC #whatsgoingon (photo)

Witnesses report chase on #LowerEastSide

Saw jittery woman rushing out of Bedley Hotel. Cops everywhere. Being questioned now, not shopping :-(

Police apparently hunting woman travelling with victim #nyfugitive

Another day, another death #NYC

Shit! Look at these guys storming Bedley Hotel in #NYC (photo)

In the photo Vi can see two men running past the photographer in heavy body armour, masks and helmets and carrying automatic rifles. She can practically hear their pounding feet and barked orders.

Death at Bedley Hotel, NYC? Cops at the scene

Still chaos outside Bedley Hotel. Police close road in front of hotel (photo)

Ambulance taking away victim of hotel attack (photo)

Jittery woman on the run #LowerEastSide? Taken by my glasses minutes before police op in Bedley Hotel (video)

Vi is shaking as she clicks on the video. What do these posts have to do with her mother? The jerky video, filmed from the poster's point of view, shows someone hurrying out of a building. At first there's nothing but an outline against the afternoon sun, weaving its way between pedestrians until it nearly bumps into the person filming. Now Vi can clearly recognize her mother. She's now feeling terribly anxious as she goes back to the posts. What's been going on?

Big buzz in southern #Manhattan. Police hunt murder suspect

Murder confirmed in #BedleyHotel #NYC?

No. Still waiting for police statement. Just lots of uniforms and flashing blue lights

Seven reported dead in attack on #BedleyHotel #NYC (link)

Another film of fugitive from #BedleyHotel #NYC, taken with my glasses (video)

Vi's pulse is racing as she watches this recording, which is barely half an hour old according to the time code. Her laptop speakers produce a blare of street noise. Seen from the perspective of an onlooker, her mother staggers out of the hotel, glances left and right before turning her back on the person filming, hurrying away almost at a run and swiftly disappearing. *Anyone who doesn't know Mum,* she thinks, *would find it impossible to identify her from this footage because it's too wobbly and out of focus.*

Vi checks the latest updates with a sense of rising panic.

Reports of 3 dead in explosion at Bedley Hotel #NYC via @jjkwnews

Police yet to confirm attack on Bedley Hotel #NYC Investigations ongoing

Pictures of people leaving Bedley Hotel immediately after attack. Taken with #eyeclick (photos)

What should she do? She rings the number her mother called her from earlier. After several ringtones she hears the automated voicemail message. She tries again, with the same outcome. She writes a frantic text to the number:

You're wanted! What's going on?!! Call me!

For several minutes she waits for a reply with one eye on the updates. When her phone remains stubbornly silent, she logs on to the waterfalls using the Pi again.

Guext: Have you seen what's going on with my mum?

An answer comes back almost straight away.

peekaboo777: Yes.

Guext: It wasn't her. Please help her!

peekaboo777: We're trying.

361

'What's the latest?' Alice asks. 'One dead? Three? Seven? Shoot-out? Explosion? Terror attack? Why do people post news when they haven't got a clue?'

She's standing alongside Will in front of the video wall in his office, watching the hunt for Cynthia Bonsant. 'This screen isn't a news medium. It's an incomprehensible, swirling cloud of rumours!'

Coverage from a regional TV channel is playing in one window. Alice turns the sound up, takes her glasses off, puts them away and urges Will to do the same.

Police radio (link): #NYPD wish to interview woman called @CynthiaBonsant as witness to incident at #BedleyHotel #NYC (photo)

Hotel guest Ann Tsilakis apparently missing #NYPD announces press conference at 17.00 ET following #BedleyHotelIncident in #NYC

The woman #NYPD is hunting after #BedleyHotelIncident:
@CynthiaBonsant facebook.com/Cyn . . . freemee.com/cyn . . .

'What is this?' she asks Will so quietly that her words are barely audible over the reporter's voice. 'Cynthia Bonsant finds out some Freemee secrets and suddenly she's a murder suspect?'

'We don't know what happened. It's too soon to make any assumptions.'

'This doesn't feel good to me. We have to find out as soon as possible what went on in there. And we need proof of what you told me inside the Bunker. It'd be better if we had it before you go on TV this evening so you can present it.'

'We won't get any.'

'We have to try. I think I know how.'

In her frantic rush to get on the first subway train, Cynthia didn't notice which line she was on and missed several stations while she was lost in thought. Now she studies the map above the train windows. It looks as though she's caught line 6. The next station is Hunter College. She almost certainly won't be able to go online any time soon. She can remember NBC's address without consulting her notes, and she sees that she needs to alight at Lexington Avenue/51st Street and walk for a few minutes to get to the Rockefeller Center, where the TV studios are.

She's standing by the door. All around her people are staring at their glasses, playing with their smartphones or talking to invisible people. Very few are looking around, as she is, at the other passengers. She feels almost as though they're her allies. A young man in a hoodie is staring at her quite intrusively, but he looks away when their eyes meet. A young woman in a business suit a couple of paces behind him is also gazing with some interest at Cyn through a pair of glasses. *Are they still glasses or perhaps more of a transparent data screen?* she wonders, as she has done so many times in recent days. When Cyn's eyes linger on the woman, her gaze changes from keen to bored and she stares into the middle distance instead. She notices that the young man is peering at her again. Is he flirting with her? Or is there something odd about her?

She glances around in annoyance. Two teenagers sitting on a bench to her right are hunched over a smartphone, whispering. She could swear that one of the boys just pointed at her but retracted his finger when she looked straight at him and his friend.

She spins round and catches the young man and the businesswoman in the act of looking away. She pretends she hasn't noticed and positions herself so she can see both the two individuals to her left and the pair of teenagers with their smartphone to her right out of the corners of her eyes. The boys' fingers swipe across the screen, and she's sure they keep glancing alternately down and then up at her as the train slows down and enters Hunter College station.

Welcome to paranoia, Cyn!

Think I saw #CynthiaBonsant on #NYSubway, line 6, Hunter College station (photo) #NYPD #BedleyHotelIncdt

Search for Ann Tsilakis goes on #BedleyHotelIncdt #NY Anybody seen her? (photo)

Person wanted by #NYPD in #BedleyHotelIncdt #CynthiaBonsant steals cap and glasses, from CCTV live stream @ MarinasBeauty (video)

#NYPD confirms one victim in BedleyHotelIncdt in #NY. British journalist @CynthiaBonsant supposedly no longer suspect only wanted as witness

This is what Joaquim has been waiting for. An automatic message is sent to all Freemee users in the vicinity.

Alert: The New York Police Department wants to talk to Cynthia Bonsant as a witness in a murder case. Report any sighting immediately by calling 911. Call >>
Remember that helping the police increases your data score.
Be careful, though: she may be armed!

This message is followed by a photo of Bonsant and a link to social media streams reporting on the hunt.

Saw #CynthiaBonsant leaving #Subway #Line6 north-bound at #HunterCollege (photo)

#CynthiaBonsant is a guest on #NBCTonight with #Tak-ishaWashington #AlvinKosak #WillDekkert #Freemee #NYPD

Is this #CynthiaBonsant at #HunterCollege #NY #Subway #Line6 southbound? (photo)

'She's heading to the NBC studios in the Rockefeller Center,' Joaquim tells the team. Some madmen have by now reported sightings of the woman as far away as Taiwan and Tierra del Fuego.

He's a little irritated by the algorithm's inability to predict Cynthia Bonsant's movements more accurately. He's been using a specific crime program EmerSec developed for track-ing down criminals on the run, but its forecasts are far too vague for his liking. Bonsant may be on the run, but she isn't a criminal, and so she doesn't behave like a fugitive gangster.

He's been toying with the idea of combining the crime program with other software – for example, a program for tracing runaway children, and another designed to monitor and counter critical reporters and activists – but he doesn't have time. So for the time being all available information feeds into the analysis and he lets the program draw its own conclusions and churn out ideas, even if the input includes reports from Mongolia.

What irritates him most is the analysis of the subway footage. The cameras suggest they've seen Bonsant in places where she cannot possibly be. Maybe some of the devices are outdated and the quality of their pictures too poor.

There's no doubt about it: that's her mum in the picture. Helplessly Vi watches the hunt for her mother in a faraway city. The reports on her news stream are coming so fast that she can only read every tenth one before they vanish off the bottom of her screen.

> You're all wrong! @CynthiaBonsant is here! #CentralPark-South #nypd #BedleyHotelIncdt #NYC (photo)

The woman in the picture might be her mother, but she's too far away and too blurry for Vi to be able to say so with any certainty. Between these reports, she spots an increasing number of posts containing the name of a different woman, Ann Tsilakis. She's apparently also wanted in connection with the events or been reported missing or . . . Who on earth can tell?

The only reasonably official news sources are the NYPD radio recordings unidentified people are posting online. But how can Vi be sure they're genuine and not some smartass's stupid prank? Besides, the scraps of conversation are pretty vague or else unintelligible.

She searches online for more details about this other woman but comes up with very little. It confirms what she already knows from the updates. The woman is a manager from San Francisco and two years younger than her mother. Vi can see a certain likeness, even if she can't imagine that anyone would ever mistake the two women.

Another person thinks they've seen Cyn, but on the other side of Manhattan this time. However, the woman on the corresponding photo is, like the previous one, too far away for Vi to be able to identify her for sure.

So where *is* her mother? Is there anything Vi can do?

Will looks in on Carl again before he sets off for the NBC studios.

'For the presentation I've got another couple of questions about the experiments you—'

'Shh!' Carl cuts him off, raising a finger to his lips and jumping up from his chair. He grabs Will by the upper arm, drags him out of the office and barks a single word: 'Bunker!'

Will slips his hand into his trouser pocket and turns off his smartphone's record function. They divest themselves of all their devices outside the entrance of the bug-proof room. Carl also checks Will's eyes for lenses.

'How nice to enjoy your boundless trust,' Will says laconically.

Carl has seen through him. Will ponders how literally one should take that expression nowadays. He half-heartedly asks Carl some questions, but the answers are worthless to him if he can't record them. As Carl speaks, Will tries to come up with an idea for how else he might be able to get his hands on some evidence of Carl's experiments.

'It's a good thing you're working on your presentations,' says Carl, breaking through into Will's thoughts. 'We'll do the first one the day after tomorrow.'

This takes Will by surprise. Should he not first devise a strategy to build interest for Carl's 'ActApp development', as Will tentatively calls it? Once again he feels keenly that he's only a second-class member of the board – a highly paid assistant to Carl, who's had this all mapped out for ages.

'Who will we be meeting?' he asks tersely. 'It'd be good to know so that I can tailor the presentation to their requirements.'

Carl names one of the world's largest corporations.

'But they're just the first,' Carl adds with a smug grin.

Will would love to punch him in the face.

No sooner has Carl put his glasses back on than he receives a message from Joaquim, Henry's new Freemee guard dog. He wants Carl to ring him back immediately. Carl reluctantly does as requested while Will walks along the corridor ahead of him.

Joaquim doesn't even use a picture or an avatar for his conversations via glasses. Carl has only a name to talk to.

'Will Dekkert's visit and his open discussion of the experiment were no coincidence,' Joaquim's voice tells him. 'We're inside his phone. He had a recording app switched on when he came into your office.'

'The bastard.'

'There's no way we can let him go on that talk show. Send someone else.'

'Who?'

'No idea. Alice Kinkaid has just left the office, but we couldn't have sent her anyway. Either you go or we cancel.'

'What reason do I give?'

'I don't know. The hunt for Cynthia Bonsant. Tell him he has to stay at the office to respond to any surprise events.

We must talk to him, but until we do he's not to leave the office or communicate with anyone. The best thing would be to send him to a meeting in the Bunker.'

Carl hangs up, calls security and orders them to come to his office, then strides after Will, who's just disappeared around a corner.

'You can't go on the TV show,' he says after catching up with him.

'Why not?'

'There's something important we need to discuss. Go back to the Bunker for now.'

'That means someone else has to go on TV,' says Will. 'Alice would be the best person. She has experience of talk shows.'

'Where's she going?' asks Marten.

'To get something to eat, I reckon,' says Luís.

They watch her via various shop cameras and the glasses of the three agents shadowing her. Alice has stowed her own glasses in her handbag.

'Does she always do that?'

Luís views Alice's profile and skim-reads it. 'Sometimes, but not often.'

'Has she arranged to meet someone?'

'We didn't overhear any conversations, and there's no note on her calendar about it.'

Alice disappears into a trendy café and restaurant.

'One of you go in,' Marten orders the women tailing Alice. Through the agent's glasses he sees Alice secure one of the last free tables in the restaurant. The agent is only able to obtain a seat on the far side of the room. From there she can keep an eye on Alice but is unable to watch her every movement due to the many bobbing heads and bodies between them. She'll have to content herself with this vantage point for now.

A waitress brings Alice the menu. She looks through it quickly and lays it on the table. She fishes her smart glasses out of her bag and puts them on.

'Now,' says Luís. 'Oh no,' he sighs, as all Alice does is look at a few webpages with details of the hunt for Cynthia Bonsant.

By now Detective Straiten has got used to the talking heads in front of him. The hallway outside the hotel room where the crime was committed smells of carpet cleaner. Via his glasses a colleague from the Real Time Crime Center says, 'We're receiving hundreds of tip-offs all the time. Analysis says she's in Midtown. Our cameras haven't found her in the subway yet. There's something wrong with them; they're playing up. The cap and glasses don't make it easy either. Same with the increasingly frequent photos from people claiming to have spotted her. Even on those we have to identify her ourselves, because the picture quality's too poor for facial and physical recognition software.'

The forensic scientists let Straiten into the room at last. He inspects the place where the victim was found. The hotel will have to lay new carpet. Next to the half-dried bloodstain lies a blood-smeared laptop in a transparent evidence bag.

'The victim has been identified. It is indeed Chander Argawal. The doctors estimate his chances of survival at zero.'

Straiten goes over to the window, the bottom half of which has been pulled up. He can make out the marks left by the technicians' sweep for fingerprints on the windowpanes. He peers down into the small courtyard, which is already plunged into half-light in spite of the bright blue square hanging above the high walls of the building. Four floors down, a woman crossed a room she'd entered from the fire escape. Straiten points to the fingerprints on the window and asks the nearest technician, 'Any identification yet?'

'It just came back,' replies the woman in somewhat close-fitting disposable overalls. She glances at her tablet computer. 'Prints from four people. Three room guests before Chander Argawal, and Cynthia Bonsant.'

'Find any outside?'

'Sure,' the woman says. 'Some of them are Cynthia Bonsant's too. On the fourth-floor window and door. She left her prints everywhere.'

Straiten looks at the laptop in the bag. 'The murder weapon?'

'The doctor thinks so. Hard enough to cave in somebody's skull.'

'Will that be considered the fatal wound?'

'That and a leak of cerebrospinal fluid.'

'You can spare me the precise details.'

'But we only found Bonsant's prints on the top. If she hit someone with it, then she'd either have had to be wearing gloves or placed something else between her skin and the device.'

'In which case you'd have found traces of it – were there any?'

'We can only do the analysis at the lab.'

'We've got the assessments of some surveillance cameras,' the colleague from the Real Time Crime Center announces to Straiten via his glasses.

Straiten thanks the technician and says, 'Shoot.'

His colleague plays him a video. It fills virtually Straiten's entire field of vision and superimposes itself on the hotel room. Straiten recognizes the hotel entrance, seen from perhaps fifty yards away. The picture quality isn't particularly good, and he can't really recognize Bonsant's face.

'That's Cynthia Bonsant leaving the hotel. Her path is easy to follow from then on. Of particular interest are the things she does on the way.'

The colleague sends him some further recordings. Bonsant bends down to a homeless woman begging by a wall.

'What's she doing? She's not giving her money, is she?' asks Straiten. 'Is she disposing of evidence?'

'That's what we were wondering.' He spools back to the place a couple of yards earlier where Straiten has a clear view of Bonsant's upper body and arms. 'Keep an eye on her left wrist.'

'She has a watch.'

'Correct. And now . . .'

He presses 'Play' and in the unnaturally frantic fast forward, Bonsant again bends down to the woman sitting on the floor, stands up straight and goes on her way. The images stop.

'The watch is gone,' Straiten observes.

'That's right. We've done some research. It wasn't an ordinary watch, it was a smartwatch.'

'To record her physical data?'

'Yep.'

'Why did she give it away then?'

'Wait.'

Two minutes later, Straiten knows that Cynthia Bonsant also gifted her smartphone to a pedestrian and foisted her smart glasses on a young man.

'I'd say she's trying to get rid of every device that might be used to locate and track her electronically,' Straiten concludes.

'Sure looks that way.'

'Have our people already picked up those devices?'

'They got hold of the smartwatch. We've located the girl with the smartphone and the kid with the glasses, and two patrol cars are on their way.'

'Why do it? It's pointless when we've got cameras all over the place. She must know that after her latest reports.'

'She steals a baseball cap and some sunglasses a few blocks later to fool the cameras, then disappears into the subway.'

'Once she's been sighted, a cap and glasses won't help her against such a comprehensive network. She must know that too,' his colleague responds.

'Maybe she didn't think of that. She's not a professional hitwoman. If she did kill that guy Argawal, then mentally she'll be all over the place.'

'The wristwatch and other devices will tell us where she was when the crime was committed.'

'The doctors won't be able to determine the time of the crime to the exact second.'

'Make sure you check the location data of her devices for the period around the crime too,' Straiten urges him. He knows the RTCC will do that anyway, but he wants to make sure. 'Do we know where she is right now?'

Cyn waits restlessly by the carriage door for the train to roll into Grand Central Station. As before, she has a feeling that people are watching her. Her feet hit the platform the moment the doors open. It's so crowded she can barely make any progress. The air's stuffy here too. She hopes there's a shower at the studio so she can freshen up properly. A quick wash isn't going to cut it now. Her clothes are also completely ruined. And to think she brought a smart outfit with her especially for the occasion! *It's crazy to think about my wardrobe at a time like this!*

She lets the rush-hour crowd carry her along until she finds herself out in the cavernous main hall she knows from so many films and photos. This wasn't where she intended to end up. It reminds her of a cathedral, except that here people aren't kneeling in silent devotion but scurrying in all directions at the bidding of that modern god, speed. Only a few pause briefly in front of the large departures board or take a souvenir snapshot. *Where does she go now?*

Vi is able to follow her mother's apparently aimless path through Grand Central Station on three smart-glasses live streams, filmed from different angles. She clearly doesn't have any inkling that she's been recognized by several bystanders, who are now broadcasting her whereabouts to the whole world. One of those observers isn't satisfied with keeping an eye on her but follows her at a slight distance. The amateur reporter babbles something to himself as he goes, but Vi can only make out the occasional word over the noise of the main hall.

A fourth broadcaster shows up in Vi's message stream, and she opens a new window in her browser. He's obviously standing in an elevated position from where he can look down over the station hall. He zooms in on Cyn, then out again. She's just a tiny dot among many others, but he pans his camera to make sure she remains in the centre of his screen.

All the while more messages flash up in the window in which Vi is following the news stream.

New police radio update (link): #NYPD seek #Cynthia-Bonsant as potential suspect in #BedleyHotelIncdt #NYC #nyfugitive

#NYPD still searching for Ann Tsilakis in #BedleyHotel-Incdt. Somebody saw Tsilakis in #NY (photo)

CCTV footage from Lebby's Deli: #CynthiaBonsant gives away phone (video)

#NYPD confirms one victim of #BedleyHotelIncdt #NY. Seriousness of injuries unknown. Further victims unconfirmed

#CynthiaBonsant linked to #terrorism? #Zero #0

Hello #NYPD, here's #CynthiaBonsant #GrandCentral #NY!!!

Anonym. source says victim in #BedleyHotelIncdt #CynthiaBonsant's partner in #Zero hunt, Chander Argawal

More footage from Lebby's Deli camera: #CynthiaBonsant slips a man something. What? Glasses? (video)

Ann Tsilakis: suspect or victim in #BedleyHotelIncdt? #NY Where is she? via @nycregex (link)

Another video (link) of #CynthiaBonsant stealing cap and shades. How she looks now (photo)

Vi doesn't know what to believe. She watches the two videos of her mother allegedly giving away her mobile and her glasses. Lebby's Deli's CCTV camera must date from the nineteenth century. The only way someone could tell that it's Vi's mother is if they'd followed her up to this exact spot on other surveillance cameras. In any case, Vi doesn't recognize Cyn. She can just about make out that the black dot someone's handing to someone else is a smartphone. What a load of tosh! She tries ringing again, but once more she goes through to voicemail.

'OK, the police is here,' is one glasses-wearer's audible comment in Grand Central. Vi can indeed spot two uniformed officers in the throng of travellers. The fourth broadcaster's footage gives a better view of events thanks to his elevated vantage point. On the left of the picture, two figures in uniform are shouldering their way through the crowded hall. On the right-hand side of the screen, Cyn is standing with her back to the concourse as she studies a map of the local area on an information board.

The constant stream of posts, photos and live footage gives Vi the impression that she's actually there in the station. She's every bit as engrossed in what's happening as the various reporters and her mother. Her palms are sweaty and her whole body tense as she hunches over the laptop and the Pi beside it. She instinctively wants to call out to her mother, 'Watch out for the police! They're behind you!' but she can only watch helplessly as the uniformed officers work their way closer. Cyn is the only one who hasn't noticed!

Vi clenches her fists. She frantically contemplates what she might be able to do. Zero? She's written to them already, but they're their only chance.

Using the Pi she writes:

Guext: Is there nothing you can do to help my mother?!

Peekaboo777: We're on it. Getting support from Anonymous. Already inside NY subway camera system and manipulating footage. Grand Central next. BTW, how did your mother contact you?

Guext: Phone.

Peekaboo777: Yours?

Guext: Yes.

Peekaboo777: Get out of there! If possible avoid cameras. Take the Pi with you, throw it away somewhere unobserved, destroy the SD card. Now!
—End of session—

Vi's stomach rebels and her hands start to shake. Without much pause for thought, she gathers her stuff together, pulls on a hoodie and grabs some shades. Zero advised her to avoid cameras. They're worried that Vi's being watched. Bloody hell, she's just a normal eighteen-year-old. What is all this shit? In the middle of the night, as well! Where's she meant to go?

She hesitates, then slides her smartwatch off her wrist. She leaves her smartphone behind. The back door of the flat leads out on to a narrow footpath. As far as she knows, there aren't any cameras overlooking it. It's her only chance.

'Miss Cynthia Bonsant?' asks the policeman as he reaches Cyn.

She's so startled that she answers yes. She feels queasy as she wonders how he knows her name and why he might be speaking to her.

A policewoman also steps up to her. 'Ms Bonsant, we have to ask you to come with us,' she says.

Now Cyn's nerves really start to jangle. To keep her composure she asks, 'What's this all about?'

'Our colleagues have a few questions about events at your hotel.'

So does she!

The policeman points the way and Cyn walks in the direction he's indicated with a police officer on either side.

A few onlookers slow down or stop for a second. Two people even appear to be following them at a distance as they cross the hall towards the main exit.

'What events are we talking about exactly?' asks Cyn, worried now.

'Our colleagues will tell you,' the policewoman replies.

'How did you find me?' she wonders. 'Via the surveillance cameras?'

The man shrugs. 'Presumably. We were just sent to pick you up. They said you were here and gave us a few up-to-date pictures.' He checks his mobile. 'Yep, looks like camera footage. They're all over the city. Or maybe some guy with glasses identified you.'

Cyn is fully clothed, but all of a sudden she feels as if she's stark naked. 'Listen,' she begins. 'I've got something important to tell you. In here I've got—' she says, tapping the pocket of her trousers.

The two police officers pull out their guns, and Cyn immediately holds her hands a long way from her body. Too late. The officers rush her, throw her to the floor and twist her arms behind her back.

'No, no!' she shouts. 'I'm not armed! In my pocket there's a memory stick with a video on it that you really need to check out! You or colleagues of yours who are familiar with this kind of material. It involves hundreds or even thousands of deaths!'

This news makes absolutely no impression on the police officers. 'You can tell that to our colleagues in person,' the policeman snaps. They frisk Cyn for weapons, pull her to her feet and drag her towards the exit through a crowd of excited bystanders. She's sorely tempted to resist but then drops the idea. At least they haven't handcuffed her, although the man is keeping a very tight hold of her wrist.

'I had several copies of this video,' Cyn continues. 'On a computer in my hotel room. They're all gone! The *Daily* in London should still have one. Your colleagues have to investigate.'

They emerge from the exit. The air outside is still close and humid. Very few people pay them any attention in the dense stream of pedestrians, just a handful stand watching them, as if they've been waiting for Cyn and the police officers. She's again assailed by memories of movie scenes of New York. Cars crawl along nose to tail, every other one a yellow cab. Steam rises from a sewer grating. A few yards further down the street three workmen in high-vis orange jackets huddle around a fenced-off hole in the street. The officers lead her to a patrol car waiting at the kerb.

'Can you pick up what they're saying?' Carl asks Joaquim via his glasses, as he searches among the six live-streaming onlookers for a serviceable soundtrack. He's sitting in a limousine, which is taking him to the NBC studios in the Rockefeller Center.

'No,' replies Joaquim. 'The street's way too noisy.'

The people filming are also too far away to catch the conversation between Cyn and the cops. The officers and Cyn are just approaching their car, when a black sedan suddenly pulls up alongside it, preventing the police from getting in and driving off.

'Ah, there's one guy who's gonna be popular,' Carl mocks.

'Yeah, looks like trouble,' Joaquim confirms.

The policeman does indeed shout at the sedan, from which two men and a woman get out, all of them in dark suits. He lets go of Cyn's arm, says something to his fellow officer and trudges over to the suited trio, who have by this time walked round to the other side of the police car.

Carl's eyes flick from one live stream to the other to see what's happening outside Grand Central. One of the men holds out his badge. The policeman checks his identity and hands it back. Reluctantly he guides the three people over to Cyn and his colleague.

'And who might these three be?'

'FBI,' the woman in the dark trouser suit says to Cyn. 'You're coming with us.'

At the same time the policewoman's grip on her arm tightens. Cyn looks curiously back and forth between the two women, while the other cop tries to contact his superiors by radio from inside the patrol car.

'Maybe you should make up your mind,' says Cyn. 'What do you want from me?'

'You'll soon find out,' the FBI woman says in an unfriendly voice.

'What if I don't want to come with you?'

'You have no choice,' the FBI woman snaps at her.

'These two appear to think differently,' Cyn replies, pointing to the NYPD officers. *So the absurd competition between the city police and the Feds you see in films really does exist?* 'I've had enough. I'm not going anywhere until I know why,' she states categorically. 'Or am I under arrest?'

'Indeed you are,' the FBI woman answers. 'On suspicion of terrorism.'

'This must be some kind of joke!'

The policeman emerges from his car, shoves his way between Cyn and the suited trio and pulls himself up to his full height. 'You're coming with us,' he announces. 'For suspected murder.'

'What?' Cyn cries so loudly that he puts his startled hands to his ears. 'Who am I supposed to have murdered?'

'Chander Argawal,' barks the policeman.

Chander's dead?

She watches in shock as the three FBI agents try to force their way around the police officer to get hold of her. He's more agile than she would have guessed from his stocky physique and manages to fend off the agents, especially when the policewoman comes to his aid. Within seconds all Cyn can see is a tangle of arms and heads, accompanied by lots of shoving and wrestling, swearing and shouted orders, the crackle of the patrol car's radio and then the sound of a siren, which seems to be coming from inside Grand Central Station.

In an instant her horror at Chander's death turns to white-hot rage, giving her a sudden surge of energy. The police officers are distracted by the alarm inside the railway station, and masses of people are beginning to stream out of it, so Cyn turns swiftly on her heel, melts into the pulsing crowd, which now covers the entire pavement, and walks calmly and nonchalantly away. She's only gone twenty feet or so when a quick glance over her shoulder tells her that the brawling agents have noticed her escape. Yet they're hemmed in by the panicking crowd, whereas Cyn is at the forefront of the wave of fleeing people and is free to leave. Just then the police officer's earlier words shoot through her head: 'They're all over the city. Or maybe some guy with glasses identified you.'

She has no chance of escaping. What should she do?

A few paces in front of her, a workman clambers out of the fenced-off hole in the ground.

Wanted by the FBI for terrorism and by the New York Police Department for murder. Those are absurd allegations but given what she's seen, heard and read about the two organizations, and given the accusations, she knows she doesn't want to fall into the hands of either. She's a sitting duck out on the streets, but how can she escape? *Into the underworld, like Zero in Vienna!*

She leaps over the fence, casts a quick glance down into the hole – it looks bottomless, but there are rungs on the wall leading down – and before the workmen can react, she's climbing down, almost letting herself drop, barely touching the cold metal rungs, as the echoes of the workmen's first shouts break over her head like waves.

The deeper she goes, the darker and hotter it gets. She slips, loses her footing and hangs there in the air. Looking down, she can see that this shaft opens into a larger sewer, but the bottom is still about ten feet below her in the darkness.

A look up reveals the silhouette of her first pursuer against the bright outline of the hole. She descends hand over hand to the final rung, then lets go. The landing is hard, but she picks herself up. The main conduit is ten feet high and about as wide and leads away from the bottom of the shaft in both directions. Weak cones of light from street gratings above illuminate the floor at regular intervals, allowing Cyn to see something at least. She runs off. Here at least it's dry, even if the air is as fuggy as she imagines it might be in a rainforest.

How many more people are going to climb down into the hole after this woman? Alice wonders. Along with the two men in suits and the police officers, fresh from their fight next to the patrol car, two other guys join the chase for Cynthia Bonsant, followed by many others. The hole seems literally to be sucking in a sizeable part of the crowd escaping from Grand Central. Pedestrians are standing around the work site with their glasses or smartphones, seemingly only waiting to be permitted to climb down too. The workmen have given up trying to stop them and watch the scene disinterestedly. Alice now has eleven windows showing live streams of the hunt open on her glasses. There's no way she can watch them all, because she'd either have to reduce their size even further or they'd overlap. The news stream is overflowing. From time to time, Alice looks around the restaurant. None of the other patrons strike her as suspicious. She removes her glasses and tucks them into one of the outer pockets of her blazer.

She picks up her handbag and heads to the toilets. She doesn't need to look for them – she knows this place. The toilets are very clean and tidy, and most importantly each toilet stall has a lock and solid walls, with no possibility of peeking over or under them or plastic partitions that collapse if you so much as aim a sideways glance at them. Two of the five are occupied. She locks herself into one, puts down the toilet seat and sits on it, then opens her bag and pulls out the Raspberry Pi from the side pocket where she carries it when it's not hidden somewhere else, along with the small keyboard and mini monitor. She swiftly sets up an encrypted anonymous connection with the computer nestling in the palm of her hand. One of the occupied toilets is unlocked, and Alice hears the click of high heels on the tiles outside. She begins to type. She's crafted the text carefully while eating her meal so that it's as concise and as comprehensible as possible.

'I want to know what she's doing in there!' barks Marten. Blurred images of the ladies' toilets flicker on the screen in front of him. His agent scans the locks on the stalls to check if they're bolted or not. Her hand appears in the picture as she opens the two unlocked doors and then carefully tries the three closed ones.

'Kick the doors in! Do something, anything!' Marten urges her. A second window from the perspective of the second agent shows her entering the restaurant but being detained by the manager.

The agent in the toilets whispers, 'I don't know which door she's behind.'

'These morons!' Marten hisses inaudibly under his breath. 'Then open them all!' he commands more loudly.

Through the woman's glasses he can see that the agent is sizing up the doors for weak spots. Her hand then reappears in the footage holding a credit card, and she sets to work on a door. A few practised movements, and the catch is released. She flings open the door.

A scream startles Alice so much that she almost knocks the Pi and the keyboard to the floor in panic.

'What are you doing?' a woman cries hysterically from one of the adjacent toilet stalls. Alice hears another woman's voice, but can't make out what she's saying. Her message is almost finished. She types away frantically to the sound of swearing, shouting and arguing outside. Then the voices grow quieter, and there's scratching at her door.

'Who's there?' she asks as she logs on to the waterfalls. 'This one's taken.'

A message flashes up on her screen.

ArchieT: Run!

Fuck!

'Open up!' a female voice shouts.

'Just a second!' Alice says harshly, but she's panicking now. Yet she still sends off her message to the waterfalls.

Someone bangs on the door and fiddles with the lock. 'Open up!'

With quick fingers Alice rips the SD card from the case and chucks it into the toilet bowl.

'What the hell's going on?' she complains as she does this. 'I'll be out in a second!' This is the truth. She flushes the SD card away and stows the Raspberry, keyboard and monitor in her bag just as the door slams into her back, almost sending her flying into the toilet bowl.

'Alice Kinkaid?' the voice roars.

On the monitor Marten sees Alice's startled expression, unkempt strands of hair draped across her face. She's pressing one hand against the wall of the toilet for support.

'Are you crazy?' she yells at the agent, through whose eyes Marten is following events. 'What's going on?'

'What are you doing in here?' screams the other, grabbing Alice's arm.

'What does it look like?' Alice shoots back, pressing the 'Flush' button again with her free hand.

The agent yanks her to one side so roughly that Marten hears a loud yelp of pain. The agent rushes over to the bowl and stares down at the rushing whirlpool. Two hands plunge into the water, and Marten hears a torrent of curses. Through the glasses of the second agent, who's now reached the scene, he spies the first agent's backside at the rear of the toilet stall. In the foreground Alice is crouching on the floor, using one hand as a prop and clutching her shoulder with the other. Two wet hands re-emerge from the toilet bowl – empty.

'Shit!' the first agent curses.

'You can say that again,' comments Luís.

'Have you gone completely out of your mind?' roars Alice. 'Can't a woman go to the toilet in peace any more?'

'Open your handbag!' orders the second agent.

'Not on your life! Wash your hands first!' she cries and runs out of the toilet before either of them can stop her.

Cyn doesn't have the slightest idea where she is. Somewhere in the guts of New York. As is normal for the intestines, it is wet and hot and it stinks. A distant source of light ensures that she can at least distinguish the contours of this corridor. One might think that it would be quiet underground, but there is uninterrupted rumbling and hissing, screeching, whistling and squelching, as if the city were already in the process of digesting her. She can hear voices or footsteps on all sides, but none of them sound very close. She keeps walking, as snapshots of the past few hours' events flash through her mind: the start of the madcap chase at the hotel; her instinctive escape from the strangers at Chander's door. Her intuition was correct. Who else but those men could have murdered him? But she's the one wanted by the police. Maybe they intended to attack her too. But who? And why? Freemee? They wouldn't have made her an offer if they were planning to kill her. Unless, that is, they didn't know until *after* their meeting that she wouldn't accept it . . .

The darkness is getting thicker and thicker. She has to grope her way forward. Voices and footsteps, closer now.

Suddenly it all becomes clear to her. They know! However the algorithms found out, Freemee knows that she was intending to reveal everything on the talk show tonight. That's why they're after her.

Those damn programs can read her like a book! There's more dim light somewhere up ahead. Do they know her next steps too? That would be helpful, because she doesn't have the foggiest idea what to do. If they know, though, they'll be waiting in the right place for her. But where is that? She originally planned to battle her way through to the TV station, but she has no chance of making it now, with the NYPD and the FBI both hot on her heels. They won't need computer programs to figure that out.

Again and again, she listens out in the darkness. The eerie sounds continue to reach her from all sides, whereas the voices and footsteps are a little further off now, although that may be misleading in this labyrinth.

All of a sudden it's obvious how she must act: she must be unpredictable! She must act differently than others would expect her to, and she would expect herself to do.

Is that the definition of 'creative' or just plain 'crazy'?

On the other hand, Freemee knows that she knows what the algorithms are capable of. Are they perhaps counting on the fact that she'll have precisely this reaction? If they're good at their job, they can predict unpredictability. Then again, can anyone predict unpredictability? Does unpredictability even exist any longer? And if it does, what conclusions should she draw? That she should still do what would be expected of her in such a situation, because the programs are relying on her trying to do something unusual? And what if they forecast she'll have that exact thought? Then she'd have to be unpredictable again.

Her head's about to burst! Her fingers dig into something wet and slimy that moves, and she stifles a scream and carries on at a run.

What do they expect her to do? she wonders. Run away. Go to ground – which is precisely what she's done. She's done the predictable thing ever since this nightmare started! From the hunt for Zero through to fleeing from the hotel and fleeing from the cops and the FBI. What else would a suspected criminal do, a person someone wants to frame for murder? What would a suspected terrorist do, who can expect neither a public investigation, a competent defence lawyer nor a fair trial in front of a normal court, but potentially solitary confinement, torture and special tribunals? She stops, out of breath, and bends over with her hands on her knees. Voices nearby. She can't understand what they're saying. Footsteps splash through puddles. *Time to move on!*

As soon as Detective Straiten enters Cynthia Bonsant's hotel room, he spots the open wardrobe door and inside, the open door of the safe. Straiten is accompanied by two crime-scene techs who immediately get down to work.

The safe is empty. *Maybe there was nothing in it*, Straiten thinks. He never puts anything in the room safe on his rare trips. Anyone who does is carrying too much luggage: that's his motto. A few items of clothing are lying or hanging in the wardrobe. The bed is made.

Straiten calls the manager and asks when housekeeping last cleaned Bonsant's room. That morning at about eleven, she answers after quickly consulting her staff, but Cynthia Bonsant was still in the hotel after that, as shown by camera footage from the lobby and the lift.

There's an open laptop on the small desk by the window. He puts on some latex gloves and presses a key at random. The computer is on, but a password is required. The IT experts will have to deal with it. They have to analyse the contents of Chander Argawal's computer as it is – if they can get inside it. The man was a professional, of course, and would surely have known how to protect himself against unwelcome intruders.

Straiten stands pensively in front of the empty safe, wondering what might have been locked inside it. The carefully hung and folded items of clothing suggest a tidy person. If Bonsant hadn't used the safe, speculates Straiten, its unlocked door wouldn't be wide open, and the wardrobe door would be closed too. Somebody grabbed something from the safe in a hurry.

'Good evening, ladies and gentlemen!' the talk-show host gushes to applause from the audience. 'Today's subject was always going to be the new self-enhancement and world improvement services that became a hot topic after the videos posted by the activist group Zero. However, we've had to update our debate in light of ongoing developments right here in New York City!'

In place of the usual studio set, the sole backdrop behind the presenter is now a gigantic video wall that dwarfs him, Carl and the other panellists. Nine separate sections of the wall show flickering footage from smart glasses and static surveillance cameras, recent reports, and posts and photos from social media.

'The British journalist Cynthia Bonsant was supposed to be with us to discuss surveillance and manipulation. But she's currently the subject of a very public police pursuit through the streets of New York! Our editors have put together this quick summary for you.'

Carl follows the snappy video montage with interest. It concludes with images of a horde of people pouring like millipedes into a hole in the ground in pursuit of Cynthia Bonsant.

'Ladies and gentlemen! A good ten per cent of the weekday population of Manhattan wear smart glasses. That's over three hundred and fifty thousand people! And just about everyone owns a smartphone or a mobile equipped with a camera. It looks like quite a few of them are currently racing the police to see who can find Cynthia Bonsant first!'

The wall behind him features at least two dozen small windows with live streams in which one can make out the vague outlines of people in the murky darkness underground.

'Thousands of people from all over Manhattan have already taken part in the hunt via #nyfugitive. They're still broadcasting live from their glasses and phones online! You can follow all the streams on our home page, by the way. We'll be expanding the theme tonight to a major phenomenon of our times, observation – both how we observe others and how we observe ourselves.

'Dr Syewell,' he says, turning to the guest philosopher, who reminds Carl more of a rapper, 'maybe you would like to go first and—'

'It'd be my pleasure, Lyle! I'd go further and call it surveillance. The key question is if it's a means to an end or an independent phenomenon in the same way as hypochondria or narcissism. Although here it can affect a whole culture. For many years people have talked about the narcissistic society, and I would add to that the hypochondriac society, which believes, among other things, that it can protect itself from presumed pests through a gigantic surveillance and intelligence apparatus, which is of course totally—'

Why do some people always have to see everything so negatively? thinks Carl. *There are so many positive sides to this! Progress is comfort.*

Cyn's priority is to find a way out of all these sewers. Every time she passes a street grate, she climbs up the rusty rungs set into the concrete, but she's not strong enough to push the grates aside or else they're locked. Each time, frustrated, she has to clamber back down again and continue her search for an exit. It feels as though she's been in the guts of the city for an eternity. She's already tried in vain to lift up twelve grates, but still she climbs up to the thirteenth.

The pedestrians above her create a play of light and shadow in the shaft – there are so many people walking over this grille that there's far more shadow than light. Flakes of dirt fall into her hair and eyes from the soles of people's shoes as they hurry past up above, but that's not going to stop her. She presses her shoulders and neck against the metal with every ounce of strength she has. She can feel it moving, but then weight bearing down from above almost makes her lose her grip and fall. She clings to the rungs and pushes, but the trampling feet of the passers-by drive her down again. Raging now, she climbs up another rung and wedges herself against the grate with all her remaining energy.

Suddenly the grate slides on to the asphalt with a clatter, and her head bursts into the open. As legs bang into her head and shoulders and feet crush her fingers, she heaves herself up, sits on the edge of the hole and takes a deep breath. People swerve around her and some glance at her in surprise, but nobody stops. She's emerged into a narrow street with a few shops, some offices, building sites, pubs, multistorey car parks, hotels and theatres. She drags her legs out then pushes the grate back into position so no one will fall down the hole.

'Damn, where did she come from?' the police operator at the Real Time Crime Center asks the colleague sitting next to him. The software that analyses the surveillance cameras has just flagged up what it regards as an abnormal event. The camera in question overlooks a section of West 49th Street near Broadway. The operator opens a separate window on his monitor and replays the thirty-second period prior to the alert. A grate is lifted up on a busy pavement, and a slender figure in a baseball cap climbs out. She's wearing neither a sewer worker's uniform nor a workman's protective vest.

In the main window, the person is now standing. The operator zooms in on her. The peaked cap hides all but her chin and mouth.

'Could this be the British journalist we've been searching for all over?' the other man asks. He calls up some pictures of Cynthia Bonsant before she went to ground. 'The clothes are dirtier, but otherwise . . . Bet you it's her!'

'I'll send over a few cops,' the first operator explains, already activating his radio.

'She isn't running away, so what does she plan to do? Is she jawing with people?'

Cyn doesn't exactly look as though she just came out of one of the smart stores in the neighbourhood. Still, she turns to the nearest passer-by and asks, 'Excuse me, could I borrow your phone for a second?'

The woman steps around her and continues on her way. Cyn realizes she'll have to try a different tack. There aren't going to be many opportunities in this street, whereas there's a swarm of people at the next crossroads. She makes straight for it.

The signs on the street corner tell her that she's at West 49th Street and Broadway. As far as possible, she quickly calls the city map to mind. The TV studio must be close by, but she has no idea which way to go. She could ask for directions – she tries it out. 'Forget it, you tourist!' seems to be people's general reaction.

She scans the other pedestrians as she marches along Broadway. There are gigantic billboards on some buildings, and huge screens on others up ahead. Now she only approaches people wearing smart glasses – at random, because she can't immediately tell if an individual is wearing ordinary specs or smart glasses. Five or six people hurry past her without stopping to listen or answer, but then someone grabs her by the arm from behind.

'I've got her!' a voice shouts.

Cyn spins around and tries to wriggle out of the iron grip, but by now a second hand has seized her other arm. Two young men in glasses are holding her tightly, jabbering away at her or at each other or at somebody else entirely. She catches very little of their excited exchange.

'Ladies and gentlemen,' the presenter announces, interrupting Alvin Kosak. 'Updates are coming thick and fast now, as you can see on our video wall! Two pedestrians have just identified Cynthia Bonsant on Broadway near Times Square!'

The two men's microphones are recording their conversation with Cyn, and the producers turn up the volume.

Carl acts extra cool as the spectacle unfolds on the screens.

'A laptop!' cries Cynthia Bonsant. 'I need a laptop!'

Her hand flutters into the shot, and when the camera manages to focus on it, Carl spots the memory stick.

'We have to show everyone what's on here!'

'You can show the police,' one of the men says.

'The police aren't interested!' she shouts. 'They think I murdered someone, though I didn't! But this is much more important! Thousands of deaths! A horrific experiment! A video on this stick . . .'

Not again! Carl groans inwardly. *Where did she get it from?* He puts his hand over the TV microphone and whispers to Joaquim, to whom he's connected via his glasses, and likewise Henry: 'I thought you'd destroyed all the backup copies including the one at the *Daily*.'

'Dear viewers,' the presenter cries, drowning out Joaquim's reply, 'our producers are now trying to set up a link to one of the men who caught Cynthia Bonsant! The two of them . . .'

He still doesn't get it, Carl thinks. Why would either of those men talk to some dude on TV when they can stream online, watched live by anyone on Earth with an internet connection? Dozens of media outlets must be trying to contact those guys right now.

'I didn't hear you,' Carl whispers without moving his lips.

'I said we destroyed every one of Bonsant's backup copies,' Joaquim repeats.

'So what's that in her hand?'.

'I've got a laptop,' a voice calls from the cluster of people that's now formed around Cyn and her two captors.

All she can see at first is someone waving a computer case over the onlookers' heads, but then the face of a young man bobs up. A mop of blond hair half obscures his tanned face. She immediately recognizes his chunky first-generation smart glasses.

'Here!' he calls out, tearing the computer from its sleeve and opening it.

She struggles and twists in the hands of the two men, who are still holding her fast. 'Let go of me, will you?' she orders them. 'Look around! You really think I'm going to be able to escape?'

In the meantime, the blond guy has worked his way through the crowd to them and hands her the laptop. 'Here you go.'

'Are you filming with your glasses?' she asks the two guys standing close behind her. 'And broadcasting this somewhere?'

'On my YouTube channel,' one says.

'OK,' she says, turning to the spectators. 'Everybody here wearing smart glasses should record this too and stream it live.' She pushes the stick into the laptop and raises it above her head so that at least some of the gathering can see the screen and film it. People immediately jostle and jockey for the best angle.

With bated breath Carl follows the streams of all eight smart-glasses wearers who are currently peeking at the laptop screen on Broadway. There's a steady flow of social media posts with the #nyfugitive and other hashtags in a second window. Carl's stomach is churning. That woman out there could bring everything crashing down.

'Dammit, Joaquim, can't we stop her?' Carl curses under his breath to his glasses, as Cyn uses the trackpad to click on the USB stick symbol.

From the loudspeakers comes a chorus of 'oohs' and 'aahs', punctuated by isolated cries.

'What for?' Joaquim asks.

'What now?'

'Nothing there!'

'What the hell?'

In quick succession the talk-show producers cut together the views of other onlookers filming the scene from the front. One of them catches Cyn's disappointed expression in extreme close-up, her lips opening and closing like those of a fish.

She turns to the laptop's owner. 'There's nothing there. Is that possible? Is the message wrong?'

The young man leans over the screen, presses some keys and shakes his head. 'No, everything's working. The stick's empty.'

'Now do you see what I meant?' Carl hears Joaquim say.

At the Real Time Crime Center, the police operator watches Cynthia Bonsant pull the memory stick out of the laptop and push it in again.

'Traffic hold-ups on the way to the scene,' a police officer radios in. 'What's going on?'

The operator checks the route and discovers from camera footage that traffic jams are starting to form in every street in the area. Several traffic lights have broken down.

'What's up?' he asks his colleague.

'We don't know yet,' the man says, 'but there's a problem with those lights.'

'First the subway cameras, now the stoplights. Every time this British lady's in trouble, something happens. It cannot be a coincidence!'

'I'll look into it,' his colleague says.

'Still no firearms visible,' he tells the police patrol. 'The suspect is being held by two citizens and is surrounded by about fifty other people. We've identified all the individuals. None is marked. Neighbourhood streets all jammed. You'll have to go in on foot.'

He hears a swear word, then, 'Roger that.'

Apart from a few short breaks, the operator has now been at his desk for six hours straight. His shoulders are slumping, his head has sunk slightly into his neck and he stares at the large wall of monitors in front of him with his elbows propped on the table. More head-shaking from Bonsant and the blond guy confirms that the memory stick is indeed empty.

'OK, that's enough,' one of her captors says. 'You've had your fifteen minutes of fame.'

'All right!' Bonsant cries. 'Listen to me instead! Are you listening? Are you streaming? I have something to tell you!'

'Now do you see what *I* meant?' Carl says to Joaquim with one hand cupped over the mike on his lapel, while Cyn talks about Edward Brickle's video and the statistics the boy was compiling about unexplained fatalities.

'Someone's got to stop her,' says Henry, the first words he has uttered.

'What do you want me to do?' Joaquim enquires. 'Turn off the whole electricity grid?'

They see Cyn break off for a moment and gaze in surprise at the huge advertising screens nearby, which are showing images from Eddie's video. She gestures excitedly towards the screens, and the eyes of her audience flit back and forth between her and the outsized commercials as she continues to talk.

'Jesus!' Henry hisses. 'How did those get there?' he says, just as a message at the bottom of the screen provides the answer to him and the rest of the world: 'Zero presents a film by Edward Brickle, revealed by Cynthia Bonsant.'

Carl isn't listening any longer. He's watching the movements of Cyn's lips from eleven different angles with the boy's video and Zero's introduction in the background. The crowd of listeners is swirling around her. Individual words pierce his consciousness, confirming his worst fears. She isn't talking only about Eddie's findings; Will must have told her about the experiment too. Carl might not have provided incontrovertible proof of the trials in his presentation to his fellow board members, but Bonsant's speech will have alerted journalists, the authorities and ultimately the courts, and they are not going to rest until Freemee has disclosed all its data.

Yet even if they can't compel Freemee to do that, the company is now on the defensive, and a refusal to disclose would be legitimately interpreted as deliberate concealment. Carl can't even bear to imagine how their competitors will gloat. The major data collectors in particular could pick up clues about certain aspects of the experiment via their databases. Even NBC is now playing the video with Eddie Brickle's original commentary. Where did they get it? Zero must be broadcasting it worldwide.

He notices, however, that his inner emotional turmoil is abating and his characteristic cool calculation returning. This has always been one of his great strengths.

'OK,' he says to Joaquim and Henry as unobtrusively as possible. 'The story's out. I see two alternatives. One, we undermine Bonsant's and Brickle's credibility and deny everything.'

'We'll need to undermine more than their credibility,' says Joaquim. 'People conform to Julius Caesar's old adage: "I love treason but hate a traitor." We must challenge their characters, their motives and their integrity, the same way the US administration and their allies did to Edward Snowden. By attacking his motives, his escape to China, his asylum bid in Russia and a few tactless statements he made, they got people to reassess his other actions as treason. It played perfectly with many members of the public.'

'Reassess? I thought you earned billions of dollars from this administration,' Carl interjects. His lips try to form themselves into a sober smile; after all, every camera in this damn studio is now trained on him. He's whispering through his teeth so that only his glasses can pick up the sound.

'Listen,' Joaquim says firmly. 'Character assassination might work. There are already some naysayers out there.'

Carl focuses briefly on the live transmission.

'It's all a hoax!'

'She's lying!'

'I use Freemee every day, and it's great!'

'There are some Freemee users in the mix out there,' Joaquim observes.

'Let her speak!' says someone else, though.

'Yeah, let her speak!'

'You mentioned two alternatives,' Henry reminds him.

'Offensive,' Carl says out of the side of his mouth. 'We own up to everything, choose the right words. People love what Freemee's crystal ball and ActApps do for them. We only need to remind them of the positive effects they have on their lives. Another parallel to the surveillance and data collection stories that have come out in recent years: in the end, convenience and security are more important to people than freedom and independence. They have no idea how to handle the latter anyway.'

'We'll do both,' says Henry. 'Attack Bonsant's character and at the same time promote Freemee's advantages.'

'But we can't confess to the fatalities,' Joaquim objects. 'Some of us are going to wind up in jail if we do.'

'We don't have to confess to them,' Henry contradicts him. 'It's sufficient not to deny them. In any case, it'd be almost impossible to prove any direct link to Freemee.' He laughs. 'Did you ever see the CEO of a tobacco corporation, an arms manufacturer or a bank go to jail? Customers reach for a cigarette, a pistol or an unpayable loan of their own free will. It's the same with Freemee.'

'Please stop making that kind of comparison!' Carl snaps.

'Calm down,' Henry says soothingly. 'There's one further advantage to all this: Erben Pennicott can go take a hike. When all of this comes out, he won't be able to black-mail us any more.'

'I've only just switched on,' Erben tells Jon.

'That Bonsant has flung open Pandora's box. Now I see why you're so interested in Freemee.'

'It's all over. I don't think Freemee can survive this. Their competitors will be rubbing their hands at the sight of the market leader going down in flames like this. We'll make contact with them instead.'

'Our men have withdrawn,' says Jon. 'It's swarming with cameras out there. Everyone's being watched, and that includes our people.'

'They'll need to hide under baseball caps.'

'It's getting to that point, yes,' Jon replies. 'Above all, though, our people have got to learn to cope in this kind of circumstance. In that one moment they tried to seize Bon-sant from the NYPD, they were filmed by eleven surveillance cameras and seven pedestrians with smart glasses.'

'So her attempted escape is well documented. That's almost an admission of guilt right there. Her escape is a massive embarrassment, but we've got her now.'

'Anyone watching this, either now or later, should ask Freemee for information!' Cyn declares to the mini-cameras perched on her listeners' noses. 'Or try to reconstruct the facts like Eddie Brickle did!'

'That's enough now, ma'am!' a police officer roars as he shoulders his way through the crowd with his partner in tow. 'Out of the way! Let us through!'

When Cyn catches sight of them, she tries to break free, but her captors have grabbed hold of her again.

'Facts can kill, as Eddie found out!' she shouts.

'What a nutjob!' she hears someone call out, but she ignores him. The officers are closing in. She only has seconds left. 'And who knows, maybe Freemee's Vice-President for Statistics and Strategy did too? He died in a car crash a few months ago.'

She's still speaking as the police officers announce that she's under arrest and the two men loosen their grip on her arms.

'Or Chander Argawal, whom I allegedly killed!' she cries, even louder now. 'He was alive when I last saw him!'

As the cops read out her rights and handcuff her behind her back, Cyn hears someone shout, 'Liar!'

But Cyn won't be silenced. 'Check it! Investigate!' she urges her audience over her shoulder as the policemen tug her away. A throng of people surrounds the trio, while Eddie's huge effigy goes on talking above their heads.

'Keep your mouth shut,' one of the cops snarls at her.

No way. 'An eighteen-year-old boy uncovered this, and so can you!'

By now they've reached the next junction, where a patrol car is hemmed in by two taxis. The officers push her head-first into the car, but she resists one last time and turns to face the watching crowd. 'You can find out more by working together! Find out everything!'

The first policeman eventually bundles her inside and slams the door. For a second it's very quiet inside the car. When the police officers get in the front, she catches a last snatch of her audience's voices and the sound of the city before the siren on the roof starts to blare.

Driving back to the station, Detective Straiten learns via his smart glasses that the results of the analysis of both Bonsant's and Argawal's sensory devices, glasses and smart-phones are now in.

'That was fast,' he remarks.

'Our friends say that Bonsant's devices were nearby when the Indian's glasses broke. However, they can only locate the exact site to a three-yard radius. So there's a degree of imprecision.'

'What do they mean by nearby? Near enough?'

'That same imprecision also applies to the victim's devices, which means that there's a radius of several yards.'

'Don't keep me in suspense. Do those two three-yard circles overlap at the time Argawal's glasses broke or not?'

'Yes and no.'

'Oh, come on! The facts!'

'You asked about circles. Seen from above, they do overlap. According to our previous findings, Bonsant was climbing down the fire escape, and her coordinates remained more or less constant.'

'But . . .'

'Her altitude didn't. It looks as if she was between four and eight yards from Argawal when his glasses gave up the ghost.'

'That doesn't necessarily mean anything. Maybe he only collapsed after a few seconds, and the glasses broke only when he hit the floor. By which time she was out on the fire escape.'

'The doctor says the blow was too hard for that. He must have fallen to the floor immediately.'

'Which means we might be looking for somebody else?'

'In her live appearance just now, she claimed that she'd escaped from several men in Argawal's room. Did you see it, her performance in Times Square?'

'Some of it.'

'What do you make of it?'

'No idea. Sounds pretty crazy. However, if somebody had told me three years back that we'd be communicating via our glasses, I'd have called them crazy too.'

'Dear viewers, there are only a few minutes of our show remaining!' whoops the presenter, who's been unable to sit still for some time now. 'But in light of the events in New York City, the channel has decided to extend our report, and so we will be joined by anchorwoman Tyria LeBon from our newsroom! First, though, we'll play a video analysis from Trevor Demsich's blog. Trevor is an IT specialist from Santa Fe. He's used automatic body and clothing recognition software to scan the footage from surveillance cameras and smart glasses that was streamed online this afternoon.'

The host raises his hand briefly to his ear to catch his producer's instructions through his earpiece.

'From what I'm hearing, Trevor has made an interesting discovery. Right after the alleged attack on Chander Argawal, chief suspect Cynthia Bonsant left the Bedley Hotel. In the next few minutes eight other people also left the hotel, including this man.' A man in a suit and dark glasses is circled in red on the wall of monitors.

'Followed soon afterwards by this man.' Another red circle appears around a corpulent man in shorts, a Hawaiian shirt, a beige straw hat and sunglasses. 'Trevor found camera footage tracing virtually the entire route taken by Bonsant until she vanished into the sewers. As we can see here, one of these two men always shows up on the same route a few seconds later! Look! The whole way! By accident? Trevor's convinced that these two men chased Cynthia Bonsant out of the hotel. Who are they? Are they witnesses? In that case why haven't they contacted the police? Why, if they'd found some reason to pursue Bonsant, didn't they immediately inform the police? How were they able to stay on Bonsant's trail despite losing sight of her several times?'

'Demsich is probably right,' the police operator confirms. 'We've matched his pictures with the videos from the hotel. Those two guys were caught on the lobby cameras too. The first turned up about twenty minutes before the crime, accompanied by three others.'

He plays the footage to Straiten's glasses. The guy in the Hawaiian shirt, three in suits, one in jeans and a shirt. All of them are wearing shades, two have hats and one a baseball cap. One of the hat guys goes over to reception. As he speaks to the receptionist, he briefly pushes up his sunglasses.

'Big mistake!' cries the operator.

'Did you run him through facial recognition?'

'Yep. Works for a small security firm. A subsidiary of a large one, EmerSec.'

'*The* EmerSec? The billion-dollar government contractor with deals in Iraq and God knows where else?'

'Its main shareholder, Henry Emerald, owns a stake in Freemee.'

'The same Freemee Bonsant denounced in her street sermon?'

'The very same.'

Straiten lets out a quiet whistle through his teeth.

When they reach the police station, Cyn first has to wait for a while. Her hands are still cuffed behind her back, and her arms are aching.

After a quarter of an hour she's approached by a man who must have ancestors from all five continents. He's dressed in jeans, a shirt and a crumpled jacket. He introduces himself as Detective Straiten before removing her handcuffs and leading her into an interview room.

'So tell me what happened,' Straiten asks in a soft voice, which echoes weakly off the bare walls.

'Where do I begin?'

'Well, for starters, noon today at the Bedley Hotel after you and Chander Argawal got back from Freemee.'

'Is he really dead?' she asks. She doesn't know how she feels right now. Discovering his breach of her trust has shattered her memories of a few wonderful hours together.

Straiten studies her before saying, 'Yes, he's dead.'

'It wasn't me.'

'Tell me what happened.'

'Our producers are about to play a new video,' the TV host announces. 'Apparently this one's also from Zero!'

Marten's monitor shows a photo of the President which turns into a picture of his chief of staff.

'Presidents' Day was just the beginning,' says Zero. 'Naturally we're taking a closer look not just at the President, but also at those around him. His chief of staff, Erben Pennicott, for example, who was such a hero when capturing our sweet little spider drone.'

A recording of the relevant scene morphs into footage of Erben Pennicott crossing a dark hotel lobby. 'Yesterday evening, for a few seconds, he crossed the smart lenses of a New York hotel guest. That guest of course had nothing better to do than post the video snippet on Facebook.'

Pennicott is going to tear some heads off for the mere fact that this video was even recorded, let alone posted on Facebook, Marten thinks. It isn't really his job, but since Cynthia Bonsant's appearance in Times Square, Marten has begun to think that it's time to start hunting Zero again. He phones his technicians and tells them to get a move on with analysing the new video.

Zero continues. 'A surveillance camera on a terrace in the building opposite that same hotel spotted Freemee's chairman Carl Montik at a fortieth-floor window a little later. That camera automatically transmits its footage online where it goes through the automatic facial recognition software we have rigged up to identify specific people. Might that be Erben Pennicott and Henry Emerald in the background? The footage is too blurry for facial recognition to work, but the resemblance is striking, wouldn't you say? What might those three be discussing the night before Cynthia Bonsant raises serious allegations against Freemee and is wanted by the FBI on suspicion of terrorist activities? Well, well, Erben Pennicott. You can't rip the legs off our cameras this time, because they're not our cameras.' Taking on the guise of a laughing chief of staff, Zero bids farewell with his signature last words: 'Another thing: I believe we must destroy the data krakens.'

'They haven't made any errors in the metadata this time,' the technician informs him by phone, 'and I can't find anything in the video either at first sight.'

Pennicott's going to explode, thinks Marten with a peculiar sense of satisfaction.

'That matches our findings so far,' says Detective Straiten when Cyn comes to the end of her description. He pushes a picture taken by a CCTV camera across the table to her. She recognizes the hotel lobby. At the reception counter stands a man in a hat who's pushed his shades up on to his forehead while talking to the female receptionist.

'Recognize him?' Straiten asks.

She studies the face closely, but is distracted by a woman in an ill-fitting suit who comes into the room and whispers something into Straiten's ear. He nods, and the woman goes out again.

Straiten nods enquiringly at the photo.

'No,' says Cyn. 'But I recognize the hat. One of the men who forced his way into Chander's room was wearing the same kind, or something similar at least.'

'Come with me,' he says, getting to his feet.

She hesitates. Straiten's already at the door, one hand on the handle.

'Come on, I want to show you something.'

He leads her into an office with two facing desks, both piled high with documents. At the left-hand one sits the woman who just spoke to Straiten. She's staring at her computer screen. Straiten guides Cyn into position behind her and stands next to her. He digs his hands into his pockets, as if keen to signal that he isn't unduly worried that he might have to use them to prevent a highly unlikely escape bid.

It takes Cyn a few seconds to understand what's happening on the screen. Various browser windows are showing different content. The one that strikes her most prominently is the live stream of a talk show. During a brief panning shot she recognizes Kosak and Washington. She was scheduled to be on that show right now.

'It looks like we have even more viewers than we thought!' cries the host.

What a pompous git, thinks Cyn. *People are watching the events on all kinds of channels, from Twitter to the* Daily. *Just because his show is presenting people's posts, he thinks everyone's watching TV.*

'Right after Cynthia Bonsant's arrest, hordes of viewers around the world started searching for clues that back up her allegations. Some of those people work for the world's largest data-collection companies. Those companies know just about all there is to know about us, including how, when and why the fatalities occurred. It took them barely half an hour to dig up evidence supporting Cynthia Bonsant's specific claims that there were two regional clusters of unnatural deaths among Freemee users in the US and Japan, but also evidence of others. Take a look at this!'

The producers project coloured maps, curved graphs and pie and bar charts on to the video wall.

'A few minutes later, a spontaneous international research team of IT specialists published similar data!'

'Looks like you stirred up a proper hornets' nest,' says Detective Straiten.

A few days later

The last rays of sunlight filter through the treetops around the edge of the meadow, repeatedly forcing Cyn to shut her eyes. She relishes the warm caresses on her cheeks. The dry-stone wall behind her is still radiating the heat stored up from the afternoon, but cool air is already drifting over from the field and creeping up her legs. A lamb bleats lower down in the pasture. Two other sheep join in, while the rest of the flock lower their muzzles to the grass and graze contentedly. Silence settles once more over the scene.

'Here you go.' Vi sets a drink down on the rough wooden table in front of Cyn. She's brought one for herself too. She sits down beside her mother on the bench. They clink glasses, sip their drinks and listen to the birds singing.

'Another seven calls and about a hundred emails at a quick guess,' says Vi.

Cyn doesn't reply. She closes her eyes in the hope of catching one last beam of sunshine, but the chill has now reached her upper body and is fingering at her neck and face. She found this remote cottage in the Lake District through friends of friends. She opens her eyes again and gazes at Vi, who's wearing a pair of smart glasses.

'I don't want anyone to know where I am for now,' she says eventually. 'You know that.'

'I do,' Vi sighs. At least she isn't wearing a smartwatch any longer. Cyn noticed that the moment she arrived back in London. 'No one can locate us here via my prepaid mobile phone and the network. I use privacy software and a mesh, I've dialled down my browser fingerprint, and so on.'

'Mesh?' Cyn repeats the word as a question.

'A free communications network. A sort of ad hoc wireless network – there's one in this area. Private regional initiatives that have generally grown up in areas that were too remote for the telecommunications companies. They often haven't yet been infiltrated by the intelligence services or commercial providers.'

How does she know all this stuff? Cyn wonders.

'But don't go thinking that no one can find you here if they really put their minds to it,' Vi continues. 'Neither the mesh nor that thing over there will help you if they do.' She points to the old Vauxhall they used to drive up here; it's parked next to the house. A vehicle from a time when drivers had to steer their own cars, and passengers used a map to navigate – back when there was no satnav constantly transmitting the car's position, and no on-board computer or individual parts such as brakes, axles or headlights continually informing manufacturers about their state of repair. They'd borrowed the car from friends too.

Cyn had to stay in New York City for two more days before the police would allow her to leave the country. She could easily have extended her stay by an extra week for newspaper and print profiles, photo sessions and filmed interviews, but she wanted to attend Eddie's funeral. Detectives have been hunting for the men from the surveillance camera footage ever since. Working backwards as if rewinding a film, they've managed to reconstruct the movements of the five individuals over the previous few days. Each at some stage dropped clues as to his identity, either by revealing his face, getting into a car with an identifiable registration number or touching objects from which the police have since been able to take fingerprints. Two have already been caught. Three are still on the run. The police are also investigating the links between EmerSec and the small security firm. Henry Emerald's spokesperson has denied any involvement by EmerSec in the events around Freemee, just as Erben Pennicott has insisted he has had nothing to do with the matter. Yet public opinion has been far more alert since Cyn's coup, and the media and political opposition are also pressing the two men for explanations.

'Freemee is still haemorrhaging members,' says Vi. 'Down by a quarter so far. No wonder. Everyone's calling it big data's Chernobyl, as you did in your article in the aftermath.'

Carl Montik has confessed to the experiment but without revealing the full details or its scale. He's continued to dispute that it was in any way linked to the three thousand deaths.

'What would you do if you found out you were one of Freemee's guinea pigs?' asks Cyn.

Vi says nothing for a second before replying, 'I don't know.'

'Do you even want to know?'

'I'm . . . going to take a long time to get over things as it is,' she says. 'But I don't want to be a goth any more.'

'And instead?'

'Mum, how many times have we discussed this since you got back? Freemee's finished. Public prosecutors are leading investigations in several countries. Adam's mother and others are suing the company.'

'So what? New companies will spring up and take over.'

'Will Dekkert, for example,' says Vi. 'He and some colleagues have turned their backs on Freemee. He's announced a data analysis company similar to Freemee but on an open-source basis so that everyone will be able to influence the program codes.'

'I know. He told me before I left the States. He thinks there's no going back from the world of data collection and analysis, but like this people could at least collaborate on writing the rules that will govern society in the future.'

'In theory, maybe, but in practice they have to be able to write code.'

'It's still an opportunity for public control.'

'Will has written several mails. He wants you on board for the project.'

'I don't know if I want this kind of society laid bare, with this disclosure of every relationship and connection. A world without secrets or surprises. A world where everything and everyone is for sale.'

'That's been the case for a long time already, Mum. The real question is who owns access to it and who profits from it – the intelligence services and a few secretive global companies or all of us.'

'Well, for the time being I'm just happy to be here.'

'And you're entitled to be. You have enough offers to choose from. Have you already told Anthony that you've quit?'

'Yep, from New York. It was high time,' she says with a grin.

'Zero's posted a new video. Want to see it?'

'No, thanks. I'm enjoying the peace and quiet.'

A breeze ruffles the tips of the trees. The night sky beyond the green foliage grows brighter the higher Cyn looks. Far above her, she sees the first star twinkling.

Or is it a satellite looking down at her?

ArchieT: Scenario: twenty years from now, most people will have been thoroughly analysed and will use lifestyle apps to help them through the complexities of life.

Submarine: You mean, the programs will know better than I do which job, partner and sport suit me best, what I should eat and what line of business I should be in? Will an invisible hand steer me in the right direction?

ArchieT: But you'll still believe that the algorithm's decisions are your own.

Nightowl: And who'll be steering the programs?

Teldif: Nobody. No human at least. They'll have become too complex for any human to understand.

Snowman: So, in the future, software will relieve us of any decisions, making all society's decision-makers, politicians, managers, etc., superfluous.

Peekaboo777: Oh stop! You make the scenario sound so appealing!

Glossary

This glossary contains a random selection of terms. If the one you're searching for isn't here, then look it up on internet. After all, that's what it's there for – that and many other things.

Anonymous: A group name under which internet activists and hackers carry out actions and demonstrations, both in coordinated fashion and individually. The structure of Anonymous makes it almost impossible to verify if the various messages, announcements and protests can really be attributed to them.

ARPANET: A project initiated by the Advanced Research Project Agency (ARPA) led by the US Department of Defense in partnership with a network of universities and research centres, paving the way for the internet.

Attention economy: A concept that treats attention as a scarce and valuable commodity. The more attention one attracts, the better. The concept would appear to be confirmed by a certain number of celebrities who are famous solely for being famous.

Big data: A catch-all term for the collection, storage, analysis and evaluation of gigantic amounts of data, usually via modern communications, sensor and network technologies.

Body snatchers: Extra-terrestrial invaders in Jack Finney's science-fiction novel *The Body Snatchers* of 1955 (adapted for the cinema four times). A classic example of the anti-communist and paranoid fiction of the 1950s, '60s and '70s.

Crowdsourcing: Where companies and organizations out-source to external volunteers tasks that would otherwise be dealt with in-house.

Facial recognition: Computer software able to recognize people by their facial characteristics.

FISA (Foreign Intelligence Surveillance Act): Legislation governing the surveillance of foreign intelligence infor-mation. Approved by the US Congress in 1978, it regulates matters such as the searching of homes and people in the US, but in particular the surveillance of telecommunica-tions abroad. FISA cases are handled by the specially established > **FISC.**

FISC (United States Foreign Intelligence Surveillance Court): A US court, established in 1978, that regulates surveillance activities by the US foreign intelligence agen-cies. It sits in total secrecy and is subject to no genuine democratic oversight.

Gamification: The application of game strategies to non-game contexts, e.g. for management, customer retention, learning and in other areas. It is supposed to increase the motivation of a target audience to happily carry out activities generally considered boring or monotonous.

Girolamo Savonarola: A Dominican friar and preacher in 15th-century Florence who fulminated against the immoral conduct of nobles and clerics and as a result was burned at the stake in 1498.

Guy Fawkes: Attempted to blow up the House of Lords in London in 1605 in order to put a Catholic monarch on the British throne. Executed for his crimes in 1606.

Howard Beale: Fictional character of a critical TV commentator gone mad in the 1976 satirical film *Network*, winner of four Oscars.

INDECT (Intelligent Information System Supporting Observation, Searching and Detection for Security of Citizens in Urban Environment): An EU-funded research project to develop a comprehensive surveillance system.

Monkey Wrench Gang: A term for an eco-terrorist group coined from the eponymous 1975 novel by Edward Abbey.

Panopticon: A model for prisons and factories developed by the British philosopher Jeremy Bentham (1748–1832), in which a single person is able to guard or oversee a large number of people.

Predictive analytics: Attempts to predict future events and patterns of behaviour by studying past occurrences. It is already fairly accurate thanks to modern software and is now used widely in almost every walk of life from the military and the financial and insurance industries to the medical sector, weather forecasting and marketing.

Predictive policing/pre-crime: Use of computer software to forecast locations and types of crime.

PRISM, XKEYSCORE, TEMPORA, INDECT and many more: A range of advanced surveillance technologies developed by the US and UK intelligence services.

Raspberry Pi: A simple single-board computer developed by the British Raspberry Pi Foundation to make it easy for young people to appropriate hardware and programming knowledge. Now used in many other fields.

Running Man, The: Science-fiction film (1987) adapted from the novel by Stephen King. Its forerunner, the German TV drama *The Game of Millions* (1970), was based on Robert Sheckley's short story *The Prize of Peril* (1958).

TOR (The Onion Router): A network that makes connection data anonymous and makes it possible, to a certain degree, to browse online anonymously.

V: The main character in the graphic novel *V for Vendetta*, who leads a struggle against a totalitarian surveillance state. Wears a > **Guy Fawkes** mask which has since become the emblem of > **Anonymous**.

VPN (Virtual Private Network): Allows various activities including a certain degree of anonymous or surveillance-protected movement online.

Wolfram Alpha: A semantic search engine that tries not just to find websites matching the search term, but also to provide content-based answers.

List of Main Characters

Staff at the *Daily*

Cynthia ('Cyn') Bonsant	Journalist
Anthony Heast	Editor-in-chief
Chander Argawal	IT forensic scientist
Jeff	Technology department

Freemee

Carl Montik	Chair & Head of Research, Development and Programming
Will Dekkert	Vice-President for Marketing and Communications
Alice Kinkaid	Director of Communications

Teenagers

Viola ('Vi') Bonsant	Cynthia's daughter
Adam Denham	Viola's friend
Edward Brickle	Viola's friend

Government/FBI

Erben Pennicott	White House Chief of Staff
Jonathan Stem	FBI Assistant Director
Marten Carson	FBI agent and team leader
Luís	FBI digital detective
Henry Emerald	Founder of the security firm EmerSec
Joaquim Proust	CEO of EmerSec

Marc Elsberg is a former creative director in advertising. *Code Zero* is his second global bestselling thriller. Its terrifying scenario of the perils of social media, surveillance and data theft is all too real. Marc Elsberg lives in Vienna, Austria.

Also by Marc Elsberg

BLACKOUT

and published by Black Swan

BLACKOUT
Marc Elsberg

A cold night in Milan, Piero Manzano wants to get home.

Then the traffic lights fail. Manzano is thrown from his Alfa as cars pile up. And not just on this street – every light in the city is dead.

Across Europe, controllers watch in disbelief as electricity grids collapse.

Plunged into darkness, people are freezing. Food and water supplies dry up. The death toll soars.

Former hacker and activist Manzano becomes a prime suspect. But he is also the only man capable of finding the real attackers.

Can he bring down a major terrorist network

Before it's too late?

THE GLOBAL MILLION-COPY BESTSELLER

'A dazzling debut' *The Times*

'Fast, tense, thrilling' Lee Child